"AMONG THIEVES" by Poul Anderson—The virtual dictator of his own world, would he prove the betrayer of Earth's far-flung empire?

"DOWN STYPHON!" by H. Beam Piper—A Pennsylvania State trooper, he'd been snatched out of his own world and cast into an alternate Earth, where his knowledge of gunpowder might prove the key to power. . . .

"DRAGON'S TEETH" by David Drake—How could he defeat a sorcery which could conjure invulnerable giants from the earth itself?

"WARRIOR" by Gordon R. Dickson—He was a Dorsai come to pay his respects to the brother of one of his fallen comrades.. He was the galaxy's deadliest soldier come upon a mission of doom. . . .

These are but a few of the soldiers recruited to stand against those who would tamper with the powers of magic and technology in—

ROBERT ADAMS' BOOK OF SOLDIERS

ROBERT ADAMS' BOOK OF SOLDIERS

Edited by
Robert Adams
Martin H. Greenberg and
Pamela Crippen Adams

A SIGNET BOOK

NEW AMERICAN LIBRARY

PUBLISHED BY
PENGUIN BOOKS CANADA LIMITED

Copyright © 1988 by Robert Adams, Martin H. Greenberg and Pamela Crippen
Adams

All rights reserved

Grateful acknowledgment is made to the following for permission to reprint
these stories:

"Clash by Night," by Lawrence O'Donnell. Copyright © 1943 by Street &
Smith Publications; renewed 1970 by Catherine Kuttner. Reprinted by permission of Don Congdon Associates, Inc.

"Among Thieves" by Poul Anderson. Copyright © 1980 by Poul Anderson.
Reprinted by permission of the author and the author's agents, Scott Meredith Literary Agency, Inc., 845 Third Avenue, New York, NY 10022.

"Despoilers of the Golden Empire" by Randall Garrett. Copyright © 1977
by Randall Garrett. Reprinted by permission of Scott Meredith Literary
Agency, Inc., 845 Third Avenue, New York, NY 10022.

"Down Styphon" by H. Beam Piper. Copyright © 1968 by H. Beam Piper.
Reprinted by permission of the Berkley Publishing Group.

"Three Soldiers" by D. C. Poyer. Copyright © 1978 by D. C. Poyer.
Reprinted by permission of the author and the author's agents, James Allen.

"Dragon's Teeth" by David Drake. Copyright © 1975 by Midnight Sun.
Reprinted by permission of the author.

"Cold Light" by Karl Edward Wagner. Copyright © 1973 by Karl Edward
Wagner. Reprinted by permission of the author.

"A Difficult Undertaking" by Harry Turtledove. Copyright © 1986 by TSR,
Inc. Reprinted by permission of the author and the author's agents, Scott
Meredith Agency, Inc., 845 Third Avenue, New York, NY 10022.

"Passage to Dilfar" by Roger Zelazny. Copyright © 1964 by Ziff-Davis
Publishing Co. Reprinted by permission of the author.

"Night on Mispec Moor" by Larry Niven. Copyright © 1977 by Larry
Niven. Reprinted by permission of the author.

"Warrior" by Gordon Dickson. Copyright © 1965 by Conde Nast Publications,
Inc. Reprinted by permission of the author.

First Printing, September, 1988

2 3 4 5 6 7 8 9

SIGNET TRADEMARK REG. U.S. PAT OFF. AND FOREIGN COUNTRIES
REGISTERED TRADEMARK — MARCA REGISTRADA
HECHO EN WINNIPEG, CANADA

SIGNET, SIGNET CLASSIC, MENTOR, ONYX, PLUME,
MERIDIAN and NAL BOOKS are published in Canada by Penguin
Books Canada Limited, 2801 John Street, Markham, Ontario,
Canada L3R 1B4
PRINTED IN CANADA
COVER PRINTED IN U.S.A.

For Tim Bolgeo, Jerry Pournelle,
David Drake, Joe Haldeman,
George Scithers, Gordy Dickson
and all those of my other
colleagues who have paid their
dues and seen the Elephant.

Contents

INTRODUCTION

Most well-balanced human beings ("well-balanced" means that they drool out of both sides of their mouths at once, of course) own an inbred dislike of recalling the more unpleasant and upsetting aspects of life. For this reason, ex-servicemen tend to remember fun times—the free-for-all fight that ended in a wrecked bar and a successful escape from the Snowdrops (Military Police, to you, dear reader), assorted short-sheeting episodes in barracks, what the poker-playing first-three-graders looked and sounded like as they burst out of the armored personnel carrier into which you and your buddy had dropped a purple smoke grenade one night on extended-order training, the camaraderie, the warm us-against-them feeling of you and your low-ranking buddies against all the others—the enemy, civilians, commissioned officers, first-three-graders and other NCOs, in that order.

Only the temporarily or permanently unbalanced willingly recall the most unpleasant aspects of soldiering. Despite the romanticism that some try to gloss over the experiences of combat, there never is or was any glory to general discomfort, unbearable boredom and utter physical exhaustion alternated with brief but seemingly endless episodes of sheer terror, of being literally scared crapless, of pain and suffering to a degree that those who have never experienced such frankly cannot even begin to imagine. A homeless cur lives better than did your average combat soldier has throughout most of history.

Yet wars continued to be fought, men kept becoming soldiers who were always expected to endure it all—the discomforts, hunger, thirst, filth, brutalities and/or stupidities of military superiors, agonizing, unmanning fear—to

9

fight bravely on command, to ruthlessly kill strangers and at least face, sleeping and waking, a miserable death that might be quick, sudden, painless, but was more likely to be hideous, protracted, wretched torment that would only end along with life itself.

Nonetheless, men still became and become soldiers, the ranks have been and are filled in one way or another. This book is packed with stories about some of these rank-fillers—past, present and future—many of them written by former soldiers.

If you are seeking the works of award-winning writers, then look no further. Between them, the writers represented herein have amassed no less than a score of Hugo Awards, seven Nebula Awards, and that is not to even mention the stray Skylarks, Ditmars, Gandolfs, Derleths and whatnot.

Save for the mutual theme, that of the soldier, no two of these tales are at all similar. The eleven craftsmen represented here have each spun exciting, carefully rendered tales filled with believable people and circumstances, chockfull of unforgettable scenes and events. The stories are set in both past and future, on earth, on other planets and even in parallel universes. Protagonists range from great captains to common rankers and their antagonists are male and female, human, beast, monster, living or undead corpse.

It's all here, from A(nderson) to Z(elazny), in my *Book of Soldiers*. Enjoy!

—Robert Adams

CLASH BY NIGHT

by Lawrence O'Donnell

INTRODUCTION

A half mile beneath the shallow Venusian Sea the black impervium dome that protects Montana Keep rests frowningly on the bottom. Within the Keep is carnival, for the Montanans celebrate the four-hundred-year anniversary of Earthman's landing on Venus. Under the great dome that houses the city all is light and color and gaiety. Masked men and women, bright in celoflex and silks, wander through the broad streets, laughing, drinking the strong native wines of Venus. The sea bottom has been combed, like the hydroponic tanks, for rare delicacies to grace the tables of the nobles.

Through the festival grim shadows stalk, men whose faces mark them unmistakably as members of a Free Company. Their finery cannot disguise that stamp, hard-won through years of battle. Under the domino masks their mouths are hard and harsh. Unlike the undersea dwellers, their skins are burned black with the ultraviolet rays that filter through the cloud layer of Venus. They are skeletons at the feast. They are respected but resented. They are Free Companions—

We are on Venus, nine hundred years ago, beneath the Sea of Shoals, not much north of the equator. But there is a wide range in time and space. All over the cloud planet the underwater Keeps are dotted, and life will not change for many centuries. Looking back, as we do now, from the civilized days of the Thirty-fourth Century, it is too easy to regard the men of the Keeps as savages, groping, stupid and brutal. The Free Companies have long since vanished. The islands and continents of Venus have been tamed, and there is no war.

But in periods of transition, of desperate rivalry, there is always war. The Keeps fought among themselves, each striving to draw the fangs of the others by depriving them of their reserves of korium, the power source of the day. Students of that era find pleasure in sifting the legends and winnowing out the basic social and geopolitical truths. It is fairly well known that only one factor saved the Keeps from annihilating one another—the gentleman's agreement that left war to the warriors, and allowed the undersea cities to develop their science and social cultures. That particular compromise was, perhaps, inevitable. And it caused the organization of the Free Companies, the roving bands of mercenaries, highly trained for their duties, who hired themselves out to fight for whatever Keeps were attacked or wished to attack.

Ap Town, in his monumental "Cycle of Venus," tells the saga through symbolic legends. Many historians have recorded the sober truth, which, unfortunately, seems often Mars-dry. But it is not generally realized that the Free Companions were almost directly responsible for our present high culture. War, because of them, was not permitted to usurp the place of peace-time social and scientific work. Fighting was highly specialized, and, because of technical advances, manpower was no longer important. Each band of Free Companions numbered a few thousand, seldom more.

It was a strange, lonely life they must have led, shut out from the normal life of the Keeps. They were vestigial but necessary, like the fangs of the marsupians who eventually evolved into Homo sapiens. But without those warriors, the Keeps would have been plunged completely into total war, with fatally destructive results.

Harsh, gallant, indomitable, serving the god of battles so that it might be destroyed—working toward their own obliteration—the Free Companies roar down the pages of history, the banner of Mars streaming above them in the misty air of Venus. They were doomed as Tyrannosaur Rex was doomed, and they fought on as he did, serving, in their strange way, the shape of Minerva that stood behind Mars.

Now they were gone. We can learn much by studying the place they held in the Undersea Period. For, because of them, civilization rose again to the heights it had once reached on Earth, and far beyond.

"These lords shall light the mystery
Of mastery or victory,
And these ride high in history,
But these shall not return."

The Free Companions hold their place in interplanetary literature. They are a legend now, archaic and strange. For they were fighters, and war has gone with unification. But we can understand them a little more than could the people of the Keeps.

This story, built on legends and fact, is about a typical warrior of the period—Captain Brian Scott of Doone's Free Companions. He may never have existed—

I

O, it's Tommy this, an' Tommy that, an' "Tommy, go away";
But it's "Thank you, Mr. Atkins," when the band begins to play,
The band begins to play, my boys, the band begins to play—
O, it's "Thank you, Mr. Atkins," when the band begins to play.

—Kipling

SCOTT DRANK STINGING UISQUEPLUS AND GLOWERED ACROSS the smoky tavern. He was a hard, stocky man, with thick gray-shot brown hair and the scar of an old wound crinkling his chin. He was thirty-odd, looking like the veteran he was, and he had sense enough to wear a plain suit of blue celoflex, rather than the garish silks and rainbow fabrics that were all around him.

Outside, through the transparent walls, a laughing throng was carried to and for along the movable ways. But in the tavern it was silent, except for the low voice of a harpman as he chanted some old ballad, accompanying himself on his complicated instrument. The song came to an end. There was scattered applause, and from the hot-box overhead the blaring music of an orchestra burst out. Instantly the restraint was gone. In the booths and at the bar men and women began to laugh and talk with casual unrestraint. Couples were dancing now.

The girl beside Scott, a slim, tan-skinned figure with glossy black ringlets cascading to her shoulders, turned inquiring eyes to him.

"Want to, Brian?"

Scott's mouth twisted in a wry grimace. "Suppose so, Jeana. Eh?" He rose, and she came gracefully into his arms.

Brian did not dance too well, but what he lacked in practice he made up in integration. Jeana's heart-shaped face, with its high cheekbones and vividly crimson lips, lifted to him.

"Forget Bienne. He's just trying to ride you."

Scott glanced toward a distant booth, where two girls sat with a man—Commander Fredric Bienne of the Doones. He was a gaunt, tall, bitter-faced man, his regular features twisted into a perpetual sneer, his eyes somber under heavy dark brows. He was pointing, now, toward the couple on the floor.

"I know," Scott said. "He's doing it, too. Well, the hell with him. So I'm a captain now and he's still a commander. That's tough. Next time he'll obey orders and not send his ship out of the line, trying to ram."

"That was it, eh?" Jeana asked. "I wasn't sure. There's plenty of talk."

"There always is. Oh, Bienne's hated me for years. I reciprocate. We simply don't get on together. Never did. Every time I got a promotion, he chewed his nails. Figured he had a longer service record than I had, and deserved to move up faster. But he's too much of an individualist—at the wrong times."

"He's drinking a lot," Jeana said.

"Let him. Three months we've been in Montana Keep. The boys get tired of inaction—being treated like this." Scott nodded toward the door, where a Free Companion was arguing with the keeper. "No noncoms allowed in here. Well, the devil with it."

They could not hear the conversation above the hubbub, but its importance was evident. Presently the soldier shrugged, his mouth forming a curse, and departed. A fat man in scarlet silks shouted encouragement.

"—want any . . . Companions here!"

Scott saw Commander Bienne, his eyes half closed, get up and walk toward the fat man's booth. His shoulder moved in an imperceptible shrug. The hell with civilians, anyhow. Serve the lug right if Bienne smashed his greasy face. And that seemed the probable outcome. For the fat man was accompanied by a girl, and obviously wasn't going to back down, though Bienne, standing too close to him, was saying something insulting, apparently.

The auxiliary hot-box snapped some quick syllables, lost in the general tumult. But Scott's trained ear caught the words. He nodded to Jeana, made a significant clicking noise with his tongue, and said, "This is it."

She, too, had heard. She let Scott go. He headed toward the fat man's booth just in time to see the beginning of a brawl. The civilian, red as a turkey cock, had struck out suddenly, landing purely by accident on Bienne's gaunt cheek. The commander, grinning tightly, stepped back a pace, his fist clenching. Scott caught the other's arm.

"Hold it, commander."

Bienne swung around, glaring. "What business is it of yours? Let—"

The fat man, seeing his opponent's attention distracted, acquired more courage and came in swinging. Scott reached past Bienne, planted his open hand in the civilian's face, and pushed hard. The fat man almost fell backward on his table.

As he rebounded, he saw a gun in Scott's hand. The captain said curtly, " 'Tend to your knitting, mister."

The civilian licked his lips, hesitated, and sat down. Under his breath he muttered something about too-damn-cocky Free Companions.

Bienne was trying to break free, ready to swing on the captain. Scott holstered his gun. "Orders," he told the other, jerking his head toward the hot-box. "Get it?"

"—mobilization Doonemen report to headquarters. Captain Scott to Administration. Immediate mobilization—"

"Oh," Bienne said, though he still scowled. "O.K. I'll take over. There was time for me to take a crack at that louse, though."

"You know what instant mobilization means," Scott grunted. "We may have to leave at an instant's notice. Orders, commander."

Bienne saluted halfheartedly and turned away. Scott went back to his own booth. Jeana had already gathered her purse and gloves and was applying lip juice.

She met his eyes calmly enough.

"I'll be at the apartment, Brian. Luck."

He kissed her briefly, conscious of a surging excitement at the prospect of a new venture. Jeana understood his emotion. She gave him a quick, wry smile, touched his hair lightly, and rose. They went out into the gay tumult of the ways.

Perfumed wind blew into Scott's face. He wrinkled his nose disgustedly. During carnival seasons the Keeps were less pleasant to the Free Companions than otherwise; they felt more keenly the gulf that lay between them and the undersea dwellers. Scott pushed his way through the crowd and took Jeana across the ways to the center fast-speed strip. They found seats.

At a clover-leaf intersection Scott left the girl, heading toward Administration, the cluster of taller buildings in the city's center. The technical and political headquarters were centered here, except for the laboratories, which were in suburbs near the base of the Dome. There were a few small test-domes a mile or so distant from the city, but these were used only for more precarious experiments. Glancing up, Scott was reminded of the catastrophe that had unified science into something like a free-masonry. Above him, hanging without gravity over a central plaza, was the globe of the Earth, half shrouded by the folds of a black plastic pall. In every Keep on Venus there was a similar ever-present reminder of the lost mother planet.

Scott's gaze went up farther, to the Dome, as though he could penetrate the impervium and the mile-deep layer of water and the clouded atmosphere to the white star that hung in space, one quarter as brilliant as the Sun. A star—all that remained of Earth, since atomic power had been unleashed there two centuries ago. The scourge had spread like flame, melting continents and leveling mountains. In the libraries there were wire-tape pictorial records of the Holocaust. A religious cult—Men of the New Judgment—had sprung up, and advocated the complete destruction of science; followers of that dogma still existed here and there. But the cult's teeth had been drawn when technicians unified, outlawing experiments with atomic power forever, making use of that force punishable by death, and permitting no one to join their society without taking the Minervan Oath.

"—to work for the ultimate good of mankind . . . taking all precaution against harming humanity and science . . . requiring permission from those in authority before undertaking any experiment involving peril to the race . . . remembering always the extent of the trust placed in us and remembering forever the death of the mother planet through misuse of knowledge—"

The Earth. A strange sort of world it must have been, Scott thought. Sunlight, for one thing, unfiltered by the cloud layer. In the old days, there had been few unexplored areas left on Earth. But here on Venus, where the continents had not yet been conquered—there was no need, of course, since everything necessary to life could be produced under the Domes—here on Venus, there was still a frontier. In the Keeps, a highly specialized social culture. Above the surface, a primeval world, where only the Free Companions had their fortresses and navies— the navies for fighting, the forts to house the technicians who provided the latter-day sinews of war, science instead of money. The Keeps tolerated visits from the Free Companions, but would not offer them headquarters, so violent the feeling, so sharp the schism, in the public mind, between war and cultural progress.

Under Scott's feet the sliding way turned into an escalator, carrying him into the Administration Building. He stepped to another way which took him to a lift, and, a moment or two later, was facing the door-curtain bearing the face of President Dane Crosby of Montana Keep.

Crosby's voice said, "Come in, captain," and Scott brushed through the curtain, finding himself in a medium-sized room with muraled walls and a great window overlooking the city. Crosby, a white-haired, thin figure in blue silks, was at his desk. He looked like a tired old clerk out of Dickens, Scott thought suddenly, entirely undistinguished and ordinary. Yet Crosby was one of the greatest socio-politicians on Venus.

Cinc Rhys, leader of Doone's Free Companions, was sitting in a relaxer, the apparent antithesis of Crosby. All the moisture in Rhys' body seemed to have been sucked out of him years ago by ultraviolet actinic, leaving a mummy of brown leather and whipcord sinew. There was no softness in the man. His smile was a grimace. Muscles lay like wire under the swarthy cheeks.

Scott saluted. Rhys waved him to a relaxer. The look of subdued eagerness in the cinc's eyes was significant—an eagle poising himself, smelling blood. Crosby sensed that, and a wry grin showed on his pale face.

"Every man to his trade," he remarked, semi-ironically. "I suppose I'd be bored stiff if I had too long a vacation. But you'll have quite a battle on your hands this time, Cinc Rhys."

Scott's stocky body tensed automatically. Rhys glanced at him.

"Virginia Keep is attacking, captain. They've hired the Helldivers—Flynn's outfit."

There was a pause. Both Free Companions were anxious to discuss the angles, but unwilling to do so in the presence of a civilian, even the president of Montana Keep. Crosby rose.

"The money settlement's satisfactory, then?"

Rhys nodded. "Yes, that's all right. I expect the battle will take place in a couple of days. In the neighborhood of Venus Deep, at a rough guess."

"Good. I've a favor to ask, so if you'll excuse me for a few minutes, I'll—" He left the sentence unfinished and went out through the door-curtain. Rhys offered Scott a cigarette.

"You get the implications, captain—the Helldivers?"

"Yes, sir. Thanks. We can't do it alone."

"Right. We're short on manpower and armament both. And the Helldivers recently merged with O'Brien's Legion, after O'Brien was killed in that polar scrap. They're a strong outfit, plenty strong. Then they've got their specialty—submarine attack. I'd say we'll have to use H-plan 7."

Scott closed his eyes, remembering the files. Each Free Company kept up-to-date plans of attack suited to the merits of every other Company of Venus. Frequently revised as new advances were made, as groups merged, and as the balance of power changed on each side, the plans were so detailed that they could be carried into action at literally a moment's notice. H-plan 7, Scott recalled, involved enlisting the aid of the Mob, a small but well-organized band of Free Companions led by Cinc Tom Mendez.

"Right," Scott said. "Can you get him?"

"I think so. We haven't agreed yet on the bonus. I've been telaudioing him on a tight beam, but he keeps putting me off—waiting till the last moment, when he can dictate his own terms."

"What's he asking, sir?"

"Fifty thousand cash and a fifty percent cut on the loot."

"I'd say thirty percent would be about right."

Rhys nodded. "I've offered him thirty-five. I may send you to his fort—carte blanche. We can get another Company, but Mendez has got beautiful sub-detectors—which would come in handy against the Helldivers. Maybe I can settle things by audio. If not, you'll have to fly over to Mendez and buy his services, at less than fifty per if you can."

Scott rubbed the old scar on his chin with a calloused forefinger. "Meantime Commander Bienne's in charge of mobilization. When—"

"I telaudioed our fort. Air transports are on the way now."

"It'll be quite a scrap," Scott said, and the eyes of the two men met in perfect understanding. Rhys chuckled dryly.

"And good profits. Virginia Keep has a big supply of korium . . . dunno how much, but plenty."

"What started the fracas this time?"

"The usual thing, I suppose," Rhys said disinterestedly. "Imperialism. Somebody in Virginia Keep worked out a new plan for annexing the rest of the Keeps. Same as usual."

They stood up as the door-curtain swung back, admitting President Crosby, another man, and a girl. The man looked young, his boyish face not yet toughened under actinic burn. The girl was lovely in the manner of a plastic figurine, lit from within by vibrant life. Her blond hair was cropped in the prevalent mode, and her eyes, Scott saw, were an unusual shade of green. She was more than merely pretty—she was instantly exciting.

Crosby said, "My niece, Ilene Kane—and my nephew, Norman Kane." He performed introductions, and they found seats.

"What about drinks?" Ilene suggested. "This is rather revoltingly formal. The flight hasn't started yet, after all."

Crosby shook his head at her. "You weren't invited here anyway. Don't try to turn this into a party—there isn't too much time, under the circumstances."

"O.K.," Ilene murmured. "I can wait." She eyed Scott interestedly.

Norman Kane broke in. "I'd like to join Doone's Free Companions, sir. I've already applied, but now that there's a battle coming up, I hate to wait till my application's approved. So I thought—"

Crosby looked at Cinc Rhys. "A personal favor, but the decision's up to you. My nephew's a misfit—a romanticist. Never liked the life of a Keep. A year ago he went off and joined Starling's outfit."

Rhys raised an eyebrow. "That gang? It's not a recommendation, Kane. They're not even classed as Free Companions. More like a band of guerrillas, and entirely without ethics. There've even been rumors they're messing around with atomic power."

Crosby looked startled. "I hadn't heard that."

"It's no more than a rumor. If it's ever proved, the Free Companions—all of them—will get together and smash Starling in a hurry."

Norman Kane looked slightly uncomfortable. "I suppose I was rather a fool. But I wanted to get in the fighting game, and Starling's group appealed to me—"

The cinc made a sound in his throat. "They would. Swashbuckling romantics, with no idea of what war means. They've not more than a dozen technicians. And they've no discipline —it's like a pirate outfit. War today, Kane, isn't won by romantic animals dashing at forlorn hopes. The modern soldier is a tactician who knows how to think, integrate, and obey. If you join our Company, you'll have to forget what you learned with Starling."

"Will you take me, sir?"

"I think it would be unwise. You need the training course."

"I've had experience—"

Crosby said, "It would be a favor, Cinc Rhys, if you'd skip the red tape. I'd appreciate it. Since my nephew wants to be a soldier, I'd much prefer to see him with the Doones."

Rhys shrugged. "Very well. Captain Scott will give you your orders, Kane. Remember that discipline is vitally important with us."

The boy tried to force back a delighted grin. "Thank you, sir."

"Captain—"

Scott rose and nodded to Kane. They went out together. In the anteroom was a telaudio set, and Scott called the Doone's local headquarters in Montana Keep. An integrator answered, his face looking inquiringly from the screen.

"Captain Scott calling, subject induction."

"Yes, sir. Ready to record."

Scott drew Kane forward. "Photosnap this man. He'll report to headquarters immediately. Name, Norman Kane. Enlist him without training course—special orders from Cinc Rhys."

"Acknowledged, sir."

Scott broke the connection. Kane couldn't quite repress his grin.

"All right," the captain grunted, a sympathetic gleam in his eyes. "That fixes it. They'll put you in my command. What's your specialty."

"Flitterboats, sir."

"Good. One more thing. Don't forget what Cinc Rhys said, Kane. Discipline is damned important, and you may not have realized that yet. This isn't a cloak-and-sword war. There are no Charges of Light Brigades. No grandstand plays—that stuff went out with the Crusades. Just obey orders, and you'll have no trouble. Good luck."

"Thank you, sir." Kane saluted and strode out with a perceptible swagger. Scott grinned. The kid would have *that* knocked out of him pretty soon.

A voice at his side made him turn quickly. Ilene Kane was standing there, slim and lovely in her celoflex gown.

"You seem pretty human after all, captain," she said. "I heard what you told Norman."

Scott shrugged. "I did that for his own good—and the good of the Company. One man off the beam can cause plenty of trouble, Mistress Kane."

"I envy Norman," she said. "It must be a fascinating life you lead. I'd like it—for a while. Not for long. I'm one of the useless offshoots of this civilization, not much good for anything. So I've perfected one talent."

"What's that?"

"Oh, hedonism, I suppose you'd call it. I enjoy myself. It's not often too boring. But I'm a bit bored now. I'd like to talk to you, captain."

"Well, I'm listening," Scott said.

Ilene Kane made a small grimace. "Wrong semantic term. I'd like to get inside of you psychologically. But painlessly. Dinner and dancing. Can do?"

"There's no time," Scott told her. "We may get our orders any moment." He wasn't sure he wanted to go out with this girl of the Keeps, though there was definitely a subtle fascination for him, an appeal he could not analyze. She typified the most pleasurable part of a world he did not know. The other facets of that world could not impinge on him; geopolitics or nonmilitary science held no appeal, were too alien. But all worlds touch at one point—pleasure. Scott could understand the relaxations of the undersea groups, as he could not understand or feel sympathy for their work on their social impulses.

Cinc Rhys came through the door-curtain, his eyes narrowed. "I've some telaudioing to do, captain," he said. Scott knew what implications the words held: the incipient bargain with Cinc Mendez. He nodded.

"Yes, sir. Shall I report to headquarters?"

Rhys' harsh face seemed to relax suddenly as he looked from Ilene to Scott. "You're free till dawn. I won't need you till then, but report to me at six a.m. No doubt you've a few details to clean up."

"Very well, sir." Scott watched Rhys go out. The cinc had meant Jeana, of course. But Ilene did not know that.

"So?" she asked. "Do I get a turn-down? You might buy me a drink, anyway."

There was plenty of time. Scott said, "It'll be a pleasure," and Ilene linked her arm with his. They took the dropper to ground-level.

As they came out on one of the ways, Ilene turned her head and caught Scott's glance. "I forgot something, captain. You may have a previous engagement. I didn't realize—"

"There's nothing," he said. "Nothing important."

It was true; he felt a mild gratitude toward Jeana at the realization. His relationship with her was the peculiar one rendered advisable by his career. Free-marriage was the word for it; Jeana was neither his wife nor his mistress, but something midway between. The Free Companions had no firmly grounded foundation for social life; in the Keeps they were visitors, and in their coastal forts they were—well, soldiers. One would no more bring a woman to a fort than aboard a ship of the line. So the women of the Free Companions lived in the Keeps, moving from one to another as their men did; and because of the ever-present shadow of death, ties were purposely left loose. Jeana and Scott had been free-married for five years now. Neither made demands on the other. No one expected fidelity of a Free Companion. Soldiers lived under such iron disciplines that when they were released, during the brief peacetimes, the pendulum often swung far in the opposite direction.

To Scott, Ilene Kane was a key that might unlock the doors of the Keep—doors that opened to a world of which he was not a part, and which he could not quite understand.

II

I, a stranger and afraid
In a world I never made.
　　　　　—*Housman*

There were nuances, Scott found, which he had never known existed. A hedonist like Ilene devoted her life to such nuances; they were her career. Such minor matters as making the powerful, insipid Moonflower Cocktails more palatable by filtering them through lime-soaked sugar held between the teeth. Scott was a uisqueplus man, having the average soldier's contempt for what he termed hydroponic drinks, but the cocktails Ilene suggested were quite as effective as acrid, burning amber uisqueplus. She taught him, that night, such tricks as pausing between glasses to sniff lightly at happy-gas, to mingle sensual excitement with mental by trying the amusement rides designed to give one the violent physical intoxication of breathless speed. Nuances all, which only a girl with Ilene's background could know. She was not representative of Keep life. As she had said, she was an offshoot, a casual and useless flower on the great vine that struck up inexorably to the skies, its strength in its tough, reaching tendrils—scientists and technicians and socio-politicians. She was doomed in her own way, as Scott was in his. The undersea folk served Minerva; Scott served Mars; and Ilene served Aphrodite—not purely the sexual goddess, but the patron of arts and pleasure. Between Scott and Ilene was the difference between Wagner and Strauss; the difference between crashing chords and tinkling arpeggios. In both was a muted bittersweet sadness, seldom realized by either. But that undertone was brought out by their contact. The sense of dim hopelessness in each responded to the other.

It was carnival, but neither Ilene nor Scott wore masks. Their faces were masks enough, and both had been trained to reserve, though in different ways. Scott's hard mouth kept its tight grimness even when he smiled. And Ilene's smiles came so often that they were meaningless.

Through her, Scott was able to understand more of the undersea life than he had ever done before. She was for him a catalyst. A tacit understanding grew between them, not needing words. Both realized that, in the course of progress, they would eventually die out. Mankind tolerated them because that was necessary for a little time. Each responded differently. Scott served Mars; he served actively; and the girl, who was passive, was attracted by the antithesis.

Scott's drunkenness struck physically deep. He did not show it. His stiff silver-brown hair was not disarranged, and his hard, burned face was impassive as ever. But when his

brown eyes met Ilene's green ones a spark of—something—
met between them.

Color and light and sound. They began to form a pattern
now, were not quite meaningless to Scott. They were, long
past midnight, sitting in an Olympus, which was a private
cosmos. The walls of the room in which they were seemed
nonexistent. The gusty tides of gray, faintly luminous clouds
seemed to drive chaotically past them, and, dimly, they
could hear the muffled screaming of an artificial wind. They
had the isolation of the gods.

*And the Earth was without form, and void; and darkness
was upon the face of the deep*— That was, of course, the
theory of the Olympus room. No one existed, no world
existed, outside of the chamber; values automatically shifted,
and inhibitions seemed absurd.

Scott relaxed on a translucent cushion like a cloud. Beside
him, Ilene lifted the bit of a happy-gas tube to his nostrils.
He shook his head.

"Not now, Ilene."

She let the tube slide back into its reel. "Nor I. Too much
of anything is unsatisfactory, Brian. There should always be
something untasted, some anticipation left— You have that.
I haven't."

"How?"

"Pleasures—well, there's a limit. There's a limit to human
endurance. And eventually I build up a resistance psychi-
cally, as I do physically, to everything. With you, there's
always the last adventure. You never know when death will
come. You can't plan. Plans are dull; it's the unexpected
that's important."

Scott shook his head slightly. "Death isn't important either. It's an automatic cancellation of values. Or, rather—"
He hesitated, seeking words. "In this life you can plan, you
can work out values, because they're all based on certain
conditions. On—let's say—arithmetic. Death is a change to
a different plane of conditions, quite unknown. Arithmetical
rules don't apply as such to geometry."

"You think death has its rules?"

"It may be a lack of rules, Ilene. One lives realizing that
life is subject to death; civilization is based on that. That's
why civilization concentrates on the race instead of the
individual. Social self-preservation."

She looked at him gravely. "I didn't think a Free Companion could theorize that way."

Scott closed his eyes, relaxing. "The Keeps know nothing about Free Companions. They don't want to. We're men. Intelligent men. Our technicians are as great as the scientists under the Domes."

"But they work for war."

"War's necessary," Scott said. "Now, anyway."

"How did you get into it? Should I ask?"

He laughed a little at that. "Oh, I've no dark secrets in my past. I'm not a runaway murderer. One—drifts. I was born in Australia Keep. My father was a tech, but my grandfather had been a soldier. I guess it was in my blood. I tried various trades and professions. Meaningless. I wanted something that . . . hell, I don't know. Something, maybe, that needs all of a man. Fighting does. It's like a religion. Those cultists—Men of the New Judgment—they're fanatics, but you can see that their religion is the only thing that matters to them."

"Bearded, dirty men with twisted minds, though."

"It happens to be a religion based on false premises. There are others, appealing to different types. But religion was too passive for me, in these days."

Ilene examined his harsh face. "You'd have preferred the church militant—the Knights of Malta, fighting Saracens."

"I suppose. I had no values. Anyhow, I'm a fighter."

"Just how important is it to you? The Free Companions?"

Scott opened his eyes and grinned at the girl. He looked unexpectedly boyish.

"Damn little, really. It has emotional appeal. Intellectually, I know that it's a huge fake. Always has been. As absurd as the Men of the New Judgment. Fighting's doomed. So we've no real purpose. I suppose most of us know there's no future for the Free Companions. In a few hundred years—well!"

"And still you go on. Why? It isn't money."

"No. There is a . . . a drunkenness to it. The ancient Norsemen had their berserker madness. We have something similar. To a Dooneman, his group is father, mother, child, and God Almighty. He fights the other Free Companions when he's paid to do so, but he doesn't hate the others. They serve the same toppling idol. And it *is* toppling, Ilene. Each battle we win or lose brings us closer to the end. We fight to protect the culture that eventually will wipe us out.

The Keeps—when they finally unify, will they need a military arm? I can see the trend. If war was an essential part of civilization, each Keep would maintain its own military. But they shut us out—a necessary evil. If they would end war now!" Scott's fist unconsciously clenched. "So many men would find happier places in Venus—undersea. But as long as the Free Companions exist, there'll be new recruits."

Ilene sipped her cocktail, watching the gray chaos of clouds flow like a tide around them. In the dimly luminous light Scott's face seemed like dark stone, flecks of brightness showing in his eyes. She touched his hand gently.

"You're a soldier, Brian. You wouldn't change."

His laugh was intensely bitter. "Like hell I wouldn't, Mistress Ilene Kane! Do you think fighting's just pulling a trigger? I'm a military strategist. That took ten years. Harder cramming than I'd have had in a Keep Tech-Institute. I have to know everything about war from trajectories to mass psychology. This is the greatest science the System has ever known, and the most useless. Because war will die in a few centuries at most. Ilene—you've never seen a Free Company's fort. It's science, marvelous science, aimed at military ends only. We have our psych-specialists. We have our engineers, who plan everything from ordnance to the frictional quotient on flitterboats. We have the foundries and mills. Each fortress is a city made for war, as the Keeps are made for social progress."

"As complicated as that?"

"Beautifully complicated and beautifully useless. There are so many of us who realize that. Oh, we fight—it's a poison. We worship the Company—that is an emotional poison. But we live only during wartime. It's an incomplete life. Men in the Keeps have full lives; they have their work, and their relaxations are geared to fit them. We don't fit."

"Not all the undersea races," Ilene said. "There's always the fringe that doesn't fit. At least you have a *raison d'être*. You're a soldier. I can't make a lifework out of pleasure. But there's nothing else for me."

Scott's fingers tightened on hers. "You're the product of a civilization, at least. I'm left out."

"With you, Brian, it might be better. For a while. I don't think it would last for long."

"It might."

"You think so now. It's quite a horrible thing, feeling yourself a shadow."

"I know."

"I want you, Brian," Ilene said, turning to face him. "I want you to come to Montana Keep and stay here. Until our experiment fails. I think it'll fail presently. But, perhaps, not for some time. I need your strength. I can show you how to get the most out of this sort of life—how to enter into it. True hedonism. You can give me —companionship perhaps. For me the companionship of hedonists who know nothing else isn't enough."

Scott was silent. Ilene watched him for a while.

"Is war so important?" she asked at last.

"No," he said, "it isn't at all. It's a balloon. And it's empty, I know that. Honor of the regiment!" Scott laughed. "I'm not hesitating, really. I've been shut out for a long time. A social unit shouldn't be founded on an obviously doomed fallacy. Men and women are important, nothing else, I suppose."

"Men and women—or the race?"

"Not the race," he said with abrupt violence. "Damn the race! It's done nothing for me. I can fit myself into a new life. Not necessarily hedonism. I'm an expert in several lines; I have to be. I can find work in Montana Keep."

"If you like. I've never tried. I'm more of a fatalist, I suppose. But . . . what about it, Brian?"

Her eyes were almost luminous, like shining emerald, in the ghostly light.

"Yes," Scott said. "I'll come back. To stay."

Ilene said, "Come back? Why not stay now?"

"Because I'm a complete fool, I guess. I'm a key man, and Cinc Rhys needs me just now."

"Is it Rhys or the Company?"

Scott smiled crookedly. "Not the Company. It's just a job I have to do. When I think how many years I've been slaving, pretending absurdities were important, knowing that I was bowing to a straw dummy—No! I want your life—the sort of life I didn't know could exist in the Keeps. I'll be back, Ilene. It's something more important than love. Separately we're halves. Together we may be a complete whole."

She didn't answer. Her eyes were steady on Scott's. He kissed her.

*   *   *

Before morning bell he was back in the apartment. Jeana had already packed the necessary light equipment. She was asleep, her dark hair cascading over the pillow, and Scott did not waken her. Quietly he shaved, showered, and dressed. A heavy, waiting silence seemed to fill the city like a cup brimming with stillness.

As he emerged from the bathroom, buttoning his tunic, he saw the table had been let down and two places set at it. Jeana came in, wearing a cool morning frock. She set cups down and poured coffee.

"Morning, soldier," she said. "You've time for this, haven't you?"

"Uh-huh." Scott kissed her, a bit hesitantly. Up till this moment, the breaking with Jeana had seemed easy enough. She would raise no objections. That was the chief reason for free-marriage. However—

She was sitting in the relaxer, sweetening the coffee, opening a fresh celopack of cigarettes. "Hung over?"

"No. I vitamized. Feel pretty good." Most bars had a vitamizing chamber to nullify the effects of too much stimulant. Scott was, in fact, feeling fresh and keenly alert. He was wondering how to broach the subject of Ilene to Jeana.

She saved him the trouble.

"If it's a girl, Brian, just take it easy. No use doing anything till this war's over. How long will it take?"

"Oh, not long. A week at most. One battle may settle it, you know. The girl—"

"She's not a Keep girl."

"Yes."

Jeana looked up, startled. "You're crazy."

"I started to tell you," Scott said impatiently. "It isn't just—her. I'm sick of the Doones. I'm going to quit."

"Hm-m-m. Like that?"

"Like that."

Jeana shook her head. "Keep women aren't tough."

"They don't need to be. Their men aren't soldiers."

"Have it your own way. I'll wait till you get back. Maybe I've got a hunch. You see, Brian, we've been together for five years. We fit. Not because of anything like philosophy or psychology— it's a lot more personal. It's just us. As man and woman, we get along comfortably. There's love, too. Those close emotional feelings are more important, really, than the long view. You can get excited about futures, but you can't live them."

Scott shrugged. "Could be I'm starting to forget about futures. Concentrating on Brian Scott."

"More coffee . . . there. Well, for five years now I've gone with you from Keep to Keep, waiting every time you went off to war, wondering if you'd come back, knowing that I was just a part of your life, but—I sometimes thought—the most important part. Soldiering's seventy-five percent. I'm the other quarter. I think you need that quarter—you need the whole thing, in that proportion, actually. You could find another woman, but she'd have to be willing to take twenty-five percent."

Scott didn't answer. Jeana blew smoke through her nostrils.

"O.K., Brian. I'll wait."

"It isn't the girl so much. She happens to fit into the pattern of what I want. You—"

"I'd never be able to fit that pattern," Jeana said softly. "The Free Companions need women who are willing to be soldiers' wives. Free-wives, if you like. Chiefly it's a matter of not being too demanding. But there are other things. No, Brian. Even if you wanted that, I couldn't make myself over into one of the Keep people. It wouldn't be me. I wouldn't respect myself, living a life that'd be false to me; and you wouldn't like me that way either. I couldn't and wouldn't change. I'll have to stay as I am. A soldier's wife. As long as you're a Dooneman, you'll need me. But if *you* change—" She didn't finish.

Scott lit a cigarette, scowling. "It's hard to know, exactly."

"I may not understand you, but I don't ask questions and I don't try to change you. As long as you want that, you can have it from me. I've nothing else to offer you. It's enough for a Free Companion. It's not enough—or too much—for a Keep-dweller."

"I'll miss you," he said.

"That'll depend, too. I'll miss you." Under the table her fingers writhed together, but her face did not change. "It's getting late. Here, let me check your chronometer." Jeana leaned across the table, lifted Scott's wrist, and compared his watch with the central-time clock on the wall. "O.K. On your way, soldier."

Scott stood up, tightening his belt. He bent to kiss Jeana, and, though she began to turn her face away, after a moment she raised her lips to his.

They didn't speak. Scott went out quickly, and the girl sat motionless, the cigarette smoldering out unheeded between her fingers. Somehow it did not matter so much, now, that Brian was leaving her for another woman and another life. As always, the one thing of real importance was that he was going into danger.

Guard him from harm, she thought, not knowing that she was praying. *Guard him from harm*!

And now there would be silence, and waiting. That, at least, had not changed. Her eyes turned to the clock.

Already the minutes were longer.

III

'E's the kind of a giddy harumfrodite—soldier an' sailor too!

—*Kipling*

Commander Bienne was superintending the embarkation of the last Dooneman when Scott arrived at headquarters. He saluted the captain briskly, apparently untired by his night's work of handling the transportation routine.

"All checked, sir."

Scott nodded. "Good. Is Cinc Rhys here?"

"He just arrived." Bienne nodded toward a door-curtain. As Scott moved away, the other followed.

"What's up, commander?"

Bienne pitched his voice low. "Bronson's laid up with endemic fever." He forgot to say "sir." "He was to handle the left wing of the fleet. I'd appreciate that job."

"I'll see if I can do it."

Bienne's lips tightened, but he said nothing more. He turned back to his men, and Scott went on into the cinc's office. Rhys was at the telaudio. He looked up, his eyes narrowed.

"Morning, captain. I've just heard from Mendez."

"Yes, sir?"

"He's still holding out for a fifty percent cut on the korium ransom from Virginia Keep. You'll have to see him. Try and get the Mob for less than fifty if you can. Telaudio me from Mendez's fort."

"Check, sir."

"Another thing. Bronson's in sick bay."

"I heard that. If I may suggest Commander Bienne to take his place at left-wing command—"

But Cinc Rhys raised his hand. "Not this time. We can't

afford individualism. The commander tried to play a lone hand in the last war. You know we can't risk it till he's back in line—thinking of the Doones instead of Fredric Bienne."

"He's a good man, sir. A fine strategist."

"But not yet a good integrating factor. Perhaps next time. Put Commander Geer on the left wing. Keep Bienne with you. He needs discipline. And—take a flitterboat to Mendez."

"Not a plane?"

"One of the technicians just finished a new tight-beam camouflager for communications. I'm having it installed immediately on all our planes and gliders. Use the boat; it isn't far to the Mob's fort—that long peninsula on the coast of Southern Hell."

Even on the charts that continent was named Hell—for obvious reasons. Heat was only one of them. And, even with the best equipment, a party exploring the jungle there would soon find itself suffering the tortures of the damned. On the land of Venus, flora and fauna combined diabolically to make the place uninhabitable to Earthmen. Many of the plants even exhaled poisonous gases. Only the protected coastal forts of the Free Companies could exist—and that was because they *were* forts.

Cinc Rhys frowned at Scott. "We'll use H-plan 7 if we can get the Mob. Otherwise we'll have to fall back on another outfit, and I don't want to do that. The Helldivers have too many subs, and we haven't enough detectors. So do your damnedest."

Scott saluted. "I'll do that, sir." Rhys waved him away, and he went out into the next room, finding Commander Bienne alone. The officer turned an inquiring look toward him.

"Sorry," Scott said. "Geer gets the left-wing command this time."

Bienne's sour face turned dark red. "I'm sorry I didn't take a crack at you before mobilization," he said. "You hate competition, don't you?"

Scott's nostrils flared. "If it had been up to me, you'd have got that command, Bienne."

"Sure. I'll bet. All right, captain. Where's my bunk? A flitterboat?"

"You'll be on right wing, with me. Control ship *Flintlock*."

"With you. Under you, you mean," Bienne said tightly. His eyes were blazing. "Yeah."

Scott's dark cheeks were flushed too. "Orders, commander," he snapped. "Get me a flitterboat pilot. I'm going topside."

Without a word Bienne turned to the telaudio. Scott, a tight, furious knot in his stomach, stamped out of headquarters, trying to fight down his anger. Bienne was a jackass. A lot he cared about the Doones—

Scott caught himself and grinned sheepishly. Well, he cared little about the Doones himself. But while he was in the Company, discipline was important—integration with the smoothly running fighting machine. No place for individualism. One thing he and Bienne had in common; neither had any sentiment about the Company.

He took a lift to the ceiling of the Dome. Beneath him Montana Keep dropped away, shrinking to doll size. Somewhere down there, he thought, was Ilene. He'd be back. Perhaps this war would be a short one—not that they were ever much longer than a week, except in unusual cases where a Company developed new strategies.

He was conducted through an air lock into a bubble, a tough, transparent sphere with a central vertical core through which the cable ran. Except for Scott, the bubble was empty. After a moment it started up with a slight jar. Gradually the water outside the curving walls changed from black to deep green, and thence to translucent chartreuse. Sea creatures were visible, but they were nothing new to Scott; he scarcely saw them.

The bubble broke surface. Since air pressure had been constant, there was no possibility of the bends, and Scott opened the panel and stepped out on one of the buoyant floats that dotted the water above Montana Keep. A few sightseers crowded into the chamber he had left, and presently it was drawn down, out of sight.

In the distance Free Companions were embarking from a larger float to an air ferry. Scott glanced up with a weather eye. No storm, he saw, though the low ceiling was, as usual, torn and twisted into boiling currents by the winds. He remembered, suddenly, that the battle would probably take place over Venus Deep. That would make it somewhat harder for the gliders—there would be few of the thermals found, for instance, above the Sea of Shallows here.

A flitterboat, low, fast, and beautifully maneuverable, shot in toward the quay. The pilot flipped back the overhead shell and saluted Scott. It was Norman Kane, looking shipshape in his tight-fitting gray uniform, and apparently ready to grin at the slightest provocation.

Scott jumped lightly down into the craft and seated himself beside the pilot. Kane drew the transparent shell back over them. He looked at Scott.

"Orders, captain?"

"Know where the Mob's fort is? Good. Head there. Fast."

Kane shot the flitterboat out from the float with a curtain of v-shaped spray rising from the bow. Drawing little water, maneuverable, incredibly fast, these tiny craft were invaluable in naval battle. It was difficult to hit one, they moved so fast. They had no armor to slow them down. They carried high explosive bullets fired from small-caliber guns, and were, as a rule, two-man craft. They complemented the heavier ordnance of the battlewagons and destroyers.

Scott handed Kane a cigarette. The boy hesitated.

"We're not under fire," the captain chuckled. "Discipline clamps down during a battle, but it's O.K. for you to have a smoke with me. Here!" He lit the white tube for Kane.

"Thanks sir. I guess I'm a bit—over-anxious?"

"Well, war has its rules. Not many, but they mustn't be broken." Both men were silent for a while, watching the blank gray surface of the ocean ahead. A transport plane passed them, flying low.

"Is Ilene Kane your sister?" Scott asked presently.

Kane nodded. "Yes, sir."

"Thought so. If she'd been a man, I imagine she'd have been a Free Companion."

The boy shrugged. "Oh, I don't know. She doesn't have the— I don't know. She'd consider it too much effort. She doesn't like discipline."

"Do you?"

"It's fighting that's important to me. Sir." That was an afterthought. "Winning, really."

"You can lose a battle even though you win it," Scott said rather somberly.

"Well, I'd rather be a Free Companion than do anything else I know of. Not that I've had much experience—"

"You've had experience of war with Starling's outfit, but you probably learned some dangerous stuff at the same time. War isn't swashbuckling piracy these days. If the Doones tried to win battles by that sort of thing, there'd be no more Doones in a week or so."

"But—" Kane hesitated. "Isn't that sort of thing rather necessary? Taking blind chances, I mean—"

"There are desperate chances," Scott told him, "but there are no blind chances in war—not to a good soldier. When I was green in the service, I ran a cruiser out of the line to ram. I was demoted, for a very good reason. The enemy ship I rammed wasn't as important to the enemy as our cruiser was to us. If I'd stayed on course, I'd have helped sink three or four ships instead of disabling one and putting my cruiser out of action. It's the great god integration we worship, Kane. It's much more important now than it ever was on Earth, because the military has consolidated. Army, navy, air, undersea—they're all part of one organization now. I suppose the only important change was in the air."

"Gliders, you mean? I knew powered planes couldn't be used in battle."

"Not in the atmosphere of Venus," Scott agreed. "Once powered planes get up in the cloud strata, they're fighting crosscurrents and pockets so much they've got no time to do accurate firing. If they're armored, they're slow. If they're light, detectors can spot them and antiaircraft can smash them. Unpowered gliders are valuable not for bombing but for directing attacks. They get into the clouds, stay hidden, and use infrared telecameras which are broadcast on a tight beam back to the control ships. They're the eyes of the fleet. They can tell us— *White water ahead, Kane! Swerve!*"

The pilot had already seen the ominous boiling froth foaming out in front of the bow. Instinctively he swung the flitterboat in a wrenching turn. The craft heeled sidewise, throwing its occupants almost out of their seats.

"Sea beast?" Scott asked, and answered his own question. "No, not with these spouts. It's volcanic. And it's spreading fast."

"I can circle it, sir," Kane suggested.

Scott shook his head. "Too dangerous. Backtrack."

Obediently the boy sent the flitterboat racing out of the area of danger. Scott had been right about the extent of the danger; the boiling turmoil was widening almost faster than the tiny ship could flee. Suddenly the line of white water caught up with them. The flitterboat jounced like a chip, the wheel being nearly torn from Kane's grip. Scott reached over and helped steady it. Even with two men handling the wheel, there was a possibility that it might wrench itself free. Steam rose in veils beyond the transparent shell. The water had turned a scummy brown under the froth.

Kane jammed on the power. The flitterboat sprang forward like a ricocheting bullet, dancing over the surface of the seething waves. Once they plunged head-on into a swell, and a screaming of outraged metal vibrated through the craft. Kane, tight-lipped, instantly slammed in the auxiliary, cutting out the smashed motor unit. Then, unexpectedly, they were in clear water, cutting back toward Montana Keep.

Scott grinned. "Nice handling. Lucky you didn't try to circle. We'd never have made it."

"Yes, sir." Kane took a deep breath. His eyes were bright with excitement.

"Circle now. Here." He thrust a lighted cigarette between the boy's lips. "You'll be a good Dooneman, Kane. Your reactions are good and fast."

"Thanks, sir."

Scott smoked silently for a while. He glanced toward the north, but, with the poor visibility, he could not make out the towering range of volcanic peaks that were the backbone of Southern Hell. Venus was a comparatively young planet, the internal fires still bursting forth unexpectedly. Which was why no forts were ever built on islands—they had an unhappy habit of disappearing without warning!

The flitterboat rode hard, at this speed, despite the insulating system of springs and shock absorbers. After a ride in one of these "spankers"—the irreverent name the soldiers had for them—a man needed arnica if not a chiropractor. Scott shifted his weight on the soft air cushions under him, which felt like cement.

Under his breath he hummed:

> *"It ain't the 'eavy 'aulin' that 'urts the 'orses' 'oofs,*
> *It's the 'ammer, 'ammer, 'ammer on the 'ard 'ighway!"*

The flitterboat scooted on, surrounded by monotonous sea and cloud, till finally the rampart of the coast grew before the bow, bursting suddenly from the fog-veiled horizon. Scott glanced at his chronometer and sighed with relief. They had made good time, in spite of the slight delay caused by the subsea volcano.

The fortress of the Mob was a huge metal and stone castle on the tip of the peninsula. The narrow strip that separated it from the mainland had been cleared, and the pockmarks of shell craters showed where guns had driven back on-slaughts from the jungle—the reptilian, ferocious giants of Venus, partially intelligent but absolutely untractable because of the gulf that existed between their methods of thinking and the culture of mankind. Overtures had been made often enough; but it had been found that the reptile-folk were better left alone. They would not parley. They were blindly bestial savages, with whom it was impossible to make truce. They stayed in the jungle, emerging only to hurl furious attacks at the forts—attacks doomed to failure, since fang and talon were matched against lead-jacketed bullet and high explosive.

As the flitterboat shot in to a jetty, Scott kept his eyes straight ahead—it was not considered good form for a Free Companion to seem too curious when visiting the fort of another Company. Several men were on the quay, apparently waiting for him. They saluted as Scott stepped out of the boat.

He gave his name and rank. A corporal stepped forward.

"Cinc Mendez is expecting you, sir. Cinc Rhys telaudioed an hour or so back. If you'll come this way—"

"All right, corporal. My pilot—"

"He'll be taken care of, sir. A rubdown and a drink, perhaps, after a spanker ride."

Scott nodded and followed the other into the bastion that thrust out from the overhanging wall of the fort. The sea gate was open, and he walked swiftly through the courtyard in the corporal's wake, passing a door-curtain, mounting an escalator, and finding himself, presently, before another curtain that bore the face of Cinc Mendez, plump, hoglike, and bald as a bullet.

Entering, he saw Mendez himself at the head of a long table, where nearly a dozen officers of the Mob were also seated. In person Mendez was somewhat more prepossessing than in effigy. He looked like a boar rather than a pig—a fighter, not a gourmand. His sharp black eyes seemed to drive into Scott with the impact of a physical blow.

He stood up, his officers following suit. "Sit down, captain. There's a place at the foot of the table. No reflections on rank, but I prefer to be face to face with the man I'm dealing with. But first—you just arrived? If you'd like a quick rubdown, we'll be glad to wait."

Scott took his place. "Thank you, no, Cinc Mendez. I'd prefer not to lose time."

"Then we'll waste none on introductions. However, you can probably stand a drink." He spoke to the orderly at the door, and presently a filled glass stood at Scott's elbow.

His quick gaze ran along the rows of faces. Good soldiers, he thought—tough, well trained, and experienced. They had been under fire. A small outfit, the Mob, but a powerful one.

Cinc Mendez sipped his own drink. "To business. The Doonemen wish to hire our help in fighting the Helldivers. Virginia Keep has bought the services of the Helldivers to attack Montana Keep." He enumerated on stubby fingers. "You offer us fifty thousand cash and thirty-five percent of the korium ransom. So?"

"That's correct."

"We ask fifty percent."

"It's high. The Doones have superior manpower and equipment."

"To us, not to the Helldivers. Besides, the percentage is contingent. If we should lose, we get only the cash payment."

Scott nodded. "That's correct, but the only real danger from the Helldivers is their submarine corps. The Doones have plenty of surface and air equipment. We might lick the Helldivers without you."

"I don't think so." Mendez shook his bald head. "They have some new underwater torpedoes that make hash out of heavy armor plate. But we have new sub-detectors. We can blast the Helldivers' subs for you before they get within torpedo range."

Scott said bluntly, "You've been stalling, Cinc Mendez. We're not that bad off. If we can't get you, we'll find another outfit."

"With sub-detectors?"

"Yardley's Company is good at undersea work."

A major near the head of the table spoke up. "That's true, sir. They have suicide subs—not too dependable, but they have them."

Cinc Mendez wiped his bald head with his palms in a slow circular motion. "Hm-m-m. Well, captain, I don't know. Yardley's Company isn't as good as ours for this job."

"All right," Scott said. "I've *carte blanche*. We don't know how much korium Virginia Keep has in her vaults. How would this proposition strike you: the Mob gets fifty percent of the korium ransom up to a quarter of a million; thirty-five percent above that."

"Forty-five."

"Forty, above a quarter of a million; forty-five below that sum."

"Gentlemen?" Cinc Mendez asked, looking down the table. "Your vote?"

There were several ayes, and a scattering of nays. Mendez shrugged.

"Then I have the deciding vote. Very well. We get forty-five percent of the Virginia Keep ransom up to a quarter of a million; forty percent on any amount above that. Agreed. We'll drink to it."

Orderlies served drinks. As Mendez rose, the others followed his example. The cinc nodded to Scott.

"Will you propose a toast, captain?"

"With pleasure. Nelson's toast, then—a willing foe and sea room!"

They drank to that, as Free Companions had always drunk that toast on the eve of battle. As they seated themselves once more, Mendez said, "Major Matson, please telaudio Cinc Rhys and arrange details. We must know his plans."

"Yes, sir."

Mendez glanced at Scott. "Now how else may I serve you?"

"Nothing else. I'll get back to our fort. Details can be worked out on the telaudio, on tight beam."

"If you're going back in that flitterboat," Mendez said sardonically, "I strongly advise a rubdown. There's time to spare, now we've come to an agreement."

Scott hesitated. "Very well. I'm ... uh ... starting to ache." He stood up. "Oh, one thing I forgot. We've heard rumors that Starling's outfit is using atomic power."

Mendez's mouth twisted into a grimace of distaste. "Hadn't heard that. Know anything about it, gentlemen?"

Heads were shaken. One officer said, "I've heard a little talk about it, but only talk, so far."

Mendez said, "After this war, we'll investigate further. If there's truth in the story, we'll join you, of course, in mopping up the Starlings. No court-martial is necessary for *that* crime!"

"Thanks. I'll get in touch with other Companies and see what they've heard. Now, if you'll excuse me—"

He saluted and went out, exultation flaming within him. The bargain had been a good one—for the Doonemen badly needed the Mob's help against the Helldivers. Cinc Rhys would be satisfied with the arrangement.

An orderly took him to the baths, where a rubdown relaxed his aching muscles. Presently he was on the quay again, climbing into the flitterboat. A glance behind him showed that the gears of war were beginning to grind. There was little he could see, but men were moving about through the courtyard with purposeful strides, to the shops, to administration, to the laboratories. The battlewagons were anchored down the coast, Scott knew, in a protected bay, but they would soon move out to their rendezvous with the Doones.

Kane, at the controls of the flitterboat, said, "They repaired the auxiliary unit for us, sir."

"Courtesies of the trade." Scott lifted a friendly hand to the men on the quay as the boat slid toward open water. "The Doone fort, now. Know it?"

"Yes, sir. Are . . . are the Mob fighting with us, if I may ask?"

"They are. And they're a grand lot of fighters. You're going to see action, Kane. When you hear battle stations next, it's going to mean one of the sweetest scraps that happened on Venus. Push down that throttle—we're in a hurry!"

The flitterboat raced southwest at top speed, its course marked by the flying V of spray.

"One last fight," Scott thought to himself. "I'm glad it's going to be a good one."

IV

We eat and drink our own damnation.
            —*Book of Common Prayer*

The motor failed when they were about eight miles from the Doone fort.

It was a catastrophe rather than merely a failure. The overstrained and overheated engine, running at top speed, blew back. The previous accident, at the subsea volcano, had brought out hidden flaws in the alloy which the Mob's repair men had failed to detect, when they replaced the smashed single unit. Sheer luck had the flitterboat poised on a swell when the crack-up happened. The engine blew out and down, ripping the bow to shreds. Had they been bow-deep, the blast would have been unfortunate for Scott and the pilot—more so than it was.

They were perhaps a half mile from the shore. Scott was deafened by the explosion and simultaneously saw the horizon swinging in a drunken swoop. The boat turned turtle, the shell smacking into water with a loud cracking sound. But the plastic held. Both men were tangled together on what had been their ceiling, sliding forward as the flitterboat began to sink bow first. Steam sizzled from the ruined engine.

Kane managed to touch one of the emergency buttons. The shell was, of course, jammed, but a few of the segments slid aside, admitting a gush of acrid sea water. For a moment they struggled there, fighting the cross-currents till the air had been displaced. Scott, peering through cloudy green gloom, saw Kane's dark shadow twist and kick out through a gap. He followed.

Beneath him the black bulk of the boat dropped slowly and was gone. His head broke surface, and he gasped for breath, shaking droplets from his lashes and glancing around. Where was Kane?

The boy appeared, his helmet gone, sleek hair plastered to his forehead. Scott caught his eye and pulled the trigger on his life vest, the inflatable undergarment which was always worn under the blouse on sea duty. As chemicals mixed, light gas rushed into the vest, lifting Scott higher in the water. He felt the collar cushion inflate against the back of his head—the skull-fitting pillow that allowed shipwrecked men to float and rest without danger of drowning in their sleep. But he had no need for this now.

Kane, he saw, had triggered his own life vest. Scott hurled himself up, searching for signs of life. There weren't any. The gray-green sea lay desolate to the misty horizon. A half mile away was a mottled chartreuse wall that marked the jungle. Above and beyond that dim sulphurous red lit the clouds.

Scott got out his leaf-bladed smatchet, gesturing for Kane to do the same. The boy did not seem worried. No doubt this was merely an exciting adventure for him, Scott thought wryly. Oh, well.

Gripping the smatchet between his teeth, the captain began to swim shoreward. Kane kept at his side. Once Scott warned his companion to stillness and bent forward, burying his face in the water and peering down at a great dim shadow that coiled away and was gone—a sea snake, but, luckily, not hungry. The oceans of Venus were perilous with teeming, ferocious life. Precautions were fairly useless. When a man was once in the water, it was up to him to get out of it as rapidly as possible.

Scott touched a small cylinder attached to his belt and felt bubbles rushing against his palm. He was slightly relieved. When he had inflated the vest, this tube of compressed gas had automatically begun to release, sending out a foul-smelling vapor that permeated the water for some distance around. The principle was that of the skunk adjusted to the environment of the squid, and dangerous undersea life was supposed to be driven away by the Mellison tubes; but it didn't work with carrion eaters like the snakes. Scott averted his nose. The gadgets were named Mellison tubes, but the men called them Stinkers, a far more appropriate term.

Tides on Venus are unpredictable. The clouded planet has no moon, but it is closer to the Sun than Earth. As a rule the tides are mild, except during volcanic activity, when tidal waves sweep the shores. Scott, keeping a weather eye out for danger, rode the waves in toward the beach, searching the strip of dull blackness for signs of life.

Nothing.

He scrambled out at last, shaking himself like a dog, and instantly changed the clip in his automatic for high explosive. The weapon, of course, was watertight—a necessity on Venus. As Kane sat down with a grunt and deflated his vest, Scott stood eyeing the wall of jungle thirty feet away. It stopped there abruptly, for nothing could grow on black sand.

The rush and whisper of the waves made the only sound. Most of the trees were liana-like, eking out a precarious existence, as the saying went, by taking in each other's washing. The moment one of them showed signs of solidity, it was immediately assailed by parasitic vines flinging themselves madly upward to reach the filtered sunlight of Venus. The leaves did not begin for thirty feet above the ground; they made a regular roof up there, lying like crazy shingles, and would have shut out all light had they not been of light translucent green. Whitish tendrils crawled like reaching serpents from tree to tree, tentacles of vegetable octopi.

There were two types of Venusian fauna: the giants who could crash through the forest, and the supple, small ground-dwellers—insects and reptiles mostly—who depended on poison sacs for self-protection. Neither kind was pleasant company.

There were flying creatures, too, but these lived in the upper strata, among the leaves. And there were ambiguous horrors that lived in the deep mud and the stagnant pools under the forest, but no one knew much about these.

"Well," Scott said, "that's that."

Kane nodded. "I guess I should have checked the motors."

"You wouldn't have found anything. Latent flaws—it would have taken black night to bring 'em out. Just one of those things. Keep your gas mask handy, now. If we get anywhere near poison flowers and the wind's blowing this way, we're apt to keel over like that." Scott opened a waterproof wallet and took out a strip of sensitized litmus, which he clipped to his wrist. "If this turns blue, that means gas, even if we don't smell it."

"Yes, sir. What now?"

"We-el—the boat's gone. We can't telaudio for help." Scott fingered the blade of his smatchet and slipped it into the belt sheath. "We head for the fort. Eight miles. Two hours, if we can stick to the beach and if we don't run into trouble. More than that if Signal Rock's ahead of us, because we'll have to detour inland in that case." He drew out a collapsible single-lenser telescope and looked southwest along the shore. "Uh-huh. We detour."

A breath of sickening sweetness gusted down from the jungle roof. From above, Scott knew, the forest looked surprisingly lovely. It always reminded him of an antique candlewick spread he had once bought Jeana—immense rainbow flowers scattered over a background of pale green. Even among the flora competition was keen; the plants vied in producing colors and scents that would attract the winged carriers of pollen.

There would always be frontiers, Scott thought. But they might remain unconquered for a long time, here on Venus. The Keeps were enough for the undersea folk; they were self-sustaining. And the Free Companions had no need to carve out empires on the continents. They were fighters, not agrarians. Land hunger was no longer a part of the race. It might come again, but not in the time of the Keeps.

The jungles of Venus held secrets he would never know.

Men can conquer lands from the air, but they cannot hold them by that method. It would take a long, slow period of encroachment, during which the forest and all it represented would be driven back, step by painful step—and that belonged to a day to come, a time Scott would not know. The savage world would be tamed. But not now—not yet.

At the moment it was untamed and very dangerous. Scott stripped off his tunic and wrung water from it. His clothing would not dry in this saturated air, despite the winds. His trousers clung to him stickily, clammy coldness in their folds.

"Ready, Kane?"

"Yes, sir."

"Then let's go."

They went southwest, along the beach, at a steady, easy lope that devoured miles. Speed and alertness were necessary in equal proportion. From time to time Scott scanned the sea with his telescope, hoping to sight a vessel. He saw nothing. The ships would be in harbor, readying for the battle; and planes would be grounded for installation of the new telaudio device Cinc Rhys had mentioned.

Signal Rock loomed ahead, an outthrust crag with eroded, unscalable sides towering two hundred feet and more. The black strip of sand ended there. From the rock there was a straight drop into the deep water, cut up by a turmoil of currents. It was impossible to take the sea detour; there was nothing else for it but to swerve inland, a dangerous but inevitable course. Scott postponed the plunge as long as possible, till the scarp of Signal Rock, jet black with leprous silvery patches on its surface, barred the way. With a quizzical look at Kane he turned sharply to his right and headed for the jungle.

"Half a mile of forest equals a hundred miles of beach hiking," he remarked.

"That bad, sir? I've never tackled it."

"Nobody does, unless they have to. Keep your eyes open and your gun ready. Don't wade through water, even when you can see bottom. There are some little devils that are pretty nearly transparent—vampire fish. If a few of those fasten on you, you'll need a transfusion in less than a minute. I wish the volcanoes would kick up a racket. The beasties generally lie low when that happens.

Under a tree Scott stopped, seeking a straight, long limb.

It took a while to find a suitable one, in that tangle of coiling lianas, but finally he succeeded, using his smatchet blade to hack himself a light five-foot pole. Kane at his heels, he moved on into the gathering gloom.

"We may be stalked," he told the boy. "Don't forget to guard the rear."

The sand had given place to sticky whitish mud that plastered the men to their calves before a few moments had passed. A patina of slickness seemed to overlay the ground. The grass was colored so much like the mud itself that it was practically invisible, except by its added slipperiness. Scott slowly advanced keeping close to the wall of rock on his left where the tangle was not so thick. Nevertheless he had to use the smatchet more than once to cut a passage through vines.

He stopped, raising his hand, and the squelch of Kane's feet in the mud paused. Silently Scott pointed. Ahead of them in the cliff base, was the mouth of a burrow.

The captain bent down, found a small stone, and threw it toward the den. He waited, one hand lightly on his gun, ready to see something flash out of that burrow and race toward them. In the utter silence a new sound made itself heard—tiny goblin drums, erratic and resonant in a faraway fashion. Water, dropping from leaf to leaf, in the soaked jungle ceiling above them. *Tink, tink, tink-tink, tink, tink, tink-tink*—

"OK.," Scott said quietly. "Watch it, though." He went on, gun drawn, till they were level with the mouth of the burrow. "Turn, Kane. Keep your eye on it till I tell you to stop." He gripped the boy's arm and guided him, holstering his own weapon. The pole, till now held between biceps and body, slipped into his hand. He used it to probe the slick surface of the mud ahead. Sinkhole and quicksands were frequent, and so were traps, camouflaged pits built by mudwolves—which, of course, were not wolves, and belonged to no known genus. On Venus, the fauna had more subdivisions than on old Earth, and lines of demarcation were more subtle.

"All right now."

Kane, sighing with relief, turned his face forward again. "What was it?"

"You never know what may come out of those holes," Scott told him. "They come fast, and they're usually poisonous. So you can't take chances with the critters. Slow down here. I don't like the looks of that patch ahead."

Clearings were unusual in the forest. There was one here, twenty feet wide, slightly saucer-shaped. Scott gingerly extended the pole and probed. A faint ripple shook the white mud, and almost before it had appeared the captain unholstered his pistol and was blasting shot after shot at the movement.

"Shoot, Kane!" he snapped. "Quick! Shoot at it!"

Kane obeyed, though he had to guess at his target. Mud geysered up, suddenly crimson-stained. Scott, still firing, gripped the boy's arm and ran him back at a breakneck pace.

The echoes died. Once more the distant elfin drums whispered through the green gloom.

"We got it," Scott said, after a pause.

"We did?" the other asked blankly. "What—"

"Mud-wolf, I think. The only way to kill those things is to get 'em before they get out of the mud. They're fast and they die hard. However—" He warily went forward. There was nothing to see. The mud had collapsed into a deeper saucer, but the holes blasted by the high-x bullets had filled in. Here and there were traces of thready crimson.

"Never a dull moment," Scott remarked. His crooked grin eased the tension. Kane chuckled and followed the captain's example in replacing his half-used clip with a full one.

The narrow spine of Signal Rock extended inland for a quarter mile before it became scalable. They reached that point finally, helping each other climb, and finding themselves, at the summit, still well below the leafy ceiling of the trees. The black surface of the rock was painfully hot, stinging their palms as they climbed, and even striking through their shoe soles.

"Halfway point, captain?"

"Yeah. But don't let that cheer you. It doesn't get any better till we hit the beach again. We'll probably need some fever shots when we reach the fort, just in case. Oh-oh. Mask, Kane, quick." Scott lifted his arm. On his wrist the band of litmus had turned blue.

With trained accuracy they donned the respirators. Scott felt a faint stinging on his exposed skin, but that wasn't serious. Still, it would be painful later. He beckoned to Kane, slid down the face of the rock, used the pole to test

the mud below, and jumped lightly. He dropped in the
sticky whiteness and rolled over hastily, plastering himself
from head to foot. Kane did the same. Mud wouldn't neu-
tralize the poison flowers' gas, but it would absorb most of it
before it reached the skin.

Scott headed toward the beach, a grotesque figure. Mud
dripped on the eye plate, and he scrubbed it away with a
handful of white grass. He used the pole constantly to test
the footing ahead.

Nevertheless the mud betrayed him. The pole broke
through suddenly, and as Scott automatically threw his weight
back, the ground fell away under his feet. He had time for a
crazy feeling of relief that this was quicksand, not a mud-
wolf's den, and then the clinging, treacherous stuff had
sucked him down knee-deep. He fell back, keeping his grip
on the pole and swinging the other end in an arc toward
Kane.

The boy seized it in both hands and threw himself flat.
His foot hooked over an exposed root. Scott, craning his
neck at a painfully awkward angle and trying to see through
the mud-smeared vision plates, kept a rattrap grip on his
end of the pole, hoping its slickness would not slip through
his fingers.

He was drawn down farther, and then Kane's anchorage
began to help. The boy tried to pull the pole toward him,
hand over hand. Scott shook his head. He was a good deal
stronger than Kane, and the latter would need all his strength
to keep a tight grip on the pole.

Something stirred in the shadows behind Kane. Scott
instinctively let go with one hand, and, with the other, got
out his gun. It had a sealed mechanism, so the mud hadn't
harmed the firing, and the muzzle had a one-way trap. He
fired at the movement behind Kane, heard a muffled tumult, and waited till it had died. The boy, after a startled
look behind him, had not stirred.

After that, rescue was comparatively easy. Scott simply
climbed along the pole, spreading his weight over the surface of the quicksand. The really tough part was pulling his
legs free of that deadly grip. Scott had to rest for five
minutes after that.

But he got out. That was the important thing.

Kane pointed inquiringly into the bushes where the creature had been shot, but Scott shook his head. The nature of
the beast wasn't a question worth deciding, as long as it was

apparently *hors de combat*. Readjusting his mask, Scott turned toward the beach, circling the quicksand, and Kane kept at his heels.

Their luck had changed. They reached the shore with no further difficulty and collapsed on the black sand to rest. Presently Scott used a litmus, saw that the gas had dissipated, and removed his mask. He took a deep breath.

"Thanks, Kane," he said. "You can take a dip now if you want to wash off that mud. But stay close inshore. No, don't strip. There's no time."

The mud clung like glue and the black sand scratched like pumice. Still, Scott felt a good deal cleaner after a few minutes in the surf, while Kane stayed on guard. Slightly refreshed, they resumed the march.

An hour later a convoy plane, testing, sighted them, telaudioed the fort, and a flitterboat came racing out to pick them up. What Scott appreciated most of all was the stiff shot of uisqueplus the pilot gave him.

Yeah. It was a dog's life, all right!

He passed the flask to Kane.

Presently the fort loomed ahead, guarding Doone Harbor. Large as the landlocked bay was, it could scarcely accommodate the fleet. Scott watched the activity visible with an approving eye. The flitterboat rounded the sea wall, built for protection against tidal waves, and shot toward a jetty. Its almost inaudible motor died; the shell swung back.

Scott got out, beckoning to an orderly.

"Yes, sir?"

"See that this soldier gets what he needs. We've been in the jungle."

The man didn't whistle sympathetically, but his mouth pursed. He saluted and helped Kane climb out of the flitterboat. As Scott hurried along the quay, he could hear an outburst of friendly profanity from the men on the dock, gathering around Kane.

He nodded imperceptibly. The boy would make a good Free Companion—always granted that he could stand the gaff under fire. That was the acid test. Discipline was tightened then to the snapping point. If it snapped—well, the human factor always remained a variable, in spite of all the psychologists could do.

He went directly to his quarters, switching on the telaudio

to call Cinc Rhys. The cinc's seamed, leathery face resolved itself on the screen.

"Captain Scott reporting for duty, sir."

Rhys looked at him sharply. "What happened?"

"Flitterboat crack-up. Had to make it here on foot."

The cinc called on his God in a mild voice. "Glad you made it. Any accident?"

"No, sir. The pilot's unharmed, too. I'm ready to take over, after I've cleaned up."

"Better take a rejuvenation—you probably need it. Everything's going like clockwork. You did a good job with Mendez—a better bargain than I'd hoped for. I've been talking with him on the telaudio, integrating our forces. We'll go into that later, though. Clean up and then make general inspection."

"Check, sir."

Rhys clicked off. Scott turned to face his orderly.

"Hello, Briggs. Help me off with these duds. You'll probably have to cut 'em off."

"Glad to see you back, sir. I don't think it'll be necessary to cut—" Blunt fingers flew deftly over zippers and clasps. "You were in the jungle?"

Scott grinned wryly. "Do I look as if I'd been gliding?"

"Not all the way, sir—no."

Briggs was like an old bulldog—one of those men who proved the truth of the saying: "Old soldiers never die; they only fade away." Briggs could have been pensioned off ten years ago, but he hadn't wanted that. There was always a place for old soldiers in the Free Companies, even those who were unskilled. Some became technicians; others, military instructors; the rest, orderlies. The forts were their homes. Had they retired to one of the Keeps, they would have died for lack of interests.

Briggs, now—he had never risen above the ranks, and knew nothing of military strategy, ordnance, or anything except plain fighting. But he had been a Dooneman for forty years, twenty-five of them on active service. He was sixty-odd now, his squat figure slightly stooped like an elderly bear, his ugly face masked with scar tissue.

"All right. Start the shower, will you?"

Briggs stumped off, and Scott, stripped of his filthy, sodden garments, followed. He luxuriated under the stinging spray, first hot soapy water, then alcomix, and after that plain water, first hot, then cold. That was the last task he had to do himself. Briggs took over, as Scott relaxed on the slab, dropping lotion into the captain's burning eyes, giving him a deft but murderous rubdown, combining osteopathic and chiropractic treatment, adjusting revitalizing lamps, and measuring a hypo shot to nullify fatigue toxins. When the orderly was finished, Scott was ready to resume his duties with a clear brain and a refreshed body.

Briggs appeared with fresh clothing. "I'll have the old uniform cleaned, sir. No use throwing it away."

"You can't clean that," Scott remarked, slipping into a singlet. "Not after I rolled in mud. But suit yourself. I won't be needing it for long."

The orderly's fingers, buttoning Scott's tunic, stopped briefly and then resumed their motion. "Is that so, sir?"

"Yeah. I'm taking out discharge papers."

"Another Company, sir?"

"Don't get on your high horse," Scott told the orderly. "It's not that. What would you do if it were? Court-martial me yourself and shoot me at sunrise?"

"No, sir. Begging your pardon, sir, I'd just think you were crazy."

"Why I stand you only the Lord knows," Scott remarked. "You're too damn independent. There's no room for new ideas in that plastic skull of yours. You're the quintessence of dogmatism."

Briggs nodded. "Probably, sir. When a man's lived by one set of rules for as long as I have, and those rules work out, I suppose he might get dogmatic."

"Forty years for you—about twelve for me."

"You came up fast, captain. You'll be cinc here yet."

"That's what you think."

"You're next in line after Cinc Rhys."

"But I'll be out of the Doones," Scott pointed out. "Keep that under your belt, Briggs."

The orderly grunted, "Can't see it, sir. If you don't join another Company, where'll you go?"

"Ever heard of the Keeps?"

Briggs permitted himself a respectful snort. "Sure. They're fine for a binge, but—"

"I'm going to live in one. Montana Keep."

"The Keeps were built with men and machines. I helped at the building of Doone fort. Blood's mixed with the plastic here. We had to hold back the jungle while the technicians were working. Eight months, sir, and never a day passed without some sort of attack. And attacks always meant casualities then. We had only breastworks. The ships laid down a barrage, but barrages aren't impassable. That was a fight, captain."

Scott thrust out a leg so that Briggs could lace his boots. "And a damn good one. I know." He looked down at the orderly's baldish, brown head where white hairs straggled.

"You know, but you weren't there, captain. I was. First we dynamited. We cleared a half circle where we could dig in behind breastworks. Behind us were the techs, throwing up a plastic wall as fast. as they could. The guns were brought in on barges. Lying offshore were the battlewagons. We could hear the shells go whistling over our heads—it sounded pretty good, because we knew things were O.K. as long as the barrage kept up. But it couldn't be kept up day and night. The jungle broke through. For months the smell of blood hung here, and that drew the enemy."

"But you held them off."

"Sure, we did. Addison Doone was cinc then—he'd formed the Company years before, but we hadn't a fort. Doone fought with us. Saved my life once, in fact. Anyhow—we got the fort built, or rather the techs did. I won't forget the kick I got out of it when the first big gun blasted off from the wall behind us. There was a lot to do after that, but when that shell was fired, we knew we'd done the job."

Scott nodded. "You feel a proprietary interest in the fort, I guess."

Briggs looked puzzled. "The fort? Why, that doesn't mean much, captain. There are lots of forts. It's something more than that; I don't quite know what it is. It's seeing the fleet out there—breaking in the rookies—giving the old toasts at mess—knowing that—" He stopped, at a loss.

Scott's lips twisted wryly. "You don't really know, do you, Briggs?"

"Know what, sir?"

"Why you stay here. Why you can't believe I'd quit."

Briggs gave a little shrug. "Well—it's the Doones," he said. "That's all, captain. It's just that."

"And what the devil will it matter, in a few hundred years?"

"I suppose it won't. No, sir. But it isn't our business to think about that. We're Doonemen, that's all."

Scott didn't answer. He could easily have pointed out the

fallacy of Briggs' argument, but what was the use? He stood up, the orderly whisking invisible dust off his tunic.

"All set, sir. Shipshape."

"Check, Briggs. Well, I've one more scrap, anyhow. I'll bring you back a souvenir, eh?"

The orderly saluted, grinning. Scott went out, feeling good. Inwardly he was chuckling rather sardonically at the false values he was supposed to take seriously. Of course many men had died when Doone fort had been built. But did that, in itself, make a tradition? What good was the fort? In a few centuries it would have outlived its usefulness. Then it would be a relic of the past. Civilization moved on, and, these days, civilization merely tolerated the military.

So—what was the use? Sentiment needed a valid reason for its existence. The Free Companions fought, bitterly, doggedly, with insane valor, in order to destroy themselves. The ancient motives for war had vanished.

What was the use? All over Venus the lights of the great forts were going out—and, this time, they would never be lit again—not in a thousand lifetimes!

V

And we are here as on a darkling plain
Swept with confused alarms of struggle and flight,
Where ignorant armies clash by night.

—Arnold

The fort was a completely self-contained unit, military rather than social. There was no need for any agrarian development, since a state of complete siege never existed. Food could be brought in from the Keeps by water and air.

But military production was important, and, in the life of the fort, the techs played an important part, from the experimental physicist to the spot welder. There were always replacements to be made, for, in battle, there were always casualties. And it was necessary to keep the weapons up-to-date, continually striving to perfect new ones. But strategy and armament were of equal importance. An outnumbered fleet had been known to conquer a stronger one by the use of practical psychology.

Scott found Commander Bienne at the docks, watching the launching of a new sub. Apparently Bienne hadn't yet got over his anger, for he turned a scowling, somber face to the captain as he saluted.

"Hello, commander," Scott said. "I'm making inspection. Are you free?"

Bienne nodded. "There's not much to do."

"Well—routine. We got that sub finished just in time, eh?"

"Yes." Bienne couldn't repress his pleasure at sight of the trim, sleek vessel beginning to slide down the ways. Scott, too, felt his pulses heighten as the sub slipped into the water, raising a mighty splash, and then settling down to a smooth, steady riding on the waves. He looked out to where the great battlewagons stood at anchor, twelve of them, gray-green monsters of plated metal. Each of them carried launching equipment for gliders, but the collapsible aircraft were stowed away out of sight as yet. Smaller destroyers lay like lean-flanked wolves among the battleships. There were two fast carriers, loaded with gliders and flitterboats. There were torpedo boats and one low-riding monitor, impregnable, powerfully armed, but slow. Only a direct hit could disable a monitor, but the behemoths had their disadvantages. The battle was usually over before they lumbered into sight. Like all monitors, this one—the *Armageddon*—was constructed on the principle of a razorback hog, covered, except for the firing ports, by a tureen-shaped shield, strongly braced from within. The *Armageddon* was divided into groups of compartments and had several auxiliary engines, so that, unlike the legendary *Rover*, when a monitor died, it did *not* die all over. It was, in effect, a dinosaur. You could blow off the monster's head, and it would continue to fight with talons and lashing tail. Its heavy guns made up in mobility for the giant's unwieldiness—but the trouble was to get the monitor into battle. It was painfully slow.

Scott scowled. "We're fighting over Venus Deep, eh?"

"Yes," Bienne nodded. "That still goes. The Helldivers are already heading toward Montana Keep, and we'll intercept them over the Deep."

"When's zero hour?"

"Midnight tonight."

Scott closed his eyes, visualizing their course on a mental chart. Not so good. When battle was joined near island groups, it was sometimes possible for a monitor to slip up under cover of the islets, but that trick wouldn't work now. Too bad—for the Helldivers were a strong outfit, more so since their recent merger with O'Brien's Legion. Even with the Mob to help, the outcome of the scrap would be anyone's guess. The *Armageddon* might be the decisive factor.

"I wonder—" Scott said. "No. It'd be impossible."

"What?"

"Camouflaging the *Armageddon*. If the Helldivers see the monitor coming, they'll lead the fight away from it, faster than the tub can follow. I was thinking we might get her into the battle without the enemy realizing it."

"She's camouflaged now."

"Paint, that's all. She can be spotted. I had some screwy idea about disguising her as an island or a dead whale."

"She's too big for a whale and floating islands look a bit suspicious."

"Yeah. But if we *could* slip the *Armageddon* in without scaring off the enemy— Hm-m-m. Monitors have a habit of turning turtle, don't they?"

"Right. They're top-heavy. But a monitor can't fight upside down. It's not such a bright idea, captain." Briefly Bienne's sunken eyes gleamed with sneering mockery. Scott grunted and turned away.

"All right. Let's take a look around."

The fleet was shipshape. Scott went to the shops. He learned that several new hulls were under way, but would not be completed by zero hour. With Bienne, he continued to the laboratory offices. Nothing new. No slip-ups; no surprises. The machine was running smoothly.

By the time inspection was completed, Scott had an idea. He told Bienne to carry on and went to find Cinc Rhys. The cinc was in his office, just clicking off the telaudio as Scott appeared.

"That was Mendez," Rhys said. "The Mob's meeting our fleet a hundred miles off the coast. They'll be under our orders, of course. A good man, Mendez, but I don't entirely trust him."

"You're not thinking of a double cross, sir?"

Cinc Rhys made disparaging noises. "Brutus is an honorable man. No, he'll stick to his bargain. But I wouldn't cut cards with Mendez. As a Free Companion, he's trustworthy. Personally— Well, how do things look?"

"Very good, sir. I've an idea about the *Armageddon*."

"I wish I had," Rhys said frankly. "We can't get that damned scow into the battle in any way I can figure out. The Helldivers will see it coming, and lead the fight away."

"I'm thinking of camouflage."

"A monitor's a monitor. It's unmistakable. You can't make it look like anything else."

"With one exception, sir. You can make it look like a disabled monitor."

Rhys sat back, giving Scott a startled glance. "That's interesting. Go on."

"Look here, sir." The captain used a stylo to sketch the outline of a monitor on a convenient pad. "Above the surface, the *Armageddon*'s dome-shaped. Below, it's a bit different, chiefly because of the keel. Why can't we put a fake superstructure on the monitor—build a false keel on it, so it'll seem capsized?"

"It's possible."

"Everybody knows a monitor's weak spot—that it turns turtle under fire sometimes. If the Helldivers saw an apparently capsized *Armageddon* drifting toward them, they'd naturally figure the tub was disabled."

"It's crazy," Rhys said. "One of those crazy ideas that might work." He used the local telaudio to issue crisp orders. "Got it? Good. Get the *Armageddon* under way as soon as the equipment's aboard. Alterations will be made at sea. We can't waste time. If we had them made in the yards, she'd never catch up with the fleet."

The cinc broke the connection, his seamed, leathery face twisting into a grin. "I hope it works. We'll see."

He snapped his fingers. "Almost forgot. President Crosby's nephew—Kane?—he was with you when you cracked up, wasn't he? I've been wondering whether I should have waived training for him. How did he show up in the jungle?"

"Quite well," Scott said. "I had my eye on him. He'll make a good soldier."

Rhys looked keenly at the captain. "What about discipline? I felt that was his weak spot."

"I've no complaint to make."

"So. Well, maybe. Starling's outfit is bad training for anyone—especially a raw kid. Speaking of Starling, did Cinc Mendez know anything about his using atomic power?"

"No, sir. If Starling's doing that, he's keeping it plenty quiet."

"We'll investigate after the battle. Can't afford that sort of thing—we don't want another holocaust. It was bad enough to lose Earth. It decimated the race. If it happened again, it'd wipe the race out."

"I don't think there's much danger of that. On Earth, it was the big atomic-power stations that got out of control. At worst, Starling can't have more than hand weapons."

"True. You can't blow up a world with those. But you know the law—no atomic power on Venus."

Scott nodded.

"Well, that's all." Rhys waved him away. "Clear weather."

Which, on this perpetually clouded world, had a tinge of irony.

After mess Scott returned to his quarters, for a smoke and a brief rest. He waved away Briggs' suggestion of a rubdown and sent the orderly to the commissary for fresh tobacco. "Be sure to get Twenty Star," he cautioned. "I don't want that green hydroponic cabbage."

"I know the brand, sir." Briggs looked hurt and departed. Scott settled back in his relaxer, sighing.

Zero hour at twelve. The last zero hour he'd ever know. All through the day he had been conscious that he was fulfilling his duties for the last time.

His mind went back to Montana Keep. He was living again those other-worldly moments in the cloud-wrapped Olympus with Ilene. Curiously, he found it difficult to visualize the girl's features. Perhaps she was a symbol—her appearance did not matter. Yet she was very lovely.

In a different way from Jeana. Scott glanced at Jeana's picture on the desk, three-dimensional and tinted after life. By pressing a button on the frame, he could have given it sound and motion. He leaned forward and touched the tiny stud. In the depths of the picture the figure of Jeana stirred, smiling. The red lips parted.

Her voice, though soft, was quite natural.

"Hello, Brian," the recording said. "Wish I were with you now. Here's a present, darling." The image blew him a kiss, and then faded back to immobility.

Scott sighed again. Jeana was a comfortable sort of person. But— Oh, hell! She wasn't willing to change. Very likely she couldn't. Ilene perhaps was equally dogmatic, but she represented the life of the Keeps—and that was what Scott wanted now.

It was an artificial life Ilene lived, but she was honest about it. She knew its values were false. At least she didn't pretend, like the Free Companions, that there were ideals worth dying for. Scott remembered Briggs. The fact that men had been killed during the building of Doone fort meant a lot to the old orderly. He never asked himself— *why*? Why had they died? Why was Doone fort built in the first place? For war. And war was doomed.

One had to believe in an ideal before devoting one's life to it. One had to feel he was helping the ideal to survive— watering the plant with his blood so eventually it would come to flower. The red flower of Mars had long since blown. How did that old poem go?

> *One thing is certain, and the rest is lies;*
> *The flower that once has blown forever dies.*

It was true. But the Free Companions blindly pretended that the flower was still in blazing scarlet bloom, refusing to admit that even the roots were withered and useless, scarcely able now to suck up the blood sacrificed to its hopeless thirst.

New flowers bloomed; new buds opened. But in the Keeps, not in the great doomed forts. It was the winter cycle, and, as the last season's blossoms faded, the buds of the next stirred into life. Life questing and intolerant. Life that fed on the rotting petals of the rose of war.

But the pretense went on, in the coastal forts that guarded the Keeps. Scott made a grimace of distaste. Blind, stupid folly! He was a man first, not a soldier. And man is essentially a hedonist, whether he identifies himself with the race or not.

Scott could not. He was not part of the undersea culture, and he could never be. But he could lose himself in the hedonistic backwash of the Keeps, the froth that always overlies any social unit. With Ilene, he could, at least, seek happiness, without the bitter self-mockery he had known for so long. Mockery at his own emotional weaknesses in which he did not believe.

Ilene was honest. She knew she was damned, because unluckily she had intelligence.

So—Scott thought—they would make a good pair.

Scott looked up as Commander Bienne came into the room. Bienne's sour, mahogany face was flushed deep red under the bronze. His lids were heavy over angry eyes. He swung the door-curtain shut after him and stood rocking on his heels, glowering at Scott.

He called Scott something unprintable.

The captain rose, an icy knot of fury in his stomach. Very softly he said, "You're drunk, Bienne. Get out. Get back to your quarters."

"Sure—you little tinhorn soldier. You like to give orders, don't you? You like to chisel, too. The way you chiseled me out of that left-wing command today. I'm pretty sick of it, Captain Brian Scott."

"Don't be a damned fool! I don't like you personally any more than you like me, but that's got nothing to do with the Company. I recommended you for that command."

"You lie," Bienne said, swaying. "And I hate your guts."

Scott went pale, the scar on his cheek flaming red. Bienne came forward. He wasn't too drunk to co-ordinate. His fist lashed out suddenly and connected agonizingly with Scott's molar.

The captain's reach was less than Bienne's. He ducked inside of the next swing and carefully smashed a blow home on the point of the other's jaw. Bienne was driven back, crashing against the wall and sliding down in a limp heap, his head lolling forward.

Scott, rubbing his knuckles, looked down, considering. Presently he knelt and made a quick examination. A knockout, that was all.

Oh, well.

Briggs appeared, showing no surprise at sight of Bienne's motionless body. The perfect orderly walked across to the table and began to refill the humidor with the tobacco he had brought.

Scott almost chuckled.

"Briggs."

"Yes, sir?"

"Commander Bienne's had a slight accident. He—slipped. Hit his chin on something. He's a bit tight, too. Fix him up, will you?"

"With pleasure, sir." Briggs hoisted Bienne's body across his brawny shoulders.

"Zero hour's at twelve. The commander must be aboard the *Flintlock* by then. And sober. Can do?"

"Certainly, sir," Briggs said, and went out.

Scott returned to his chair, filling his pipe. He should have confined Bienne to his quarters, of course. But—well, this was a personal matter. One could afford to stretch a point, especially since Bienne was a valuable man to have aboard during action. Scott vaguely hoped the commander would get his thick head blown off.

After a time he tapped the dottle from his pipe and went off for a final inspection.

At midnight the fleet hoisted anchor.

By dawn the Doones were nearing the Venus Deep.

The ships of the Mob had already joined them, seven battleships, and assorted cruisers, destroyers, and one carrier. No monitor. The Mob didn't own one—it had capsized two months before, and was still undergoing repairs.

The combined fleets sailed in crescent formation, the left wing, commanded by Scott, composed of his own ship, the *Flintlock*, and the *Arquebus*, the *Arrow*, and the *Misericordia*, all Doone battlewagons. There were two Mob ships with him, the *Navaho* and the *Zuni*, the latter commanded by Cinc Mendez. Scott had one carrier with him, the other being at right wing. Besides these, there were the lighter craft.

In the center were the battleships *Arbalest*, *Lance*, *Gatling*, and *Mace*, as well as three of Mendez's. Cinc Rhys was aboard the *Lance*, controlling operations. The camouflaged monitor *Armageddon* was puffing away valiantly far behind, well out of sight in the mists.

Scott was in his control room, surrounded by telaudio screens and switchboards. Six operators were perched on stools before the controls, ready to jump to action when orders came through their earphones. In the din of battle spoken commands often went unheard, which was why Scott bore a hush-mike strapped to his chest.

His eyes roved over the semicircle of screens before him.

"Any report from the gliders yet?"

"No, sir."

"Get me air-spotting command."

One of the screens flamed to life; a face snapped into view on it.

"Report."

"Nothing yet, captain. Wait." There was a distant thunder. "Detectors clamped on a telaudio tight-beam directly overhead."

"Enemy glider in the clouds?"

"Apparently. It's out of the focus now."

"Try to relocate it."

A lot of good that would do. Motored planes could easily

be detected overhead, but a glider was another matter. The only way to spot one was by clamping a detector focus directly on the glider's telaudio beam—worse than a needle in a haystack. Luckily the crates didn't carry bombs.

"Report coming in, sir. One of our gliders."

Another screen showed a face. "Pilot reporting, sir. Located enemy."

"Good. Switch in the telaudio, infra. What sector?"

"V.D. eight hundred seven northwest twenty-one."

Scott said into his hush-mike, "Get Cinc Rhys and Commander Geer on tight-beam. And Cinc Mendez."

Three more screens lit up, showing the faces of the three officers.

"Cut in the pilot."

Somewhere over Venus Deep the glider pilot was arcing his plane through the cloud-layer, the automatic telaudio-camera, lensed to infrared, penetrating the murk and revealing the ocean below. On the screen ships showed, driving forward in battle formation.

Scott recognized and enumerated them mentally. The *Orion*, the *Sirius*, the *Vega*, the *Polaris*—uh-huh. Lighter ships. Plenty of them. The scanner swept on.

Cinc Rhys said, "We're outnumbered badly. Cinc Mendez, are your sub-detectors in operation?"

"They are. Nothing yet."

"We'll join battle in half an hour, I judge. We've located them, and they've no doubt located us."

"Check."

The screens blanked out. Scott settled back, alertly at ease. Nothing to do now but wait, keeping ready for the unexpected. The *Orion* and the *Vega* were the Helldivers' biggest battleships, larger than anything in the line of the Doones—or the Mob. Cinc Flynn was no doubt aboard the *Orion*. The Helldivers owned a monitor, but it had not showed on the infrared aërial scanner. Probably the behemoth wouldn't even show up in time for the battle.

But even without the monitor, the Helldivers had an overwhelming surface display. Moreover, their undersea fleet was an important factor. The sub-detectors of Cinc Mendez might—probably would—cut down the odds. But possibly not enough.

The *Armageddon*, Scott thought, might be the point of decision, the ultimate argument. And, as yet, the camouflaged monitor was lumbering through the waves far in the wake of the Doones.

Commander Bienne appeared on a screen. He had frozen into a disciplined, trained robot, personal animosities forgotten for the time. Active duty did that to a man.

Scott expected nothing different, however, and his voice was completely impersonal as he acknowledged Bienne's call.

"The flitterboats are ready to go, captain."

"Send them out in fifteen minutes. Relay to left wing, all ships carrying flitters."

"Check."

For a while there was silence. A booming explosion brought Scott to instant alertness. He glanced up at the screens.

A new face appeared. "Helldivers opening up. Testing for range. They must have gliders overhead. We can't spot 'em."

"Get the men under cover. Send up a test barrage. Prepare to return fire. Contact our pilots over the Helldivers."

It was beginning now—the incessant, racking thunder that would continue till the last shot was fired. Scott cut in to Cinc Rhys as the latter signaled.

"Reporting, sir."

"Harry the enemy. We can't do much yet. Change to R-8 foundation."

Cinc Mendez said, "We've got three enemy subs. Our detectors are tuned up to high pitch."

"Limit the range so our subs will be outside the sphere of influence."

"Already did that. The enemy's using magnetic depth charges, laying an undersea barrage as they advance."

"I'll talk to the sub command." Rhys cut off. Scott listened to the increasing fury of explosions. He could not yet hear the distinctive *clap-clap* of heat rays, but the quarters were not yet close enough for those undependable, though powerful, weapons. It took time for a heat ray to warm up, and during that period a well-aimed bullet could smash the projector lens.

"Casualty, sir. Direct hit aboard destroyer *Bayonet*."

"Extent of damage?"

"Not disabled. Complete report later."

After a while a glider pilot came in on the beam.

"Shell landed on the *Polaris*, sir."

"Use the scanner."

It showed the Helldivers' battlewagon, part of the super-structure carried away, but obviously still in fighting trim. Scott nodded. Both sides were getting the range now. The hazy clouds still hid each fleet from the other, but they were nearing.

The sound of artillery increased. Problems of trajectory were increased by the violent winds of Venus, but accurate aiming was possible. Scott nodded grimly as a crash shook the *Flintlock*.

They were getting it now. Here, in the brain of the ship, he was as close to the battle as any member of a firing crew. The screens were his eyes.

They had the advantage of being able to use infrared, so that Scott, buried here, could see more than he could have on deck, with his naked eye. Something loomed out of the murk and Scott's breath stopped before he recognized the lines of the Doone battlewagon *Misericordia*. She was off course. The captain used his hush-mike to snap a quick reprimand.

Flitterboats were going out now, speedy hornets that would harry the enemy fleet. In one of them, Scott remembered, was Norman Kane. He thought of Ilene and thrust the thought back, out of his mind. No time for that now.

Battle stations allowed no time for wool gathering.

The distant vanguard of the Helldivers came into sight on the screens. Cinc Mendez called.

"Eleven more subs. One got through. Seems to be near the *Flintlock*. Drop depth bombs."

Scott nodded and obeyed. Shuddering concussions shook the ship. Presently a report came in: fuel slick to starboard.

Good. A few well-placed torpedoes could do a lot of damage.

The *Flintlock* heeled incessantly under the action of the heavy guns. Heat rays were lancing out. The big ships could not easily avoid the searing blasts that could melt solid metal, but the flitterboats, dancing around like angry insects, sent a rain of bullets at the projectors. But even that took integration. The rays themselves were invisible, and could only be traced from their targets. The camera crews were working overtime, snapping shots of enemy ships, tracing the rays' points of origin, and telaudioing the information to the flitterboats.

"Helldivers' *Rigel* out of action."

On the screen the big destroyer swung around, bow pointing forward. She was going to ram. Scott snapped orders. The *Flintlock* went hard over, guns pouring death into the doomed *Rigel*.

The ships passed, so close that men on the *Flintlock*'s decks could see the destroyer lurching through the haze. Scott judged her course and tried desperately to get Mendez. There was a delay.

"QM—QM—emergency! Get the *Zuni*!"

"Here she answers, sir."

Scott snapped, "Change course. QM. Destroyer *Rigel* bearing down on you."

"Check." The screen blanked. Scott used a scanner. He groaned at the sight. The *Zuni* was swinging fast, but the *Rigel* was too close—too damned close.

She rammed.

Scott said, "Hell." That put the *Zuni* out of action. He reported to Cinc Rhys.

"All right, captain. Continue R-8 formation."

Mendez appeared on a screen. "Captain Scott. We're disabled. I'm coming aboard. Have to direct sub-strafing operations. Can you give me a control board?"

"Yes, sir. Land at Port Sector 7."

Hidden in the mist, the fleets swept on in parallel courses, the big battlewagons keeping steady formation, pouring heat rays and shells across the gap. The lighter ships strayed out of line at times, but the flitterboats swarmed like midges, dog-fighting when they were not harrying the larger craft. Gliders were useless now, at such close quarters.

The thunder crashed and boomed. Shudders rocked the *Flintlock*.

"Hit on Helldivers' *Orion*. Hit on *Sirius*."

"Hit on Mob ship *Apache*."

"Four more enemy subs destroyed."

"Doone sub X-16 fails to report."

"Helldivers' *Polaris* seems disabled."

"Send out auxiliary flitterboats, units nine and twenty."

Cinc Mendez came in, breathing hard. Scott waved him to an auxiliary control unit seat.

"Hit on *Lance*. Wait a minute. Cinc Rhys a casualty, sir."

Scott froze. "Details."

"One moment— Dead, sir."

"Very well," Scott said after a moment. "I'm assuming command. Pass it along."

He caught a sidelong glance from Mendez. When a Company's cinc was killed, one of two things happened—promotion of a new cinc, or a merger with another Company. In this case Scott was required, by his rank, to assume temporarily the fleet's command. Later, at the Doone fort, there would be a meeting and a final decision.

He scarcely thought of that now. Rhys dead! Tough, unemotional old Rhys, killed in action. Rhys had a free-wife in some Keep, Scott remembered. The Company would pension her. Scott had never seen the woman. Oddly, he wondered what she was like. The question had never occurred to him before.

The screens were flashing. Double duty now—or triple. Scott forgot everything else in directing the battle.

It was like first-stage anaesthesia—it was difficult to judge time. It might have been an hour or six since the battle had started. Or less than an hour, for that matter.

"Destroyer disabled. Cruiser disabled. Three enemy subs out of action—"

It went on, endlessly. At the auxiliaries Mendez was directing substrafing operations. Where in hell's the *Armageddon*, Scott thought? The fight would be over before that overgrown tortoise arrived.

Abruptly a screen flashed QM. The lean, beak-nosed face of Cinc Flynn of the Helldivers showed.

"Calling Doone command."

"Acknowledging," Scott said. "Captain Scott, emergency command."

Why was Flynn calling? Enemy fleets in action never communicated, except to surrender.

Flynn said curtly, "You're using atomic power. Explanation, please."

Mendez jerked around. Scott felt a tight band around his stomach.

"Done without my knowledge or approval, of course, Cinc Flynn. My apologies. Details?"

"One of your flitterboats fired an atomic-powered pistol at the *Orion*."

"Damage?"

"One seven-unit gun disabled."

"One of ours, of the same caliber, will be taken out of action immediately. Further details, sir?"

"Use your scanner, captain, on Sector Mobile 18 south *Orion*. Your apology is accepted. The incident will be erased from our records."

Flynn clicked off. Scott used the scanner, catching a Doone flitterboat in its focus. He used the enlarger.

The little boat was fleeing from enemy fire, racing back toward the Doone fleet, heading directly toward the *Flintlock*, Scott saw. Through the transparent shell he saw the bombardier slumped motionless, his head blown half off. The pilot, still gripping an atomic-fire pistol in one hand, was Norman Kane. Blood streaked his boyish, strained face.

So Starling's outfit did have atomic power, then. Kane must have smuggled the weapon out with him when he left. And, in the excitement of battle, he had used it against the enemy.

Scott said coldly, "Gun crews starboard. Flitterboat Z-19-4. Blast it."

Almost immediately a shell burst near the little craft. On the screen Kane looked up, startled by his own side firing upon him. Comprehension showed on his face. He swung the flitterboat off course, zigzagging, trying desperately to dodge the barrage.

Scott watched, his lips grimly tight. The flitterboat exploded in a rain of spray and debris.

Automatic court-martial.

After the battle, the Companies would band together and smash Starling's outfit.

Meantime, this was action. Scott returned to his screens, erasing the incident from his mind.

Very gradually, the balance of power was increasing with the Helldivers. Both sides were losing ships, put out of action rather than sunk, and Scott thought more and more often of the monitor *Armageddon*. She could turn the battle now. But she was still far astern.

Scott never felt the explosion that wrecked the control room. His senses blacked out without warning.

He could not have been unconscious for long. When he opened his eyes, he stared up at a shambles. He seemed to be the only man left alive. But it could not have been a direct hit, or he would not have survived either.

He was lying on his back, pinned down by a heavy crossbeam. But no bones were broken. Blind, incredible luck had helped him there. The brunt of the damage had been borne by the operators. They were dead, Scott saw at a glance.

He tried to crawl out from under the beam, but that was impossible. In the thunder of battle his voice could not be heard.

There was a movement across the room, halfway to the door. Cinc Mendez stumbled up and stared around, blinking. Red smeared his plump cheeks.

He saw Scott and stood, rocking back and forth, staring. Then he put his hand on the butt of his pistol.

Scott could very easily read the other's mind. If the Doone captain died now, the chances were that Mendez could merge with the Doones and assume control. The politico-military balance lay that way.

If Scott lived, it was probable that he would be elected cinc.

It was, therefore, decidedly to Mendez's advantage to kill the emprisoned man.

A shadow crossed the doorway. Mendez, his back to the newcomer, did not see Commander Bienne halt on the threshold, scowling at the tableau. Scott knew that Bienne understood the situation as well as he himself did. The commander realized that in a very few moments Mendez would draw his gun and fire.

Scott waited. The cinc's fingers tightened on his gun butt.

Bienne, grinning crookedly, said, "I thought that shell had finished you, sir. Guess it's hard to kill a Dooneman."

Mendez took his hand off the gun, instantly regaining his poise. He turned to Bienne.

"I'm glad you're here, commander. It'll probably take both of us to move that beam."

"Shall we try, sir?"

Between the two of them, they managed to shift the weight off Scott's torso. Briefly the latter's eyes met Bienne's. There was still no friendliness in them, but there was a look of wry self-mockery.

Bienne hadn't saved Scott's life, exactly. It was, rather, a question of being a Dooneman. For Bienne was, first of all, a soldier, and a member of the Free Company.

Scott tested his limbs; they worked.

"How long was I out, commander?"

"Ten minutes, sir. The *Armageddon*'s in sight."

"Good. Are the Helldivers veering off?"

Bienne shook his head. "So far they're not suspicious."

Scott grunted and made his way to the door, the others at his heels. Mendez said, "We'll need another control ship."

"All right. The *Arquebus*. Commander, take over here. Cinc Mendez—"

A flitterboat took them to the *Arquebus*, which was still in good fighting trim. The monitor *Armageddon*, Scott saw, was rolling helplessly in the trough of the waves. In accordance with the battle plan, the Doone ships were leading the Helldivers toward the apparently capsized giant. The technicians had done a good job; the false keel looked shockingly convincing.

Aboard the *Arquebus*, Scott took over, giving Mendez the auxiliary control for his substrafers. The Cinc beamed at Scott over his shoulder.

"Wait till that monitor opens up, captain."

"Yeah . . . we're in bad shape, though."

Neither man mentioned the incident that was in both their minds. It was tacitly forgotten—the only thing to do now.

Guns were still bellowing. The Helldivers were pouring their fire into the Doone formation, and they were winning. Scott scowled at the screens. If he waited too long, it would be just too bad.

Presently he put a beam on the *Armageddon*. She was in a beautiful position now, midway between two of the Helldivers' largest battleships.

"Unmask. Open fire."

Firing ports opened on the monitor. The sea titan's huge guns snouted into view. Almost simultaneously they blasted, the thunder drowning out the noise of the lighter guns.

"All Doone ships attack," Scott said. "Plan R-7."

This was it. *This was it!*

The Doones raced in to the kill. Blasting, bellowing, shouting, the guns tried to make themselves heard above the roaring of the monitor. They could not succeed, but that savage, invincible onslaught won the battle.

It was nearly impossible to maneuver a monitor into battle formation, but, once that was accomplished, the only thing that could stop the monster was atomic power.

But the Helldivers fought on, trying strategic formation. They could not succeed. The big battlewagons could not get out of range of the *Armageddon*'s guns. And that meant—

Cinc Flynn's face showed on the screen.

"Capitulation, sir. Cease firing."

Scott gave orders. The roar of the guns died into humming, incredible silence.

"You gave us a great battle, cinc."

"Thanks. So did you. Your strategy with the monitor was excellent."

So—that was that. Scott felt something go limp inside of him. Flynn's routine words were meaningless; Scott was drained of the vital excitement that had kept him going till now.

The rest was pure formula.

Token depth charges would be dropped over Virginia Keep. They would not harm the Dome, but they were the rule. There would be the ransom, paid always by the Keep which backed the losing side. A supply of korium, or its negotiable equivalent. The Doone treasury would be swelled. Part of the money would go into replacements and new keels. The life of the forts would go on.

Alone at the rail of the *Arquebus*, heading for Virginia Keep, Scott watched slow darkness change the clouds from pearl to gray, and then to invisibility. He was alone in the night. The wash of waves came up to him softly as the *Arquebus* rushed to her destination, three hundred miles away.

Warm yellow lights gleamed from ports behind him, but he did not turn. This, he thought, was like the cloud-wrapped Olympus in Montana Keep, where he had promised Ilene—many things.

Yet there was a difference. In an Olympus a man was like a god, shut away completely from the living world. Here, in the unbroken dark, there was no sense of alienage. Nothing could be seen—Venus has no moon, and the clouds hide the stars. And the seas are not phosphorescent.

Beneath these waters stand the Keeps, Scott thought. They hold the future. Such battles as were fought today are fought so that the Keeps may not be destroyed.

And men will sacrifice. Men have always sacrificed, for a social organization or a military unit. Man must create his own ideal. "If there had been no God, man would have created Him."

Bienne had sacrificed today, in a queer, twisted way of loyalty to his fetish. Yet Bienne still hated him, Scott knew.

The Doones meant nothing. Their idea was a false one. Yet, because men were faithful to that ideal, civilization would rise again from the guarded Keeps. A civilization that would forget its doomed guardians, the watchers of the seas of Venus, the Free Companions yelling their mad, futile battle cry as they drove on—as this ship was driving—into a night that would have no dawn.

Ilene.

Jeana.

It was no such simple choice. It was, in fact, no real choice at all. For Scott knew, very definitely, that he could never, as long as he lived, believe wholeheartedly in the Free Companions. Always a sardonic devil deep within him would be laughing in bitter self-mockery.

The whisper of the waves drifted up.

It wasn't sensible. It was sentimental, crazy, stupid, sloppy thinking.

But Scott knew, now, that he wasn't going back to Ilene.

He was a fool.

But he was a soldier.

AMONG THIEVES

by Poul Anderson

His Excellency M'Katze Unduma, Ambassador of the Terrestrial Federation to the Double Kingdom, was not accustomed to being kept waiting. But as the minutes dragged into an hour, anger faded before a chill deduction.

In this bleakly clock-bound society a short delay was bad manners, even if it were unintentional. But if you kept a man of rank cooling his heels for an entire sixty minutes, you offered him an unforgivable insult. Rusch was a barbarian, but he was too canny to humiliate Earth's representative without reason.

Which bore out everything that Terrestrial Intelligence had discovered. From a drunken junior officer, weeping in his cups because Old Earth, Civilization, was going to be attacked and the campus where he had once learned and loved would be scorched to ruin by *his* fire guns—to the battle plans and annotations thereon, which six men had died to smuggle out of the Royal War College—and now, this degradation of the ambassador himself—everything fitted.

The Margrave of Drakenstane had sold out Civilization.

Unduma shuddered, beneath the iridescent cloak, embroidered robe, and ostrich-plume headdress of his rank. He swept the antechamber with the eyes of a trapped animal.

This castle was ancient, dating back some eight hundred years to the first settlement of Norstad. The grim square massiveness of it, fused stone piled into a turreted mountain, was not much relieved by modern fittings. Tableservs, loungers, drapes, jewel mosaics, and biomurals only clashed with those fortress walls and ringing flagstones; fluorosheets did not light up all the dark corners, there was perpetual

69

dusk up among the rafters where the old battle banners hung.

A dozen guards were posted around the room, in breast-plate and plumed helmet but with very modern blast rifles. They were identical seven-foot blonds, and none of them moved at all, you couldn't even see them breathe. It was an unnerving sight for a Civilized man.

Unduma snubbed out his cigar, swore miserably to himself, and wished he had at least brought along a book.

The inner door opened on noiseless hinges and a shavepate officer emerged. He clicked his heels and bowed at Unduma. "His Lordship will be honored to receive you now, excellency."

The ambassador throttled his anger, nodded, and stood up. He was a tall thin man, the relatively light skin and sharp features of Bantu stock predominant in him. Earth's emissaries were normally chosen to approximate a local ideal of beauty—hard to do for some of those weird little cultures scattered through the galaxy—and Norstad-Ostarik had been settled by a rather extreme Caucasoid type which had almost entirely emigrated from the home planet.

The aide showed him through the door and disappeared. Hans von Thoma Rusch, Margrave of Drakenstane, Law-man of the Western Folkmote, Hereditary Guardian of the White River Gates, et cetera, et cetera, et cetera, sat wait-ing behind a desk at the end of an enormous black-and-red tile floor. He had a book in his hands, and didn't close it till Unduma, sandals whispering on the great chessboard squares, had come near. Then he stood up and made a short ironic bow.

"How do you do, your excellency," he said. "I am sorry to be so late. Please sit." Such curtness was no apology at all, and both of them knew it.

Unduma lowered himself to a chair in front of the desk. He would *not* show temper, he thought, he was here for a greater purpose. His teeth clamped together.

"Thank you, your lordship," he said tonelessly. "I hope you will have time to talk with me in some detail. I have come on a matter of grave importance."

Rusch's right eyebrow tilted up, so that the archaic mono-cle he affected beneath it seemed in danger of falling out. He was a big man, stiffly and solidly built, yellow hair cropped to a wiry brush around the long skull, a scar puck-ering his left cheek. He wore Army uniform, the gray high-collared tunic and old-fashioned breeches and shiny boots of his planet; the trident and suns of a primary general; a sidearm, its handle worn smooth from much use. If ever the iron barbarian with the iron brain had an epitome, thought Unduma, here he sat!

"Well, your excellency," murmured Rusch—though the harsh Norron language did not lend itself to murmurs—"of course I'll be glad to hear you out. But after all, I've no standing in the Ministry, except as unofficial advisor, and—"

"Please." Unduma lifted a hand. "Must we keep up the fable? You not only speak for all the landed warlords—and the Nor-Samurai are still the most powerful single class in the Double Kingdom—but you have the General Staff in your pouch, and, ah, you are well thought of by the royal family. I think I can talk directly to you."

Rusch did not smile, but neither did he trouble to deny what everyone knew, that he was the leader of the fighting aristocracy, friend of the widowed Queen Regent, virtual step-father of her eight-year-old son King Hjalmar—in a word, that he was the dictator. If he preferred to keep a small title and not have his name unnecessarily before the public, what difference did that make?

"I'll be glad to pass on whatever you wish to say to the proper authorities," he answered slowly. "Pipe." That was an order to his chair, which produced a lit briar for him.

Unduma felt appalled. This series of—informalities—was like one savage blow after another. Till now, in the three-hundred-year history of relations between Earth and the Double Kingdom, the Terrestrial ambassador had ranked everyone but God and the royal family.

No human planet, no matter how long sundered from the main stream, no matter what strange ways it had wandered, failed to remember that Earth was Earth, the home of man and the heart of Civilization. No *human* planet—had Norstad-Ostarik, then, gone the way of Kolresh?

Biologically, no, thought Unduma with an inward shudder. Nor culturally—yet. But it shrieked at him, from every insolent movement and twist of words, that Rusch had made a political deal.

"Well?" said the Margrave.

Unduma cleared his throat, desperately, and leaned forward. "Your lordship," he said, "my embassy cannot help taking notice of certain public statements, as well as certain military preparations and other matters of common knowledge—"

"And items your spies have dug up," drawled Rusch.

Unduma started. "My lord!"

"My good ambassador," grinned Rusch, "it was you who suggested a straightforward talk. I know Earth has spies here. In any event, it's impossible to hide so large a business as the mobilization of two planets for war."

Unduma felt sweat trickle down his ribs.

"There is . . . you . . . your Ministry has only announced it is a defense measure," he stammered. "I had hoped . . . frankly, yes, till the last minute I hoped you . . . your people might see fit to join us against Kolresh."

There was a moment's quiet. *So* quiet, thought Unduma. A redness crept up Rusch's cheeks, the scar stood livid and his pale eyes were the coldest thing Unduma had ever seen.

Then, slowly, the Margrave got it out through his teeth: "For a number of centuries, your excellency, our people hoped Earth might join them."

"What do you mean?" Unduma forgot all polished inanities. Rusch didn't seem to notice. He stood up and went to the window.

"Come here," he said. "Let me show you something."

The window was a modern inset of clear, invisible plastic, a broad sheet high in the castle's infamous Witch Tower. It looked out on a black sky, the sun was down and the glacial forty-hour darkness of northern Norstad was crawling toward midnight.

Stars glittered mercilessly keen in an emptiness which seemed like crystal, which seemed about to ring thinly in contracting anguish under the cold. Ostarik, the companion planet, stood low to the south, a gibbous moon of steely blue; it never moved in that sky, the two worlds forever faced each other, the windy white peaks of one glaring at the warm lazy seas of the other. Northward, a great curtain of aurora flapped halfway around the cragged horizon.

From this dizzy height, Unduma could see little of the town Drakenstane: a few high-peaked roofs and small glowing windows, lamps lonesome above frozen streets. There wasn't much to see anyhow—no big cities on either planet, only the small towns which had grown from scattered thorps, each clustered humbly about the manor of its lord. Beyond lay winter fields, climbing up the valley walls to the hard green blink of glaciers. It must be blowing out there, he saw snowdevils chase ghostly across the blue-tinged desolation.

Rusch spoke roughly: "Not much of a planet we've got here, is it? Out on the far end of nowhere, a thousand light-years from your precious Earth, and right in the middle of a glacial epoch. Have you ever wondered why we don't set up weather-control stations and give this world a decent climate?"

"Well," began Unduma, "of course, the exigencies of—"

"Of war." Rusch sent his hand upward in a chopping motion, to sweep around the alien constellations. Among them burned Polaris, less than thirty parsecs away, huge and cruelly bright. "We never had a chance. Every time we thought we could begin, there would be war, usually with Kolresh, and the labor and materials would have to go for that. Once, about two centuries back, we did actually get stations established, it was even beginning to warm up a little. Kolresh blasted them off the map.

"Norstad was settled eight hundred years ago. For seven of those centuries, we've had Kolresh at our throats. Do you wonder if we've grown tired?"

"My lord, I . . . I can sympathize," said Unduma awkwardly. "I am not ignorant of your heroic history. But it would seem to me . . . after all, Earth has also fought—"

"At a range of a thousand light-years!" jeered Rusch. "The forgotten war. A few underpaid patrolmen in obsolete rustbucket ships to defend unimportant outposts from sporadic Kolreshite raids. We live on their borders!"

"It would certainly appear, your lordship, that Kolresh is your natural enemy," said Unduma. "As indeed it is of all Civilization, of Homo sapiens himself. What I cannot credit are the, ah, the rumors of an, er, alliance—"

"And why shouldn't we?" snarled Rusch. "For seven hundred years we've held them at bay, while your precious so-called Civilization grew fat behind a wall of our dead young men. The temptation to recoup some of our losses by helping Kolresh conquer Earth is very strong!"

"You don't mean it!" The breath rushed from Unduma's lungs.

The other man's face was like carved bone. "Don't jump to conclusions," he answered. "I merely point out that from our side there's a good deal to be said for such a policy. Now if Earth is prepared to make a different policy worth our while—do you understand? Nothing is going to happen in the immediate future. You have time to think about it."

"I would have to . . . communicate with my government," whispered Unduma.

"Of course," said Rusch. His bootheels clacked on the floor as he went back to his desk. "I've had a memorandum prepared for you, an unofficial informal sort of protocol, points which his majesty's government would like to make the basis of negotiations with the Terrestrial Federation. Ah, here!" He picked up a bulky folio. "I suggest you take a leave of absence, your excellency, go home and show your superiors this, ah—"

"Ultimatum," said Unduma in a sick voice.

Rusch shrugged. "Call it what you will." His tone was empty and remote, as if he had already cut himself and his people out of Civilization.

As he accepted the folio, Unduma noticed the book beside it, the one Rusch had been reading: a local edition of Schakspier, badly printed on sleazy paper, but in the original Old Anglic. Odd thing for a barbarian dictator to read. But then, Rusch was a bit of an historical scholar, as well as an enthusiastic kayak racer, meteor polo player, chess champion, mountain climber, and . . . and all-around scoundrel!

Norstad lay in the grip of a ten-thousand year winter, while Ostarik was a heaven of blue seas breaking on warm island sands. Nevertheless, because Ostarik harbored a peculiarly nasty plague virus, it remained an unattainable paradise in the sky till a bare two hundred fifty years ago. Then a research team from Earth got to work, found an effective vaccine, and saw a mountain carved into their likeness by the Norron folk.

It was through such means—and the sheer weight of example, the liberty and wealth and happiness of its people—that the Civilization centered on Earth had been propagating itself among colonies isolated for centuries. There were none which lacked reverence for Earth the Mother, Earth the Wise, Earth the Kindly: none but Kolresh, which had long ceased to be human.

Rusch's private speedster whipped him from the icicle walls of Festning Drakenstane to the rose gardens of Sorgenlos in an hour of hell-bat haste across vacuum. But it was several hours more until he and the queen could get away from their courtiers and be alone.

They walked through geometric beds of smoldering blooms, under songbirds and fronded trees, while the copper spires of the little palace reached up to the evening star and the hours-long sunset of Ostarik blazed gold across great quiet waters. The island was no more than a royal retreat, but lately it had known agonies.

Queen Ingra stooped over a mutant rose, tiger striped and a foot across; she plucked the petals from it and said close to weeping: "But I liked Unduma. I don't want him to hate us."

"He's not a bad sort," agreed Rusch. He stood behind her in a black dress uniform with silver insignia, like a formal version of death.

"He's more than that, Hans. He stands for decency—Norstad froze our souls, and Ostarik hasn't thawed them. I thought Earth might—" Her voice trailed off. She was slender and dark, still young, and her folk came from the rainy dales of Norstad's equator, a farm race with gentler ways than the miners and fishermen and hunters of the red-haired ice ape who had bred Rusch. In her throat, the Norron language softened to a burring music; the Drakenstane men spat their words out rough-edged.

"Earth might what?" Rusch turned a moody gaze to the west. "Lavish more gifts on us? We were always proud of paying our own way."

"Oh, no," said Ingra wearily. "After all, we could trade with them, furs and minerals and so on, if ninety per cent of our production didn't have to go into defense. I only thought they might teach us how to be human."

"I had assumed we were still classified Homo sapiens," said Rusch in a parched tone.

"Oh, you know what I mean!" She turned on him, violet eyes suddenly aflare. "Sometimes I wonder if *you're* human, Margrave Hans von Thoma Rusch. I mean free, free to be something more than a robot, free to raise children knowing they won't have their lungs shoved out their mouths when a Kolreshite cruiser hulls one of our spaceships. What is our whole culture, Hans? A layer of brutalized farmhands and factory workers—serfs! A top crust of heel-clattering aristocrats who live for nothing but war. A little folk art, folk music, folk saga, full of blood and treachery. Where are our symphonies, novels, cathedrals, research laboratories . . . where are people who can say what they wish and make what they will of their lives and be happy?"

* * *

Rusch didn't answer for a moment. He looked at her, unblinking behind his monocle, till she dropped her gaze and twisted her hands together. Then he said only: "You exaggerate."

"Perhaps. It's still the basic truth." Rebellion rode in her voice. "It's what all the other worlds think of us."

"Even if the democratic assumption—that the eternal verities can be discovered by counting enough noses—were true," said Rusch, "you cannot repeal eight hundred years of history by decree."

"No. But you could work toward it," she said. "I think you're wrong in despising the common man, Hans . . . when was he ever given a chance, in this kingdom? We could make a beginning now, and Earth could send psychotechnic advisors, and in two or three generations—"

"What would Kolresh be doing while we experimented with forms of government?" he laughed.

"Always Kolresh." Her shoulders, slim behind the burning-red cloak, slumped. "Kolresh turned a hundred hopeful towns into radioactive craters and left the gnawed bones of children in the fields. Kolresh killed my husband, like a score of kings before him. Kolresh blasted your family to ash, Hans, and scarred your face and your soul—" She whirled back on him, fists aloft, and almost screamed: "Do you want to make an ally of Kolresh?"

The Margrave took out his pipe and began filling it. The saffron sundown, reflected off the ocean to his face, gave him a metal look.

"Well," he said, "we've been at peace with them for all of ten years now. Almost a record."

"Can't we find allies? Real ones? I'm sick of being a figurehead! I'd befriend Ahuramazda, New Mars, Lagrange— We could raise a crusade against Kolresh, wipe every last filthy one of them out of the universe!"

"Now who's a heel-clattering aristocrat?" grinned Rusch.

He lit his pipe and strolled toward the beach. She stood for an angry moment, then sighed and followed him.

"Do you think it hasn't been tried?" he said patiently. "For generations we've tried to build up a permanent alliance directed at Kolresh. What temporary ones we achieved have always fallen apart. Nobody loves us enough—and, since we've always taken the heaviest blows, nobody hates Kolresh enough."

He found a bench on the glistening edge of the strand, and sat down and looked across a steady march of surf, turned to molten gold by the low sun and the incandescent western clouds. Ingra joined him.

"I can't really blame the others for not liking us," she said in a small voice. "We are overmechanized and undercultured, arrogant, tactless, undemocratic, hard-boiled . . . oh, yes. But their own self-interest—"

"They don't imagine it can happen to them," replied Rusch contemptuously. "And there are even pro-Kolresh elements, here and there." He raised his voice an octave: "Oh, my dear sir, my dear Margrave, what are you *saying*? Why, of *course* Kolresh would never attack us! They made a *treaty* never to attack us!"

Ingra sighed, forlornly. Rusch laid an arm across her shoulders. They sat for a while without speaking.

"Anyway," said the man finally, "Kolresh is too strong for any combination of powers in this part of the galaxy. We and they are the only ones with a military strength worth mentioning. Even Earth would have a hard time defeating them, and Earth, of course, will lean backward before undertaking a major war. She has too much to lose; it's so much more comfortable to regard the Kolreshite raids as mere piracies, the skirmishes as 'police actions.' She just plain will not pay the stiff price of an army and a navy able to whip Kolresh and occupy the Kolreshite planets."

"And so it is to be war again." Ingra looked out in desolation across the sea.

"Maybe not," said Rusch. "Maybe a different kind of war, at least—no more black ships coming out of *our* sky."

He blew smoke for a while, as if gathering courage, then spoke in a quick, impersonal manner. "Look here. We Norrons are not a naval power. It's not in our tradition. Our navy has always been inadequate and always will be. But we can breed the toughest soldiers in the known galaxy, in unlimited numbers; we can condition them into fighting machines, and equip them with the most lethal weapons living flesh can wield.

"Kolresh, of course, is just the opposite. Space nomads, small population, able to destroy anything their guns can reach but not able to dig in and hold it against us. For seven hundred years, we and they have been the elephant and the whale. Neither could ever win a real victory over the other;

war became the normal state of affairs, peace a breathing spell. Because of the mutation, there will always be war, as long as one single Kolreshite lives. We can't kill them, we can't befriend them—all we can do is to be bled white to stop them."

A wind sighed over the slow thunder on the beach. A line of sea birds crossed the sky, thin and black against glowing bronze.

"I know," said Ingra. "I know the history, and I know what you're leading up to. Kolresh will furnish transportation and naval escort; Norstad-Ostarik will furnish men. Between us, we may be able to take Earth."

"We will," said Rusch flatly. "Earth has grown plump and lazy. She can't possible rearm enough in a few months to stop such a combination."

"And all the galaxy will spit on our name."

"All the galaxy will lie open to conquest, once Earth has fallen."

"How long do you think we would last, riding the Kolresh tiger?"

"I have no illusions about them, my dear. But neither can I see any way to break this eternal deadlock. In a fluid situation, such as the collapse of Earth would produce, we might be able to create a navy as good as theirs. They've never yet given us a chance to build one, but perhaps—"

"Perhaps not! I doubt very much it was a meteor which wrecked my husband's ship, five years ago. I think Kolresh knew of his hopes, of the shipyard he wanted to start, and murdered him."

"It's probable," said Rusch.

"And you would league us with them." Ingra turned a colorless face on him. "I'm still the queen. I forbid any further consideration of this . . . this obscene alliance!"

Rusch sighed. "I was afraid of that, your highness." For a moment he looked gray, tired. "You have a veto power, of course. But I don't think the Ministry would continue in office a regent who used it against the best interests of—"

She leaped to her feet. "You wouldn't!"

"Oh, you'd not be harmed," said Rusch with a crooked smile. "Not even deposed. You'd be in a protective custody, shall we say. Of course, his majesty, your son, would have to be educated elsewhere, but if you wish—"

Her palm cracked on his face. He made no motion.

"I . . . won't veto—" Ingra shook her head. Then her

back grew stiff. "Your ship will be ready to take you home, my lord. I do not think we shall require your presence here again."

"As you will, your highness," mumbled the dictator of the Double Kingdom.

Though he returned with a bitter word in his mouth, Unduma felt the joy, the biological rightness of being home, rise warm within him. He sat on a terrace under the mild sky of Earth, with the dear bright flow of the Zambezi River at his feet and the slim towers of Capital City rearing as far as he could see, each gracious, in its own green park. The people on the clean quiet streets wore airy blouses and colorful kilts—not the trousers for men, ankle-length skirts for women, which muffled the sad folk of Norstad. And there was educated conversation in the gentle Tierrans language, music from an open window, laughter on the verandas and children playing in the parks: freedom, law, and leisure.

The thought that this might be rubbed out of history, that the robots of Norstad and the snake-souled monsters of Kolresh might tramp between broken spires where starved Earthmen hid, was a tearing in Unduma.

He managed to lift his drink and lean back with the proper casual elegance. "No, sir," he said, "they are not bluffing."

Ngu Chilongo, Premier of the Federation Parliament, blinked unhappy eyes. He was a small grizzled man, and a wise man, but this lay beyond everything he had known in a long lifetime and he was slow to grasp it.

"But surely—" he began. "Surely this . . . this Rusch person is not insane. He cannot think that his two planets, with a population of, what is it, perhaps one billion, can overcome four billion Terrestrials!"

"There would also be several million Kolreshites to help," reminded Unduma. "However, they would handle the naval end of it entirely—and their navy *is* considerably stronger than ours. The Norron forces would be the ones which actually landed, to fight the air and ground battles. And out of those paltry one billion, Rusch can raise approximately one hundred million soldiers."

Chilongo's glass crashed to the terrace. "What!"

"It's true, sir." The third man present, Mustafa Lefarge, Minister of Defense, spoke in a miserable tone. "It's a question of every able-bodied citizen, male and female, being a trained member of the armed forces. In time of war, virtually everyone not in actual combat is directly contributing to some phase of the effort—a civilian economy virtually ceases to exist. They're used to getting along for years at a stretch with no comforts and a bare minimum of necessities." His voice grew sardonic. "By necessities, they mean things like food and ammunition—not, say, entertainment or cultural activity, as we assume."

"A hundred million," whispered Chilongo. He stared at his hands. "Why, that's ten times our *total* forces!"

"Which are ill-trained, ill-equipped, and ill-regarded by our own civilians," pointed out Lefarge bitterly.

"In short, sir," said Unduma, "while we could defeat either Kolresh or Norstad-Ostarik in an all-out war—though with considerable difficulty—between them they can defeat us."

Chilongo shivered. Unduma felt a certain pity for him. You had to get used to it in small doses, this fact which Civilization screened from Earth: that the depths of hell are found in the human soul. That no law of nature guards the upright innocent from malice.

"But they wouldn't dare!" protested the Premier. "Our friends . . . everywhere—"

"All the human-colonized galaxy will wring its hands and send stiff notes of protest," said Lefarge. "Then they'll pull the blankets back over their heads and assure themselves that now the big bad aggressor has been sated."

"This note—of Rusch's." Chilongo seemed to be grabbing out after support while the world dropped from beneath his feet. Sweat glistened on his wrinkled brown forehead. "Their terms . . . surely we can make some agreement?"

"Their terms are impossible, as you'll see for yourself when you read," said Unduma flatly. "They want us to declare war on Kolresh, accept a joint command under Norron leadership, foot the bill and—No!"

"But if we have to fight anyway," began Chilongo, "it would seem better to have at least one ally—"

"Has Earth changed that much since I was gone?" asked Unduma in astonishment. "Would our people really consent to this . . . this extortion . . . letting those hairy barbarians write our foreign policy for us— Why, jumping into war, making the first declaration ourselves, it's unconstitutional! It's *un-Civilized*!"

Chilongo seemed to shrink a little. "No," he said. "No, I don't mean that. Of course it's impossible; better to be honestly defeated in battle. I only thought, perhaps we could bargain—"

"We can try," said Unduma skeptically, "but I never heard of Hans Rusch yielding an angstrom without a pistol at his head."

Lefarge struck a cigar, inhaled deeply, and took another sip from his glass. "I hardly imagine an alliance with Kolresh would please his own people," he mused.

"Scarcely!" said Unduma. "But they'll accept it if they must."

"Oh? No chance for us to get him overthrown—assassinated, even?"

"Not to speak of. Let me explain. He's only a petty aristocrat by birth, but during the last war with Kolresh he gained high rank and a personal following of fanatically loyal young officers. For the past few years, since the king died, he's been the dictator. He's filled the key posts with his men: hard, able, and unquestioning. Everyone else is either admiring or cowed. Give him credit, he's no megalomaniac—he shuns publicity—but that simply divorces his power all the more from responsibility. You can measure it by pointing out that everyone knows he will probably ally with Kolresh, and everyone has a nearly physical loathing of the idea—but there is not a word of criticism for Rusch himself, and when he orders it they will embark on Kolreshite ships to ruin the Earth they love."

"It could almost make you believe in the old myths," whispered Chilongo. "About the Devil incarnate."

"Well," said Unduma, "this sort of thing has happened before, you know."

"Hm-m-m?" Lefarge sat up.

Unduma smiled sadly. "Historical examples," he said. "They're of no practical value today, except for giving the cold consolation that we're not uniquely betrayed."

"What do you mean?" asked Chilongo.

"Well," said Unduma, "consider the astropolitics of the situation. Around Polaris and beyond lies Kolresh territory, where for a long time they sharpened their teeth preying on backward autochthones. At last they started expanding toward the richer human-settled planets. Norstad happened

to lie directly on their path, so Norstad took the first blow—
and stopped them.

"Since then, it's been seven hundred years of stalemated
war. Oh, naturally Kolresh outflanks Norstad from time to
time, seizes this planet in the galactic west and raids that
one to the north, fights a war with one to the south and
makes an alliance with one to the east. But it has never
amounted to anything important. It can't, with Norstad
astride the most direct line between the heart of Kolresh
and the heart of Civilization. If Kolresh made a serious
effort to by-pass Norstad, the Norrons could—and would—
disrupt everything with an attack in the rear.

"In short, despite the fact that interstellar space is three-
dimensional and enormous, Norstad guards the northern
marches of Civilization."

He paused for another sip. It was cool and subtle on his
tongue, a benediction after the outworld rotgut.

"Hm-m-m, I never thought of it just that way," said
Lefarge. "I assumed it was just a matter of barbarians
fighting each other for the usual barbarian reasons."

"Oh, it is, I imagine," said Unduma, "but the result is
that Norstad acts as the shield of Earth.

"Now if you examine early Terrestrial history—and Rusch,
who has a remarkable knowledge of it, stimulated me to do
so—you'll find that this is a common thing. A small semicivi-
lized state, out on the marches, holds off the enemy while
the true civilization prospers behind it. Assyria warded Mesopotamia, Rome defended Greece, the Welsh border lords
kept England safe, the Transoxanian Tartars were the shield
of Persia, Prussia blocked the approaches to western Europe . . . oh, I could add a good many examples. In every
instance, a somewhat backward people on the distant frontier of a civilization, receive the worst hammer-blows of the
really alien races beyond, the wild men who would leave
nothing standing if they could get at the protected cities of
the inner society."

He paused for breath. "And so?" asked Chilongo.

"Well, of course, suffering isn't good for people," shrugged
Unduma. "It tends to make them rather nasty. The marchmen
react to incessant war by becoming a warrior race, uncouth
peasants with an absolute government of ruthless militarists.
Nobody loves them, neither the outer savages nor the inner
polite nations.

"And in the end, they're all too apt to turn inward. Their

military skill and vigor need a more promising outlet than
this grim business of always fighting off an enemy who
always comes back and who has even less to steal than the
sentry culture.

"So Assyria sacks Babylon; Rome conquers Greece; Percy
rises against King Henry; Tamerlane overthrows Bajazet;
Prussia clanks into France—"

"And Norstad-Ostarik falls on Earth," finished Lefarge.

"Exactly," said Unduma. "It's not even unprecedented
for the border state to join hands with the very tribes it
fought so long. Percy and Owen Glendower, for instance
. . . though in that case, I imagine both parties were considerably more attractive than Hans Rusch or Klerak Belug."

"What are we going to do?" Chilongo whispered it toward
the blue sky of Earth, from which no bombs had fallen
for a thousand years.

Then he shook himself, jumped to his feet, and faced the
other two. "I'm sorry, gentlemen. This has taken me rather
by surprise, and I'll naturally require time to look at this
Norron protocol and evaluate the other data. But if it turns
out you're right"—he bowed urbanely—"as I'm sure it will—"

"Yes?" said Unduma in a tauntening voice.

"Why, then, we appear to have some months, at least,
before anything drastic happens. We can try to gain more
time by negotiation. We do have the largest industrial complex in the known universe, and four billion people who
have surely not had courage bred out of them. We'll build
up our armed forces, and if those barbarians attack we'll
whip them back into their own kennels and kick them through
the rear walls thereof!"

"I hoped you'd say that," breathed Unduma.

"I hope we'll be granted time," Lefarge scowled. "I assume Rusch is not a fool. We cannot rearm in anything less
than a glare of publicity. When he learns of it, what's to
prevent him from cementing the Kolresh alliance and attacking at once, before we're ready?"

"Their mutual suspiciousness ought to help," said Unduma.
"I'll go back there, of course, and do what I can to stir up
trouble between them."

He sat still for a moment, then added as if to himself:
"Till we do finish preparing, we have no resources but hope."

The Kolreshite mutation was a subtle thing. It did not
show on the surface: physically, they were a handsome

people, running to white skin and orange hair. Over the centuries, thousands of Norron spies had infiltrated them, and frequently gotten back alive; what made such work unusually difficult was not the normal hazards of impersonation, but an ingrained reluctance to practice cannibalism and worse.

The mutation was a psychic twist, probably originating in some obscure gene related to the endocrine system. It was extraordinarily hard to describe—every categorical statement about it had the usual quota of exceptions and qualifications. But one might, to a first approximation, call it extreme xenophobia. It is normal for Homo sapiens to be somewhat wary of outsiders till he has established their bona fides; it was normal for Homo Kolreshi to *hate* all outsiders, from first glimpse to final destruction.

Naturally, such an instinct produced a tendency to inbreeding, which lowered fertility, but systematic execution of the unfit had so far kept the stock vigorous. The instinct also led to strongarm rule within the nation; to nomadism, where a planet was only a base like the oasis of the ancient Bedouin, essential to life but rarely seen; to a cult of secrecy and cruelty, a religion of abominations; to an ultimate goal of conquering the accessible universe and wiping out all other races.

Of course, it was not so simple, nor so blatant. Among themselves, the Kolreshites doubtless found a degree of tenderness and fidelity. Visiting on neutral planets—i.e., planets which it was not yet expedient to attack—they were very courteous and had an account of defending themselves against one unprovoked aggression after another, which some found plausible. Even their enemies stood in awe of their personal heroism.

Nevertheless, few in the galaxy would have wept if the Kolreshites all died one rainy night.

Hans von Thomas Rusch brought his speedster to the great whaleback of the battleship. It lay a light-year from his sun, hidden by cold emptiness; the co-ordinates had been given him secretly, together with an invitation which was more like a summons.

He glided into the landing cradle, under the turrets of guns that could pound a moon apart, and let the mechanism suck him down below decks. When he stepped out into the high, coldly lit debarkation chamber, an honor guard in red presented arms and pipes twittered for him.

He walked slowly forward, a big man in black and silver, to meet his counterpart, Klerak Belug, the Overman of Kolresh, who waited rigid in a blood-colored tunic. The cabin bristled around him with secret police and guns.

Rusch clicked heels. "Good day, your dominance," he said. A faint echo followed his voice. For some unknown reason, this folk liked echoes and always built walls to resonate.

Belug, an aging giant who topped him by a head, raised shaggy brows. "Are you alone, your lordship?" he asked in atrociously accented Norron. "It was understood that you could bring a personal bodyguard."

Rusch shrugged. "I would have needed a personal dreadnought to be quite safe," he replied in fluent Kolra, "so I decided to trust your safe conduct. I assume you realize that any harm done to me means instant war with my kingdom."

The broad, wrinkled lion-face before him split into a grin. "My representatives did not misjudge you, your lordship. I think we can indeed do business. Come."

The Overman turned and led the way down a ramp toward the guts of the ship. Rusch followed, enclosed by guards and bayonets. He kept a hand on his own sidearm—not that it would do him much good, if matters came to that.

Events were approaching their climax, he thought in a cold layer of his brain. For more than a year now, negotiations had dragged on, hemmed in by the requirement of secrecy, weighted down by mutual suspicion. There were only two points of disagreement remaining, but discussion had been so thoroughly snagged on those that the two absolute rulers must meet to settle it personally. It was Belug who had issued the contemptuous invitation.

And he, Rusch, had come. Tonight the old kings of Norstad wept worms in their graves.

The party entered a small, luxuriously chaired room. There were the usual robots, for transcription and reference purposes, and there were guards, but Overman and Margrave were essentially alone.

Belug wheezed his bulk into a seat. "Smoke? Drink?"

"I have my own, thank you." Rusch took out his pipe and a hip flask.

"That is scarcely diplomatic," rumbled Belug.

Rusch laughed. "I'd always understood that your dominance had no use for the mannerisms of Civilization. I daresay we'd both like to finish our business as quickly as possible."

The Overman snapped his fingers. Someone glided up with wine in a glass. He sipped for a while before answering: "Yes. By all means. Let us reach an executive agreement now and wait for our hirelings to draw up a formal treaty. But it seems odd, sir, that after all these months of delay, you are suddenly so eager to complete the work."

"Not odd," said Rusch. "Earth is rearming at a considerable rate. She's had almost a year now. We can still whip her, but in another six months we'll no longer be able to; give her automated factories half a year beyond *that*, and she'll destroy us!"

"It must have been clear to you, sir, that after the Earth Ambassador—what's his name, Unduma—after he returned to your planets last year, he was doing all he could to gain time."

"Oh, yes," said Rusch. "Making offers to me, and then haggling over them—brewing trouble elsewhere to divert our attention—a gallant effort. But it didn't work. Frankly, your dominance, you've only yourself to blame for the delays. For example, your insisting that Earth be administered as Kolreshite territory—"

"My dear sir!" exploded Belug. "It was a talking point. Only a talking point. Any diplomatist would have understood. But you took six weeks to study it, then offered that preposterous counter-proposal that everything should revert to *you*, loot and territory both— Why, if you had been truly willing to co-operate, we could have settled the terms in a month!"

"As you like, your dominance," said Rusch carelessly. "It's all past now. There are only these questions of troop transport and prisoners, then we're in total agreement."

Klerak Belug narrowed his eyes and rubbed his chin with one outsize hand. "I do not comprehend," he said, "and neither do my naval officers. We have regular transports for your men, nothing extraordinary in the way of comfort, to be sure, but infinitely more suitable for so long a voyage than . . . than the naval units you insist we use. Don't you understand? A transport is for carrying men or cargo; a ship of the line is to fight or convoy. You do *not* mix the functions!"

"I do, your dominance," said Rusch. "As many of my soldiers as possible are going to travel on regular warships furnished by Kolresh, and there are going to be Double Kingdom naval personnel with them for liaison."

"But—" Belug's fist closed on his wineglass as if to splinter it. "Why?" he roared.

"My representatives have explained it a hundred times," said Rusch wearily. "In blunt language, I don't trust you. If . . . oh, let us say there should be disagreement between us while the armada is en route . . . well, a transport ship is easily replaced, after its convoy vessels have blown it up. The fighting craft of Kolresh are a better hostage for your good behavior." He struck a light to his pipe. "Naturally, you can't take our whole fifty-million-man expeditionary force on your battle wagons; but I want soldiers on every warship as well as in the transports."

Belug shook his ginger head. "No."

"Come now," said Rusch. "Your spies have been active enough on Norstad and Ostarik. Have you found any reason to doubt my intentions? Bearing in mind that an army the size of ours cannot be alerted for a given operation, without a great many people knowing the fact—"

"Yes, yes," grumbled Belug. "Granted." He smiled, a sharp flash of teeth. "But the upper hand is mine, your lordship. I can wait indefinitely to attack Earth. You can't."

"Eh?" Rusch drew hard on his pipe.

"In the last analysis, even dictators rely on popular support. My Intelligence tells me you are rapidly losing yours. The queen has not spoken to you for a year, has she? And there are many Norrons whose first loyalty is to the Crown. As the thought of war with Earth seeps in, as men have time to comprehend how little they like the idea, time to see through your present anti-Terrestrial propaganda—they grow angry. Already they mutter about you in the beer halls and the officers' clubs, they whisper in ministry cloakrooms. My agents have heard.

"Your personal cadre of young key officers are the only ones left with unquestioning loyalty to you. Let discontent grow just a little more, let open revolt break out, and your followers will be hanged from the lamp posts.

"You can't delay much longer."

Rusch made no reply for a while. Then he sat up, his monocle glittering like a cold round window on winter.

"I can always call off this plan and resume the normal state of affairs," he snapped.

Belug flushed red. "War with Kolresh again? It would take you too long to shift gears—to reorganize."

"It would not. Our war college, like any other, has prepared military plans for all foreseeable combinations of circumstances. If I cannot come to terms with you, Plan No. So-and-So goes into effect. And obviously *it* will have popular enthusiasm behind it!"

He nailed the Overman with a fish-pale eye and continued in frozen tones: "After all, your dominance, I would prefer to fight you. The only thing I would enjoy more would be to hunt you with hounds. Seven hundred years have shown this to be impossible. I opened negotiations to make the best of an evil bargain—since you cannot be conquered, it will pay better to join with you on a course of mutually profitable imperialism.

"But if your stubbornness prevents an agreement, I can declare war on you in the usual manner and be no worse off than I was. The choice is, therefore, yours."

Belug swallowed. Even his guards lost some of their blankness. One does not speak in that fashion across the negotiators' table.

Finally, only his lips stirring, he said: "Your frankness is appreciated, my lord. Some day I would like to discuss that aspect further. As for now, though . . . yes, I can see your point. I am prepared to admit some of your troops to our ships of the line." After another moment, still sitting like a stone idol: "But this question of returning prisoners of war. We have never done it. I do not propose to begin."

"*I* do not propose to let poor devils of Norrons rot any longer in your camps," said Rusch. "I have a pretty good idea of what goes on there. If we're to be allies, I'll want back such of my countrymen as are still alive."

"Not many are still sane," Belug told him deliberately.

Rusch puffed smoke and made no reply.

"If I give in on the one item," said Belug, "I have a right to test your sincerity by the other. We keep our prisoners."

Rusch's own face had gone quite pale and still. It grew altogether silent in the room.

"Very well," he said after a long time. "Let it be so."

Without a word, Major Othkar Graaborg led his company into the black cruiser. The words came from the spaceport, where police held off a hooting, hissing, rock-throwing mob.

It was the first time in history that Norron folk had stoned their own soldiers.

His men tramped stolidly behind him, up the gangway and through the corridors. Among the helmets and packs and weapons, racketing boots and clashing body armor, their faces were lost, they were an army without faces.

Graaborg followed a Kolreshite ensign, who kept looking back nervously at these hereditary foes, till they reached the bunkroom. It had been hastily converted from a storage hold, and was scant cramped comfort for a thousand men.

"All right, boys," he said when the door had closed on his guide. "Make yourselves at home."

They got busy, opening packs, spreading bedrolls on bunks. Immediately thereafter, they started to assemble heavy machine guns, howitzers, even a nuclear blaster.

"You, there!" The accented voice squawked indignantly from a loudspeaker in the wall. "I see that. I got video. You not put guns together here."

Graaborg looked up from his inspection of a live fission shell. "Obscenity you," he said pleasantly. "Who are you, anyway?"

"I executive officer. I tell captain."

"Go right ahead. My orders say that according to treaty, as long as we stay in our assigned part of the ship, we're under our own discipline. If your captain doesn't like it, let him come down here and talk to us." Graaborg ran a thumb along the edge of his bayonet. A wolfish chorus from his men underlined the invitation.

No one pressed the point. The cruiser lumbered into space, rendezvoused with her task force, and went into nonspatial drive. For several days, the Norron army contingent remained in its den, more patient with such stinking quarters than the Kolreshites could imagine anyone being. Nevertheless, no spaceman ventured in there: meals were fetched at the galley by Norron squads.

Graaborg alone wandered freely about the ship. He was joined by Commander von Brecca of Ostarik, the head of the Double Kingdom's naval liaison on this ship: a small band of officers and ratings, housed elsewhere. They conferred with the Kolreshite officers as the necessity arose, on routine problems, rehearsal of various operations to be performed when Earth was reached a month hence— but they did not mingle socially. This suited their hosts.

The fact is the Kolreshites were rather frightened of them.

A spaceman does not lack courage, but he is a gentleman among warriors. His ship either functions well, keeping him clean and comfortable, or it does not function at all and he dies quickly and mercifully. He fights with machines, at enormous ranges.

The ground soldier, muscle in mud, whose ultimate weapon is whetted steel in bare hands, has a different kind of toughness.

Two weeks after departure, Graaborg's wrist chronometer showed a certain hour. He was drilling his men in full combat rig, as he had been doing every "day" in spite of the narrow quarters.

"Ten-SHUN!" The order flowed through captains, lieutenants, and sergeants; the bulky mass of men crashed to stillness.

Major Graaborg put a small pocket amplifier to his lips. "All right, lads," he said casually, "assume gas masks, radiation shields, all gun squads to weapons. Now let's clean up this ship."

He himself blew down the wall with a grenade.

Being perhaps the most thoroughly trained soldiers in the universe, the Norron men paused for only one amazed second. Then they cheered, with death and hell in their voices, and crowded at his heels.

Little resistance was met until Graaborg had picked up von Brecca's naval command, the crucial ones, who could sail and fight the ship. The Kolreshites were too dumbfounded. Thereafter the nomads rallied and fought gamely. Graaborg was handicapped by not having been able to give his men a battle plan. He split up his forces and trusted to the intelligence of the noncoms.

His faith was not misplaced, though the ship was in poor condition by the time the last Kolreshite had been machinegunned.

Graaborg himself had used a bayonet, with vast satisfaction.

M'Katze Unduma entered the office in the Witch tower. "You sent for me, your lordship?" he asked. His voice was as cold and bitter as the gale outside.

"Yes. Please be seated." Margrave Hans von Thoma Rusch looked tired. "I have some news for you."

"What news? You declared war on Earth two weeks ago. Your army can't have reached her yet." Unduma leaned over the desk. "Is it that you've found transportation to send me home?"

"Somewhat better news, your excellency." Rusch leaned over and tuned a telescreen. A background of clattering robots and frantically busy junior officers came into view.

Then a face entered the screen, young, and with more life in it than Unduma had ever before seen on this sullen planet. "Central Data headquarters—Oh yes, your lordship." Boyishly, against all rules: "We've got her! The *Bheoka* just called in . . . she's ours!"

"Hm-m-m. Good." Rusch glanced at Unduma. "The *Bheoka* is the superdreadnought accompanying Task Force Two. Carry on with the news."

"Yes, sir. She's already reducing the units we failed to capture. Admiral Sorrens estimates he'll control Force Two entirely in another hour. Bulletin just came in from Force Three. Admiral Gundrup killed in fighting, but Vice Admiral Smitt has assumed command and reports three-fourths of the ships in our hands. He's delaying fire until he sees how it goes aboard the rest. Also—"

"Never mind," said Rusch. "I'll get the comprehensive report later. Remind Staff that for the next few hours all command decisions had better be made by officers on the spot. After that, when we see what we've got, broader tactics can be prepared. If some extreme emergency doesn't arise, it'll be a few hours before I can get over to HQ."

"Yes, sir. Sir, I . . . may I say " So might the young Norron have addressed a god.

"All right, son, you've said it." Rusch turned off the screen and looked at Unduma. "Do you realize what's happening?"

The ambassador sat down; his knees seemed all at once to have melted. "What have you done?" It was like a stranger speaking.

"What I planned quite a few years ago," said the Margrave.

He reached into his desk and brought forth a bottle. "Here, your excellency. I think we could both use a swig. Authentic Terrestrial Scotch. I've saved it for this day."

But there was no glory leaping in him. It is often thus, you reach a dream and you only feel how tired you are.

Unduma let the liquid fire slide down his throat.

"You understand, don't you?" said Rusch. "For seven centuries, the Elephant and the Whale fought, without being able to get at each other's vitals. I made this alliance against Earth solely to get our men aboard their ships. But a really large operation like that can't be faked. It has to be genuine—

the agreements, the preparations, the propaganda, everything. Only a handful of officers, men who could be trusted to . . . to infinity"—his voice cracked over, and Unduma thought of war prisoners sacrificed, hideous casualties in the steel corridors of spaceships, Norron gunners destroying Kolreshite vessels and the survivors of Norron detachments which failed to capture them—"only a few could be told, and then only at the last instant. For the rest, I relied on the quality of our troops. They're good lads, every one of them and, therefore, adaptable. They're especially adaptable when suddenly told to fall on the men they'd most like to kill."

He tilted the bottle afresh. "It's proving expensive," he said in a slurred, hurried tone. "It will cost us as many casualties, no doubt, as ten years of ordinary war. But if I hadn't done this, there could easily have been another seven hundred years of war. Couldn't there? Couldn't there have been? As it is, we've already broken the spine of the Kolreshite fleet. She has plenty of ships yet, to be sure, still a menace, but crippled. I hope Earth will see fit to join us. Between them, Earth and Norstad-Ostarik can finish off Kolresh in a hurry. And after all, Kolresh *did* declare war on you, had every intention of destroying you. If you won't help, well, we can end it by ourselves, now that the fleet is broken. But I hope you'll join us."

"I don't know," said Unduma. He was still wobbling in a new cosmos. "We're not a . . . a hard people."

"You ought to be," said Rusch. "Hard enough, anyway, to win a voice for yourselves in what's going to happen around Polaris. Important frontier, Polaris."

"Yes," said Unduma slowly. "There is that. It won't cause any hosannahs in our streets, but . . . yes, I think we will continue the war, as your allies, if only to prevent you from massacring the Kolreshites. They can be rehabilitated, you know."

"I doubt that," grunted Rusch. "But it's a detail. At the very least, they'll never be allowed weapons again." He raised a sardonic brow. "I suppose we, too, can be rehabilitated, once you get your peace groups and psychotechs out here. No doubt you'll manage to demilitarize us and turn us into good plump democrats. All right, Unduma, send your Civilizing missionaries. But permit me to give thanks that I won't live to see their work completed!"

The Earthman nodded, rather coldly. You couldn't blame Rusch for treachery, callousness, and arrogance—he was what his history had made him—but he remained unpleasant company for a Civilized man. "I shall communicate with my government at once, your lordship, and recommend a provisional alliance, the terms to be settled later," he said. "I will report back to you as soon as . . . ah, where will you be?"

"How should I know?" Rusch got out of his chair. The winter night howled at his back. "I have to convene the Ministry, and make a public telecast, and get over to Staff, and— No. The devil with it! If you need me inside the next few hours, I'll be at Sorgenlos on Ostarik. But the matter had better be urgent!"

DESPOILERS OF THE GOLDEN EMPIRE

by *Randall Garrett*

I

In the seven centuries that had elapsed since the Second Empire had been founded on the shattered remnants of the First, the nobles of the Imperium had come slowly to realize that the empire was not to be judged by the examples of its predecessor. The First Empire had conquered most of the known universe by political intrigue and sheer military strength; it had fallen because that same propensity for political intrigue had gained over every other strength of the Empire, and the various branches and sectors of the First Empire had begun to use it against one another.

The Second Empire was politically unlike the First; it tried to balance a centralized government against the autonomic governments of the various sectors, and had almost succeeded in doing so.

But, no matter how governed, there are certain essentials which are needed by any governmental organization.

Without power, neither Civilization nor the Empire could hold itself together, and His Universal Majesty, the Emperor Carl, well knew it. And power was linked solidly to one element, one metal, without which Civilization would collapse as surely as if it had been blasted out of existence. Without the power metal, no ship could move or even be built; without it, industry would come to a standstill.

In ancient times, even as far back as the early Greek and Roman civilizations, the metal had been known, but it had been used, for the most part, as decoration and in the manufacture of jewelry. Later, it had been coined as money.

It had always been relatively rare, but now, weight for

weight, atom for atom, it was the most valuable element on Earth. Indeed, the most valuable in the known universe.

The metal was Element Number Seventy-nine—gold.

To the collective mind of the Empire, gold was the prime object in any kind of mining exploration. The idea of drilling for petroleum, even if it had been readily available, or of mining coal or uranium would have been dismissed as impracticable and even worse than useless.

Throughout the Empire, research laboratories worked tirelessly at the problem of transmuting commoner elements into Gold-197, but thus far none of the processes was commercially feasible. There was still, after thousands of years, only one way to get the power metal: extract it from the ground.

So it was that, across the great gulf between the worlds, ship after ship moved in search of the metal that would hold the far-flung colonies of the Empire together. Every adventurer who could manage to get aboard was glad to be cooped up on a ship during the long months it took to cross the empty expanses, was glad to endure the hardships on alien terrain, on the chance that his efforts might pay off a thousand or ten thousand fold.

Of these men, a mere handful were successful, and of these one or two stand well above the rest. And for sheer determination, drive, and courage, for the will to push on toward his goal, no matter what the odds, a certain Commander Frank had them all beat.

II

Before you can get a picture of the commander—that is, as far as his personality goes—you have to get a picture of the man physically.

He was enough taller than the average man to make him stand out in a crowd, and he had broad shoulders and a narrow waist to match. He wasn't heavy; his was the hard, tough, wirelike strength of a steel cable. The planes of his tanned face showed that he feared neither exposure to the elements nor exposure to violence; it was seamed with fine wrinkles and the thin white lines that betray scar tissue. His mouth was heavy-lipped, but firm, and the lines around it showed that it was unused to smiling. The commander could laugh, and often did—a sort of roaring explosion that burst forth suddenly whenever something struck him as particularly uproarious. But he seldom just smiled; Commander Frank rarely went halfway in anything.

His eyes, like his hair, were a deep brown—almost black, and they were set well back beneath heavy brows that tended to frown most of the time.

Primarily, he was a military man. He had no particular flair for science, and, although he had a firm and deep-seated grasp of the essential philosophy of the Universal Assembly, he had no inclination towards the kind of life necessarily led by those who would become higher officers of the Assembly. It was enough that the Assembly was behind him; it was enough to know that he was a member of the only race in the known universe which had a working knowledge of the essential, basic Truth of the Cosmos. With a weapon like that, even an ordinary soldier had little to fear, and Commander Frank was far from being an ordinary soldier.

He had spent nearly forty of his sixty years of life as an explorer-soldier for the Emperor, and during that time he'd kept his eyes open for opportunity. Every time his ship had landed, he'd watched and listened and collected data. And now he knew.

If his data were correct—and he was certain that they were—he had found his strike. All he needed was the men to take it.

III

The expedition had been poorly outfitted and undermanned from the beginning. The commander had been short of money at the outset, having spent almost all he could raise on his own, plus nearly everything he could beg or borrow, on his first two probing expeditions, neither of which had shown any real profit.

But they *had* shown promise; the alien population of the target which the commander had selected as his personal claim wore gold as ornaments, but didn't seem to think it was much above copper in value, and hadn't even progressed to the point of using it as coinage. From the second probing expedition, he had brought back two of the odd-looking aliens and enough gold to show that there must be more where that came from.

The old, hopeful statement, "There's gold in them thar hills," should have brought the commander more backing than he got, considering the Empire's need of it and the commander's evidence that it was availabe; but people are always more ready to bet on a sure thing than to indulge in speculation. Ten years before, a strike had been made in a sector quite distant from the commander's own find, and most of the richer nobles of the Empire preferred to back an established source of the metal than to sink money into what might turn out to be the pursuit of a wild goose.

Commander Frank, therefore, could only recruit men who were willing to take a chance, who were willing to risk anything, even their lives, against tremendously long odds.

And, even if they succeeded, the Imperial Government would take twenty per cent of the gross without so much as a by-your-leave. There was no other market for the metal except back home, so the tax could not be avoided; gold was no good whatsoever in the uncharted wilds of an alien world.

Because of his lack of funds, the commander's expedition was not only dangerously undermanned, but illegally so. It was only by means of out-and-out trickery that he managed to evade the official inspection and leave port with too few men and too little equipment.

There wasn't a scientist worthy of the name in the whole outfit, unless you call the navigator, Captain Bartholomew, an astronomer, which is certainly begging the question. There was no anthropologist aboard to study the semibarbaric civilization of the natives; there was no biologist to study the alien flora and fauna. The closest thing the commander had to physicists were engineers who could take care of the ship itself—specialist technicians, nothing more.

There was no need for armament specialists; each and every man was a soldier, and, as far as his own weapons went, an ordnance expert. As far as Commander Frank was concerned, that was enough. It had to be.

Mining equipment? He took nothing but the simplest testing apparatus. How, then, did he intend to get the metal that the Empire was screaming for?

The commander had an answer for that, too, and it was as simple as it was economical. The natives would get it for him.

They used gold for ornaments; therefore, they knew where the gold could be found. And, therefore, they would bloody well dig it out for Commander Frank.

IV

Due to atmospheric disturbances, the ship's landing was several hundred miles from the point the commander had originally picked for the debarkation of his troops. That meant a long, forced march along the coast and then inland, but there was no help for it; the ship simply wasn't built for atmospheric navigation.

That didn't deter the commander any. The orders rang through the ship: "All troops and carriers prepare for landing!"

Half an hour later, they were assembled outside the ship, fully armed and armored, and with full field gear. The sun, a yellow G-O star, hung hotly just above the towering mountains to the east. The alien air smelled odd in the men's nostrils, and the weird foliage seemed to rustle menacingly. In the distance, the shrieks of alien fauna occasionally echoed through the air.

A hundred and eighty-odd men and some thirty carriers stood under the tropic blaze for forty-five minutes while the commander checked over their equipment with minute precision. Nothing faulty or sloppy was going into that jungle with him if he could prevent it.

When his hard eyes had inspected every bit of equipment, when he had either passed or ordered changes in the manner of its carrying or its condition, when he was fully satisfied that every weapon was in order—then, and only then, did he turn his attention to the men themselves.

He climbed atop a little hillock and surveyed them carefully, letting his penetrating gaze pass over each man in turn. He stood there, his fists on his hips, with the sunlight gleaming from his burnished armor, for nearly a full minute before he spoke.

Then his powerful voice rang out over the assembled adventurers.

"My comrades-at-arms! We have before us a world that is ours for the taking! It contains more riches than any man on Earth ever dreamed existed, and those riches, too, are ours for the taking. It isn't going to be a picnic, and we all knew that when we came. There are dangers on every side—from the natives, from the animals and plants, and from the climate.

"But there is not one of these that cannot be overcome by the onslaught of brave, courageous, and determined men!

"Ahead of us, we will find the Four Horsemen of the Apocalypse arrayed against our coming—Famine, Pestilence, War, and Death. Each and all of these we must meet and conquer as brave men should, for at their end we will find wealth and glory!"

A cheer filled the air, startling the animals in the forest into momentary silence.

The commander stilled it instantly with a raised hand.

"Some of you know this country from our previous expeditions together. Most of you will find it utterly strange. And not one of you knows it as well as I do.

"In order to survive, you must—and *will*—follow my orders to the letter—and beyond.

"First, as to your weapons. We don't have an unlimited supply of charges for them, so there will be no firing of any power weapon unless absolutely necessary. You have your swords and your pikes—use them."

Several of the men unconsciously gripped the hafts of the long steel blades at their sides as he spoke the words, but their eyes never left the commanding figure on the hummock.

"As for food," he continued, "we'll live off the land. You'll find that most of the animals are edible, but stay away from the plants unless I give the O.K.

"We have a long way to go, but, by Heaven, I'm going to get us there alive! Are you with me?"

A hearty cheer rang from the throats of the men. They shouted the commander's name with enthusiasm.

"All right!" he bellowed. "There is one more thing! Anyone who wants to stay with the ship can do so; anyone who feels too ill to make it should consider it his duty to stay behind, because sick men will simply hold us up and weaken us more than if they'd been left behind. Remember, we're not going to turn back as a body, and an individual would never make it alone." He paused.

"Well?"

Not a man moved. The commander grinned—not with humor, but with satisfaction. "All right, then: let's move out."

V

Of them all, only a handful, including the commander, had any real knowledge of what lay ahead of them, and that knowledge only pertained to the periphery of the area the intrepid band of adventurers were entering. They knew that the aliens possessed a rudimentary civilization—they did not, at that time, realize they were entering the outposts of a powerful barbaric empire—an empire almost as well-organized and well-armed as that of First Century Rome, and, if anything, even more savage and ruthless.

It was an empire ruled by a single family who called themselves the Great Nobles; at their head was the Greatest Noble—the Child of the Sun Himself. It has since been conjectured that the Great Nobles were mutants in the true sense of the word; a race apart from their subjects. It is impossible to be absolutely sure at this late date, and the commander's expedition, lacking any qualified geneticists or genetic engineers, had no way of determining—and, indeed, no real *interest* in determining—whether this was or was not true. None the less, historical evidence seems to indicate the validity of the hypothesis.

Never before—not even in ancient Egypt—had the historians ever seen a culture like it. It was an absolute monarchy that would have made any Medieval king except the most saintly look upon it in awe and envy. The Russians and the Germans never even approached it. The Japanese tried to approximate it at one time in their history, but they failed.

Secure in the knowledge that theirs was the only civilizing force on the face of the planet, the race of the Great Nobles spread over the length of a great continent, conquering the lesser races as they went.

Physically, the Great Nobles and their lesser subjects were quite similar. They were, like the commander and his men, human in every sense of the word. That this argues some ancient, prehistoric migration across the empty gulfs that separate the worlds cannot be denied, but when and how that migration took place are data lost in the mists of time. However it may have happened, the fact remains that these people *were* human. As someone observed in one of the reports written up by one of the officers: "They could pass for Indians, except their skins are of a decidedly redder hue."

The race of the Great Nobles held their conquered subjects in check by the exercise of two powerful forces: religion and physical power of arms. Like the feudal organizations of Medieval Europe, the Nobles had the power of life and death over their subjects, and to a much greater extent than the European nobles had. Each family lived on an allotted parcel of land and did a given job. Travel was restricted to a radius of a few miles. There was no money; there was no necessity for it, since the government of the Great Nobles took all produce and portioned it out again according to need. It was communism on a vast and—incomprehensible as it may seem to the modern mind—*workable*—scale. Their minds were as different from ours as their bodies were similar; the concept "freedom" would have been totally incomprehensible to them.

They were sun-worshipers, and the Greatest Noble was the Child of the Sun, a godling subordinate only to the Sun Himself. Directly under him were the lesser Great Nobles, also Children of the Sun, but to a lesser extent. They exercised absolute power over the conquered peoples, but even they had no concept of freedom, since they were as tied to the people as the people were tied to them. It was a benevolent dictatorship of a kind never seen before or since.

At the periphery of the Empire of the Sun-Child lived still unconquered savage tribes, which the Imperial forces were in the process of slowly taking over. During the centuries, tribe after tribe had fallen before the brilliant leadership of the Great Nobles and the territory of the Empire had slowly expanded until, at the time the invading Earthmen came, it covered almost as much territory as had the Roman Empire at its peak.

The Imperial Army, consisting of upwards of fifty thousand troops, was extremely mobile in spite of the handicap of having no form of transportation except their own legs. They had no cavalry; the only beasts of burden known to them—the flame-beasts—were too small to carry more than a hundred pounds, in spite of their endurance. But the wide, smooth roads that ran the length and breadth of the Empire enabled a marching army to make good time, and messages carried by runners in relays could traverse the Empire in a matter of days, not weeks.

And into this tight-knit, well-organized, powerful barbaric world marched Commander Frank with less than two hundred men and thirty carriers.

VI

It didn't take long for the men to begin to chafe under the constant strain of moving through treacherous and unfamiliar territory. And the first signs of chafing made themselves apparent beneath their armor.

Even the best designed armor cannot be built to be worn for an unlimited length of time, and, at first, the men could see no reason for the order. They soon found out.

One evening, after camp had been made, one young officer decided that he had spent his last night sleeping in full armor. It was bad enough to have to march in it, but sleeping in it was too much. He took it off and stretched, enjoying the freedom from the heavy steel. His tent was a long way from the center of camp, where a small fire flickered, and the soft light from the planet's single moon filtered only dimly through the jungle foliage overhead. He didn't think anyone would see him from the commander's tent.

The commander's orders had been direct and to the point: "You will wear your armor at all times; you will march in it, you will eat in it, you will sleep in it. During such times as it is necessary to remove a part of it, the man doing so will make sure that he is surrounded by at least two of his companions in full armor. There will be no exceptions to this rule!"

The lieutenant had decided to make himself an exception.

He turned to step into his tent when a voice came out of the nearby darkness.

"Hadn't you better get your steel plates back on before the commander sees you?"

The young officer turned quickly to see who had spoken. It was another of the junior officers.

"Mind your own business," snapped the lieutenant.

The other grinned sardonically. "And if I don't?"

There had been bad blood between these two for a long time; it was an enmity that went back to a time even before the expedition had begun. The two men stood there for a long moment, the light from the distant fire flickering uncertainly against their bodies.

The young officer who had removed his armor had not been foolish enough to remove his weapons too; no sane man did that in hostile territory. His hand went to the haft of the blade at his side.

"If you say a single word—"

Instinctively, the other dropped his hand to his own sword.

"Stop! Both of you!"

And stop they did; no one could mistake the crackling

authority in that voice. The commander, unseen in the moving, dim light, had been circling the periphery of the camp, to make sure that all was well. He strode toward the two younger men, who stood silently, shocked into immobiliity. The commander's sword was already in his hand.

"I'll split the first man that draws a blade," he snapped.

His keen eyes took in the situation at a glance.

"Lieutenant, what are you doing out of armor?"

"It was hot, sir, and I—"

"Shut up!" The commander's eyes were dangerous. "An asinine statement like that isn't even worth listening to! Get that armor back on! *Move!*"

He was standing approximately between the two men, who had been four or five yards apart. When the cowed young officer took a step or two back toward his tent, the commander turned toward the other officer. "And as for you, if—"

He was cut off by the yell of the unarmored man, followed by the sound of his blade singing from its sheath.

The commander leaped backwards and spun, his own sword at the ready, his body settling into a swordsman's crouch.

But the young officer was not drawing against his superior. He was hacking at something ropy and writhing that squirmed on the ground as the lieutenant's blade bit into it. Within seconds, the serpentine thing gave a convulsive shudder and died.

The lieutenant stepped back clumsily, his eyes glazing in the flickering light. "Dropped from th' tree," he said thickly. "Bit me."

His hand moved to a dark spot on his chest, but it never reached its goal. The lieutenant collapsed, crumpling to the ground.

The commander walked over, slammed the heel of his heavy boot hard down on the head of the snaky thing, crushing it. Then he returned his blade to its sheath, knelt down by the young man, and turned him over on his face.

The commander's own face was grim.

By this time, some of the nearby men, attracted by the yell, had come running. They came to a stop as they saw the tableau before them.

The commander, kneeling beside the corpse, looked up at them. With one hand, he gestured at the body. "Let this be a lesson to all of you," he said in a tight voice. "This man died because he took off his armor. That"—he pointed at the butchered reptile—"thing is full of as deadly a poison as you'll ever see, and it can move like lightning. *But it can't bite through steel!*

"Look well at this man and tell the others what you saw. I don't want to lose another man in this idiotic fashion."

He stood up and gestured.

"Bury him."

VII

They found, as they penetrated deeper into the savage-infested hinterlands of the Empire of the Great Nobles, that the armor fended off more than just snakes. Hardly a day passed but one or more of the men would hear the sharp *spang*! of a blowgun-driven dart as it slammed ineffectually against his armored back or chest. At first, some of the men wanted to charge into the surrounding forest, whence the darts came, and punish the sniping aliens, but the commander would have none of it.

"Stick together," he ordered. "They'll do worse to us if we're split up in this jungle. Those blowgun darts aren't going to hurt you as long as they're hitting steel. Ignore them and keep moving."

They kept moving.

Around them, the jungle chattered and muttered, and occasionally, screamed. Clouds of insects, great and small, hummed and buzzed through the air. They subsided only when the drizzling rains came, and then lifted again from their resting places when the sun came out to raise steamy vapors from the moist ground.

It was not an easy march. Before many days had passed, the men's feet were cracked and blistered from the effects of fungus, dampness, and constant marching. The compact military marching order which had characterized the first few days of march had long since deteriorated into a straggling column, where the weaker were supported by the stronger.

Three more men died. One simply dropped in his tracks. He was dead before anyone could touch him. Insect bite? Disease? No one knew.

Another had been even less fortunate. A lionlike carnivore had leaped on him during the night and clawed him badly before one of his companions blasted the thing with a power weapon. Three days later, the wounded man was begging to be killed; one arm and one leg were gangrenous. But he died while begging, thus sparing any would-be executioner from an unpleasant duty.

The third man simply failed to show up for roll call one morning. He was never seen again.

But the rest of the column, with dauntless courage, followed the lead of their commander.

It was hard to read their expressions, those reddened eyes that peered at him from swollen, bearded faces. But he knew his own face looked no different.

"We all knew this wasn't going to be a fancy-dress ball when we came," he said. "Nobody said this was going to be the easiest way in the world to get rich."

The commander was sitting on one of the carriers, his eyes watching the men, who were lined up in front of him. His voice was purposely held low, but it carried well.

"The marching has been difficult, but now we're really going to see what we're made of.

"We all need a rest, and we all deserve one. But when I lie down to rest, I'm going to do it in a halfway decent bed, with some good, solid food in my belly.

"Here's the way the picture looks: An hour's march from here, there's a good-sized village." He swung partially away from them and pointed south. "I think we have earned that town and everything in it."

He swung back, facing them. There was a wolfish grin on his face. "There's gold there, too. Not much, really, compared with what we'll get later on, but enough to whet our appetites."

The men's faces were beginning to change now, in spite of the swelling.

"I don't think we need worry too much about the savages that are living there now. With God on our side, I hardly see how we can fail."

He went on, telling them how they would attack the town, the disposition of men, the use of the carriers, and so forth. By the time he was through, every man there was as eager as he to move in. When he finished speaking, they set up a cheer:

"For the Emperor and the Universal Assembly!"

*   *   *

The natives of the small villages had heard that some sort of terrible beings were approaching through the jungle. Word had come from the people of the forest that the strange monsters were impervious to darts, and that they had huge dragons with them which were terrifying even to look at. They were clad in metal and made queer noises as they moved.

The village chieftain called his advisers together to ponder the situation. What should they do with these strange things? What were the invaders' intentions?

Obviously, the things must be hostile. Therefore, there were only two courses open—fight or flee. The chieftain and his men decided to fight. It would have been a good thing if there had only been some Imperial troops in the vicinity, but all the troops were farther south, where a civil war was raging over the right of succession of the Greatest Noble.

Nevertheless, there were two thousand fighting men in the village—well, two thousand men at any rate, and they would certainly all fight, although some were rather young and a few were too old for any really hard fighting. On the other hand, it would probably not come to that, since the strangers were outnumbered by at least three to one.

The chieftain gave his orders for the defense of the village.

The invading Earthmen approached the small town cautiously from the west. The commander had his men spread out a little, but not so much that they could be separated. He saw the aliens grouped around the square, boxlike buildings, watching and waiting for trouble.

"We'll give them trouble," the commander whispered softly. He waited until his troops were properly deployed, then he gave the signal for the charge.

The carriers went in first, thundering directly into the massed alien warriors. Each carrier-man fired a single shot from his power weapon, and then went to work with his carrier, running down the terrified aliens, and swinging a sword with one hand while he guided with the other. The commander went in with that first charge, aiming his own carrier toward the center of the fray. He had some raw, untrained men with him, and he believed in teaching by example.

The aliens recoiled at the onslaught of what they took to be horrible living monsters that were unlike anything ever seen before.

Then the commander's infantry charged in. The shock effect of the carriers had been enough to disorganize the aliens, but the battle was not over yet by a long shot.

There were yells from other parts of the village as some of the other defenders, hearing the sounds of battle, came running to reinforce the home guard. Better than fifteen hundred men were converging on the spot.

The invading Earthmen moved in rapidly against the armed natives, beating them back by the sheer ferocity of their attack. Weapons of steel clashed against weapons of bronze and wood.

The power weapons were used only sparingly; only when the necessity to save a life was greater than the necessity to conserve weapon charges was a shot fired.

The commander, from the center of the fray, took a glance around the area. One glance was enough.

"They're dropping back!" he bellowed, his voice carrying well above the din of the battle. "Keep 'em moving!" He singled out one of his officers at a distance, and yelled: "Hernan! Get a couple of men to cover that street!" He waved toward one of the narrow streets that ran off to one side. The others were already being attended to.

The commander jerked around swiftly as one of the natives grabbed hold of the carrier and tried to hack at the commander with a bronze sword. The commander spitted him neatly on his blade and withdrew it just in time to parry another attack from the other side.

By this time, the reinforcements from the other parts of the village were beginning to come in from the side streets, but they were a little late. The warriors in the square—what was left of them—had panicked. In an effort to get away from the terrible monsters with their deadly blades and their fire-spitting weapons, they were leaving by the same channels that the reinforcements were coming in by, and the resultant jam-up was disastrous. The panic communicated itself like wildfire, but no one could move fast enough to get away from the sweeping, stabbing, glittering blades of the invading Earthmen.

"All right," the commander yelled, "we've got 'em on the run now! Break up into squads of three and clear those streets! Clear 'em out! Keep 'em moving!"

After that, it was the work of minutes to clear the town.

The commander brought his carrier to a dead stop, reached out with his sword, and snagged a bit of cloth from one of the fallen native warriors. He began to wipe the blade of his weapon as Lieutenant Commander Hernan pulled up beside him.

"Casualties?" the commander asked Hernan without looking up from his work.

"Six wounded, no dead," said Hernan. "Or did you want me to count the aliens, too?"

The commander shook his head. "No. Get a detail to clear out the carrion, and then tell Frater Vincent I want to talk to him. We'll have to start teaching these people the Truth.

VIII

"Have you anything to say in your defense?" the commander asked coldly.

For a moment, the accused looked nothing but hatred at the commander, but there was fear behind that hatred. At last he found his voice. "It was mine. You promised us all a share."

Lieutenant Commander Hernan picked up a leather bag that lay on the table behind which he and the commander were sitting. With a sudden gesture, he upended it, dumping its contents on the flat, wooden surface of the table.

"No," said the accused soldier. "Why should I? It's mine. Rightfully mine. I fought for it. I found it. I kept it. It's mine." He glanced to either side, towards the two guards who flanked him, then looked back at the commander.

The commander ran an idle finger through the pound or so of golden trinkets that Hernan had spilled from the bag. He knew what the trooper was thinking. A man had a right to what he had earned, didn't he?

The commander picked up one of the heavier bits of primitive jewelry and tossed it in his hand. Then he stood up and looked around the town square.

The company had occupied the town for several weeks. The stored grains in the community warehouse, plus the relaxation the men had had, plus the relative security of the town, had put most of the men back into condition. One had died from a skin infection, and another from wounds sustained in the assault on the town, but the remainder were in good health.

And all of them, with the exception of the sentries guarding the town's perimeter, were standing in the square, watching the court-martial. Their eyes didn't seem to blink, and their breathing was soft and measured. They were waiting for the commander's decision.

The commander, still tossing the crude golden earring, stood tall and straight, estimating the feeling of the men surrounding him.

"Gold," he said finally. "Gold. That's what we came here for, and that's what we're going to get. Five hundred pounds of the stuff would make any one of you wealthy for the rest of his life. Do you think I blame any of you for wanting it? Do you think I blame this man here? Of course not." He laughed—a short, hard bark. "Do I blame myself?"

He tossed the bauble again, caught it. "But wanting it is one thing; getting it, holding it, and taking care of it wisely are something else again.

"I gave orders. I have expected—and still expect—that they will be obeyed. But I didn't give them just to hear myself give orders. There was a reason, and a good one.

"Suppose we let each man take what gold he could find. What would happen? The lucky ones would be wealthy, and the unlucky would still be poor. And then some of the lucky ones would wake up some morning without the gold they'd taken because someone else had relieved them of it while they slept.

"And others wouldn't wake up at all, because they'd be found with their throats cut.

"I told you to bring every bit of the metal to me. When this thing is over, every one of you will get his share. If a man dies, his share will be split among the rest, instead of being stolen by someone else or lost because it was hidden too well."

He looked at the earring in his hand; then, with a convulsive sweep of his arm, he tossed it out into the middle of the square.

"There! Seven ounces of gold! Which of you wants it?"

Some of the men eyed the circle of metal that gleamed brightly on the sunlit ground, but none of them made any motion to pick it up.

"So." The commander's voice was almost gentle. He turned his eyes back toward the accused. "You know the orders. You knew them when you hid this." He gestured negligently toward the small heap of native-wrought metal. "Suppose you'd gotten away with it. You'd have ended up with your own share, *plus* this, thereby cheating the others out of—" He glanced at the pile. "Hm-m-m—say, twenty-five each. And that's only a little compared with what we'll get from now on."

He looked back at the others. "Unless the shares are taken care of my way, the largest shares will go to the dishonest, the most powerful, and the luckiest. Unless the division is made as we originally agreed, we'll end up trying to cut each other's heart out."

There was hardness in his voice when he spoke to the accused, but there was compassion there, too.

"First: You have forfeited your share in this expedition. All that you have now, and all that you might have expected will be divided among the others according to our original agreement.

"Second: I do not expect any man to work for nothing. Since you will not receive anything from this expedition, there is no point in your assisting the rest of us or working with us in any way whatsoever.

"Third: We can't have anyone with us who does not carry his own weight."

He glanced at the guards. "Hang him." He paused. "Now."

As he was led away, the commander watched the other men. There was approval in their eyes, but there was something else there, too—a wariness, a concealed fear.

The condemned man turned suddenly and began shouting at the commander, but before he could utter more than three syllables, a fist smashed him down. The guards dragged him off.

"All right, men," said the commander carefully, "let's search the village. There might be more gold about; I have a hunch that this isn't all he hid. Let's see if we can find the rest of it." He sensed the relief of tension as he spoke.

The commander was right. It was amazing how much gold one man had been able to stash away.

IX

They couldn't stay long in any one village; they didn't have the time to sit and relax any more than was necessary. Once they had reached the northern marches of the native empire, it was to the commander's advantage to keep his men moving. He didn't know for sure how good or how rapid communications were among the various native provinces, but he had to assume that they were top-notch, allowing for the limitations of a barbaric society.

The worst trouble they ran into on their way was not caused by the native warriors, but by disease.

The route to the south was spotted by great strips of sandy barrenness, torn by winds that swept the grains of sand into the troopers' eyes and crept into the chinks of their armor. Underfoot, the sand made a treacherous pathway; carriers and men alike found it heavy going.

The heat from the sun was intense; the brilliant beams from the primary seemed to penetrate through the men's armor and through the insulation underneath, and made the marching even harder.

Even so, in spite of the discomfort, the men were making good time until the disease struck. And that stopped them in their tracks.

What the disease was or how it was spread is unknown and unknowable at this late date. Virus or bacterium, amoeba or fungus—whatever it was, it struck.

Symptoms: Lassitude, weariness, sickness, and pain.

Signs: Great, ulcerous, wartlike, blood-filled blisters that grew rapidly over the body.

A man might go to sleep at night feeling reasonably tired, but not ill, and wake up in the morning to find himself unable to rise, his muscles too weak to lift him from his bed.

If the blisters broke, or were lanced, it was almost impossible to stop the bleeding, and many died, not from the toxic effect of the disease itself, but from simple loss of blood.

But, like many epidemics, the thing had a fairly short life span. After two weeks, it had burned itself out. Most of those who got it recovered, and a few were evidently immune.

Eighteen men remained behind in shallow graves.

The rest went on.

X

No man is perfect. Even with four decades of training behind him, Commander Frank couldn't call the turn every time. After the first few villages, there were no further battles. The natives, having seen what the invaders could do, simply showed up missing when the commander and his men arrived. The villages were empty by the time the column reached the outskirts.

Frater Vincent, the agent of the Universal Assembly, complained in no uncertain terms about this state of affairs.

"As you know, commander," he said frowningly one morning, "it's no use trying to indoctrinate a people we can't contact. And you can't subject a people by force of arms alone; the power of the Truth—"

"I know, Frater," the commander interposed quickly. "But we can't deal with these savages in the hinterlands. When we get a little farther into this barbarian empire, we can take the necessary steps to—"

"The Truth," Frater Vincent interrupted somewhat testily, "is for all men. It works, regardless of the state of civilization of the society."

The commander looked out of the unglazed window of the native hut in which he had established his temporary headquarters, in one of the many villages he had taken—or, rather, walked into without a fight because it was empty. "But you'll admit, Frater, that it takes longer with savages."

"True," said Frater Vincent.

"We simply haven't the time. We've got to keep on the move. And, besides, we haven't even been able to contact any of the natives for quite a while; they get out of our way. And we have taken a few prisoners—" His voice was apologetic, but there was a trace of irritation in it. He didn't want to offend Frater Vincent, of course, but dammit, the Assemblyman didn't understand military tactics at all. Or, he corrected himself hastily, at least only slightly.

"Yes," admitted Frater Vincent, "and I've had considerable success with the prisoners. But, remember—we're not here just to indoctrinate a few occasional prisoners, but to change the entire moral and philosophical viewpoint of an entire race."

"I realize that, Frater," the commander admitted. He turned from the window and faced the Assemblyman. "We're getting close to the Great Bay now. That's where our ship landed on the second probing expedition. I expect we'll be more welcome there than we have been, out here in the countryside. We'll take it easy, and I think you'll have a chance to work with the natives on a mass basis."

The Frater smiled. "Excellent, commander. I . . . uh . . . want you to understand that I'm not trying to tell you your business; you run this campaign as you see fit. But don't lose sight of the ultimate goal of life."

"I won't. How could I? It's just that my methods are not, perhaps, as refined as yours."

Frater Vincent nodded, still smiling. "True. You are a great deal more direct. And—in your own way—just as effective. After all, the Assembly could not function without the military, but there were armies long before the Universal Assembly came into being."

The commander smiled back. "Not any armies like this, Frater."

Frater Vincent nodded. The understanding between the two men—at least on that point—was tacit and mutual. He traced a symbol in the air and left the commander to his thoughts.

Mentally, the commander went through the symbol-patterns that he had learned as a child—the symbol-patterns that brought him into direct contact with the Ultimate Power, the Power that controlled not only the spinning of atoms and the whirling of electrons in their orbits, but the workings of probability itself.

Once indoctrinated into the teachings of the Universal Assembly, any man could tap that Power to a greater or lesser degree, depending on his mental control and ethical attitude. At the top level, a first-class adept could utilize that Power for telepathy, psychokinesis, levitation, teleportation, and other powers that the commander only vaguely understood.

He, himself, had no such depth of mind, such iron control over his will, and he knew he'd never have it. But he could and did tap that Power to the extent that his physical body was under near-perfect control at all times, and not even the fear of death could shake his determination to win, or his great courage.

He turned again to the window and looked at the alien sky. There was a great deal yet to be done.

The commander needed information—needed it badly. He had to know what the government of the alien empire was doing. Had they been warned of his arrival? Surely they must have, and yet they had taken no steps to impede his progress.

For this purpose, he decided to set up headquarters on an island just offshore in the Great Bay. It was a protected position, easily defended from assault, and the natives, he knew from his previous visit, were friendly.

They even helped him to get his men and equipment and the carriers across on huge rafts.

From that point, he began collecting the information he needed to invade the central domains of the Greatest Noble himself. It seemed an ideal spot—not only protection-wise, but because this was the spot he had originally picked for the landing of the ship. The vessel, which had returned to the base for reinforcements and extra supplies, would be aiming for the Great Bay area when she came back. And there was little likelihood that atmospheric disturbances would throw her off course again; Captain Bartholomew was too good a man to be fooled twice.

But landing on that island was the first—and only—mistake the commander made during the campaign. The rumors of internal bickerings among the Great Nobles of the barbarian empire were not the only rumors he heard. News of more local treachery came to his ears through the agency of natives, now loyal to the commander, who had been indoctrinated into the philosophy of the Assembly.

A group of native chieftans had decided that the invading Earthmen were too dangerous to be allowed to remain on their island, in spite of the fact that the invaders had done them no harm. There were, after all, whisperings from the north, whence the invaders had come, that the armored beings with the terrible weapons had used their power more than once during their march to the south. The chieftains were determined to rid their island of the potential menace.

As soon as the matter was brought to the commander's attention, he acted. He sent out a patrol to the place where the ringleaders were meeting, arrested them, and sentenced them to death. He didn't realize what effect that action would have on the rest of the islanders.

He almost found out too late.

XI

"There must be three thousand of them out there," said Lieutenant commander Hernan tightly, "and every one of them's crazy."

"Rot!" The commander spat on the ground and then sighted again along the barrel of his weapon. "I'm the one who's crazy. I'm a lousy politician; that's my trouble."

The lieutenant commander shrugged lightly. "Anyone can make a mistake. Just chalk it up to experience."

"I will, when we get out of this mess." He watched the gathering natives through hard, slitted eyes.

The invading Earthmen were in a village at the southern end of the eight-mile-long island, waiting inside the mud-brick huts, while the natives who had surrounded the village worked themselves into a frenzy for an attack. The commander knew there was no sense in charging into them at that point; they would simply scatter and reassemble. The only thing to do was wait until they attacked—and then smash the attack.

"Hernan," he said, his eyes still watching the outside, "you and the others get out there with the carriers after the first volley. Cut them down. They're twenty-to-one against us, so make every blow count. Move."

Hernan nodded wordlessly and slipped away.

The natives were building up their courage with some sort of war dance, whooping and screaming and making threatening gestures toward the embattled invaders. Then the pattern of the dance changed; the islanders whirled to face the mud-brick buildings which housed the invading Earthmen. Suddenly, the dance broke, and the warriors ran in a screaming charge, straight for the trapped soldiers.

The commander waited. His own shot would be the signal, and he didn't want the men to fire too quickly. If the islanders were hit too soon, they might fall back into the woods and set up a siege, which the little company couldn't stand. Better to mop up the natives now, if possible.

Closer. Closer—

Now!

The commander's first shot picked off one of the leaders in the front ranks of the native warriors, and was followed by a raking volley from the other power weapons, firing from the windows of the mud-brick buildings. The warriors in the front rank dropped, and those in the second rank had to move adroitly to keep from stumbling over the bodies of their fallen fellows. The firing from the huts became ragged, but its raking effect was still deadly. A cloud of heavy, stinking smoke rolled across the clearing between the edge of the jungle and the village, as the bright, hard lances of heat leaped from the muzzles of the power weapons toward the bodies of the charging warriors.

The charge was gone from the commander's weapon, and he didn't bother to replace it. As Hernan and his men

charged into the melee with their carriers, the commander
went with them.

At the same time, the armored infantrymen came pouring
out of the mud-brick houses, swinging their swords, straight
into the mass of confused native warriors. A picked group
of sharp-shooters remained behind in the concealment of
the huts to pick off the warriors at the edge of the battle
with their sporadic fire.

The commander's lips were moving a little as he formed
the symbol-patterns of power almost unconsciously; a lifetime of habit had burned them into his brain so deeply that
he could form them automatically while turning the thinking
part of his mind to the business at hand.

He soon found himself entirely surrounded by the alien
warriors. Their bronze weapons glittered in the sunlight as
they tried to fight off the onslaught of the invaders. And
those same bronze weapons were sheared, nicked, blunted,
bent, and broken as they met the harder steel of the commander's sword.

Then the unexpected happened. One of the warriors,
braver than the rest, made a grab for the commander's
sword arm. At almost the same moment, a warrior on the
other side of the carrier aimed a spear thrust at his side.

Either by itself would have been ineffectual. The spear
clanged harmlessly from the commander's armor, and the
warrior who had attempted to pull him from the carrier died
before he could give much of a tug. But the combination,
plus the fact that the heavy armor was a little unwieldy,
overbalanced him. He toppled to the ground with a clash of
steel as he and the carrier parted company.

Without a human hand at its controls, the carrier automatically moved away from the mass of struggling fighters
and came to a halt well away from the battle.

The commander rolled as he hit and leaped to his feet, his
sword moving in flickering arcs around him. The natives had
no knowledge of effective swordplay. Like any barbarians,
they conceived of a sword as a cutting instrument rather
than a thrusting one. They chopped with them, using small
shields to protect their bodies as they tried to hack the
commander to bits.

But the commander had no desire to become mincemeat
just yet. Five of the barbarians were coming at him, their
swords raised for a downward slash. The commander lunged
forward with a straight stop-thrust aimed at the groin of the

nearest one. It came as a complete surprise to the warrior, who doubled up in pain.

The commander had already withdrawn his blade and was attacking the second as the first fell. He made another feint to the groin and then changed the aim of his point as the warrior tried to cover with his shield. A buckler is fine protection against a man who is trying to hack you to death with a chopper, because a heavy cutting sword and a shield have about the same inertia, and thus the same maneuverability. But the shield isn't worth anything against a light stabbing weapon. The warrior's shield started downward and he was unable to stop it and reverse its direction before the commander's sword pierced his throat.

Two down, three to go. No, four. Another warrior had decided to join the little battle against the leader of the invading Earthmen.

The commander changed his tactics just slightly with the third man. He slashed with the tip of his blade against the descending sword-arm of his opponent—a short, quick flick of his wrist that sheared through the inside of the wrist, severing tendons, muscles, veins and arteries as it cut to the bone. The sword clanged harmlessly off the commander's shoulder. A quick thrust, and the third man died.

The other three slowed their attack and began circling warily, trying to get behind the commander. Instead of waiting, he charged forward, again cutting at the sword arm of his adversary, severing fingers this time. As the warrior turned, the commander's sword pierced his side.

How long it went on, he had no idea. He kept his legs and his sword-arm moving, and his eyes ever alert for new foes as man after man dropped beneath that snake-tonguing blade. Inside his armor, perspiration poured in rivulets down his skin, and his arms and legs began to ache, but not for one second did he let up. He could not see what was going on, could not tell the direction of the battle nor even allow his mind to wonder what was going on more than ten paces from him.

And then, quite suddenly, it seemed, it was all over. Lieutenant commander Hernan and five other men pulled up with their carriers, as if from nowhere, their weapons dealing death, clearing a space around their commander.

"You hurt?" bawled Hernan.

The commander paused to catch his breath. He knew

there was a sword-slash across his face, and his right leg felt as though there was a cut on it, but otherwise—

"I'm all right," he said. "How's it going?"

"They're breaking," Hernan told him. "We'll have them scattered within minutes."

Even as he spoke, the surge of battle moved away from them, toward the forest. The charge of the carriers, wreaking havoc on every side, had broken up the battle formation the aliens had had; the flaming death from the horrible weapons of the invaders, the fearless courage of the foot soldiers, and the steel-clad monsters that were running amuck among them shattered the little discipline they had. Panicky, they lost their anger, which had taken them several hours to build up. They scattered, heading for the forest.

Shortly, the village was silent. Not an alien warrior was to be seen save for the hundreds of mute corpses that testified to the carnage that had been wrought.

Several of the commander's men had been wounded, and three had died. Lieutenant commander Hernan had been severely wounded in the leg by a native javelin, but the injury was a long way from being fatal.

Hernan gritted his teeth while his leg was being bandaged. "The angels were with us on that one," he said between winces.

The commander nodded. "I hope they stick with us. We'll need 'em to get off this island."

XII

For a while, it looked as though they were trapped on the island. The natives didn't dare to attack again, but no hunting party was safe, and the food supply was dropping. They had gotten on the island only by the help of the natives, who had ferried them over on rafts. But getting off was another thing, now that the natives were hostile. Cutting down trees to build rafts might possibly be managed, but during the loading the little company would be too vulnerable to attack.

The commander was seated bleakly in the hut he had taken as his headquarters, trying to devise a scheme for getting to the mainland, when the deadlock was finally broken.

There was a flurry of footsteps outside, a thump of heavy boots as one of the younger officers burst into the room.

"Commander!" he yelled. "Commander! Come outside!"

The commander leaped to his feet. "Another attack?"

"No, sir! Come look!"

The commander strode quickly to the door. His sight followed the line of the young officer's pointing finger.

There, outlined against the blue of the sky, was a ship!

The news from home was encouraging, but it was a long way from being what the commander wanted. Another hundred men and more carriers had been added to the original company of now hardened veterans, and the recruits, plus the protection of the ship's guns, were enough to enable the entire party to leave the island for the mainland.

By this time, the commander had gleaned enough information from the natives to be able to plan the next step in his campaign. The present Greatest Noble, having successfully usurped the throne from his predecessor, was still not in absolute control of the country. He had won a civil war, but his rule was still too shaky to allow him to split up his armies, which accounted for the fact that, thus far, no action had been taken by the Imperial troops against the invading Earthmen.

The commander set up a base on the mainland, near the coast, left a portion of his men there to defend it, and, with the remainder, marched inland to come to grips with the Greatest Noble himself.

As they moved in toward the heart of the barbarian empire, the men noticed a definite change in the degree of civilization of the natives—or, at least, in the degree of technological advancement. There were large towns, not small villages, to be dealt with, and there were highways and bridges that showed a knowledge of engineering equivalent to that of ancient Rome.

The engineers of the Empire of the Great Nobles were a long way above the primitive. They could have, had they had any reason to, erected a pyramid the equal of great Khufu's in size, and probably even more neatly constructed. Militarily speaking, the lack of knowledge of iron hampered them, but it must be kept in mind that a well-disciplined and reasonably large army, armed with bronze-tipped spears, bronze swords, axes, and maces, can make a formidable foe, even against a much better equipped group.

The Imperial armies were much better disciplined and much better armed than any of the natives the commander had thus far dealt with, and there were reputed to be more than ten thousand of them with the Greatest Noble in his mountain stronghold. Such considerations prompted the commander to plan his strategy carefully, but they did not deter him in the least. If he had been able to bring aircraft and perhaps a thermonuclear bomb or two for demonstration purposes, the attack might have been less risky, but neither had been available to a man of his limited means, so he had to work without them.

But now, he avoided fighting if at all possible. Working with Frater Vincent, the commander worked to convince the natives on the fertile farms and in the prosperous villages that he and his company were merely ambassadors of good will—missionaries and traders. He and his men had come in peace, and if they were received in peace, well and good. If not . . . well, they still had their weapons.

The commander was depending on the vagueness of the information that may have filtered down from the north. The news had already come that the invaders were fierce and powerful fighters, but the commander gave the impression that the only reason any battles had taken place was because the northern tribes had been truculent in the extreme. He succeeded fairly well; the natives he now met considered their brethren of the northern provinces to be little better than savages, and therefore to be expected to treat strangers inhospitably and bring about their own ruin. The southern citizens of the empire eyed the strangers with apprehension, but they offered very little resistance. The commander and his men were welcomed warily at each town, and, when they left, were bid farewell with great relief.

It took a little time for the commander to locate the exact spot where the Greatest Noble and his retinue were encamped. The real capital of the empire was located even farther south, but the Greatest Noble was staying, for the nonce, in a city nestled high in the mountains, well inland from the seacoast. The commander headed for the mountains.

The passage into the mountains wasn't easy. The passes were narrow and dangerous, and the weather was cold. The air became thinner at every step. At eight thousand feet, mountain climbing in heavy armor becomes more than just hard work, and at twelve thousand it becomes exhausting torture. But the little company went on, sparked, fueled, and driven by the personal force of their commander, who stayed in the vanguard, his eyes ever alert for treachery from the surrounding mountains.

When the surprise came, it was an entirely different kind than he had expected. The commander's carrier came over a little rise, and he brought it to an abrupt halt as he saw the valley spread out beneath him. He left the carrier, walked over to a boulder near the edge of the cliff, and looked down at the valley.

It was an elongated oval of verdant green, fifteen miles long by four wide, looking like an emerald set in the rocky granite of the surrounding peaks that thrust upward toward the sky. The valley ran roughly north-and-south, and to his right, at the southern end, the commander could see a city, although it was impossible to see anyone moving in it at this distance.

To his left, he could see great clouds of billowing vapor that rolled across the grassy plain—evidently steam from the volcanic hot springs which he had been told were to be found in this valley.

But, for the moment, it was neither the springs nor the city that interested him most.

In the heart of the valley, spreading over acre after acre, were the tents and pavilions of a mighty army encampment. From the looks of it, the estimate of thirty thousand troops which had been given him by various officials along the way was, if anything, too small.

It was a moment that might have made an ordinary man stop to think, and, having thought, to turn and go. But the commander was no ordinary man, and the sheer remorseless courage that had brought him this far wouldn't allow him to turn back. So far, he had kept the Greatest Noble off balance with his advancing tactics; if he started to retreat, the Greatest Noble would realize that the invaders were not invincible, and would himself advance to crush the small band of strangers.

The Greatest Noble had known the commander and his men were coming; he was simply waiting to find out what they were up to, confident that he could dispose of them at his leisure. The commander knew that, and he knew he couldn't retreat now. There was no decision to be made, really—only planning to be done.

He turned back from the boulder to face the officers who had come to take a look at the valley.

"We'll go to the city first," he said.

XIII

The heavy tread of the invaders' boots as they entered the central plaza of the walled city awakened nothing but echoes from the stone walls that surrounded the plaza. Like the small villages they had entered farther north, the city seemed devoid of life.

There is nothing quite so depressing and threatening as a deserted city. The windows in the walls of the buildings seemed like blank, darkened eyes that watched—and waited. Nothing moved, nothing made a sound, except the troopers themselves.

The men kept close to the walls; there was no point in bunching up in the middle of the square to be cut down by arrows from the windows of the upper floors.

The commander ordered four squads of men to search the buildings and smoke out anyone who was there, but they turned up nothing. The entire city was empty. And there were no traps, no ambushes—nothing.

The commander, with Lieutenant Commander Hernan and another officer, climbed to the top of the central building of the town. In the distance, several miles away, they could see the encampment of the monarch's troops.

"The only thing we can do," the commander said, his face hard and determined, "is to call their bluff. You two take about three dozen men and go out there with the carriers and give them a show. Go right into camp, as if you owned the place. Throw a scare into them, but don't hurt anyone. Then, very politely, tell the Emperor, or whatever he calls himself, that I would like him to come here for dinner and a little talk."

The two officers looked at each other, then at the commander.

"Just like that?" asked Hernan.

"Just like that," said the commander.

The demonstration and exhibition went well—as far as it had gone. The native warriors had evidently been quite impressed by the onslaught of the terrifying monsters that had thundered across the plain toward them, right into the great camp, and come to a dead halt directly in front of the magnificent pavilion of the Greatest Noble himself.

The Greatest Noble put up a good face. He had obviously been expecting the visitors, because he and his lesser nobles were lined up before the pavilion, the Greatest Noble ensconced on a sort of portable throne. He managed to look perfectly calm and somewhat bored by the whole affair, and didn't seem to be particularly affected at all when Lieutenant Commander Hernan bowed low before him and requested his presence in the city.

And the Greatest Noble's answer was simple and to the point, although it was delivered by one of his courtiers.

"You may tell your commander," said the noble, "that His Effulgence must attend to certain religious duties tonight, since he is also High Priest of the Sun. However, His Effulgence will most graciously deign to speak to your commander tomorrow. In the meantime, you are requested to enjoy His Effulgence's gracious hospitality in the city, which has been emptied for your convenience. It is yours, for the nonce."

Which left nothing for the two officers and their men to do but go thundering back across the plain to the city.

The Greatest Noble did not bring his whole army with him, but the pageant of barbaric splendor that came tootling and drumming its way into the city the next evening was a magnificent sight. His Effulgence himself was dressed in a scarlet robe and a scarlet, turbanlike headcovering with scarlet fringes all around it. About his throat was a necklace of emerald-green gems, and his clothing was studded with more of them. Gold gleamed everywhere. He was borne on an ornate, gilded palanquin, carried high above the crowd on the shoulders of a dozen stalwart nobles, only slightly less gorgeously-dressed than the Greatest Noble. The nobility that followed was scarcely less showy in its finery.

When they came into the plaza, however, the members of the procession came to a halt. The singing and music died away.

The plaza was absolutely empty.

No one had come out to greet the Emperor.

There were six thousand natives in the plaza, and not a sign of the invaders.

The commander, hiding well back in the shadows in one of the rooms of the central building, watched through the window and noted the evident consternation of the royal entourage with satisfaction. Frater Vincent, standing beside him, whispered, "Well?"

"All right," the commander said softly, "they've had a

taste of what we got when we came in. I suppose they've had enough. Let's go out and act like hosts."

The commander and a squad of ten men, along with Frater Vincent, strode majestically out of the door of the building and walked toward the Greatest Noble. They had all polished their armor until it shone, which was about all they could do in the way of finery, but they evidently looked quite impressive in the eyes of the natives.

"Greetings, Your Effulgence," said the commander, giving the Greatest Noble a bow that was hardly five degrees from the perpendicular. "I trust we find you well."

In the buildings surrounding the square, hardly daring to move for fear the clank of metal on metal might give the whole plan away, the remaining members of the company watched the conversation between their commander and the Greatest Noble. They couldn't hear what was being said, but that didn't matter; they knew what to do as soon as the commander gave the signal. Every eye was riveted on the commander's right hand.

It seemed an eternity before the commander casually reached up to his helmet and brushed a hand across it—once—twice—three times.

Then all hell broke loose. The air was split by the sound of power weapons throwing their lances of flame into the massed ranks of the native warriors. The gunners, safe behind the walls of the buildings, poured a steady stream of accurately directed fire into the packed mob, while the rest of the men charged in with their blades, thrusting and slashing as they went.

The aliens, panic-stricken by the sudden, terrifying assault, tried to run, but there was nowhere to run to. Every exit had been cut off to bottle up the Imperial cortege. Within minutes, the entrances to the square were choked with the bodies of those who tried to flee.

As soon as the firing began, the commander and his men began to make their way toward the Greatest Noble. They had been forced to stand a good five yards away during the parlay, cut off from direct contact by the Imperial guards. The commander, sword in hand, began cutting his way through to the palanquin.

The palanquin bearers seemed frozen; they couldn't run, they couldn't fight, and they didn't dare drop their precious cargo.

The commander's voice bellowed out over the carnage. "Take him prisoner! I'll personally strangle the idiot who harms him!" And then he was too busy to yell.

Two members of the Greatest Noble's personal guard came for him, swords out, determined to give their lives, if necessary, to preserve the sacred life of their monarch. And give them they did.

The commander's blade lashed out once, sliding between the ribs of the first guard. He toppled and almost took the sword with him, but the commander wrenched it free in time to parry the downward slash of the second guard's bronze sword. It was a narrow thing, because the bronze sword, though of softer stuff than the commander's steel, was also heavier, and thus hard to deflect. As it sang past him, the commander swung a chop at the man's neck, cutting it halfway through. He stepped quickly to one side to avoid the falling body and thrust his blade through a third man, who was aiming a blow at the neck of one of the commander's officers. There were only a dozen feet separating the commander from his objective, the palanquin of the Greatest Noble, but he had to wade through blood to get there.

The palanquin itself was no longer steady. Three of the twelve nobles who had been holding it had already fallen, and there were two of the commander's men already close enough to touch the royal person, but they were too busy fighting to make any attempt to grab him. The Greatest Noble, unarmed, could only huddle in his seat, terrified, but it would take more than two men to snatch him from his bodyguard. The commander fought his way in closer.

Two more of the palanquin bearers went down, and the palanquin itself began to topple. The Greatest Noble screamed as he fell toward the commander.

One of the commander's men spun around as he heard the scream so close to him, and, thinking that the Greatest Noble was attacking his commander, lunged out with his blade.

It was almost a disaster. Moving quickly, the commander threw out his left arm to deflect the sword. He succeeded, but he got a bad slash across his hand for his trouble.

He yelled angrily at the surprised soldier, not caring what he said. Meanwhile, the others of the squad, seeing that the Greatest Noble had fallen, hurried to surround him. Two minutes later, the Greatest Noble was a prisoner, being half carried, half led into the central building by four of the men, while the remaining six fought a rear-guard action to hold off the native warriors who were trying to rescue the sacred person of the Child of the Sun.

Once inside, the Greatest Noble was held fast while the doors were swung shut.

Outside, the slaughter went on. All the resistance seemed to go out of the warriors when they saw their sacred monarch dragged away by the invading Earthmen. It was every man for himself and the Devil take the hindmost. And the Devil, in the form of the commander's troops, certainly did.

Within half an hour after it had begun, the butchery was over. More than three thousand of the natives had died, and an unknown number more had been badly wounded. Those who had managed to get out and get away from the city kept on going. They told the troops who had been left outside what had happened, and a mass exodus from the valley began.

Safely within the fortifications of the central building, the commander allowed himself one of his rare grins of satisfaction. Not a single one of his own men had been killed, and the only wound which had been sustained by anyone in the company was the cut on his own hand. Still smiling, he went into the room where the Greatest Noble, dazed and shaken, was being held by two of the commander's men. The commander bowed—this time, very low.

"I believe, Your Effulgence, that we have an appointment for dinner. Come, the banquet has been laid."

And, as though he were still playing the gracious host, the commander led the half-paralyzed Child of the Sun to the room where the banquet had been put on a table in perfect diplomatic array.

"Your Effulgence may sit at my right hand," said the commander pleasantly.

XIV

As MacDonald said of Robert Wilson, "This is not an account of how Boosterism came to Arcadia. It's a devil of a long way from it." And once the high point of a story has been reached and passed, it is pointless to prolong it too much. The capture of the Greatest Noble broke the power of the Empire of the Great Nobles forever. The loyal subjects were helpless without a leader, and the disloyal ones, near the periphery of the Empire, didn't care. The crack Imperial troops simply folded up and went home. The Greatest Noble went on issuing orders, and they were obeyed; the people were too used to taking orders from authority to care whether they were really the Greatest Noble's own idea or not.

In a matter of months, two hundred men had conquered an empire, with a loss of thirty-five or forty men. Eventually, they had to execute the old Greatest Noble and put his more tractable nephew on the throne, but that was a mere incident.

Gold? It flowed as though there were an endless supply. The commander shipped enough back on the first load to make them all wealthy.

The commander didn't go back home to spend his wealth amid the luxuries of the Imperial court, even though Emperor Carl appointed him to the nobility. That sort of thing wasn't the commander's meat. There, he would be a fourth-rate noble; here, he was the Imperial Viceroy, responsible only to the distant Emperor. There, he would be nothing; here, he was almost a king.

Two years after the capture of the Greatest Noble, he established a new capital on the coast and named it Kingston. And from Kingston he ruled with an iron hand.

As has been intimated, this was *not* Arcadia. A year after the founding of Kingston, the old capital was attacked, burned, and almost fell under siege, due to a sudden uprising of the natives under the new Greatest Noble, who had managed to escape. But the uprising collapsed because of the approach of the planting season; the warriors had to go back home and plant their crops or the whole of the agriculture-based country would starve—except the invading Earthmen.

Except in a few instances, the natives were never again any trouble.

But the commander—now the Viceroy—had not seen the end of his troubles.

He had known his limitations, and realized that the governing of a whole planet—or even one continent—was too much for one man when the population consists primarily of barbarians and savages. So he had delegated the rule of a vast area to the south to another—a Lieutenant Commander James, known as "One-Eye," a man who had helped finance the original expedition, and had arrived after the conquest.

One-Eye went south and made very small headway against the more barbaric tribes there. He did not become rich, and he did not achieve anywhere near the success that the Viceroy had. So he came back north with his army and decided to unseat the Viceroy and take his place. That was five years after the capture of the Greatest Noble.

One-Eye took Center City, the old capital, and started to work his way northward, toward Kingston. The Viceroy's forces met him at a place known as Salt Flats and thoroughly trounced him. He was captured, tried for high treason, and executed.

One would think that the execution ended the threat of Lieutenant Commander James, but not so. He had a son, and he had followers.

XV

Nine years. Nine years since the breaking of a vast empire. It really didn't seem like it. The Viceroy looked at his hands. They were veined and thin, and the calluses were gone. Was he getting soft, or just getting old? A little bit—no, *a great deal* of both.

He sat in his study, in the Viceregal Palace at Kingston, chewing over the events of the past weeks. Twice, rumors had come that he was to be assassinated. He and two of his councilors had been hanged in effigy in the public square not long back. He had been snubbed publicly by some of the lesser nobles.

Had he ruled harshly, or was it just jealousy? And was it, really, as some said, caused by the Southerners and the followers of Young Jim?

He didn't know. And sometimes, it seemed as if it didn't matter.

Here he was, sitting alone in his study, when he should have gone to a public function. And he had stayed because of fear of assassination.

Was it—

There was a knock at the door.

"Come in."

A servant entered. "Sir Martin is here, my lord."

The Viceroy got to his feet. "Show him in, by all means."

Sir Martin, just behind the servant, stepped in, smiling,

and the Viceroy returned his smile. "Well, everything went off well enough without you," said Sir Martin.

"Any sign of trouble?"

"None, my lord; none whatsoever. The—"

"Damn!" the Viceroy interrupted savagely. "I should have known! What have I done but display my cowardice? I'm getting yellow in my old age!"

Sir Martin shook his head. "Cowardice, my lord? Nothing of the sort. Prudence, I should call it. By the by, the judge and a few others are coming over." He chuckled softly. "We thought we might talk you out of a meal."

The Viceroy grinned widely. "Nothing easier. I suspected all you hangers-on would come around for your handouts. Come along, my friend; we'll have a drink before the others get here."

There were nearly twenty people at dinner, all, presumably, friends of the Viceroy. At least, it is certain that they were friends in so far as they had no part in the assassination plot. It was a gay party; the Viceroy's friends were doing their best to cheer him up, and were succeeding pretty well. One of the nobles, known for his wit, had just essayed a somewhat off-color jest, and the others were roaring with laughter at the punch line when a shout rang out.

There was a sudden silence around the table.

"What was that?" asked someone. "What did—"

"*Help!*" There was the sound of footsteps pounding up the stairway from the lower floor.

"*Help! The Southerners have come to kill the Viceroy!*"

From the sounds, there was no doubt in any of the minds of the people seated around the table that the shout was true. For a moment, there was shock. Then panic took over.

There were only a dozen or so men in the attacking party; if the "friends" of the Viceroy had stuck by him, they could have held off the assassins with ease.

But no one ran to lock the doors that stood between the Viceroy and his enemies, and only a few drew their weapons to defend him. The others fled. Getting out of a window from the second floor of a building isn't easy, but fear can lend wings, and, although none of them actually flew down, the retreat went fast enough.

Characteristically, the Viceroy headed, not for the window, but for his own room where his armor—long unused, except for state functions—hung waiting in the closet. With him went Sir Martin.

But there wasn't even an opportunity to get into the armor. The rebel band charged into the hallway that led to the bedroom, screaming: "*Death to the Tyrant! Long live the Emperor!*"

It was personal anger, then, not rebellion against the Empire which had appointed the ex-commander to his post as Viceroy.

"Where is the Viceroy? Death to the Tyrant!" The assassins moved in.

Swords in hand, and cloaks wrapped around their left arms, Sir Martin and the Viceroy moved to meet the oncoming attackers.

"Traitors!" bellowed the Viceroy. "Cowards! Have you come to kill me in my own house?"

Parry, thrust! Parry, thrust! Two of the attackers fell before the snake-tongue blade of the fighting viceroy. Sir Martin accounted for two more before he fell in a flood of his own blood.

The Viceroy was alone, now. His blade flickered as though inspired, and two more died under its tireless onslaught. Even more would have died if the head of the conspiracy, a supporter of Young Jim named Rada, hadn't pulled a trick that not even the Viceroy would have pulled.

Rada grabbed one of his own men and shoved him toward the Viceroy's sword, impaling the hapless man upon that deadly blade.

And, in the moment while the Viceroy's weapon was buried to the hilt in an enemy body, the others leaped around the dying man and ran their blades through the Viceroy.

He dropped to the floor, blood gushing from half a dozen wounds.

Even so, his fighting heart still had seconds more to beat. As he propped himself up on one arm, the assassins stood back; even they recognized that they had killed something bigger and stronger than they. A better man than any of them lay dying at their feet.

He clawed with one hand at the river of red that flowed from his pierced throat and then fell forward across the stone floor. With his crimson hand, he traced the great symbol of his Faith on the stone—the Sign of the Cross. He bent his head to kiss it, and, with a final cry of "*Jesus!*" he died. At the age of seventy, it had taken a dozen men to kill him with treachery, something all the hell of nine years of conquest and rule had been unable to do.

And thus died Francisco Pizarro, the Conqueror of Peru.

Despoilers is, of course, a takeoff on history. It was actually the brainchild of John W. Campbell, Jr., the great editor who guided Astounding Science Fiction *from 1938, through its metamorphosis into* Analog *in 1962, until his untimely death in 1971.*

I was in his office one day, and he said: "There may be supermen in the future; have there ever been any in the past?"

Anyone who ever worked with John knows that that was a trick question. It, and others like it, were designed to make one think.

I hedged. (We all did.) "It's possible."

"Possible?" He sniffed. "Historical evidence shows that it was true."

I, of course, was thinking of "superman" in terms of Kimball Kinnison, Jommy Cross, or even Clark Kent. "You mean Biblical— "

"I mean historical. Four hundred years ago!" He paused. Then, in a low voice: "Do you realize that less than five hundred men conquered the Empire of Peru?"

Well—hell—with that to go on, what else could I do but write the story?

DOWN STYPHON!

by H. Beam Piper

In the quiet of the Innermost Circle, in Styphon's House Upon Earth, the great image looked down, and Sesklos, Supreme Priest and Styphon's Voice, returned the carven stare as stonily. Sesklos did not believe in Styphon, or in any other god; if he had, he would not be sitting here. The policies of Styphon's House were too important to entrust to believers. The image, he knew, was of a man—the old high priest who, by discovering the application of a half-forgotten secret, had taken the cult of a minor healer-god out of its mean back-street temples and made it the power that ruled the rulers of all the Five Great Kingdoms. If it had been in Sesklos to worship anything, he would have worshiped that man's memory.

And now, the first Supreme Priest looked down upon the last one. He lowered his eyes, flattened the parchment on the table in front of him, and read again:

PTOSPHES, *Prince of Hostigos*, to SESKLOS, *calling himself Styphon's Voice, these:*

False priest of a false god, impudent swindler, liar and cheat!

Know that we in Hostigos, by simple mechanic arts, now make for ourselves that fireseed which you pretend to be the miracle of your fraudulent god, and that we propose to teach these arts to all, that hereafter Kings and Princes minded to make war may do so for their own defense and advancement, and not to the enrichment of Styphon's House of Iniquities.

In proof thereof, we send you fireseed of our own make, enough for twenty musket charges, and set forth how it is made, thus:

To three parts of refined saltpeter add three fifths of one

132

*part of charcoal and two fifths of one part of sulfur, all
ground to the fineness of bolted wheat flour. Mix these thoroughly, moisten the mixture and work it to a heavy dough,
then press the dough to cakes and dry them, and when they
are dry, grind and sieve them.*

*And know that we hold you and all in Styphon's House of
Iniquities to be our mortal enemies, and the enemies-general
of all men, to be dealt with as Wolves are, and that we will
not rest content until Styphon's House of Iniquities is utterly
cast down and ruined.*

PTOSPHES

That had been the secret of the power of Styphon's House.
No ruler, Great King or petty lord, could withstand his
enemies if they had fireseed and he had none. Given here,
armies marched to victory; withheld there, terms of peace
were accepted. In every council of state, Styphon's House
had spoken the deciding word. Wealth had poured in, to be
lent out at usury and return more wealth.

And now, the contemptible prince of a realm a man could
ride across without tiring his horse was bringing it down,
and Styphon's House had provoked him to it. There were
sulfur springs in Hostigos, and of Styphon's Trinity, sulfur
was hardest to get. When the land around the springs had
been demanded of him, Ptosphes had refused, and since
none could be permitted to defy Styphon's House, his enemy, Prince Gormoth of Nostor, had been raised against
him, with subsidies to hire mercenaries and gifts of fireseed.
When Gormoth had conquered Hostigos, he was pledged to
give the sulfur springs to Styphon's House. Things like that
were done all the time.

But now, Ptosphes was writing thus, to Styphon's Voice
Himself. For a moment, the impiety of it shocked Sesklos.
Then he pushed aside Ptosphes' letter and looked again at
the one from Vyblos, the high priest of the temple at Nostor
Town. Three moons ago, a stranger calling himself Kalvan
and claiming to be an exiled prince from a far country—the
boast of every needy adventurer—had appeared in Hostigos.
A moon later, Ptosphes had made his Kalvan commander of
his soldiers, and had set guards on all the ways out of
Hostigos, allowing any to enter but none to leave. He had
been informed of that at the time, but had thought nothing
of it.

Then, six days ago, the Hostigi had captured Tarr-Dombra,
the castle guarding Gormoth's easiest way into Hostigos.

The castellan, a Count Pheblon, cousin to Gormoth, had been released on ransom-oath, with a letter to Gormoth in which Ptosphes had offered peace and friendship and the teaching of fireseed making. A priest of Styphon, a black-robe believer, who had been at the castle, had also been released, to bear Ptosphes' letter of defiance to him.

It had, of course, been the stranger, Kalvan, who had taught Ptosphes' people the fireseed secret. He wondered briefly if he could be a renegade from Styphon's House. No; only yellow-robe priests of the Inner Circle knew the full secret as Ptosphes had written it, and had one of these absconded, the news would have reached him as swiftly as galloping relays of horses could bring it. Some Inner Circle priest could have written it down, a thing utterly forbidden, and the writing fallen into unconsecrated hands, but he questioned that. The proportions were different, more salt-peter and less charcoal. He would have Ptosphes' sample tried; it might be better than their own.

A man, then, who had re-discovered the secret? That could be, though it had taken many years and many experiments to perfect the processes, especially the caking and grinding. He shrugged. That was not important; the important thing was that the secrecy was broken. Soon anyone could make fireseed, and then Styphon's House would be only a name, and a name of mockery.

Perhaps, though, he could postpone the end for as long as mattered. He was near his ninetieth year; soon he would die, and for each man, when he dies, the world ends.

Letters of urgency to the Archpriests of the five Great Temples, telling them all. A story to be circulated among the secular rulers that fireseed, stolen by bandits, was being smuggled and sold. Prompt investigation of all stories of anyone collecting sulfur or saltpeter or building or altering grinding mills. Immediate death by assassination for anyone suspected of knowing the secret.

And, of course, destruction of Hostigos; none in it to be spared, even for slavery. Gormoth had been waiting until his crops were harvested; he must be made to strike now. And as Archpriest of Styphon's House Upon Earth to Nostor, this was quite beyond poor Vyblos' capacities, with more silver, and fireseed and arms, for Gormoth.

He glanced again at Vyblos' letter. A copy of Ptosphes' letter to him had been sent to Gormoth; why, then, Gormoth knew the fireseed secret himself! It had been daring, and fiendishly clever, of Ptosphes to give this deadly gift to his enemy.

And with the archpriest, fifty mounted Guardsmen of the Temple, their captain to be an Inner Circle priest without robe, and more silver to corrupt Gormoth's nobles and his mercenary captains.

And a special letter to the high priest of the temple at Sask Town. It had been planned to use Prince Sarrask of Sask as a counterpoise to Gormoth, when Gormoth had grown too mighty by the conquest of Hostigos. The time for that was now. Gormoth was needed to destroy Hostigos; then he, too, must be destroyed, before he began making fireseed in Nostor.

He struck the gong thrice, and as he did he thought again of the mysterious Kalvan. That was nothing to shrug off; it was important to learn whence he had come before he appeared—he was intrigued by Vyblos' choice of that word—in Hostigos, and with whom he had been in contact. He could have come from some distant country, in which fireseed was commonly made by all. He knew of none such, but it could well be that the world was larger than he thought.

Or could there be other worlds? The idea had occurred to him, now and then, as an idle speculation.

It was one of those small late-afternoon gatherings, with nobody seeming to have a care in the world, lounging indolently, smoking, sipping tall drinks, nibbling canapes, talking and laughing. Verkan Vall, who would be Chief of Paratime Police after Year-End Day, flicked his lighter and held it for his wife, Hadron Dalla, then applied it to his own cigarette. Across the low table, Tortha Karf, the retiring chief, was mixing another drink, with the concentrated care of an alchemist compounding the Elixir of Life. The Dhergabar University people—the elderly gentleman who was head of the department of Paratemporal Theory, the lady who was professor of Outtime History (IV), and the young man who was director of outtime study operations— were all smiling like three pussycats at a puddle of spilled milk.

"You'll have it all to yourselves," he told them. "The Paratime Commission has declared that time-line a study area, and it's absolutely quarantined to everybody but University personnel and accredited students. And five adjoining, near-identical, time-lines for comparison study. And I will make it my personal business to see that the quarantine is rigidly enforced."

Tortha Karf looked up. "After I retire, I'll have a seat on the Commission, myself," he said. "I'll make it my business to see that the quarantine isn't revoked or diluted."

"I wish we could account for those four hours after he was caught in the transposition field and before he came to that peasant's farm," the paratemporal theorist fretted. "We have no idea what he was doing."

"Wandering in the woods, trying to orient himself," Dalla said. "I'd say, sitting and thinking, for a couple of hours, trying to figure out what happened to him. A paratemporal shift like that is a pretty shattering experience for an outtimer. I don't think he was changing history all by himself, if that's what you're worrying about."

"You can't say that," the paratemporal theorist reproved. "He might have killed a rattlesnake which would otherwise have fatally bitten a child who would otherwise have grown up to be an important personage. That sounds farfetched and trivial, but paratemporal alternate probability is built on such trifles. Who knows what started the Aryan migration eastward instead of westward on that sector? Some chief's hangover, some tribal wizard's nightmare."

"Well, that's why you're getting those five control-study time-lines," the operations direction said. "And that reminds me; our people stay out of Hostigos on all of them for a while. We don't want them massacred along with the resident population by Gormoth's gang, or forced to use First Level weapons in self-defense."

"What bothers me," the lady professor said over the rim of her glass, "is Vall's beard."

"It bothers me, too," Dalla said, "but I'm getting used to it."

"He grew it when he went out to that time-line, and he hasn't shaved it off since. It begins to look like a permanent fixture. And Dalla's a blonde, now; blondes are less conspicuous on Aryan-Transpacific. They're both going to be on and off that time-line all the time, now."

"Well, your exclusive rights don't exclude the Paratime Police. I told you I was going to give that time-line my personal attention."

*   *   *

"Well, you'll not introduce a lot of probability contamination, will you?" the paratemporal theorist asked anxiously. "We want to observe the effect of this man''s appearance on that time-line—"

"No, of course not. But I'm already established with these people. I am Verkan, a free-trader from Grefftscharr, that's the kingdom around the Great Lakes. I am now supposed to be traveling on horseback to Zygros, about where Quebec is on Europo-American; I have promised Lord Kalvan to recruit brass-founders to teach the Hostigi how to cast brass cannon. He needs light field-pieces badly."

"Don't they have cannon of their own?" the historian asked. "I thought you said—"

"Wrought iron, welded up and strengthened with shrunk-on rings. They have iron works, there's a lot of bog iron mined in that section, but no brass foundries. There are some at Zygros, they get their copper and tin by water from the west." He turned to the operations director. "I won't be able to get back, plausibly, for another thirty days. Can you have your first study team ready by then? They'll be the Zygrosi brass founders."

The young man nodded. "They have everything now but local foundry techniques and correct Zygrosi accent. They'll need practice, you can't get manual dexterity by hypno-mech. Yes, thirty days'll be plenty."

"Good. We have two Paratime Police agents in Hostigos now, a supposed blind minstrel and a supposed half-witted boy. As soon as I show up with your crowd, they can take off their coats and go to work, and they won't even have to hunt for coathooks. And I'll set up a trading depot to mask your conveyor-head. After that, you'll be in business."

"But you're helping him win," the paratemporal theorist objected. "That's probability contamination."

"No, it isn't. If I didn't bring in fake Zygrosi brass founders, he'd send somebody else to get real ones. I will give him information, too, just what any other wandering pack trader would. I may even go into battle with him, as I did at Tarr-Dombra, with a local flintlock. But I want *him* to win. I admire the man too much to hand him an unearned victory."

"He sounds like quite a man," the lady historian said. "I'd like to meet him, myself."

"Better not, Eldra," Dalla warned. "This princess of his is handy with a pistol."

"Yes. The man's a genius. Only a police corporal on his own timeline, which shows how outtimers let genius go to waste. We investigated his previous history. Only son of a clergyman; father named him for a religious leader, and wanted him to be a clergyman, too. As a boy, he resisted, passively; scamped all his studies at college except history, and particularly military history, in which he was much interested. Then they had this war, in Korea, you know what that was, and it offered him an escape from the career he was being forced into. Father died while he was at war, mother a year later. After the war he entered the Pennsylvania State Police. Excellent record, as far as his opportunities went; held down by routine because nobody recognized him for what he was. Then he blundered into the field of that conveyor, just when it went weak, and—"

Three months ago—no, just "at another time," he was sure of that—he had been Corporal Calvin Morrison, Pennsylvania State Police. Now he was the Lord Kalvan, in command of the army of Prince Ptosphes of Hostigos, and soon he would marry Ptosphes' daughter Rylla and become heir-matrimonial to the princely throne. That couldn't have happened in his own world.

Hostigos, of course, was no vast realm. It was only as big as Centre and Union Counties, Pennsylvania, with snips of Clinton and Lycoming. That was precisely what it was, too, except that here-and-now there was no Commonwealth of Pennsylvania, it was part of the Great Kingdom of Hos-Harphax—*Hos*-meant great—ruled by a King Kaiphranos. No, just reigned over lightly; outside his own capital at the mouth of the Susquehannna, Kaiphranos' authority was non-existent, the present situation for example.

When he was less evident. Going to arrest a perfectly routine hillybilly murderer; he had entered what could only have been a time-machine; emerging from it, he had landed on what could only have been another time-dimension. He had theorized a little about that, and his theories had demolished themselves half constructed. Then he had given it up and dismissed the whole subject. He had other things to think about.

Rylla, for one; it was hard not to think about her all the time. And commanding an army, once he got it made into one. And manufacturing gunpower in competition with Styphon's House. And fighting a war, against uncomfortably steep odds. And, at the moment, a meeting of the General Staff, all of whom were new at it. So, for that matter, was he, but he had a few vague ideas of military staff organization which put him several up on any of the others. And he was hot and sweat-sticky, because he was wearing close to thirty pounds of armor, to accustom himself to the weight.

They all stood around the big table, looking at the relief map of Hostigos and surroundings which covered the entire top. Just to show you, none of this crowd had ever realized that maps were weapons of war. Maps, here-and-now, were illuminated parchment scrolls, highly artistic and wildly inaccurate. This one had taken over a month, he and Rylla doing most of the work, from what he remembered of the U.S. Geological Survey maps he'd used on the State Police, from hundreds of talks with peasants, soldiers, woodsmen and landlords, and from a good deal of personal horseback reconnaissance.

"The bakeries in Nostor work night and day." That was old Xentos, the blue-robed priest of Dralm, who was also Prince Ptosphes' chancellor and because of contacts with his co-religionists in Nostor, head of espionage and fifth-column operations. "And milk cannot be bought at any price, it is all being made into cheese, and most of the meat is being ground for smoked sausages."

Field rations, stuff a soldier could carry in his haversack and eat uncooked. That could be stored, but Xentos also had reports of wagons and oxen being commandeered and peasants impressed as drivers. That wouldn't be done too long in advance.

"Then they'll strike soon," somebody said. "Taking Tarr-Dombra hasn't stopped Gormoth at all."

"It delayed him," Prince Ptosphes said. "He'd be pouring troops in through Sevenhills Valley now if we hadn't."

There was a smile on the thin lips, between the pointed gray mustache and the small chin-beard. Ptosphes had been learning to smile again, since the powder mill had gone into production. He hadn't, before.

Chartiphon, bulky and grizzle-bearded, stood glowering at the map. He had been chief captain of Hostigos for as long as Ptosphes had been Prince; now he was second in command— Field Marshal and Chief of Operations—and gratifyingly unresentful at Lord Kalvan being placed over him. His idea of war was to hit every head you saw, and whoever hit the most heads first won. All this staff-stuff, maps and fifth columns and logistics and intelligence and security, he did not understand, and he was happy to let somebody do it who did. He'd been informed that Lord Kalvan had been hurled into the past from a thousand years in the future by sorcery, and he probably half suspected that Lord Kalvan was a sorcerer, himself.

"Yes, but where?" he wanted to know.

Ptosphes drew his sword. It was a rapier; the bladesmiths at Tarr-Hostigos had been swamped with orders for rapiers, since this crowd had learned that a sword has a point and that a thrust beats a swinging cut. He used his point now to trace the course of the West Branch—the Athan, here-and-now—from the otherwhen site of Muncy down to where Milton ought to be. The point rested on the river midway between them.

"Marax Ford," he said.

"Oh, no, Prince!" Chartiphon growled. "Go all the way around the mountain and all the way up East Hostigos? He won't do that. Here's where he'll try to come in."

He drew his own sword—long, heavy and double-edged, none of these newfangled pokers for him—and pointed to the juncture of Bald Eagle Creek and the river, at the site of Lock Haven.

"Listra Mouth," he said. "He can move his whole army west along the river, cross here—if we let him—and go up the Listra Valley to the Saski border. And that's where all our ironworks are."

Now that was something. Not so long ago, Chartiphon had taken weapons for granted. Now he was realizing they had to be produced.

That started an argument. Somebody thought Gormoth would try to force one of the gaps. Not Dombra—Antes Gap—that was too strong. Maybe Vryllos—McElhattan—or the gap back of where South Williamsport ought to be.

"He'll attack where he can best use his cavalry," young Harmakros, who was a cavalryman himself, declared. "That's what he has the most of."

That was true. Gormoth's cavalry superiority was something to worry, not to say be frightened, about.

"He'll attack where we don't expect him to."

That was Rylla, in male riding dress, a big dagger on her belt and a pheasant feather in her cap, leaning forward on the map table across from him.

Rylla was the nicest of many nice things, here-and-now. She was beautiful—blond hair almost shoulder-length, laughing blue eyes, impudent tilty little nose dusted with golden freckles—gay and fun-loving. She was utterly fearless; he'd first seen her riding into a cavalry skirmish at the head of her father's troopers. But best of all, after the wonderful very-best that she loved him and was going to marry him, the girl had a brain and wasn't afraid to use it.

"That's right," he agreed. "Where don't we expect him?"

"You know what that means?" Ptosphes asked. He had a pretty good brain, himself. "It means we'll have to be strong enough to resist everywhere." His rapier point swung almost from one end of the map to the other.

"With five thousand, and that counts boys with bows and arrows and peasant grandfathers with pitchforks?" Chartiphon demanded. "Don't joke about such things, Prince."

It came to a little over that but not much. Twenty-five hundred regular infantry, meaning organized into something like companies and given a modicum of drill, a thousand arquebusiers and calivermen, with fifteen hundred pikemen to keep the cavalry off them. Two thousand militia, peasant levies, anybody who could do an hour's foot-drill without dropping dead, armed with anything at all. And slightly less than a thousand cavalry, with steel cuirasses, helmets and thigh-guards. And against that, Prince Gormoth had four thousand of his own subjects, including neither the senile nor the adolescent and none of them armed with bows or agricultural implements, and six thousand mercenaries, of whom four thousand were cavalry.

"Then we'll just have to be able to move what men we have around faster," Rylla said.

Well, good girl! She'd grasped what neither her father nor Harmakros had, that mobility can make up for a numerical inferiority.

"Yes. Harmakros, how many horses can you find to mount our infantry? They don't have to be good horses, just good enough to get the men where they can fight on foot."

Harmakros was scandalized. Mounted soldiers were *cavalry*; anybody ought to know it took years to train a cavalryman. So was Chartiphon; infantry were *foot* soldiers, and had no business on horseback.

"It'll mean one out of four holding horses in a battle, but they'll get to the battle before it's over, and they can wear heavier armor. Now, how many infantry can we mount?"

Harmakros looked at him, decided that he was serious, and was silent for a while. It always took Harmakros a little to recover from the shock of a new idea. Then he grinned and nodded. "I'll find out," he said, grabbing the remount officer by the arm and pulling him off to the side. Rylla joined them with a slate and a piece of soapstone. Rylla was the math wizard; she'd learned how to do up to long division in Arabic numeration. While they argued, he began talking to Ptosphes and Chartiphon about artillery.

That was the one really hopeful thing about the situation. Here-and-now cannon didn't have trunnions. The guns were bedded into timbers like huge gunstocks, or timber frames for the heavier pieces. What passed for field artillery was mounted on four-wheeled carts, usually ox-powered. He blamed Styphon's House for that. They did the weaponeering, and they didn't want bloody and destructive wars, which were bad for business, or decisive wars which established peace, which were worse. They wanted a lot of little wars, all the time, to burn a lot of fireseed.

In the past two months, along with everything else and by methods which would have made Simon Legree look like the Model Employer, he had ordered six new four-pounders built, with trunnions, on field carriages with limbers. Drawn by four horses apiece, they would keep up with cavalry on any sort of decent ground. He had also had trunnions welded onto some old pieces, mostly eight-pounders, and mounted them on makeshift field carriages. They would *not* keep up with cavalry, but they were five hundred per cent better than anything Gormoth had ever heard of.

They were still talking when Harmakros and Rylla came over.

"Two thousand," Rylla said. "They all have four legs. We think they were all alive yesterday evening."

"We'll need some for pack train and replacements. Sixteen hundred mounted infantry. Eight hundred arquebusiers, with arquebuses, not rabbit guns, and eight hundred pikemen, with pikes, not hunting spears or those scythe-blade things." He turned to Chartiphon. "Can you manage that?"

Chartiphon could. Men who wouldn't fall off their horses, too.

"And all the riflemen." Fifty of them, all the muskets and calivers and arquebuses he'd been able to get rifled to date. That was fifty more than the combined rifle strength of all

five Great Kingdoms. "And five hundred cavalry, swords
and pistols, no lances or musketoons."

Everybody heard that, and everybody howled. There
weren't that many, not uncommitted. Swords flashed over
the map, pointing to places where there were only half
enough now. One of these days, somebody was going to use
a sword in one of these arguments for something beside
map-pointing. Finally, they scraped up five hundred cavalry
for the new Mobile Force.

"You'll command," he told Harmakros. "You'll have all
six four-pounders, and the best four eights. You'll be based
in Sevenhills Valley; be ready at any notice to move either
east or west from there."

"As soon as I get it organized, which will be tomorrow
afternoon at latest, I'll be ready to go to Sevenhills. I can
promise I'll be there by noon the next day."

That meant he'd be there before that; that was another
thing about Harmakros.

"Oh, and before I forget." He addressed them all. "Battle cries." They had to be shouted constantly, to keep from
being killed by your friends. "Beside 'Ptosphes!' and
'Hostigos!' we will also shout, '*Down Styphon!*' "

That met with general approval. They all knew who the
real enemy was

Gormoth, Prince of Nostor, set down the goblet and
wiped his bearded lips on the back of his hand. The candles
in front of him and down the long tables to the side flickered slightly. Tableware clattered, voices were loud.

"Lost everything!" The speaker was a baron driven from
Sevenhills Valley when Tarr-Dombra had fallen. "My house,
a score of farms, a village—"

"You think we've lost nothing? They crossed at Vryllos
and burned everything on my land; it was a Styphon's miracle I got out at all."

"For shame!" Vyblos the high priest cried rebukingly.
"What of the Sevenhills temple farm, a holy place pillaged
and desecrated? What of the blood of fifteen consecrated
priests and novices and a score of lay guards, all cruelly
murdered 'Dealt with as wolves are,' " he quoted.

"Well, we have an army, haven't we?" somebody at the
side table on the left hectored. "Why don't we use it?"

Weapons clattered outside, and somebody else sneered,
"That's Ptosphes, now; under the tables, everybody." A

man in black leather entered, advancing and saluting; the captain of the dungeon guards.

"Lord Prince," he said, "the special prisoner will tell all."

"Ha!" He knew what that meant. Then he laughed at the anxious faces along the tables; not a few of his nobles dreaded the thought that somebody was telling all about something. He drew his poniard and cut a line across the candle in front of him, a thumbnail's length from the top.

"You bring good news. I'll hear him in that time."

He nodded in dismissal. As the captain backed away, he rapped loudly on the table with the dagger-pommel.

"Be silent, all of you. I've little time, so give heed." He turned to Klestreus, the elected captain-general of the mercenaries. "You have four thousand horse, two thousand foot, and ten cannon. Add to them a thousand of my infantry, choose which you will, and such cannon of mine as you need. You'll cross the river at Marax Ford. Be on the road before the dew's off the grass tomorrow before dawn the next day, take and hold the ford, put the best of your cavalry across, and let the others follow as speedily as they can.

"Netzigon," he addressed his own chief captain, "you'll gather every man you can, down to the very peasant rabble, and such cannon as Klestreus leaves you. With half of them, confront all the gaps into Nostor, from Nirfe up. You'll take the others opposite Listra-Mouth and Vryllos Gap. As Klestreus moves west through Hostigos, he will attack each gap from behind. When he does, your men will cross the river and attack from the north. Dombra we'll have to starve out; the rest must be stormed. When Klestreus is back of Vryllos Gap, the force you have at Listra-Mouth will cross and move up Listra Valley. After that, we'll have Tarr-Hostigos to take, Galzar only knows how long we'll be at that, but by the end of the moon-half, all else in Hostigos should be ours."

There was a gratified murmur along the tables; this made good hearing to all. Only the high priest, Vyblos, was ill-pleased.

"But why so soon, Prince?" he asked.

"Soon?" he roared. "By the mace of Galzar, you've been bawling for it like a weaned calf! Well, now you have your invasion; thank your god for it."

"A few more days would not be too much, Lord Prince," Vyblos said mildly. "Today I had word from Styphon's

House Upon Earth, from the pen of His Divinity Himself. An Archpriest, His Holiness Krastokles, is coming here to Nostor, with rich gifts of fireseed and money, and the blessing of Styphon's Voice. It were poor reverence not to await His Holiness' coming."

He turned to the two captains. "You heard me," he said. "I rule here, not the priest. Be about it; send orders at once. You move tomorrow."

Then he rose, pushing back his chair before the servant could withdraw it. The line was still visible at the top of the candle.

Guards with torches attended him down the winding stairs into the dungeons. The air stank. His breath congealed; the heat of summer never penetrated here. From the torture chambers shrieks told of some wretch being questioned; idly he wondered who. Stopping at an iron-bound oaken door, he unlocked it with a key from his belt and entered alone, closing it behind him.

The room within was large, warmed by a fire on the hearth in the corner and lighted by a great lantern from above. Under it, a man bent over a littered table. He had a bald head and a straggling beard, and wore a most unprisoner-like dagger on his belt. A key for the door lay on the table, and a pair of heavy horseman's pistols He straightened, turning.

"Greetings, Prince. It's done. I tried it; it's as good as they make in Hostigos, and better than the priests' trash."

"And no prayers to Styphon, Skranga?" he asked sarcastically.

Skranga was chewing tobacco. He spat brownly on the floor.

"In the face of Styphon! Try it yourself, Prince; the pistols are empty."

There was a dish half full of fireseed on the table. He measured in a charge, loaded and wadded a bullet on top of it, primed the pan and readied the striker, then fired into a billet of wood by the fire and went to probe the hole with a straw. The bullet had gone in almost a little finger's length; Styphon's powder wouldn't do that. He carried the pistol back and laid it on the table.

"Well, Skranga," he laughed. "You'll have to bide here a while, but from this hour you're first nobleman of Nostor after me. Style yourself Duke. There'll be rich lands for you in Hostigos, when Hostigos is mine."

"And the Styphon temple farm of Nostor," Skranga grinned. "If I'm to make your fireseed, there's all there that I'll need."

"Yes, that too, by Galzar! After I've downed Ptosphes, I'll deal with Vyblos, and he'll envy Ptosphes before I let him die."

Snatching up a pewter cup without looking to see if it were clean, he went to the wine keg and drew for himself, tasted the wine, then spat it out.

"Is this the swill they've given you?" he demanded. "By Galzar, whoever's at fault won't see tomorrow's sun set!" He flung open the door and bellowed into the hall: "Wine! Wine for Prince Gormoth and Duke Skranga! And silver cups! And see it's fit for nobles to drink!"

Mobile Force HQ had been the mansion of a Nostori noble driven from Sevenhills Valley on D-for-Dombra Day; his name had been shouted ahead as he rode through the troop-crowded village, and Harmakros and his officers met him at the door.

"Great Dralm, Kalvan!" Harmakros laughed, clasping his hand. "Are you growing wings on horses, now? Our messengers only got off an hour and a half ago."

"I know; I met them back of Vryllos Gap." They crossed the outer hall and through the doorway to the big room beyond. "We got the news at Tarr-Hostigos just after dark. What have you heard since?"

At least fifty candles burned in the great central chandelier. Evidently the cavalry had arrived here before the peasants, and hadn't looted the place too destructively themselves. Harmakros led him to an inlaid table on which a map, scorched with hot needles on white doeskin, was spread.

"We have reports from all the watchtowers along the mountain. They're too far back to see anything but dust, but the column's three miles long; first cavalry, then infantry, then wagons and guns, and then more infantry and cavalry. They halted at Nirfe at dusk and built hundreds of campfires. Whether they left them burning and marched on after dark, and how far ahead the cavalry are, we don't know. We expect them at Marax Ford by dawn."

"We got a little more than that. The priest of Dralm at Nostor Town got a messenger off a little after noon; it was dusk before he could get across the river. Your column's commanded by Klestreus. Four thousand mercenary cavalry, two thousand mercenary infantry, a thousand of Gormoth's infantry, fifteen guns, he didn't say what kind, and a wagon train that must be creaking with loot. At the same time, Netzigon's moving west, probably toward Listra-Mouth and we don't know what with. The messenger had to dodge his troops all the way up to Vryllos. Chartiphon's going to Listra-Mouth with what he can scrape up; Prince Ptosphes is occupying Vryllos Gap."

"That's it; a double attack," Harmakros said. "We can't help Chartiphon, can we?"

"We can help him by beating Klestreus." He got out his pipe; as soon as he had filled it, one of the officers provided a light. "Thank you. What have you done so far?"

"I started my wagons and the eight-pounders down the main road. They'll stop just short of Fitra, here"—he pointed on the map—"and wait for us. As soon as I'm all collected, I'm taking the cavalry and mounted infantry and the four-pounders down the back road. After we're on the main road, the wagons and the eights will follow on. I have two hundred militia, the usual odds-and-ends, marching with the wagons."

"That was smart."

Puffing on his pipe, he looked at the map. The back road, adequate for horsemen and the four-pounders but not for wagons, followed the mountains and then bent south away from them to join the main valley road at the village of Fitra. Harmakros had started his slow stuff first, and could overtake without being impeded by it, and he was waiting till he had all his striking force in hand and not dribbling it in to be chopped up by detail.

"Where had you thought of fighting?"

"Why, on the Athan, of course." Harmakros was surprised that he should ask. "Klestreus will have some cavalry over before we get there, that can't be helped, but we'll wipe them out or chase them back, and then defend the line of the river."

"Huh-uh." He touched the Fitra road-junction with his pipe stem. "We fight here."

"But that's miles inside Hostigos!" one of the officers cried. Maybe he owned an estate down there. "We can't let them get that far."

"Lord Kalvan," Harmakros began stiffly. He was going to

be insubordinate, he never bothered with titles otherwise. "We must not give up one foot of ground; the honor of Hostigos forbids it."

Here we are, back in the Middle Ages! He seemed to hear the voice of a history professor, inside his head, calling a roll of battles lost on points of honor. Mostly by the French; they'd been the worst, though not the only, offenders. He decided to fly into a rage.

"To Styphon with that!" he yelled, banging his fist on the table. "Honor won't win this war, and real estate won't win this war. The only thing that'll win this war is killing Nostori!

"Now here," he continued, quietly, the rage having served its purpose, "is where we can kill the most of them, and get the fewest of our own men killed doing it. Klestreus will cross the Athan here, at Marax Ford." That would be a little below where he remembered Watsontown to have been. "He'll rush his best cavalry ahead to secure the ford, and the rest of the cavalry will cross next. They'll want to get in on the best looting ahead of the infantry; they'll push ahead without waiting. By the time the infantry are over, they'll be stringing west in bunches.

"Now, that army Klestreus has could walk all over us, if they were all together. But they won't be. And they'll be tired, and we'll have reached Fitra by daylight, have our position prepared, our men and horses will be rested, we'll even be able to give everybody a hot meal. And Klestreus will be strung out for ten miles by the time his advance elements come up to us. Now, what kind of troops have we east of here?"

"A hundred cavalry along the river, and a hundred and fifty regular infantry and about twice as many militia; about five hundred, militia and regulars, at posts in the gaps."

"All right; get riders off at once. Somebody who won't be argued with. Have all that force along the river moved back; to Fitra if possible, and if not they can reinforce the posts at the gaps. The gaps'll have to look out for themselves, we can't help them. The cavalry will keep just in front of Klestreus, skirmishing but doing nothing to delay him."

Harmakros looked at the map, thought for a little, and nodded.

"East Hostigos," he said, "will be the graveyard of the Nostori."

That was all right; that took care of the honor of Hostigos.

"Well, mercenaries from Hos-Agrys and Hos-Ktemnos, anyhow." That reminded him of something. "Who hired those mercenaries; Gormoth, or Styphon's House?"

"Why, Gormoth. The money came from Styphon's House, but the mercenaries contracted with Gormoth; they serve him."

"The reason I asked, the Rev. Whatshisname in Nostor included a bit of gossip in his message. It seems that this morning Gormoth had one of his under-stewards put to death. Had a funnel forced into his mouth and half a keg of wine poured into him. The wine was of inferior quality, and had been given to a prisoner for whom Gormoth had commanded good treatment."

One of the officers made a face. "Sounds like Gormoth," he commented. Another laughed and said he could think of a few tavern keepers in Hostigos Town who deserved that.

"Who was the prisoner?" Harmakros asked. "Count Pheblon?"

"Oh, no. Pheblon's out of favor, but he isn't a prisoner. You know this fellow. Agrysi horse-trader named Skranga."

"Yes, he got caught in Hostigos during the Iron Curtain." Like Fifth Column, Iron Curtain was now part of the Hostigi vocabulary. Then he blinked. "He was working in the fireseed mill, while he was here! You think he might be making fireseed for Gormoth?"

"He is if he's doing what I told him to." There was an outcry at that. He laughed. "And if Gormoth begins making his own fireseed, Styphon's House'll hear about it, and you know what'll happen then. That's why I asked about those mercenaries. I was wondering whether Gormoth would use them against Styphon's House, or Styphon's House against Gormoth." He shrugged. "Not that it matters. If everybody does his job tomorrow, nobody'll use those mercenaries. Except, maybe, us. That's another thing. We don't bother with Nostori prisoners, but take all the mercenaries who'll surrender. We may need them later."

Dawn was only a pallor in the east, and the whitewashed walls were blurs under dark thatches, but the village of Fitra was awake, light pouring from open doors and a fire blazing on the small common. There was a crowd, villagers, and cavalrymen who had ridden ahead. Behind him, hoofs thudded and armor and equipment clattered; away back, he could hear the four-pounders thumping over the pole bridge at the mill. The shouting started, of course: "Lord Kalvan! Dralm bless Lord Kalvan!" He was used to it, now; it didn't give him the thrill it had at first. He had to make a speech, while orders were shouted and re-shouted to the rear, and men and horses got off to the sides of the road to make way for the guns.

Then he and Harmakros and four or five of the officers turned left and cantered down the main road, reining in where it began to dip. The eastern pallor had become a bar of yellow light. The Mountains of Hostigos were blackly plain on the left, and the jumble of ridges to the right were taking shape. Nearby trees began to detach themselves from the obscurity. In a few hours, they'd all be down. He pointed to the right.

"Send two hundred cavalry around that ridge, over there, to where those three farms are clumped together," he told Harmakros. "They're not to make fires or let themselves be seen. They're to wait till we're engaged and the second mob of Nostori cavalry come up; then they'll come out and hit them from the flank and rear."

An officer galloped away to the rear to attend to it. The yellow light was spreading upward in the east, only the largest and brightest stars were still visible. In front, the ground fell away into a little hollow, with a brook running through it to the left, to join a larger stream at the foot of the mountain, which rose steeply, then sloped up to the summit. On the right was broken ground, mostly wooded. A few trees around them, in the hollow, and on the slope beyond; open farmland in front. This couldn't have been better if he'd had Dralm create it to order.

The yellow light was past the zenith, and the eastern horizon was a dazzle. Harmakros squinted at it and said something about fighting with the sun in their eyes.

"No such thing; it'll be overhead before they get here. Now, you go take a nap. I'll wake you in time to give me some sack-time. As soon as the wagons get here, we'll give everybody a hot meal."

An ox cart appeared on the brow of the little hill across the hollow, piled high, a woman and a boy trudging beside the team and another woman and more children riding. Before they were down to where the road crossed the stream, a wagon was coming up.

"Have them turned aside," he ordered. "Don't let them get into the village." This was only the start; there'd be a perfect stream of them before long. They couldn't be allowed on the main road past Fitra, not till the wagons and the eight-pounders got through. "And use wagons for barricades, and the oxen to help drag trees."

The village peasants were coming out, now, leading four- and six-ox teams, chains dragging. Axes began thudding. One thing, if anybody was alive here then, this village wouldn't have to worry about winter firewood. More refugees were coming in; loud protests at being diverted, and at the seizure of wagons and teams. The axemen were across the hollow, now, and men shouted at straining oxen as trees were dragged in to build an abatis.

He strained his eyes against the sunrise; he couldn't see any smoke. Too far away. He was sure, though, that the mercenary cavalry was across the Athan, and they ought to be burning things. Pyromania was as fixed in the mercenary character as kleptomania. Of course, he could be misjudging here-and-now mercenaries; all he knew was what he'd learned reading Sir Charles Oman's "History of the Art of War," when he should have been studying homiletics and scriptural exegesis and youth-organization methods at college, but there were universal constants. One was that mercenary soldiers' hearts were full of larceny. Another was that they liked being alive to spend their loot. He was pretty confident of what Klestreus' cavalry were doing down toward the river.

The abatis began to take shape, trees dragged into line, the tops to the front, with spaces for three of the four-pounders on either side of the road, and a barricade of peasants' wagons at either end. He rode forward a couple of times, to get an enemy's eye-view of it; he didn't want it to look too formidable. He made sure that none of the guns would be visible. Finally, he noticed smears of smoke against the horizon, maybe five or six miles down the valley. Klestreus' mercenaries weren't going to disappoint him, after all.

A company of regular infantry, a hundred and fifty, three pikes to two calivers, came up in good order. They'd marched all the way from the Athan, reported firing behind them, and were disgusted at marching away from it. He told them they'd get all the firing they wanted by noon, and to fall out and rest. A couple of hundred militia dribbled in, some with crossbows. There were a few more smokes in the east, but he still couldn't hear anything. At seven-thirty, the supply wagons and the eight-pounders, and the two hundred militia wagon-guards, came in from the west. That was good; the refugees, now a steady stream, could be sent on up the main road.

He found Harmakros asleep in one of the village cottages, wakened him, and gave him the situation to date.

"Good; I'll get the men fed. When do you want me to wake you?"

"As soon as you see smoke two miles down the valley, as soon as our cavalry from the east begin coming in, and in any case in two hours."

Then he pulled off his boots and helmet, unbuckled his belt, and lay down in the rest of his armor on the cornshuck tick Harmakros had vacated, hoping that it had no small inhabitants or, if so, that none of them would move in under his arming-doublet. It was comparatively cool in here, behind the stone walls and under the thick thatch; the wet heat of his body became a clammy chill. He shifted positions a couple of times, finally deciding that fewer things dug into him if he lay flat on his back.

So far, everything had gone nicely; all he was worried about was who would let him down, and how badly. If some valiant fool got a rush of honor to the head and charged at the wrong moment—

If he could bring this off just half as well as he'd planned it, which would be about par for the course for any battle, he could go to Valhalla when he died and drink at the same table with Richard Coeur-de-Lion and the Black Prince and Henry of Navarre. A complete success would entitle him to take a salute from Stonewall Jackson. He fell asleep receiving the commendation of George S. Patton.

An infantry captain wakened him a little before ten.

"They're burning Systros, now." That was a town, about two thousand, two and a half miles away. "A couple of the cavalry who've been keeping just in front of them came in. The first batch are about fifteen hundred; there's another lot, maybe a thousand, two miles behind them. We don't know where the infantry and the wagons are, but we've been hearing those big bombards at Narza Gap."

That would be Klestreus' infantry on this side, probably supported by Netzigon's ragtag-and-bobtail from the other side. He pulled on his boots and buckled on his sword, and, after eating a bowl of beef stew with plenty of onion in it, he put on his helmet and drank a mug of wine. Somebody brought his horse, and he rode up to the line. On the way, he noticed that the village priest of Dralm and the Mobile Force priest of Galzar had set up a field hospital on the village common and that pole-and-blanket stretchers were being prepared. No anesthetics, here-and-now, though the priests of Galzar used sandbags. He hoped he wouldn't be wounded, himself. The last time had been bad enough.

A big column of smoke dirtied the sky above Systros. Silly buggers; first crowd into it had fired it, here-and-now mercenaries were the same as any other, and now the ones behind would have to bypass it. They'd be handling Klestreus' army in retail lots.

The abatis was finished, over a hundred felled trees ox-dragged into line, butts to the rear and tops to the front. Between them, men sat smoking or eating, or lay on the ground resting. The horse lines were back of the side road, with the more poorly-armed militiamen holding horses. At each end of the abatis were two of the four eight-pounders, then an opening big enough for cavalry to sortie out through, and then barricades of farm carts.

He could hear a distant, and then not so distant, popping of small arms. Away off, one of the bombards at Narza Gap boomed, and, after a while, the other. Good; they were still holding out. Cavalry came drifting up the road, some re-loading pistols. The shots grew louder, and more cavalry, in more of a hurry, arrived. Finally, a dozen or so topped the rise across the hollow and galloped down; the last one fired a pistol over his shoulder. By the time he was splashing across the brook, Nostori cavalry appeared, ten or fifteen of them.

Immediately, an eight-bore rifled musket bellowed from behind the abatis. His horse dance-stepped daintily; another, and another, roared. Across the hollow, a horse went down kicking, and another just went down. Another, with an empty saddle, trotted down to the stream and stopped to drink. The Nostori turned and galloped back out of sight. Nobody else had fired; riflemen were a law to themselves, but the arquebusiers were waiting for orders. He was wondering where the rest of the rifles were when a row of white smoke puffs blossomed along the edge of the bench above the creek on the left, and shots banged like a string of firecrackers. There were yells from out of sight across the hollow, and musketoons thumped in reply.

Wasting Styphon's good fireseed; four hundred yards, they couldn't hit Grant's Tomb at that range with smoothbores. Along the abatis, everybody was on his feet, crowding into position; there were a few yells of "Hostigos!" and "Down Styphon!" More confused noise from the dead ground beyond the brow of the other hill, a steady whipcracking of rifles, fired as fast as they could be reloaded and aimed, from the bench. He wished he had five hundred rifles up there.

Hell, while he was wishing, why not wish for twenty medium tanks and a dozen Sabre-Jets?

Then the mercenary cavalry came up in a solid front on the brow of the hill, black and orange lance-pennons and helmet-plumes and scarves, polished breastplates. Lancers all in front, musketoonmen behind. A shiver ran along the line as the lances came down; the advance paused to dress front.

As though that had been the signal, which it had been, six four-pounders and four eight-pounders went off as one, not a noise but a palpable blow on the ears. His horse started to buck; by the time he had him under control again, the smoke was billowing out over the hollow, and several perfect rings floated up against the blue, and everybody was yelling, *"Down Styphon!"*

Roundshot; he could see the furrows it had plowed into the block of black and orange cavalry; men yelling, horses rearing, or down and screaming horribly as only wounded horses can. The charge had stopped, briefly, before it had started. On either side of him, gun captains were shouting, "Grapeshot! Grapeshot!" and cannoneers were jumping to their pieces before they had stopped recoiling with doubleheaded swabs, one end wet to quench lingering powder-bag sparks and the other dry.

The charge slid forward in broken chunks, down the dip into the hollow. When they were twenty yards short of the brook, four hundred arquebuses blazed; the whole front went down, horses behind tripping over fallen horses in front. The arquebusiers stepped back, drawing the stoppers of their powder flasks with their teeth. *Memo: self-measuring spring powder flask; start making them as soon as possible.* When they were half reloaded, the other four hundred arquebuses crashed. The way those cavalry were jammed, down there, every bullet must have hit something. The smoke was clogging the hollow like spilled cotton, now; through it he could see another wave of cavalry come up on the brow of the hill. A four-pounder spewed grape into them, and then another. *Down Styphon!* Before they could begin the descent, another four-pounder went off.

Gustavus Adolphus' four-pounder crews could load and fire faster than musketeers, a dry lecture-room voice was telling him. Lord Kalvan's weren't going quite that well, but almost. The first one had fired close on the heels of the third arquebus volley. Then one of the eight-pounders fired, and that was a small miracle.

A surprising number of Klestreus' cavalry had survived the fall of their horses. Well, horses were bigger targets, and they didn't wear breastplates. Having nowhere else to go, they were charging up on foot, their lances for pikes. Some of them were shot in front of the abatis, quite a few were piked trying to get through it. A few did get through. As he galloped to help deal with one party of these, he could see militiamen with scythe-blade things, he had never decided on the correct name for those weapons, and billhooks and axes, running forward from the horse lines. At that moment, a trumpet sounded on the right, and another on the left, and there were great shouts of *"Down Styphon!"* at both ends. Harmakros and the cavalry.

Then he was in front of a dozen Nostori mercenaries, pulling up his horse and aiming a pistol at them.

"Yield, comrades! We spare mercenaries!"

An undecided second and a half, then one raised his reverse musketoon over his head.

"We yield; oath to Galzar."

That they would keep. Galzar didn't like oath-breaking soldiers; he always let them get killed at the next opportunity. *Memo: cult of Galzar; encourage.*

Some peasants ran up, brandishing axes. He waved them back.

"Keep your weapons," he told the mercenaries. "I'll find somebody to guard you."

He found a couple of Mobile Force arquebusiers, and then had to save a couple more mercenaries from having their throats cut. Damn these civilians! Have to detail prisoner guards. Disarm the mercenaries, and the peasants would butcher them; leave them armed in the rear, and maybe the temptation would be too great even for the fear of Galzar.

Along the abatis, the firing had stopped, but the hollow below was a perfect hell's bedlam—*Down Styphon!* and, occasionally, *Gormoth!* Pistol shots, clashing steel. Over his shoulder, he could see villagers, even women and children, replacing the militia at the horse lines. Captains were shouting, "Pikes forward," and pikemen were dodging out among the felled trees. Dimly, through the smoke, he saw red and blue colors on horsemen at the brow of the opposite hill. The road had been left open; he trotted forward and down toward the brook.

What he saw in the hollow made his stomach heave. After being demobbed on the West Coast, he had made a side trip into Mexico on the way home, and seen a bullfight in Juarez. One horse gored to death by a bull hadn't bothered him much, but this would have sickened the most hardened *aficionado*. The infantrymen, going forward, were stopping to brain wounded horses or cut their throats or shoot them with pistols from saddle holsters. They oughtn't to stop to do that, but he couldn't blame them. The Hostigi soldier was a farmer and couldn't let horses suffer.

Stretcher-bearers were coming forward, too, and so were villagers to loot. Corpse-robbing was the only way the civil population, here-and-now, had of getting some of their own back after a battle. Most of them had clubs or hatchets, to make sure that what they were robbing really were corpses. A lot of good weapons lying around, too. They ought to be collected before they rusted into uselessness, but no time to do that now. Stopping to do that, once, had been one of Stonewall Jackson's few mistakes.

Away ahead, there was another uproar of battle, and more *Down Styphon!* That would be the two hundred cavalry from the far right hitting the second batch of mercenaries, who would be disorganized, by now, by fugitives from the fight at the hollow. Gormoth wasn't going to have to pay a lot of mercenaries, if this kept up. The infantry were beginning to form up on the opposite hill, blocks of pikemen with smaller blocks of arquebusiers between, and some were running back to fetch the horses. And Nostori cavalry were coming in in small groups, holding their helmets up on their sword points and crying, "We yield; oath to Galzar." One of the officers of the flanking party, with four men, was bringing in close to a hundred of them. He was regretful that so many had escaped. The riflemen on the bench were drifting east, firing as they went. All the infantry from the Athan and many of the militia had mounted themselves on captured horses.

There was a clatter behind him, and he got his horse off the road to let the four-pounders pass in column. Their captain waved to him and told him, laughing, that the eights would be along in a day or so.

"Where do we get some more shooting?" he asked.

"Down the road a piece. Just follow along; we'll show you."

He looked at his watch. It was still ten minutes till noon, Hostigos Standard Sundial Time.

By 1700, they were well down the road, and there had been a lot of shooting on the way. Now they were two miles west of the Athan, where Klestreus' wagons and cannon were strung out for half a mile each way along the road, and he was sitting, with his helmet off, on an upended wine keg, at a table made by laying a shed door across a couple of boxes, with Harmakros' pyrographed doeskin map spread in front of him and a mug where he could reach it. There were some burned-out farm-buildings beside the road, and the big oaks which shaded him had been yellowed on one side by the heat. Several hundred prisoners were squatting in the field beyond, eating food from their own wagons. Harmakros, and the chief captain of mounted infantry, he'd be about two-star rank, and the major-equivalent Galzar chaplain, and the brigadier in direct command of the cavalry, sat or squatted around him. The messenger from Sevenhills Valley, who had just caught up with him, was trying to walk the stiffness out of his legs, carrying a mug from which he drank as he paced and talked.

"That's all we know," he said. "All morning, there was cannon fire up the river, and then small-arms fire, a lot of it, and when the wind was right, we could hear shouting. A little after noon, some cavalry who had been patrolling the strip between the river and the mountain came in; they said Netzigon was across in force in front of Vryllos Gap, and they couldn't get through to Ptosphes and Princess Rylla."

He cursed; some of it was comprehensible in local cursing terms. "Is she at Vryllos, too?"

Harmakros laughed. "You ought to know her by now, Kalvan. Try and keep that girl out of a battle."

He'd probably be doing that the rest of his life. Or hers, which mightn't be so long, if she wasn't careful. The messenger stopped, taking a deep drink, then continued:

"Finally, a rider came in from this side of the mountain. He said that the Nostori were over the river and pushing Prince Ptosphes back into the gap. He wanted to know if the captain at Tarr-Dombra could help him."

"Well?"

"We only had two hundred regulars and two hundred and fifty militia, and it's ten miles up to Vryllos along the river, and the Styphon's own way around the mountains on the south side. So the captain left a few cripples and kitchen women to hold the castle, and took everything else he had across the river. They were just starting when he sent me off. I heard cannon fire when I was crossing Sevenhills Valley."

"That was about the best thing he could do."

There'd be a couple of hundred Nostori at Dyssa—about Jersey Shore—just a holding force. If they could run them out, burn the town, and start enough of a scare, it might take some of the weight off Ptosphes at Vryllos and Chartiphon at Listra-Mouth.

"I hope nobody expects any help from us," Harmakros said. "Our horses are ridden into the ground; half our men are mounted on captured horses, and they're in worse shape now than the ones of our own we have left."

"Some of my men are riding two on a horse," Phrames, the mounted infantry CO, said. "You figure what kind of a march they can make."

"It would be midnight before any of us could get to Vryllos Gap," he said. "That would be less than a thousand."

"Five hundred, I'd call it," the cavalry brigadier said. "We've been losing by attrition all the way east."

"But I'd heard that your losses had been very light."

"You heard? From whom?"

"Why, from the men guarding prisoners. Great Dralm, Lord Kalvan, I never saw so many—"

"That's our losses; prisoner-guard details, every one as much out of it as though he'd been shot through the head."

But Klestreus' army had simply ceased to exist. It was not improbable that as many as five hundred had safely crossed the Athan at Marax Ford. There would be several hundred more, singly and in small bands, dodging through the woods to the south. And some six hundred had broken through at Narza Gap. The rest had either been killed or captured.

First, there had been the helter-skelter chase east from Fitra. For instance, twenty-five riflemen, firing from behind trees and rocks, had stopped and turned back two hundred cavalry who were making for the next gap down. Mostly, anybody who was overtaken held up an empty hand or a reversed sword and invoked Galzar. He only had to fight once, himself; he and two Mobile Force cavalrymen caught up with ten fleeing mercenaries and charged them, shouting to them to yield. Maybe the ten were tired of running, maybe they thought it was insulting for three men to try to capture them, or maybe they were just contrary. Instead, they had turned and charged. He had half-dodged and half-parried a lance and spitted the lancer through the throat, and had been thrusting and parrying with two swordsmen when a dozen mounted infantrymen came up.

Then, they had fought a small battle half a mile west of Systros. Fifteen hundred infantry and five hundred cavalry, all mercenaries, had just returned to the main road after passing around both sides of the burning town and were forming up when the wrecks of the cavalry from Fitra had come pelting into them. Their own cavalry and the fugitives were trying to force a way of escape, and the infantry were trying to pike them off, when the Hostigi arrived, mounted infantrymen dismounting to fight on foot. Then the four-pounders arrived and began throwing case-shot, leather tubes full of pistol bullets. Gormoth's mercenaries had never been exposed to case-shot before. Several hundred were killed, and the rest promptly hoisted their helmets, tore off Gormoth's colors, and cried for quarter.

That had been where the mercenary general, Klestreus, had surrendered. Phrames had attended to that; he and Harmakros had kept on with the cavalry, now down to three hundred; pistoling and cutting down fugitives. A lot of these turned left toward Narza Gap.

Hestophes, the Hostigi CO there—about United States captain equivalent, he'd be a full colonel this time tomorrow—had been a real cool cat. He'd had two hundred and fifty men, mostly regulars with calivers, two old twenty-pound bombards, and several smaller pieces. Klestreus' infantry had attacked Nirfe gap, the one below him, and, with the aid of Netzigon's men from the other side, had swamped it. A few survivors had escaped along the mountain top and brought the news to Narza. An hour later, Hestophes' position was under attack from both sides, too.

He had beaten off three assaults, a probable total of a thousand men. Then his lookout on the mountain reported seeing the Fitra-Systros fugitives streaming east. Hestophes promptly spiked his guns and pulled his men up out of the gap. The infantry who had been besieging him were swept along with the fleeing cavalry; from the mountainside, Hestophes spattered them with caliver bullets to discourage loitering and let them escape to spread panic on the other side. By now, they would be spreading it in Nostor Town.

Fitra had been a turkey shoot, Systros had been a roundup, and the rest of it had been a fox hunt. Then they had run into the guns and wagon train, inching along under ox power. There had been, with the train, a thousand of Gormoth's own infantry, and five hundred mercenary cavalry. This had been Systros all over, but a massacre. The fugitive cavalry had tried to force their way through, the infantry had resisted, and then the four-pounders—only five, one was off the road below Systros with a broken axle—had arrived and begun firing case-shot, and then one of the eight-pounders arrived. Some of the mercenaries tried to put up a serious fight; when they found the pay chests in one of the wagons they understood why. The Nostori infantry simply emptied their calivers and threw them away and ran. Along with *Down Styphon!* the pursuers were now shouting, *Dralm and No Quarter!* He wondered what Xentos would have thought of that. Dralm wasn't supposed to be that kind of a god.

"You know," he said, getting out his pipe and tobacco, "we didn't have a very big army to start with. Just what do we have now?"

"Five hundred here, and four hundred at the river," Phrames said. "The rest are guarding prisoners all the way back to Fitra."

"Well, I think we can help Ptosphes and Chartiphon best from here," he said. "That gang Hestophes let through at Narza will be panting out their story all the way to Nostor Town." He looked at his watch again. If he ever broke that thing, he'd be sunk! "By this time, Gormoth will be getting ready to fight the Battle of Nostor." He turned to Phrames. "How many men do you absolutely need, here?" he asked. "Two hundred?"

Phrames looked up and down the road, and at the prisoners in the field, and then, out of the corner of his eye, at the boxes under the shed door that formed the table top. They hadn't got around to weighing all that silver yet, but there was too much to be careless with.

"I ought to have twice that many, Lord Kalvan."

"The prisoners are mercenaries, and they have agreed to take Prince Ptosphes' colors," the priest of Galzar said. "Of course, they cannot bear arms against Gormoth or against any in his service until released from their oaths to him by the end of the war. In the sight of the Wargod, helping you to guard these wagons would be bearing arms against Gormoth, for it would free your own soldiers to do so. But I will speak to them, and I will answer that they will not break their oath of surrender. You will need no guards for them."

"Two hundred, then," Phrames said. "I can use walking wounded for some things."

"All right; take two hundred, the ones with the worst beat up horses, and mind the store. Harmakros, you take three hundred and two of the four-pounders and cross at the next ford down. I'll take four hundred across at Marax and work east and north. You can divide into two columns of a hundred men and one gun apiece, but no smaller. There will be companies and parts of companies over there trying to reform. Break them up. And burn the whole country out, set fire to everything that'll make a smoke, or a blaze after dark. Any refugees going north, give them a good scare, but don't stop them. We want Gormoth to think we have three or four thousand men across the river. That'll take the pressure off Vryllos Gap and Listra-Mouth."

He rose, and Phrames took his seat. Horses were brought; he and Harmakros and the others mounted. The messenger from Sevenhills Valley refilled his mug and sat down, stretching his legs in front of him. He rode along the line of wagons, full of food the people of Nostor wouldn't eat this winter, and curse Gormoth for the lack, and kegs of fireseed the slaves in Styphon's temple farms would have to toil to replace. He came to the guns, and saw one at which he stopped. A long brass eighteen-pounder, on a two-wheeled cart, with a four-wheeled cart for ammunition and to support the tail of the heavy timber stock. There was another behind it, and an officer in gilded armor sitting on the cart, morosely smoking a pipe.

"Your guns, captain?" he asked.

"They were. Prince Ptosphes' guns, now."

"They're still yours, and good pay for their use. Gormoth of Nostor isn't our only enemy."

The mercenary artilleryman grinned. "Then I'll take Ptosphes' colors, and my guns with me. You're Lord Kalvan? Is it really true that you make your own fireseed?"

"What do you think we were shooting at you today, sawdust?" He looked at the guns again. "We don't see brass guns around here."

They'd been made, as he suspected, in Zygros. He looked at them again, critically; there wasn't a thing wrong with Zygrosi brass-casting. The captain was proud of them, and glad he wasn't going to lose them; he boasted about good shots they had made.

"Well, you'll find one of my officers, Count Phrames, back by that burned house and those big trees. Tell him I sent you. He's to do what he can to help you get those guns to Hostigos Town. Where are your men?"

"Some of them got killed, before we cried quits. The rest are back there with the others. They'll all take the red and blue along with me."

"I'll talk to you later. Good luck, captain, and glad to have you with us."

There were dead infantry all along the road, mostly killed from behind, while running. Infantry who stood firm had a chance, usually a very good one, against cavalry. Infantry who ran had none at all. It grew progressively worse until he came to the river, where the four-pounder crews were swabbing and polishing their pieces, and dark birds rose cawing and croaking and squawking when disturbed at their feast. Must be every crow and raven and buzzard in Hos-Harphax; he even saw a few eagles.

And the river, horse-knee deep at the ford, was tricky. Crossing, their mounts stumbled continuously on armor-weighted corpses. This one had been a real baddie for Nostor.

"So your boy did it, all by himself," the lady history professor was saying.

Verkan Vall nodded, grinning. They were in a seminar room at the University, lounging in seats facing a big map of Fourth Level Aryan-Transpacific Hostigos, Nostor, northeastern Sask and northern Beshta.

"Didn't I tell you he's a genius?"

"Just how much genius did it take to lick a bunch of

klunks like that?" the operations director challenged. "From all the reports I got on it, they licked themselves."

"Well, a great deal, accurately to predict the mistakes they'd make, and then plan to take advantage of them," the elderly professor of paratemporal probability theory pronounced. He saw it was a brilliant theoretical accomplishment, vindicated by experiment. "I agree with Chief's Assistant Verkan; the man is a genius. Wait till we get this worked up a little more completely!"

"He knew the military history of his own time line," the historian said. "And he knew how to apply it." She wasn't going to let her own subject be ignored. "Actually, I think Gormoth planned a good campaign—against Ptosphes and Chartiphon. Without Kalvan, they'd never have won."

"Well, Ptosphes and Chartiphon fought a battle of their own and won, didn't they?"

"More or less. Netzigon was supposed to wait across the river till Klestreus got up to Vryllos Gap, but Chartiphon started cannonading him—ordnance engineering by Kalvan—and Netzigon couldn't take it."

"Well, why didn't he pull back out of range? He knew Chartiphon couldn't get his cannon over the river."

"Oh, that wouldn't have been honorable. Besides, he didn't want the mercenaries to win the war, he wanted the honor of winning it."

"How often I've heard *that* one!" the historian laughed. "But don't the Hostigi go in for this honor jazz, too? On that cultural level—"

"Sure, till Kalvan talked them out of it. As soon as he started making better-than-Styphon's powder, he gained a moral ascendancy over them. Indispensable Man. And then, the new swordplay, the new tactics, the artillery improvements; now it's 'Trust Lord Kalvan; Lord Kalvan is always right.' "

"He'll have to keep working at that. He won't dare make any mistakes. But what happened to Netzigon?"

"He made three attempts to cross a hundred yards of river in the face of an artillery superiority. That was when he lost most of his cavalry. Then he threw his infantry across at Vryllos, pushed Ptosphes back into the gap, and started a flank attack on Chartiphon up the south bank of the river. Ptosphes didn't stay pushed; he counter-attacked and flanked Netzigon. Then the girl, Rylla, took a hundred-odd cavalry across, burned Netzigon's camp, slaughtered a lot of camp followers, and started a panic in Netzigon's rear."

"That was too bad about Rylla," the lady historian said.

He shrugged. "That can happen in battles, any size. That's why Dalla's always worried when she hears I've been in one. Well, then everything went to pieces and the pieces began breaking up. We had a couple of conveyors in on antigrav last night. They had to stay above twenty thousand feet, we didn't want any heavenly portents on top of everything else, but they got some good infrared telephoto pictures. Fires all over the western end of Nostor, and for a two-mile radius around Dyssa, and in the southeast, that was Kalvan and Harmakros. And a lot of entrenching and fortifying around Nostor Town; Gormoth thinks he's going to have to fight the next battle there."

"That's ridiculous!" the operations director declared. "It'll be a couple of weeks before Kalvan has his army reorganized, after those two battles. And powder; how much do you suppose he has left?"

"Five or six tons. That just came in a little after noon, from our people in Hostigos Town. After he crossed the river, Harmakros captured a wagon train. An Archpriest of Styphon's House, on his way to Nostor Town, with four tons of fireseed for Gormoth—and seven thousand ounces of gold."

The operations director whistled. "Man! That's making war support war, now!"

"And another ton or so in Klestreus' supply train, and Klestreus' pay chest," he added. "Hostigos came out of this deal pretty well."

"Wait till we get this all worked up," the paratemporal probability theorist was cackling. "Absolute proof of the decisive effect of one superior individual on the course of history. Kalthar Morth and his Historical Inevitability, and his vast, impersonal, social forces, indeed!"

Gormoth of Nostor stood with an arm over his companion's shoulder—nobly clad, freshly bathed and barbered, with a gold chain about his neck, Duke Skranga looked nothing like the vagrant horse trader who had come to Nostor half a moon ago. Together they stared at the crowd in the Presence Chamber. Netzigon, who had come stumbling in after midnight with all his guns and half his army lost and the rest a frightened rabble; his cousin Pheblon, his ransom still unpaid; the nobles of the Elite Guard who had attended him yesterday, waiting with him for news of victory until news of defeat had come; three officers of Klestreus' mercenaries who had got through Narza Gap, and several more who had managed to cross at Marax Ford alive. And Vyblos, the high priest, and with him Krastokles, the Archpriest of Styphon's House Upon Earth, and his black-armored guard captain, who had arrived with half a dozen men on broken-down horses at dawn.

He hated the sight of all of them, and the two priests most of all, and wasted no words on them.

"This is Duke Skranga. Next to me, he is first nobleman of Nostor. He takes precedence of all here." The faces in front of him went slack with amazement, then stiffened angrily. A mutter of protest was hushed almost as it began. "Do any object? Then he'd better be one who's served me half as well as Skranga, and I see none such here." He turned to Vyblos. "What do you want here, and who's this with you?"

"His Sanctity the Archpriest Krastokles, sent by His Divinity Styphon's Voice," Vyblos began angrily. "And how has he fared, coming here? Set upon by Hostigi heathens, hounded through the hills like a deer, his people murdered, his wagons pillaged—"

"His wagons, by the mace of Galzar! My gold and fireseed, sent me by Styphon's Voice in his care, and look how he cared for it! He and Styphon between them!"

"Blasphemy!" A dozen voices said it at once. Vyblos', and Krastokles', and the guard captain's. And, among others, Netzigon's.

Now, by Galzar, didn't he have a fine right to open his mouth here? Anger sickened him; in a moment he thought he would vomit pure bile. He strode to Netzigon, snatching the golden chief captain's chain from over his shoulders and striking him in the face with it, reviling him with obscenity upon malediction.

"Out of my sight! I told you to wait at Listra-Mouth for Klestreus, not to throw your army away with his. By Galzar, I ought to flay you alive! Go, now, while you can!"

"Speak not of your fireseed and your gold," Krastokles told him. "They were the god's gold and fireseed, to be given to you for use in the god's service at my discretion."

"And lost at your indiscretion; you witless fool in a yellow bed-gown. Didn't you know a battle when you saw one in front of you? Vyblos, take this fellow you brought, and get you back to your temple with him, and come here again at my bidding or at your peril. Now go!"

He looked at the golden chain in his hand, then tossed it over the head of his cousin Pheblon.

"I still don't thank you for losing me Tarr-Dombra, but that's a handful of dried peas to what that son of a horseleech's daughter's lost me. Now, Galzar help you, you'll have to make an army out of what he's left you."

"My ransom still needs paying," Pheblon reminded him. "Till that's done, I'm still oath-bound."

"So you are. Twenty thousand ounces of silver, do you know where I can find it? I don't."

"I do, Prince," Skranga said. "There should be five times that much in the treasure vault of the temple of Styphon, here."

His horse stumbled, jerking him awake, and he got back onto the road. Behind him clattered fifty-odd men, most more or less wounded, but none seriously. There had been a score on horse-litters or barely able to cling to their mounts, but they had been left at the base hospital in Sevenhills Valley. He couldn't remember how long it had been since he had had his clothes off, or even all his armor. Except for pauses of a quarter-hour now and then, he hadn't been out of the saddle since daybreak, when he had crossed the Athan with the smoke of southern Nostor behind him.

That had been as bad as Phil Sheridan in the Shenandoah, but every time some peasant's thatch blazed up, he knew it was burning holes in Prince Gormoth's morale. He had felt better about it after seeing the mile-wide swath of devastation along the main road in East Hostigos; at Systros, there wasn't a house unburned. It stopped dramatically short at Fitra, and that made him feel best of all.

And the story Harmakros' stragglers had told him—fifteen eight-horse wagons, four tons of fireseed, seven thousand ounces of gold, that was at least one hundred fifty thousand dollars, three hundred new calivers and six hundred pistols; a wagon-load of plate armor. Too bad that archpriest got away, his execution would have been a big public attraction in Hostigos Town.

He had passed prisoners marching west, mercenaries, under arms and in good spirits, at least one pike or lance in each detachment sporting red and blue colors. Some of them shouted "Down Styphon!" as he rode past. The back road from Fitra to Sevenhills Valley had not been so bad, but now, in what he had formerly known as Nittany Valley, the traffic became heavy again. Militia from Listra-Mouth and Vryllos, marching like regulars, which was what they were, now. Lines of farm wagons, piled with sacks and barrels and furniture that must have come from manor houses. Droves of cattle, and droves of prisoners not in good spirits and not armed, under heavy guard; Nostori headed for labor camps and intensive Styphon-is-a-fake indoctrination. And guns, on four-wheel carts, that he couldn't remember from any Hostigi ordnance inventory.

Hostigos Town was in an all-time record traffic jam. He ran into the mercenary artillery captain, wearing his sword and dagger, with a strip of blue cloth that seemed to have been torn from a bedspread and a red strip from the bottom of a petticoat. He was magnificently drunk.

"Lord Kalvan!" he shouted. "I saw your guns; they're wonderful! What god taught you that? Can you mount mine that way?"

"I think so. I'll have to talk with you about it tomorrow, if I'm awake then."

Harmakros was on his horse in the square, his rapier drawn, trying to untangle the chaos of wagons and carts and riders. He shouted to him above the din:

"What the Styphon; when did we start using three-star generals for traffic cops around here?"

MP's, of course; how the devil had he forgotten about that. *Memo: Organize, soonest.*

"Just till I can get a detail here. I sent all my own crowd up to the castle with the wagons." He started to say something else, stopped, and asked: "Did anybody tell you about Rylla?"

He went cold under his scalding armor. "Great Dralm, no. What about her?" It seemed eternity before Harmakros answered:

"She was hurt; late yesterday, across the river. Her horse threw her, or something; I only know what one of Chartiphon's aides told me. She's at the castle—"

"Thanks; I'll see you later."

He plowed his horse into the crowd. People got out of his way and yelled to those beyond. Outside town, the road was choked with things too big and slow to get out of the way, and mostly he rode in the ditch. The wagons Harmakros had captured were going up to Tarr-Hostigos, huge covered things like Conestogas with the drivers riding the nigh horses. He thought he'd never get past them, there was always another one ahead. Finally, he rode through the outer gate of Tarr-Hostigos.

Throwing his reins to somebody, he stumbled up the steps to the keep and through the door. From the Staff Room he heard laughing voices, Ptosphes' among them. For an instant he was horrified, then a little reassured. If Ptosphes could laugh, maybe it wasn't so bad.

He was mobbed as soon as he entered; everybody was shouting his name and thumping him on the back, he was glad for his armor. A goblet of wine was thrust into his hand. Ptosphes, Xentos, Chartiphon, most of the General Staff—and a dozen officers decked with red and blue, whom he had never seen before.

"Kalvan, this is General Klestreus," Ptosphes was saying, to introduce a big man with gray hair and a florid face.

"An honor, General; you fought most brilliantly and valiantly." He'd fought like a damned imbecile, and his army had been chopped to hamburger, but let's be polite. He raised his goblet to the mercenary and drank. It was winter wine, set out in tubs to freeze and the ice thrown off until it was almost as strong as brandy. Maybe sixty proof, the closest they had to spirits here-and-now. It made him feel better, and he drank more.

"Rylla; what happened to her?" he asked her father.

"Why, she broke a leg," Ptosphes began.

That scared him. People had died of broken legs in his former world, when the level of the medical art was at least up to here-and-now. They used to amputate—

"She's all right, Kalvan," Xentos was saying. "None of us would be here if she were in any danger. Brother Mytron is with her. If she's awake, she'll want to see you."

"Then I'll go to her." He finished his wine and put the goblet down; drew off his helmet and coif and put them beside it, stuffed his gloves through his belt. "You'll all excuse me—"

Rylla, whom he had expected to find gasping her last, sat propped against a pile of pillows in bed, smoking a pipe with a cane stem and a silver-inlaid redstone bowl. She wore a loose gown, and her right leg was buckled into a huge contraption of saddle-leather. Mytron, the chubby priest-physician, was with her, as were several of the women who functioned as midwives, herb-boilers, hexers and general nurses. Rylla saw him first; her face lighted like sunrise.

"Hi, Kalvan! Are you all right? When did you get in? How was the battle?"

"Rylla, darling!" The women sprayed away from in front of him like grasshoppers. She flung her arms around his neck as he bent over her; he thought Mytron stepped in to relieve her of the pipe. "What happened to you?"

"You stopped in the Staff Room," she told him, between kisses. "I smell it on you."

"Well, what did happen?"

"Oh, my horse fell on me. We were burning a Nostori village, and he stepped on a hot ember." Yes, just like William the Conqueror. Nantes, 1087, the history professor in the back of his mind reminded him. "He almost threw me, and then fell over something, and down we both went. I had an extra pair of pistols down my boot-tops; I fell on one of them. The horse broke a leg, too, and they shot him."

"How is she, Mytron?"

"Nothing to worry about, Lord Kalvan! It's a beautiful fracture. A priest of Galzar set it—"

"And gave me a Styphon's own lump on the head, too. And now, it'll be a couple of moons till we can have a wedding."

"Why, we could have it now—"

"I will not be married in my bedroom. I will be married in the temple, and I won't be on crutches."

"It's your wedding, Princess." He hoped that the war with Sask everybody expected would be out of the way before she was back in the saddle. "Somebody," he said over his shoulder, "go and have a hot bath brought to my room, and tell me when it's ready. I must stink to the very throne of Dralm."

"I was wondering when you'd mention that, darling."

Sesklos, Supreme Priest and Styphon's Voice, rested his elbows on the table and palmed his smarting eyes. Around him pens scratched and parchments rustled and tablets clattered. He longed for the cool quiet of the Innermost Circle, but there was so much to do.

The letter from the Archpriest of the Great Temple of Hos-Agrys lay before him. News of the defeat of Prince Gormoth's armies was spreading, and with it rumors that Ptosphes of Hostigos was making fireseed for himself. Agentsinquisitory reported that the ingredients and even the proportions and processes were being bandied in the taverns. To kill everyone who knew the secret was quite out of the question; even a pestilence couldn't do that. And how to check the spread of the secret without further divulging it?

He opened his eyes. Admit it; better that than deny it and later be proven liars. Let everyone, even the lay guards, know the full secret, but, for believers, insist that special prayers and rites, which only yellow-robe priests could perform, were necessary.

But why? Soon it would be known to all that fireseed made by unconsecrated hands would fire as well.

Well, there were malignant demons of the netherworld. Everybody knew that. He smiled, imagining them thronging about, scrawny bodies, bat wings, bristling beards, clawed and fanged. In fireseed there were many of them, and only the prayers of anointed priests of Styphon could slay them. If this were not done, as soon as the fireseed was exploded, they would be set free into the world of men, to work manifold evils and frights. And, of course, the curse of Styphon was upon all who made fireseed unconsecrated.

But Ptosphes had made fireseed and had not been smitten, and he had pillaged a temple-farm and massacred the priests, and after that he had defeated the armies of Prince Gormoth, who marched with Styphon's blessing. How about that, now?

But wait!- Gormoth was no better than Ptosphes. He had made fireseed himself, both Krastokles and Vyblos were sure of it, and he had blasphemed Styphon, and despitefully used a holy archpriest, and forced a hundred thousand ounces of silver from the Nostor temple, at as close to pistol-point as didn't matter. To be sure, most of that had been after the battle, but who outside Nostor would know that? Gormoth had suffered defeat for his sins.

He was smiling happily, now. Of course, Hostigos must be utterly destroyed and ruined, and all in it put to the sword; the world must see, once and for all, what befell a land that turned its back on Styphon. Sarrask of Sask would have to do that; Gormoth couldn't, even if he could be trusted to. Sarrask, and Balthar, Prince of Beshta; Sarrask had been seeking a Beshtan alliance, and now was offering his daughter, Amnita, in marriage to Prince Balthar's younger brother, Balthames. An idea began to seep up into his mind.

Balthames wanted to be a Prince, too. It needed only a poisoned cup or a hired dagger to make him Prince of Beshta, and Balthar knew it. He wanted Balthames and his ambitions removed; should have had him killed long ago. Now, suppose Balthames married this wench of Sarrask's; suppose Sarrask gave up a little corner of Sask, and Balthar a little corner of Beshta, both adjoining Hostigos. Call it the Princedom of Sashta. To it could be added all western Hostigos south of the mountains; why, that would be a nice little princedom for any young couple. He smiled benevolently. And the father of the bride and the brother of the groom could recompense themselves, respectively, with the Listra Valley, rich in iron, and East Hostigos.

That should be done immediately, before winter set it; then, in the spring, Sarrask, Balthames and Balthar could hurl their combined armies out of conquered Hostigos into Nostor. He'd send out another archpriest of Styphon's House Upon Earth . . . let's see who that should be . . . to Sask, to make arrangements—with lavish gifts of money and fireseed for Sarrask and Balthar. And this time, make sure the treasures of Styphon's House did not fall into the hands of the infidel.

THREE SOLDIERS

by D. C. Poyer

The blackness opened, and von Rheydt swam up through inky velvet to a consciousness that he had never expected to see again.

He did not move, not even opening his eyes.

Von Rheydt remembered falling face down in the snow, fingers clutching the sudden wetness in the pit of his stomach, hearing the soft crunch of millions of six-pointed ice crystals as his face sank toward the Russian earth.

Hauptmann (Captain) von Rheydt noticed, without surprise, that he did not feel particularly cold, nor could he feel anything where the bullet had struck him. He was waiting, eyes closed and mind blank, for a Russian bayonet.

The white-coated troops who followed the tanks always checked the fallen Germans for signs of life. That, he thought remotely, must be why he was now face up. One of the Red troops must have turned him over while he was unconscious to check on the seriousness of his wound.

It must be bad if they hadn't bothered to use a bayonet, he thought. Maybe that was why he couldn't feel anything in his stomach.

Minutes passed. Von Rheydt waited. It was very quiet.

Too quiet, he thought suddenly. He could hear nothing but his heart. No machine-gun fire, neither the *tap-tap-tap* of the Degtyarevs nor the high cloth-ripping sound of the German guns. No grunting of tank engines, no shouts of "Oooray!" as the Red Army charged. Not even—and this was the strangest of all—not even the sighing of the wind over the plains of Stalingrad in this year of struggle 1942.

He opened his eyes, tensing himself for the bayonet. Above him was a gray ceiling.

A hospital, he thought. German or Russian? That was easy to answer. The Soviets did not waste hospital space on wounded enemy officers. So he was in friendly hands. A smile creased his thin, blond-stubbled face, and he sat up without thinking. And stared down at the crisp, unstained gray of his battle-dress tunic. No holes. No blood. After several seconds he touched his stomach with one hand. He was unwounded.

Captain Werner von Rheydt, German Army, thirty years old, educated at Göttingen . . . *memory's all right*, he thought confusedly, still looking down at his stomach. Had he dreamed it, then? His brow furrowed. The University . . . the war . . . the draft . . . the Polish campaign, then France, then Yugoslavia, and so to the Russian Front. To Stalingrad with the 44th Infantry, Sixth Army, after four years of war. To the madness of Stalingrad in winter, an entire army surrounded, abandoned, but still fighting. . . .

No, it was not a dream, von Rheydt concluded silently. Line "Violet" had fallen; and in the fighting retreat to "Sunflower," the Soviet tanks had broken through. He had led a counterattack and had fallen, badly wounded, on a snowy battlefield two thousand miles from home. And he was now—here.

He swung his boots over the edge of the bunk and noticed it for the first time. It was a plain Reichsheer-issue steel bunk, standard thin pallet mattress with a dingy pillow and a gray wool blanket.

He stood up and the momentary sense of reassurance the familiar-looking bunk had given him disappeared. He stared around at a room that was far too strange for a dream.

It's gray, he thought, but the gray was strange. Not a painted color, but a hard shininess like the dull sheen of polished metal. But the shape—it was the shape of the room that was different. He stood at the bottom of an octagon and at the center of one; the room had eight walls, and its cross-section was an octagon as well. He counted, came up with a total of twenty-six facets.

A pile of what looked like military equipment was stuck oddly to one of the eight vertical walls. Von Rheydt walked forward to investigate, stepped up on a slanted facet of the room to reach up—and found the pile on a slanted face just in front of him. He looked back at the bunk. It too was on a slanted face and looked as if it should come sliding down on him at any moment.

And there was no question but that the facet he had stepped up on was now at the bottom of the room.

Queer, thought von Rheydt. He walked on, stood next to the pile. Now that facet was the floor, and the bunk hung ludicrously on a vertical wall.

Feeling a touch of nausea, he bent to the heap of equipment. It was not his own, he saw, but it was all standard army. Helmet, battle, one, white-painted for winter wear. Canteen. Pack ration. An officer's dress dagger, which he examined closely, scowling as he saw the double lightning strokes of the SS; the army and Himmler's thugs had never gotten along, and of late there had been rumors . . . shadowy but horrible rumors. A dress sword, plain but of good Solingen steel. At the very bottom of the heap he found what he had been hoping for: a Luger. A quick investigation revealed six cartridges in its magazine.

Von Rheydt smiled as he buckled on the pistol belt. Having a weapon made him feel much more confident *wherever* he was. He buckled on the dagger too, and began walking again, continuing around the room. His boots clicked arrogantly on the hard surface.

Halfway around—the "floor," inexplicably, still underneath his feet—he noticed a grille set into its surface. He bent to look into it.

A black, grimacing face, horribly furrowed with scars and paint, stared back him, teeth bared. Von Rheydt recoiled, drawing the dagger. At his motion, the face disappeared, drawn back from the grille.

Beyond wonder, he walked on. In the next facet of the room was a door, or hatch, set flush with the gray surface and of the same material. There was no knob or handle, and he was unable to get the point of the dagger far enough into the seam to pry it open. He went on and had almost reached the bunk again before he saw something else on the smooth sameness of gray.

It was another grille. This one he approached with dagger drawn, but there was no one at it. He bent and peered through it, seeing on the other side another room like his own.

"Anyone there?" he called loudly.

The quick pad of footsteps came up to the grille and a moment later a hard-looking, tanned face stared out. A second or so passed, and then the man barked out a question.

It took several seconds for von Rheydt to realize that the

strong-jawed, dark-haired man on the other side of the grille had said, "Who are you?"—*in Latin.*

Von Rheydt searched his mind for the moldly words he had struggled over at Göttingen. "*Ego sum . . .* von Rheydt," he said haltingly. "Ah . . . *sum miles Germanicus . . . amicus. Amicus,* friend *Et tu?*"

The other man spoke rapidly; not classical Latin, but a rough, corrupt-sounding tongue with a Spanish rhythm. Von Rheydt caught a word here and there, enough to piece the sense together. "Roman soldier . . . Nineteenth Legion. Into the forest, the battle against Arminius . . . spear wound . . . slept." The Roman passed a hand over his close-cropped, dark hair, looking puzzled as if trying to remember something. "Slept. . . ."

Von Rheydt started to speak in German, stopped, said in Latin: "You are a *Roman soldier?*"

"*Centurio,*" corrected the man, showing a massive gold ring on his powerful-looking hand. "Junius Cornelius Casca, centurion second rank, Nineteenth Legion, General Varus commanding."

"Centurion Casca . . . what year is this?"

The other man—Casca—frowned through the grille. "Year? What year? Why, 762, *ab urbe condita,* and thirty-eighth year of the principate of Augustus." His heavy brows drew together. "Where are we, German? What prison is this?"

Von Rheydt did not answer immediately for he was chasing a phrase down dusty corridors of his mind. *Ab urbe condita . . .* literally, from founding the city . . . yes, he remembered. The legendary founding of Rome, 753 B.C., the date used to reckon time by the Empire. This man Casca, then, could be . . . almost two thousand years old?

And then something else clicked in his mind. P. Quintilius Varus, leading the Nineteenth Legion into Gaul. Sent to crush the Chirusci revolt under Arminius. *Surrounded and massacred without a survivor, late in the reign of Augustus Caesar. . . .*

"*Non certe scire*—I don't know," he said slowly, trying to match stale school Latin to the cadence the other man used. The Roman laughed, a short, bitter sound.

Von Rheydt looked up from the grille. He looked at the bunk that stuck to the wall like a fly, at the strangeness of the gray metal walls, at the light that filled the room without visible source. He remembered the gravity that followed wherever he walked.

He had been wounded in 1942, on the frozen plains of Stalingrad. Just as this Casca, this Roman, had been wounded in the forests of Teutoburgium in nine A.D. They had been snatched away. *But to where?* he asked himself. *And what year is it in this strange cell—9, or 1942 A.D.?*

The Roman had left the grille, and von Rheydt slowly stood up. He looked vacantly around the room, then walked back to the bunk and sat down.

Fifteen minutes later he got up and went to the first grille, the one at which he had seen the black man. He was there again, big hands wrapped around the gray metal bars that separated the rooms. Von Rheydt wondered whether the other man was kneeling too, and if so—where did the room's gravity come from? From the gray metal of its walls?

"Verstehen Sie Deutsch?"

The man looked at him without expression, and von Rheydt sat back on his haunches and studied him. The face was broad, thick-lipped and strong; though the paint stripes were obviously meant for adornment or intimidation, the scars looked like battle scars rather than tattoo or ritual mutilation. The man's hair was done up in a doughnut-shaped ring atop the wide skull, and his eyes, dark and intelligent, were studying the German with every bit as much interest as they were being given. Von Rheydt tried Latin after a time, and then French, of which he had picked up a few words during the 1940 campaign.

No luck. The man was listening intently though, and when von Rheydt paused, he placed his outstretched fingers on his broad, bare chest and said several words in a gutteral, clicking language:

"Ngi wum Zulu."

Von Rheydt tried to understand but ended by shaking his head in frustration. Did *ngi* mean "My name is"? If only they had a few words of *some* language in common!

"You . . . are English?"

Von Rheydt started. His roommate at school had been English; he had picked up a fair amount of the language. "No. German. Who are you?"

The warrior placed his hand on his chest again and said slowly, "Mbatha. Of . . . the Zulu. This is . . . gaol?"

The language lesson lasted for about an hour.

By the time he was fully awake, von Rheydt had rolled out of the bunk and had the Luger in his hand—safety off;

Stalingrad reflexes. He scrutinized his surroundings from a crouch before he stood up, holstering the pistol. The room was as empty, the light as steady, as when he had gone to sleep. Only one thing was different: The door had opened. He approached it cautiously, one hand still on the butt of the weapon.

As far as he could make out, the door had disappeared. There were no hinges, and the inside of the jamb was smooth and featureless; it could not have slid inside the wall. He remembered how impressed he'd been with the automatic doors he'd seen before the war in Berlin department stores, and grinned humorlessly.

Feeling a little like a cautious ape, von Rheydt stepped through the door. He looked to either side, down a long, narrow, gray-lit corridor with four welcome right angles to the walls. To his left the corridor fell away into darkness; to his right it was lit with the same sourceless brightness, stretching away into the distance.

There was a high, almost musical note behind him . . . the sound, he realized, that had awakened him. He turned and found the door in place, locked. He could see no way to open it.

Shrugging, he loosened the dagger in its sheath, placed his hand near the pistol and walked down the corridor to the right. He passed the outline of another door, and then another. A thought struck him, and he tried to step up on a wall; no good. The every-wall-a-floor device wasn't used in corridors, then.

Octagonal rooms . . . doors . . . square corridors . . . the layout of the place came into focus as he walked. Von Rheydt visualized a grid of octagons, side to side, their corners forming four-sided longitudinal corridors. The corridors would lead the length of . . . what? The arrangement was an inhumanly efficient utilization of space, so space must be at a premium here. He walked along, staying alert, but thinking as well.

As a boy he had read Hermann Oberth's and Willy Ley's books about interplanetary flight. Read them avidly, until his father had thrown them all away and forbidden him to read such trash. Was he aboard such an interplanetary rocket? Or . . . and von Rheydt felt uneasy at the thought . . . was he, and the Zulu and the Roman, trapped in something as far beyond his imagination as Stukas and Königpanzer tanks were beyond Casca's?

He came to an open hatch, stepped in and snapped to rigid attention, a look of surprise flashing across his face.

The room was gray and octagonal; but in the center of it sat a desk, and at the desk stood a man. A hard-looking man of middle age, dressed in the high-collared tunic and red-striped trousers of a general of the O.K.W.—the General Staff. A man with sharp eyes and a rocklike chin, who nodded to von Rheydt's astounded salute and motioned to a chair.

"Sit down, Captain," he said in clear, Prussian-accented German. "Smoke?"

Von Rheydt sat, shook his head. "Thank you, no, Herr General."

"Well," said the general, studying him for a moment while taking a long cigar from a box on the desk, lighting it carefully and exhaling a puff of aromatic smoke. "You are a bit confused, no doubt."

"That is an understatement, Herr General."

"I suppose so. We expected that you would be—you and your two companions. We owe you an explanation. You are here, Captain von Rheydt, because you are a brave man."

"For Leader and Reich," said von Rheydt automatically.

The man in the general's uniform glanced at him sharply. "Yes. Of course. But tell me, Captain. Would you fight as bravely as you fought at Stalingrad—surrounded, outnumbered, abandoned by your leader—if, say the future of your species was at stake?"

"I beg the general's pardon?" said von Rheydt.

"How did you come here, Captain?"

"Here . . . I don't know, Herr General. The last thing I recall is leading an infantry counterattack against Soviet tanks. . . ."

"Against *tanks*?"

"Those were my orders, Herr General," said von Rheydt. "And then a strange thing happened. I thought that I was wounded."

"That is not quite correct. You were killed."

"Killed . . . but I am alive!"

"Are you, Captain?"

Frozen, von Rheydt stared at the general's face. He felt his heart beating, felt the breath that rustled in his throat and the hunger that was beginning to stir in his bowels. "Yes, Herr General, I am alive."

"You died at Stalingrad in 1942, Captain. I am sorry."

Von Rheydt gripped the arms of his chair. "Explain yourself, Herr General. This is going beyond a joke!"

The older man chuckled. "This is not a joke, Captain. And I am not a general. Those of your time would not even consider me a man. Especially—you will pardon the emphasis—am I not a German."

"Not a German . . ." began von Rheydt, presentiment growing in his mind. "You are not of my time?"

"Nor of your species," said the general. "But—just as one stoops down when addressing a child—I am addressing you in a form that you can understand, one that, to your mind, embodies authority and command. As a general officer of the O.K.W."

"What do you want?" asked von Rheydt harshly.

"Simply this," said the officer, rising from the desk. His chrome leather boots clicked on the floor as he paced back and forth, hands interlocked behind his back, a cloud of cigar smoke trailing behind him. He began to speak, looking sharply at the seated captain each time he turned. "You are familiar with war, Hauptmann von Rheydt. As are your two comrades. Well, envision, if you can, a war that encompasses a galaxy and that has lasted for well over a million of your years. A war in which entire races are developed, deployed and used as weapons, as you develop new tanks or rifles."

In spite of what it meant, von Rheydt knew the man was telling the truth. He shook his head. "And the fact that, as you say, I am dead?"

"You *were* dead," the general corrected gravely. "Until we intervened. But we are offering you, and your companions, the chance to return."

"How?"

"By fighting."

"Fighting for you? In this war of yours?"

"Not quite. Let me explain a little further." The general stopped pacing, crossed his arms and looked down at the captain. A wreath of cigar smoke gradually encircled the hard features. "Your race has always been puzzled by its own killer instincts, plagued by its own love for war. To you it was tragic, inexplicable. It seemed contrary to all the laws of evolution, for it killed off not the old and weak, but the young and strong. Correct?"

"Yes."

"Your race, Captain, has been, shall we say, in development. Forced development. To forge a warlike race, one must have wars."

"That is obvious, Herr General. The Fuhrer has said that himself."

"Yes," said the general, looking at the ceiling. "The Fuhrer . . . we will have to recall him soon and cover his disappearance in some convincing manner. But back to the subject at hand. Your species has developed very promisingly. It can be very useful, to us, if . . ."

"If?"

"If you prove yourselves to be an effective weapon in a test. Tell me, Captain, if your army had developed two types of hand grenade and wished to determine which of the two would prove a more effective weapon, how would it go about it?"

"Well, the answer would be to conduct a comparative evaluation," began von Rheydt, and then he saw it. "There is another race of warriors," he said flatly. "Another one of your 'weapons projects.' "

"Very good!" said the general, smiling. "Correct. Please go on."

"Somehow, I don't know how, you've been able to . . . go back in time and pick up the other two men, Casca and Mbatha. Roman and Zulu and German—your choice for the most warlike races of earth's history, I suppose. And now you will match us against the others, I suppose."

"Exactly," said the general, raising his eyebrows in pleased surprise and perching one leg on the edge of his desk. "An intelligent species as well as a warlike one. Very good, Captain."

"But why pick us?" asked von Rheydt. "Front-line soldiers, all three of us. If you had all history to choose from, why not Napoleon, or Caesar, or Frederick the Great? They were true men of war."

"Not quite," said the general. He tapped the cigar into a glass ashtray and examined the glowing tip. "The men you name were leaders, not soldiers. Since, in this war, *we* will provide all necessary leadership, they would be of little value to us. No, what we value in our weapons is different. Take the three of you. Stalingrad, Teutoburgium, and Ulundi—all battles in which a body of professional soldiers, abandoned, almost leaderless, and greatly outnumbered, stood and fought to the death *because they valued obedience above life.*"

Von Rheydt sat motionless. The general went on: "We need soldiers like that. So far in your history your three cultures have shown us what we can expect from the human race at its most disciplined, most obedient and most un-thinking best."

"As you say," said von Rheydt slowly. "We are soldiers, then. But what good will our victory do for our race? Make mankind a pawn in a struggle we know nothing about?"

"It is that or extinction," said the general quietly. "To put it in army terms, Captain, the Human project is at the crossroads. It must now either be put into full production or it must be liquidated and the resources shifted to another project. I'm sure you realize, Captain, that in total war there is no other way."

Von Rheydt stood up stiffly, put one hand on his dagger and clicked his heels. His other hand shot out in a quivering salute.

"You will find us good soldiers," he said.

"I hope so," said the general. "Tell the others, Captain. Ten hours from now, the three of you will fight. I suggest that you all get some sleep." The high-pitched note of an opening hatch came from behind the rigid German. "Dismissed!"

Von Rheydt pivoted smartly and marched out. Outside, in the corridor, he turned. The door was not yet closed, and he caught a glimpse, not of a stiff O.K.W. general at a German army desk, but of something that sent him, mind reeling, stumbling down the corridor.

Von Rheydt's school Latin seemed to be coming back; Casca, listening at the grille, nodded slowly and frowned as he finished his explanation of the upcoming test. "I have been thinking, German. The *framea* (spear?) could not have healed like this." He drew up a dirty tunic and showed von Rheydt a smooth, unmarked chest covered with curly black hair. "When will we go into battle?"

"About nine hours from now."

"I am ready," said the centurion. "I found some arms in my room. I will sleep, I think, before the contest of the gods."

"The gods? . . . Yes," said von Rheydt, realizing the inadequacy of his Latin to explain alien races and galactic wars to a man who thought the earth flat. "Yes, sleep well, Junius."

Mbatha was not at his grille. Von Rheydt drew his dagger, stuck it through the bars and rattled it to attract the Zulu's attention. An instant later he froze as the point of a broad-bladed, razor-sharp *assegai* touched his throat.

Von Rheydt smiled as he let go of the dagger, which the African took and examined critically, at last pulling back the *assegai* and returning the knife to the German.

"We must fight soon, Mbatha," said von Rheydt in English. "You, me, and Casca, the other man with us. We must win. If we lose, we die."

"Fight English? Fight you and Casca?"

"No, you do not fight us," said von Rheydt desperately, thinking that the three of them might have to act as a team in a very few hours; having one man suspicious of the other two might kill them all. The Zulu had fallen fighting white men; to him all whites were the hated English. "I am not English. Casca is not English. We three men fight three . . . devils."

"Devils?" said the African.

"Spirits. Ghosts."

"Ghosts," repeated the Zulu, deadpan. "Warriors cannot fight ghosts, u-Rheydt."

"We don't have a choice, Mbatha. We fight in the morning—in one sleep."

"I sleep now, u-Rheydt," said Mbatha and left the grating. A scraping sound came from his room for a few minutes, and then silence.

Von Rheydt went back to his bunk and sat down, eased his boots off. He had a light meal of tinned sausage and biscuit from the ration pack and found what tasted like vodka in the canteen. When he had finished his meal, he lay back on the bunk, placed the Luger under his pillow and fell into a heavy sleep.

"Captain von Rheydt," said the voice in his dream, and he jerked away. "It is time," said the voice, and as its meaning sank in, he came slowly back to reality.

He went to the grilles and made sure that Mbatha and Casca were both awake. They were, looking around their rooms; they must have heard the voice as well. As von Rheydt pulled on his boots, he wondered, *In what language had it spoken to them?*

He stood up, stamped his feet into the boots and walked to the pile of gear. He buckled on the scabbard of the dress saber over his pistol belt and stuck the dagger under it. He tightened the belt of his uniform trousers and tucked the cuffs into his boots. Finally he walked back to his bunk, took the pistol from under his pillow, checked the chamber, tucked the gun into its holster and buttoned the leather flap over it.

He was tightening the leather chinstrap of his helmet when the door bonged. With a last look around, he picked up the canteen, slung it from his shoulder and stepped out into the corridor.

Mbatha was already there waiting, and von Rheydt's eyebrows rose.

The Zulu was big —muscular as well as tall. His broad, bare chest was crisscrossed with dark, puckered scars. A short skirt of animal pelt fell from waist to mid-thigh, and at elbow and knee blossomed fringes of white feathers. The African was carrying a short thrusting spear at his waist, a slightly longer one in his right hand and an oval cowhide shield on his back. A necklace of yellow animal teeth clicked against his chest.

Before von Rheydt could speak, there was a rattle of metal, and the German turned to see Junius Cornelius Casca raise a hand in greeting to the Zulu.

The centurion's dirty tunic was gone, hidden by a burnished corselet of horizontal hoops of steel. Leather padding showed under half-hoops of deeply gouged metal protecting the shoulders; the swelling muscles of his arms were bare. A coarse brown-woolen skirt or kilt fell to his knees, and he wore heavy sandals. One big, tanned hand rested on the sheath of a short sword and the other was curled negligently around a square shield, embossed with a wing-and-thunderbolt design. A short, plain dagger rode at his waist, and in spite of the Roman's short stature, the plumes of his centurion's helmet nodded above the taller men. Casca reached out an arm and gripped their hands solemnly, one at a time.

Von Rheydt looked at the two of them, the tall Zulu and the stocky Roman. "If it is the fate of a soldier to die," he said aloud in his own tongue, "to do it with such men as you is an honor."

They did not understand his harsh German, but they understood that it was a compliment and they nodded grimly. At that moment, one end of the corridor went dark, and they began to march three abreast in the direction of the light. The clang of bronze and steel echoed away in front of them.

The hatch closed behind them, and von Rheydt whispered, "My God." A low grunt of surprise came from Casca. The three men stared around.

They were in a gigantic amphitheater, and it was empty. Von Rheydt looked back, seeing a high wall without a trace of the door through which they had entered. Firm sand grated under their feet, and a red sun above them cast a bloody glow over empty tiers of gray metal seats, stretched to meet a deep violet sky.

Metal scraped as Casca grew the short sword and balanced it at waist level. "In your country, German, do you have the circus?" he asked in his strangely corrupt Latin. "That is what this is like. I have seen the gladiators fight in the imperial city. And now we fight—before the throne of Jove."

Von Rheydt looked at Mbatha, who returned his look without visible expression. "The u-Fasimba do not fight ghosts," said the African slowly. Then the short spear pointed with the speed of a striking snake. "But those . . . those are not ghosts."

Across the flatness of sand, through the atmosphere shimmering with heat, three dark figures stood against the wall of the amphitheater.

Von Rheydt unslung the canteen from his shoulder, took a mouthful of vodka and handed the canteen to the Zulu. When Casca handed it back to him, it was empty, and he dropped it to the sand and drew his saber.

Mbatha started forward at a jog-trot, and Casca and von Rheydt followed, their steps thudding on the hard-packed sand. The figures opposite them swung into motion too, and the two groups, men and Others, closed rapidly.

Fifty meters apart, they both stopped, and von Rheydt's eyes narrowed.

The enemy was not human. From a distance they had resembled men, upright, bipedal, two-armed. But from this distance the differences were horribly evident.

The aliens were taller and thinner than men, but there was no appearance of fragility. They had long hair of a brassy color. *Skin tone?* von Rheydt wondered. Thick, small footpads, like a camel's. The necks were long, leading to a ridiculously small knob of a head. There was no clearly defined face, though he could make out large, dark eyes fixed on the men.

A sound next to him made him turn his head. Casca, eyes fixed on the enemy, had fronted his sword and was murmuring a prayer; when he caught von Rheydt's eyes on him, he grinned but didn't stop. Mbatha had been silent, scrutinizing the enemy; but then he turned his back contemptuously to them and addressed the German.

"We fight, u-Rheydt?" he said. "You—Casca?"

Von Rheydt nodded. "We fight."

Casca finished his prayer and brought the square shield up to cover his breast. Mbatha turned back; and von Rheydt, drawn saber in his right hand, Luger in his left, walked between the armored Roman and the hide-shielded Zulu toward the waiting aliens.

As they closed, he could see variations in their equipment and dress. *They must be of different time too*, he thought. One of them seemed to be sheathed in a blue-metal armor and carried a long staff of the same material. Von Rheydt nudged Junius, pointed with his saber; the Roman nodded, teeth bared, and fixed his eyes on that one. Another was almost naked, and its weapons were two curved, glittering scimitars; Mbatha was already turning toward it when things began to happen.

In a second, the aliens seemed to shrink, from seven feet or so to almost human size. Von Rheydt blinked, then saw what had happened; the "heads" had been withdrawn into the deep chests, and the dark eyes peered over the edge of a protective carapace like a soldier peering from a trench. *The bruin must be inside the chest*, he thought. Well, a bullet would reach it even there.

And even while von Rheydt blinked, the blue-armored alien had lifted a long arm and something swift left the long staff and fell toward him, too fast to dodge.

There was a terrifying loud clang, and a meter-long, blue-metal rod quivered in the sand at his feet. Casca's shield twitched back and the centurion sent a mocking laugh at the being that was drawing another missile from a quiver on its back.

"*Gratias*," said von Rheydt, and then the three men separated and he found himself face to face with the third alien.

Von Rheydt's opponent stood solidly on two feet, neck stalk slightly extended, large, dark eyes fixed on the German. The smooth, brassy-looking skin was bare at the arms and legs but the trunk was covered with a flat black garment that looked incongruously like carbon paper. . . .

But these were details that the captain noted only with his subconscious, for his attention was centered on the short rod that one brassy hand was bringing up stealthily to cover him.

Von Rheydt fired twice, rapidly from the hip. The nine-millimeter jolted his hand and the flat crack of it echoed back from the circled walls of the amphitheater. His opponent reeled back, then steadied, shook itself, and stepped forward, one hand going to its chest and the other raising the rod.

Electricity snapped, and von Rheydt's whole body arced in a spasm. He fell heavily to the sand, face up but unable to move. The alien came toward him, towering up into the purple sky, and lowered the rod to point at von Rheydt's chest.

He recovered movement and brought the saber around in a whistling arc. The alien jumped back but not in time to avoid the stroke, and the German's arm tingled as if he had struck a lamp post. He scrambled back up, retrieving the automatic from the sand. The alien closed with him again, and the point of the saber grated against the black-jerkined chest. The alien backed off a little.

Von Rheydt looked at the saber point. Broken; the tip had gone with that wild slash to the legs. He looked again at his opponent, who was still backing away. Most likely it needed a little range to use the rod, which it was training on him again.

Von Rheydt switched the Luger to his right hand, aimed carefully and sent four bullets caroming off the thing's torso. None penetrated, but the sheer kinetic energy of the eight-gram bullets knocked it back with each hit, and at the last shot it fell, dropping the rod.

Von Rheydt was on the weapon in two bounds, crushing it into the sand under his boot. From the corner of his eye he caught a glimpse of Mbatha and the nearly naked alien, both weaponless, straining in hand-to-hand combat. Von Rheydt reached his alien, placed the muzzle between the wide eyes and pressed the trigger. Only at the empty click did he see that the toggle link was up; there was no more ammunition.

At the same instant a grip of iron closed around his leg and he was jerked off his feet. Dropping the saber and the uscless pistol, he fell on his enemy, hammering with his fists on its chest. He had hoped it was the garment that had deflected his bullets, but it was too flimsy; it was the carapace beneath it that was like steel, impervious to his fists and his weapons alike.

He was being crushed in a close hug when he found the ceremonial dagger in his hand and managed to slice it into the softer flesh of the "neck." The grip loosened, and the two fighters sprang apart and circled warily under the red sun.

Von Rheydt panted, wiped sweat from his eyes with the back of his dagger hand. Pain began to throb in his crushed ankle and in his chest. His opponent's sad eyes watched him unblinkingly as they circled, crouched, arms extended like wrestlers. The cuts on his half-extended neck gaped, but there was no trace of blood. The dark eyes flicked away from von Rheydt once, noting the ruin of its weapon, then slid back to follow the limping German.

Von Rheydt, circling to his right, stepped on something hard, stopped quickly and retrieved it: Mbatha's short spear. He held it low, pointed up at those sad, interested eyes.

This makes it a little more even than hand-to-hand, thought von Rheydt. He felt quite cool, as he usually did once a fight had started. But the odds certainly seemed to favor the alien; that metal-hard skin, its great strength he had felt in his leg, the lack of an exposed brain. The very deliberation with which the creature moved gave an impression of terrible strength. The deliberation of a tank. . . .

Deliberation. Could it be the deliberation not of irresistible power, but of great mass? Anything hard enough to resist a steel-jacketed bullet *must* weigh more than flesh.

At that moment von Rheydt crumpled, as if his injured ankle had given out. He fell to the sand and groaned.

The alien hesitated for a moment, then strode forward, its camellike foodpads making deep impressions on the sand.

It reached the fallen German, and the quick stride turned to a stumble as his spear entwined itself in the long legs. It began to topple over him, and von Rheydt rolled, bounding up. The neck extended as the creature fought for its balance; and then the whole frame jerked as von Rheydt swept the short spear around and rammed its butt into the back of the alien's neck.

It hit the ground so hard that little gouts of dry sand flew up. Von Rheydt reversed the spear and leaned the point into the base of the neck stalk, but the creature did not even shudder. Von Rheydt smiled tightly; there had been a major nerve from the eyes to the brain.

He glanced around for the others and saw Casca grinning at him. The Roman was bareheaded, and blood covered his scalp and the right side of his face; but he was kneeling on the chest of the blue-armored alien and his short sword was at its throat.

Where was Mbatha? He looked around and saw, about twenty meters off, the last minute of *that* combat. The giant Zulu, body shining with sweat, had both hands interlocked on his opponent's back in a powerful full nelson. The alien seemed to sag suddenly; the Zulu's back and shoulder bulged with a great effort, and with a horrible tearing sound, one of the brassy arms was bent far back.

Mbatha dropped the unconscious alien, fell to his knees and was sick in the sand, his body shaking with the aftermath of his exertion.

There was a sound of clapping from above them, and von Rheydt looked up at the general, who was sitting alone on the lowest tier of seats.

"Well done, Captain!" he called down, honest admiration in his harsh voice.

Von Rheydt looked around at his companions. Casca had raised his palm in the air in salute; he looked surprised. Mbatha had risen to his feet and extended his spear arm. *What,* von Rheydt wondered, *were they seeing in place of a general of the O.K.W.?*

"Thank you," he said to the general. "And now—your part of the bargain?"

"Of course. Return to life for all three of the victors," the general said. "Finish these three off, and then—"

"No," said von Rheydt.

The general stopped in mid-stretch, arms in the air. "What did you say, Captain?"

"I said no. This—creature—fought bravely. It is not a soldier's way to kill when his opponent, though brave, is helpless."

The general lowered his arms and laughed. "And what do your less-civilized friends say to that noble sentiment, Captain?" He said something rapid, something von Rheydt couldn't catch, and they both looked at Casca.

The Roman looked down at the blue-clad warrior, slowly raised his hand and—turned his thumb upward.

Mbatha spread his hands and walked away from his defeated opponent. Von Rheydt turned back to the general. "You see?"

"This is insane," said the general, angrily. "This primitive chivalry has no place in modern warfare. Even in your time, Captain—do your enemies give quarter to the wounded?"

"No," said von Rheydt; then his eyes fell to the sand of the arena. "Nor . . . do some of my own countrymen. But the best among us, the professional soldiers, do. Obedience is not our only code, General. We also have honor."

"That's enough," said the general, who had turned white. "Your last chance, Captain. Finish this matter properly Now."

Von Rheydt stepped forward and threw the spear violently to the ground. It stuck there, quivering. "You do it," he said flatly. "It's your war." He turned, motioned to the Roman and the Zulu. They walked away across the sand.

Von Rheydt felt the blackness coming, drawing closer to him, like a velvet curtain sweeping in to end the last act of a play. It reached him, and he sank into it.

He opened his eyes to the white coldness of snow against his face and to a warmth that glowed like fire in the pit of his stomach. His eyes blinked, focused on a face. A human face. The face of a white-clad soldier who shouted something and raised a submachine gun

It had rather enjoyed the role of a General Staff Officer, and It still retained the appearance of one as It sat down to write Its report. The battered army typewriter rattled as It typed; It paused occasionally to refer to a document from the desk or to take a draw on Its cigar. The gray octagonal room gradually filled with drifting layers of smoke as It wrote:

> . . . *the directive embodied in paragraph [4], reference [a], was fully carried out in accordance with standard testing procedures as set forth in Ordnance Manual, latest revision . . . Evaluating officer personally observed comparative combat testing and was highly impressed with performance of Human soldiers. They proved the better fighters in three of three encounters.*
>
> *However, the Humans evinced certain undesirable characteristics as far as suitability for front-line use is con-*

cerned. The most serious was a refusal to obey orders contrary to their primitive codes of fighting.

It leaned back in the chair and thought about that one for a while, absentmindedly blowing smoke rings. In all good conscience, It could not recommend immediate employment of the Humans in the Disputed Sectors; they simply wouldn't do if they couldn't take simple orders. *But then*, It thought, *there's just too much combat potential here to simply close down and start over again with some other design.*

It thought for quite some time and then stubbed out the cigar, tilted the chair forward again and typed, *Recommendations:*

What is needed for this Project is an intensified, speeded-up program of development. To effect this, it is proposed that two great power blocs be created at the conclusion of the present war and that a situation of continuous conflict be maintained for as long as is necessary to produce a deployable Human weapon. . . .

It nodded in satisfaction. Just the thing. And It could stay on to supervise, in a soft rear-echelon job, far from the front. . . .

It smiled and began to change.

DRAGON'S TEETH

by David Drake

The sound of squealing axles drifted closer on the freezing wind. The watching Roman raised his eyes an inch above the rim of his brush-screened trench. A dozen Sarmatian wagons were hulking toward him into the twilight. Their wheels of uncured oak, gapped and irregular at the fellies, rumbled complainingly as they smashed stiff grass and bushes into the unyielding soil.

A smile of grim satisfaction brushed Vettius' lips as the Sarmatians approached. He did not touch the bow that lay beside him; it was still too soon.

The enormous weight of the wagons turned every finger's breadth of rise into a steep escarpment up which the oxen had to plod. They grunted out great plumes of breath as they threw their weight into the traces. Sexless, almost lifeless in their poses of stolid acceptance, the drivers hunched on the high wagon seats. Like the oxen, they had been at their killing work since dawn. The wind slashed and eddied about the canopies of aurochs hide which covered the boxes. Tendrils of smoke from heating fires within squirmed through the peaks. They hung for a moment in the sunset before scudding off invisibly.

The last of the wagons was almost within the defile, Vettius noted. It would be very soon now.

Among the Sarmatians the whole family travelled together, even to war. The children and nursing mothers huddled inside the wagons. So did the warriors; their work, like that of the horses tethered behind each wain, was yet to come. Soon the wagons would halt and laager up in the darkness. Using night as a shroud, the reivers would mount and thunder across the frozen Danube. Laughingly they

191

would return before dawn with booty and fresh Roman ears.

The only picket Vettius could see from where he lay was a single rider slightly ahead and to the left of the wagons. Earlier in the day he might have been guide or outrider. Hours had passed. Wagons had bunched or straggled according to the strength of their teams and the temper of their drivers. Now, while the sun bled like an open wound in the western sky, the rider was almost a part of the jumbled line and no protection for it. Vettius smiled again, and his hand was on the bow.

The wind that moaned around the wagons scuffed up crystals from the snow crusts lying in undulant rills among the brush. The shaggy pony's rump and belly sparkled. The beast's torso, like its rider's, was hidden under armor of broad horn scales, each one painstakingly sewn onto a leather backing by the women of the family. Across his pommel rested a slender lance more than eighteen feet long. The Sarmatian fondled its grip as he nodded over his mount's neck, neglecting to watch the bushes that clawed spiked shadows from the sun.

A sound that trickled through the wind made him straighten; unexpected movement caught his eye. Then the Roman archer rose up from behind a bush far too small to conceal a man the way it had. The Sarmatian, spurring his horse in incredulous panic, heard the slap of the bowstring, heard the loud pop as one scale of his cuirass shattered. After the bodkin-pointed arrow ripped through his chest he heard nothing at all.

"Let's get 'em!" Vettius shouted, nocking another arrow as his first target pitched out of the saddle. The trumpeter crouching behind him set the silver-mounted warhorn to his lips and blasted out the attack. Already the shallow hillsides were spilling soldiers down on the unprepared Sarmatians.

The driver of the lead wagon stood up, screaming a warning. The nearest Roman thrust her through the body with his spear. With two slashes of his short-sword, the legionary cut open the canopy behind her and plunged inside with a howl of triumph.

Sarmatians leaped out of the second wagon, trying to reach their horses. Three legionaries met them instead. Vettius had set fifty men in ambush, all picked veterans in full armor. None of the others had bows—the legate had feared a crossfire in the dusk—but sword and spear did the butcher's work on the startled nomads. The Sarmatians were dressed for war in armor of boiled leather or aurochs horn, but they had no shields and their light swords were no match for the heavy Roman cut and thrust blades. One at a time the nomads jumped down to be stretched on the ground by a stab, a quick chop, or even the heavy smash of a shield rim. Death trebled, the legionaries stood waiting for each victim. The fading sunlight gleamed from their polished helmets and greaves and touched with fire the wheels of bronze and vermillioned leather that marked the shields.

The legate's practiced eye scanned the fighting. The wrack showed the Sarmatians had battled with futile desperation. A baby lay beside the fourth wagon. Its skull had been dashed in on the wagon box, but its nails were stained with Roman blood. The oxen bellowed, hamstrung in the yoke. One was spurting black jets through a heart-deep channel. This day was Rome's vengeance; retribution for a thousand sudden raids, a thousand comrades crumpled from a chance arrow or a dagger thrust in the night.

Only toward the rear where three wagons had bunched together was there real fighting. Vettius ran down the line of wagons though his quiver was almost emptied when he saw one of his men hurtle through the air in a lifeless somersault. The legionary crashed to the ground like a load of scrap metal. His whole chest and body armor had been caved in by an enormous blow. Measurably later the man's sword completed its own parabola and clanked thirty feet away.

"Get back!" Vettius shouted when he saw the windrow of ruined bodies strewn in front of him. "Stand clear!" Before he could say more, the killer was lumbering toward him around the back of the wagon.

The horsehair crest wobbling in the waning sunlight increased the figure's titanic height, but even bareheaded the giant would have been half again as tall as the six-foot soldier. Worse, he was much heavier built than a man, a squat dwarf taller than the wagon. He carried no shield but his whole body shone with a covering of smooth bronze plates. Both gauntleted hands gripped the haft of an iron-headed mace. The six-foot helve was as thick as a man's calf and the head could have served as an anvil.

The giant strode toward Vettius with terrifying agility.

Vettius arched his bow. The shaft of his arrow splintered on the monster's breastplate. It left only a bright scar on the metal. Vettius stepped back, nocking another missile and shifting his aim to the oddly sloped helmet. The face was completely covered except for a T-shaped slot over the eyes and nose. The light was very dim but the narrow gap stood out dead black against the helmet's luster. As the giant started to swing his mace parallel to the ground, Vettius shot again.

The arrow glanced off the bronze and howled away into the darkness.

Vettius leaped upward and fell across the wagon seat as the giant's mace hurtled toward him. The spiked head smashed into a wheel with awesome force, scattering fragments of wood and making the whole wagon shudder. As it rocked, the driver's hacked corpse tumbled to the ground leaving the Roman alone on the seat as he sighted along his last arrow.

The giant had reversed his grip on the mace. Now he swung his weapon upward with no more apparent effort than a man with a flywhisk. As the head came level with the giant's hips, the mace slipped from his fingers to fly forward and burst through the side of the wagon. The titan reeled backwards. A small tuft of feathers was barely visible where the helmet slot crossed the bridge of his nose.

The earth trembled when he fell.

Shaking with reaction himself, Vettius dropped his now-useless bow and craned his neck to peer over the wagon's canopy at the remaining fighting. Some of the wains were already burning. Confusion or the victors had spilled the heating flames from their earthenware pots and scattered coals into the cloth and straw of the bedding.

"Save me a prisoner!" Vettius bellowed against the wind. "For Mithra's sake, save me a prisoner!"

He jumped to the ground and cautiously approached the fallen giant. The helmet came off easily when he grasped it by the crest and yanked. Beneath the bronze the face was almost human. The jaw was square and massive; death's rictus had drawn thin lips back from leonine tushes, yellowed and stark. The nose squatted centrally like a smashed toad, and from it the face rose past high flat eyesockets to enormous ridges of bone. There was virtually no forehead so that the brows sloped shallowly to a point on the back of the skull. Only their short tight coils distinguished the eyebrows from the black strands that covered the rest of the head.

No wonder the helmet looked odd, Vettius thought bleakly. He would believe in the face, in a man so large, because they were there for him to touch; but he would have called another man a liar for claiming the existence of something so impossible. Perhaps believing in the impossible was the secret of the success of the Christians whose god, dead three hundred years, was now beginning to rule the Empire.

The trumpeter approached from behind with his horn slung and a bloody sword in his right hand. The torque he now wore was of gold so pure and soft that he had spread it by hand to get it off a dead nomad and rebent it around his own neck.

"Sir!" he called, "are you all right?"

"Give me a hand here," Vettius grunted unresponsively as he tugged at the mace. Together the men pulled the weapon from the fabric of the wagon. Vettius gave a curt order and hefted it alone as his subordinate stepped back. "Ha!" he snorted in disbelief. The mace weighed at least two talents, the weight of a small man or a fair-sized woman.

He let it thud to the ground and walked away from it. "May the Bull bugger me if I don't learn more about this," he swore.

The doorkeeper had difficulty slamming the door against the gust of wind that followed Vettius into the anteroom. Moist air from the baths within condensed to bead the decorated tiles and rime the soldier's cape of black bearskin. He wore the bear's head as a cowl. The beast's glass eyes usually glared out above Vettius' own; now they too were frosted and the doorkeeper, turning, shuddered at the look of blank agony they gave him.

Vettius shrugged off the cape and stamped his muddy boots on the floor. The doorkeeper sighed inwardly and picked up his twig broom. The damned man had been stomping through the muck like a common soldier instead of riding decently in a litter as befit his rank. The slave said nothing aloud as he swept, though; the legate had a reputation for violence and he already wore a dark glower this afternoon.

Walking through the door of the changing room, Vettius tossed his cape to one of the obsequious attendants and began to unlace his boots. While he sat on a bench and stripped off his thick woolen leggings, the other attendant looked delicately at the miry leather and asked with faint disdain, "Will you have these cleaned while you bathe, sir?"

"Dis, why should I?" the soldier snarled. "I've got to wear them out of here, don't I?"

The attendant started at his tone. Vettius chuckled at the man's fear and threw the filthy leggings in his face. Laying both his tunics on the bench, he surveyed the now apprehensive slaves and asked, "Either of you know where Dama is?"

"The Legate Vettius?" called a voice from the inner hallway. A third attendant stuck his head into the changing room. "Sir? If you will follow me. . . ."

The attendant's sandals slapped nervously down the hallway past steam rooms on the right and the wall of the great pool on the left. Tiles of glaucous gray covered the floors and most of the walls, set off by horizontal bands of mosaic. A craftsman of Naisso who had never been to the coast had inset octopuses and dolphins cavorting on a bright green sea. The civilization I protect, Vettius thought disgustedly. The reason I bow to fat fools.

At the corner of the hall the attendant stopped and opened one of the right-hand doors. Steam puffed out. Vettius peered in with his hand on the jamb to keep from slipping on the slick tile. He could make out two figures through the hot fog, a small man lying on a bench with a masseur beside him. The slap of hands on flesh had paused when the door opened.

"Dama?" the soldier called uncertainly.

The man on the bench raised up on his elbow. "Come on in, Lucius," he invited with genuine pleasure. "Urso, we'll have no further need of you today."

Coins jingled. The masseur bowed low to the merchant, nodded respectfully to Vettius, and thudded the door shut behind him.

"Have a bench," Dama offered. "How did it go?"

Vettius grunted. "Anyone with big ears likely to bust in here?"

"I doubt it," the merchant replied. "I think Dazos misunderstood when I told him we'd not want to be disturbed, but he knows I pay well for privacy."

The soldier stepped gingerly through the gloom. Even so his foot brushed one of the perforated tiles through which boilers in the basement forced steam into the room. He swore fiercely. The only light seeped through the skylight, a tracery of mica plaquets now virtually opaqued by the layers of ice and soot above. Even the minatory red glaze of the ducts blurred to gray in the dark.

Vettius stretched his solid form on the bench. "Why don't they light this place?" he growled.

"There's a lamp on the wall, but I think it's out of oil," his friend said. "Just lie down and relax; your eyes will adjust. Did you talk to the Count?"

The soldier swore again. He flexed his thigh and shoulder muscles, letting the anger work out through opening pores. At last he loosened and sighed. "Yeah, I talked to Celsus. Did you ever have anything to do with him, Dama?"

"Not directly. It's worth his while to let me sell silk in his region."

"The gods waste me if he's not an idiot!" Vettius snapped angrily. He sat up, swinging his legs over the side of his bench. "Look, I'm just a soldier—but I damned well know how to soldier. I keep my sector of border safe and a thousand of the toughest whoresons in the Eastern Army happy. Anybody can see I know my business!"

He paused, breathing hard. Dama too sat up, trying to scan the big man's face in the darkness. "You told him what you told me this morning?" he asked. "I mean, you told him about the giant?"

"I told him, sure," Vettius answered. He rubbed his forehead with his knuckles while he remembered. "More. We got this prisoner to talk after I left you. It's as bad as I thought it might be, maybe worse. That wasn't the only giant, and he wasn't a freak Sarmatian. Mithra, you could see from the face that he wasn't any sort of Sarmatian."

"If he wasn't a Sarmatian," Dama considered, "where could he have come from?"

"Oh, he came from Torgu," explained Vettius. "It's one of those tent villages, maybe a hundred miles across the river. In summer there's only a handful of permanent buildings and most of them wattle and daub. In the winter a thousand or so Sarmatians gather with their wagons and all their livestock, trading and drinking and going off to raid in little groups. Only there's a shaman there now who seems to have taken the place over—"

"I didn't think the Sarmatians ever let a shaman become chief," the merchant interrupted.

"I didn't either," Vettius agreed, "but that's not the last odd thing we heard about Hydaspes." The soldier chuckled evilly and added, "And I don't think the prisoner was lying by the time we were through with him.

"Hydaspes—that's the shaman—is something beyond the usual hedge wizard. His magic looks so real that the prisoner was more afraid of what the chief a hundred miles away could do to him than what we could, until he scarcely had mind left to answer questions."

Vettius fell silent. Torture was a part of his job. Sometimes following a Sarmatian raid it became more personal than that, but the successful ambush had left him feeling almost kindly toward the defeated. There had been no savor in what he and his interrogators were doing to the broken, drooling prisoner. Normally Vettius would have forgotten the incident as soon as possible.

Normally: had he not spoken to Celsus. Stupid, short-sighted Celsus with his dark suspicions of a subordinate who showed initiative. Vettius had wanted to smash his simpering commander off the delicately carven ivory stool he affected, wanted at least to clench his great fists and watch the Count pale. Self interest had held him rigid instead. In his mind though, he once again inserted the glowing rod while the Sarmatian screamed in helpless agony on the rack.

Dama said nothing. He knew why his friend's hands clamped tight on the bench. A handball game was in progress on the other side of the steam room's back wall. Words came through the masonry as little more than high-pitched squeals, but the unfaltering slap-slap-slap of the ball wove a fabric for contemplation. Either one man was practicing alone or two perfectly matched experts were having a bout as precise as a dance of oreads.

Vettius rumbled, clearing his throat in embarrassment. "I must have drifted off," he apologized, lying back down on the bench. He felt ashamed of the red savagry that had bubbled through his brain, ashamed because it was misdirected. Perhaps he would do something for the human wreckage in the detention cell, buy the fellow and send him to the steward of his British estates with a chit for a soft job. A comfortable enough life. Fear of a wizard across the Danube couldn't reach that far.

"Where did Hydaspes get a giant?" Dama prompted to divert the soldier's revery.

"Giants," Vettius corrected. "The prisoner says there were ten more at Torgu when his family was sent out with this one. Thing is, he couldn't say where they came from.

He thought it was a part of the shaman's magic, that Hydaspes was building the men out of clay and breathing life into them. That's crap, by the way; we didn't have time or transport to bring the body back, but I don't need a philosopher's word to know that he was a normal man, no statue."

"Then why did the Sarmatian think otherwise?" Dama queried.

"Well, the giants just seemed to appear," his friend replied. The question had been bothering him. "They weren't at Torgu when the family we ambushed got there in the late fall. Hydaspes was there, though, nervous as the emperor's taster and fussing around the village to look over each new arrival. He wasn't claiming much authority, either.

"About two months ago a horseman rode in from eastward alone. Our prisoner didn't talk with the fellow but he saw him give a package to Hydaspes. Nothing big—the size of a fist, he says. That was what Hydaspes had been waiting for. He laughed and capered all the way to his tent and didn't come out again for a week. When he did, he started giving orders like a king. With a nine-foot giant behind him, everyone obeyed. In back of Hydaspes' tent there was a long trench in the frozen ground and a lot of dirt was missing."

The merchant began rapping one fingertip on his bench as he pondered, beating out an unconscious counterpoint to the handball game outside the room. "So . . ." he articulated slowly. "It looks as though Hydaspes was able to dig up a giant, literally. If only one, then maybe he just knew where to dig . . . but you say there were more of them?"

"Ten more, one at a time," Vettius agreed with a nod of his head. "And there was another hole in the ground the morning each one appeared. Nobody the prisoner knew about hung about at night to see what was happening behind the shaman's tent, though. They were all scared to death by then."

"So scared that they found enough bronze to build a colossus and used it to armor Hydaspes' creations," Dama mused.

The soldier grunted assent. "Some they gave to him. A lot of it he bought from other tribes or from traders at Tyras, paying for it with raw gold."

"Gold and a giant bodyguard," Dama continued softly, "and a one-time hedge wizard had united a tribe under him. If he can do that, he might as easily become king of the whole nation. A real leader, not a figurehead like most Sarmatian kings. What would happen, Lucius, if the Sarmatians stopped squabbling among themselves and crossed the river together, obeying one man?"

The white fear that had been shimmering around the edges of Vettius' mind broke through and again all his muscles tensed. Consciously forcing himself to relax, the soldier said, "A century ago the Persians unified Mesopotamia against us. Constant fighting. Some victories, more losses. But we would accept that on one frontier—it's a big empire. On two sides at the same time . . . I can't really say what would happen."

We'd better deal with Hydaspes soon," Dama summarized flatly, or Hydaspes will deal with us."

"That's what I tried to tell Celsus," Vettius muttered. His fury had burned out and frustration had given way to bleak dispair. "The prisoner told us each of the giants was sent with a single family to raid our border posts. Messengers had gone out to call the other tribes to a meeting and he thought that if the raids were successful the others would come. I begged Celsus for a quick expedition against Torgu before Hydaspes could settle with the other chiefs."

"And?" the merchant demanded.

"The Count was more interested in criticizing the ambush I'd set.

"Yeah, that's what I said," Vettius continued over Dama's grunt of surprise. His voice rose high, taking on a mocking simper. " 'Don't you know how hard it is to find and train men, Legate? You took fifty men out into the heart of Sarmatia and despite incredible luck in getting back at all, you took heavy casualties.' Damn that man!"

The echoes of his voice shouted back at Vettius. The incongruity struck him. He began to chuckle and, while the merchant blinked, filled the rooms with peals of laughter.

"Oh Dama," the soldier gasped, clasping his friend's hands, "the sky is falling down on our heads and I'm mad. A simpleton doesn't appreciate my tactical genius, so I'm mad. Oh!

"We killed at least eighty Sarmatians, and only six of my boys didn't make it back. It could have been better but Mithra! I didn't figure on a giant. At the very best they would have done more damage if they'd have gotten to this side of the river. But Celsus didn't like the ambush and he didn't think I should have gone along anyway. Undignified for a legate, he said."

At that Dama laughed, trying to imagine Vettius too dignified for a fight.

"That's the sort he is," the soldier agreed with a rueful smile. "He expects me to keep my cutthroats in line without dirtying my boots. A popular attitude this side of the river, it seems. But Mithra, I know my men. They're so stubborn they'd not follow Venus to bed—but they'd follow me to Hell because they know I'd be leading them when the war horns blew. Leading, damn it, not in the rear sitting on a white horse."

The handball game across the partition ended with a crash of flesh on wood. The door had suddenly opened behind the players and one of them, leaping back, had struck it. A voice shrilled through the wall, "You crowbait fool, you might have killed me! I don't care who you are, you've no right to come bursting in here like that. And I never heard of your fool soldier!"

Both men in the steam room looked up sharply. Knuckles rapped on their door.

"Sirs, quickly!" Dazos hissed from outside.

Dama threw the door open for the frightened attendant. "Sirs," the slave explained, "the Count has come for the legate Vettius. I misdirected him, thinking you might want to prepare, but he'll be here any moment."

"I'll put on a tunic and meet him in the changing room," the soldier decided. "I've no desire to be arrested in the nude."

The frightened changing room attendants had disappeared into the far reaches of the building, leaving the friends to pull on their linen tunics undisturbed. Celsus burst in on them without ceremony, followed by two of his runners. He's not here to charge me after all, Vettius thought, not without at least a squad of troops. Though Mithra knew, his wishes would have supported a treason indictment.

"Where have you been?" the official stormed. His round face was almost the color of his toga's broad maroon hem.

"Right here in the bath, your excellency," Vettius replied without deference.

"Word just came by heliograph," the count sputtered. "There were ten attacks last night, **ten**! Impregnable monsters leading them—Punicum, Novae, Frasuli, Anarti—posts wiped out!"

"I told you there were other attacks planned," the soldier replied calmly. "None of them were in my sector. I told you why that was too."

"But you lied when you said you killed a monster, didn't you?" accused Celsus, stamping his foot. "At Novae they hit one with a catapult and the bolt only bounced off!"

"Then they didn't hit him squarely," Vettius retorted. "The armor isn't that heavy. And I told you, I shot mine through the viewslit in his helmet."

The count motioned his runners away. Noticing Dama for the first time he screamed, "Get out! Get out!"

The merchant bowed and exited behind the runners. He stood near the door.

"Listen," Celsus whispered, plucking at the soldier's sleeve to bring his ear lower, "you've got to do something about the giants. It'll look bad if these raids continue."

"Fine," Vettius said in surprise. "Give me my regiment and the Fifth Macedonian, and some cavalry—say the Old Germans. I'll level Torgu and everyone in it."

"Oh no," his pudgy superior gasped, "not so much. The Emperor will hear about it and the gods know what he'll think. Oh no—fifty men, that was enough before."

"Are you—" Vettius began, then rephrased his thought. "This isn't an ambush for one family, your excellency. This is disposing of a powerful chief and maybe a thousand of his followers, a hundred miles into Sarmatia. I might as well go alone as with fifty men."

"Fifty men," Celsus repeated. Then, beaming as if he were making a promise, he added, "You'll manage, I'm sure."

The two riders were within a few miles of Torgu before they were noticed.

"I shouldn't have let you come," Vettius grumbled to his companion. "Either I should have gone myself or else marched my regiment in and told Celsus to bugger himself."

Dama smiled. "You don't have any curiosity, Lucius. You only see the job to be done. Myself, I want to know where a nine-foot giant comes from."

They eyed the sprawling herd of black cattle which were finding some unimaginable pasturage beneath the snow crust. Perhaps they were stripping bark from the brush that scarred the landscape with its black rigidity. A cow scented the unfamiliar horses approaching it. The animal blatted and scrambled to its feet, splashing dung behind it. When it had bustled twenty feet away, the cow regained enough composure to turn and stare at the riders, focusing the ripple of disturbance that moved sluggishly through other bovine minds. Face after drooling, vacant face rotated toward them; after long moments, even the distant herdsman looked up from where he huddled over his fire in the lee of a hill.

Dama's chest grew tight. There was still another moment's silence while the Sarmatian made up his mind that there really were Romans riding toward Torgu through his herd. When at last he grasped the fact, he leaped to his feet yipping his amazement. For an instant he crouched bowlegged, waiting for a hostile move. When the intruders ignored him, the Sarmatian scampered to his horse and lashed it into a startled gallop for home.

The merchant chewed at his cheeks, trying to work saliva into a mouth that had gone dry when he realized they would be noticed. He'd known they were going to meet Sarmatians: that was the whole purpose of what they were doing. But now it was too late to back out. "About time we got an escort," he said with false bravado. "I'm surprised the Sarmatians don't patrol more carefully."

"Why should they?" Vettius snorted. "They know they're safe over here so long as a brainless scut like Celsus is in charge of the border."

They jogged beyond the last of the cattle. Without the Sarmatian's presence the beasts were slowly drifting away from the trampled area where they had been herded. If they wandered far they would be loose at night when the wolves hunted.

"Cows," Vettius muttered. "It's getting hard to find men, my friend."

Half a mile away on the top of the next rolling hill an armored horseman reined up in a spatter of snow. He turned his head and gave a series of short yelps that carried over the plain like bugle calls. Moments later a full score of lancers topped the brow of the hill and pounded down toward the interlopers.

"I think we'll wait here," the soldier remarked.

"Sure, give them a sitting target," Dama agreed with a tense smile.

Seconds short of slaughter the leading Sarmatian raised his lance. The rest of the troop followed his signal. The whole group swept around Vettius and Dama to halt in neighing, skidding chaos. One horse lost its footing and spilled its rider on the snow with a clatter of weapons. Cursing, the disgruntled Sarmatian lurched toward the Romans with his short, crooked sword out. From behind Dama, the leader barked a denial and laid his lance in front of the man. The merchant breathed deeply but did not relax his grip on the queerly shaped crossbow resting on his saddle until the glowering Sarmatian had remounted.

The leader rode alongside Vettius and looked up at the soldier on his taller horse. "You come with us to Torgu," he ordered in passable Greek.

"That's right," Vettius agreed in Sarmatian. "We're going to Torgu to see Hydaspes."

There was a murmur from the Sarmatians. One of them leaned forward to shake an amulet bag in the soldier's face, gabbling something too swiftly to be understood.

The leader had frowned when Vettius spoke. He snapped another order and kicked his horse forward. Romans and Sarmatians together jogged up the hill, toward the offal and frozen muck of Torgu.

On the bank of a nameless, icebound stream stood the village's central hall and only real building. Dama glanced at it as they rode past. Its roughly squared logs were gray and streaked with odd splits along the twisted grain. Any caulking there might have been in the seams had fallen out over the years. The sides rose to a flaring roof of scummed thatch, open under the eaves to emit smoke and the stink of packed bodies. The hall would have seemed crude in the most stagnant backwaters of the Empire; the merchant could scarcely believe that a people to whom it was the height of civilization could be a threat.

Around the timber structure sprawled the nomad wagons in filthy confusion. Their sloping canopies were shingled with cow droppings set out to dry in the wan sunlight before being burned for fuel. The light soot that had settled out of thousands of cooking fires permeated the camp with an unclean, sweetish odor. Nothing in the village but the untethered horses watching the patrol return looked cared for.

Long lances had been butted into the ground beside each wagon. As he stared back at the flat glazes directed at him by idle Sarmatians, Dama realized what was wrong with the scene. Normally, only a handful of each family group would have been armored lancers. The rest would be horse archers, able to afford only a bow and padded linen protection.

Most of their escort hung cased bows from their saddles, but all bore the lance and most wore scale mail.

"Lucius," the merchant whispered in Latin, "are all of these nobles?"

"You noticed that," Vettius replied approvingly. "No, you can see from their looks that almost all of them were just herdsmen recently. Somebody made them his retainers, paid for their equipment and their keep."

"Hydaspes?" the merchant queried.

"I guess. He must have more personal retainers than the king then."

"You will be silent!" ordered the Sarmatian leader.

They had ridden almost completely through the camp and were approaching a tent of gaily pennoned furs on the edge of the plains. At each corner squatted an octagonal stump of basalt a few feet high. The stones were unmarked and of uncertain significance, altars or boundary markers or both. No wains had been parked within fifty paces of the tent. A pair of guards stood before its entrance. Dama glanced at the streamers and said, "You know, there really is a market for silk in this forsaken country. A shame that—"

"Silence!" the Sarmatian repeated as he drew up in front of the tent. He threw a rapid greeting to the guards, one of whom bowed and ducked inside. He returned quickly, followed by a tall man in a robe of fine black Spanish wool. The newcomer's face was thin for a Sarmatian and bore a smile that mixed triumph and something else. On his shoulder, covered by the dark hood, clung a tiny monkey with great brown eyes. From time to time it put its mouth to its master's ear and murmured secretly.

"Hydaspes," Vettius whispered. "He always wears black."

"Have they been disarmed?" the wizard questioned. The escort's leader flushed in embarrassment at his oversight and angrily demanded the Romans' weapons. Vettius said nothing as he handed over his bow and the long cavalry bow he carried even now that he commanded an infantry unit. The merchant added his crossbow and a handful of bolts to the collection.

"What is that?" Hydaspes asked, motioning his man to hand him the crossbow.

"It comes from the east where I get my silk," Dama explained, speaking directly to the wizard. "You just drop a bolt into the tall slot on top. That holds it while you pull back on the handle, cocking it and firing it all in one motion."

"From the east? I get weapons from the east," the Sarmatian said with a nasty quirk of his lip. "But this, this is only a toy surely? The arrow is so light and scarcely a handspan long. What could a man do with such a thing?"

Dama shrugged. "I'm not a warrior. For my own part, I wouldn't care to be shot with this or anything else."

The wizard gestured an end to the conversation, setting the weapon inside his tent for later perusal. "Dismount, gentlemen, dismount," he continued in excellent Greek. "Perhaps you have heard of me?"

"Hydaspes the wizard. Yes," Vettius lied, "even within the Empire we think of you when we think of a powerful sorceror. That's why we've come for help."

"In whose name?" the Sarmatian demanded shrewdly. "Constantius the emperor?"

"Celsus, Count of Dacia," Vettius snapped back. "The Empire has suffered the absurdities of Constantius and his brothers long enough. Eunuchs run the army, priests rule the state, and the people pray to the tax gatherers. We'll have support when we get started, but first we need some standard to rally to, something to convince everyone that we have more than mere hopes behind us. We want your giants, and we'll pay you a part of the Empire to get them."

"And you, little man?" Hydaspes asked the merchant unexpectedly. Dama had been imagining the count's face if he learned his name was being linked with raw treason, but he recovered swiftly and fumbled at his sash while replying, "We merchants have little cause to love Constantius. The roads are ruinous, the coinage base; and the rapacity of local officials leaves little profit for even the most daring adventurer."

"So you came to add your promise of future gain?"

"Future? Who knows the future?" Dama grunted. Gold gleamed in his hand. A shower of coins arced unerringly from his right palm to his left and back again. "If you can supply what we need, you'll not lament your present payment."

"Ho! Such confidence," the wizard said, laughing cheerfully. The monkey chittered, stroking its master's hair with bulbous fingertips. "You really believe that I can raise giants from the past?

"I can!"

Hydaspes' face became a mask of unreason. Dama shifted nervously from one foot to the other, realizing that the wizard was far from the clever illusionist they had assumed back at Naisso he must be. This man wasn't sane enough to successfully impose on so many people, even ignorant barbarians. Or was the madness a recent thing?

"Subradas, gather the village behind my tent," Hydaspes ordered abruptly, "but leave space in the middle as wide and long as the tent itself."

The leader of the escort dipped his lance in acknowledgement. "The women, Lord?"

"All—women, slaves, everyone. I'm going to show you how I raise the giants."

"Ho!" gasped the listening Sarmatians. The leader saluted again and rode off shouting. Hydaspes turned to reenter his tent, then paused. "Take the Romans, too," he directed the guards. "Put them by the flap and watch them well.

"Yes," he continued, glancing back at Vettius, "it is a very easy thing to raise giants, if you have the equipment and the knowledge. Like drawing a bowstring for a man like you."

The Hell-lit afterimage of the wizard's eyes continued to blaze in the soldier's mind when the furs had closed behind the black figure.

As the rest of the Sarmatians dismounted and began to jostle them around the tent, Dama whispered, "This isn't working. If it gets too tight, break for the tent. You know about my bow?"

Vettius nodded, but his mind was chilled by a foretaste of death.

As the prisoner had said, eleven long trenches bristled outward from the wall of Hydaspes' tent. Each was shallow but too extensive for the wizard to have dug it in the frozen ground in one night. Dama disliked the way the surface slumped over the ditches as if enormous corpses had clawed their way out of their graves.

Which was what the wizard seemed to claim had happened.

The guards positioned the two Romans at the center of the back wall of the tent where laces indicated another entrance. Later comers crowded about anxiously, held back in a rough circle by officers with drawn swords. Twenty feet to either side of the Romans stretched the straight wall of the tent paralleled by a single row of warriors. From the basalt posts at either corner curved the rest of the tribe in milling excitement, warriors in front and women and children squirming as close as they could get before being elbowed back.

The Sarmatians were still pushing for position when Hydaspes entered the cleared space, grinning ironically at Vettius and Dama as he stepped between them. A guard laced the tent back up. In the wizard's left hand was a stoppered copper flask; his right gripped a small packet of supple cowhide.

"The life!" Hydaspes shouted to the goggle-eyed throng, waving the flask above his head from the center of the circle. He set the vessel down on the dirt and carefully unrolled the leather wrappings from the other objects.

"And the seed!" the wizard cried at last. In his palm lay a pair of teeth. They were a dull, stony gray without any of the sheen of ivory. One was a molar, human but inhumanly large. The other tooth, even less credible, seemed to be a canine fully four inches long. With one tooth in either hand, Hydaspes goat-footed about the flask in an impromptu dance of triumph.

His monkey rider clacked its teeth in glee.

The wizard stopped abruptly and faced the Romans. "Oh, yes. The seed. I got them, all thirteen teeth, from the Chinese—the people who sell you your silk, merchant. Dragon's teeth they call them—hee hee! And I plant them just like Cadmus did when he built Thebes. But I'm the greater prince, oh yes, for I'll build an empire where he built a city."

Dama licked his lips. "We'll help you build your empire," he began, but the wizard ignored him and spoke only to Vettius.

"You want my giants, Roman, my darlings? Watch!"

Hydaspes plucked a small dagger from his sash and poked a hole in the ground. Like a farmer planting a nut, the wizard popped the molar into the hole and patted the earth back down. When he straightened he shouted a few words at the sky. The villagers gasped, but Dama doubted whether they understood any more of the invocation than he did. Perhaps less—the merchant thought he recognized the language, at least, one he had heard chanted on the shores of the Persian Gulf on a dead, starless night. He shuddered.

Now the wizard was unstoppering his flask and crooning

under his breath. His cowl had fallen back to display the monkey clinging fiercely to his long oily hair. When the wizard turned, Dama could see the beast's lips miming its master obscenely.

Droplets splattered from the flask, bloody red and glowing. The merchant guessed wine or blood, changed his mind when the fluid popped and sizzled on the ground. The frozen dirt trembled like a stricken gong.

The monkey leaped from Hydaspes' shoulder, strangely unaffected by the cold. It faced the wizard across the patch of fluid-scarred ground. It was chanting terrible squeaky words that thundered back from Hydaspes.

The ground split.

The monkey collapsed. Hydaspes leaped over the earth's sudden gape and scooped up the little creature, wrapping it in his cloak.

Through the crack in the soil thrust an enormous hand. Earth heaved upward again. The giant's whole torso appeared, dribbling dirt back into the trench. Vettius recognized the same thrusting jaw, the same high flat eyesockets, as those of the giant he had killed.

The eyes were Hydaspes' own.

"Oh, yes, Roman," the wizard cackled. "The life and the seed—but the mind too, hey? There must be the mind."

The giant rose carefully in a cascade of earth. Even standing in the trench left by his body, he raised his pointed skull eight feet into the air.

"My mind!" Hydaspes shrieked, oblivious to everyone but the soldier. "Part of me in each of my darlings, you see? Flowing from me through my pet here to them."

One of the wizard's hands caressed the monkey until it murmured lasciviously. The beast's huge eyes were seas of steaming brown mud, barely flecked by pinpoint pupils.

"You said you knew me," continued the wizard. "Well, I know you too, Lucius Vettius. I saw you bend your bow, I saw you kill my darling—

"I saw you kill me, Roman!"

Vettius unclasped his cape, let it slip to the ground. Hydaspes wiped a streak of spittle from his lips and stepped back to lay a hand on the giant's forearm. "Kill me again, Roman," the wizard said softly. "Go ahead; no one will interfere. But this time you don't have a bow.

"Watch the little one!" he snapped to the guard on Dama's right. The Sarmatian gripped the merchant's shoulder.

Then the giant charged.

Vettius dived forward at an angle, rolling beyond the torn up section of the clearing. The giant spun, stumbled in a ditch that had cradled one of his brothers. The soldier had gained the room he wanted in the center of the open space and waited in a loose-armed crouch. The giant sidled toward him splay footed.

"Hey!" the Roman shouted and lunged for his opponent's dangling genitalia. The giant struck with shocking speed, swatting Vettius in midair like a man playing handball. Before the Roman's thrusting fingers could make contact, the giant's open-handed blow had crashed into his ribs and hurled him a dozen feet away. Only the giant's clumsy rush saved Vettius from being pulped before he could jump to his feet again. The soldier was panting heavily but his eyes were fixed on the giant's. A thread of blood dribbled off the point of his jaw. Only a lip split on the hard ground—thus far. The giant charged.

Two faces in the crowd were not fixed on the one-sided battle. Dama fingered the hem of his cloak unobtrusively, following the fight only from the corners of his eyes. It would be pointless to watch his friend die. Instead the merchant watched Hydaspes, who had dug another hole across the clearing and inserted the last and largest tooth into it. The wizard seemed to ignore the fighting. If he watched at all, it was through the giant's eyes as he claimed; and surely, mad as he was, Hydaspes would not have otherwise turned his back on his revenge. For the first time Dama thought he recognized an unease about the monkey which rode again on the wizard's shoulder. It might have been only fatigue. Certainly Hydaspes seemed to notice nothing unusual as he tamped down the soil and began his thirteenth invocation.

Dama's guard was wholly caught up in the fight. He began to pound the merchant on the back in excitement, yelling bloodthirsty curses at Vettius. Dama freed the slender stiletto from his cloak and palmed it. He did not turn his head lest the movement catch the guard's attention. Instead he raised his hand to the Sarmatian's neck, delicately fingering his spine. Before the moth-light touch could register on the enthusiastic Sarmatian, Dama slammed the thin blade into the base of his brain and gave it a twist. The guard died instantly. The merchant supported the slumping body, guiding it back against the tent. Hydaspes continued chanting a litany with the monkey, though the noise of the crowd drowned out his words. The wizard formed the inaudible syllables without noticing either Dama or the stumbling way his beast answered him. There was a look of puzzlement, almost fear, in the monkey's eyes. The crowd continued to cheer as the merchant opened the flap with a quick slash and backed inside Hydaspes' tent.

Inside a pair of chalcedony oil lamps burned with tawny light. The floor was covered with lush furs, some of which draped wooden benches. On a table at one end rested a pair of human skulls, unusually small but adult in proportions. More surprising were the cedar book chests holding parchments and papyri and even the strange pleated leaf-books of India. Dama's crossbow stood beside the front entrance. He ran to it and loosed the bundle of stubby, unfletched darts beside it. From his wallet came a vial of pungent tarry matter into which he jabbed the head of each dart. The uncovered portions of the bronze points began to turn green. Careful not to touch the smears of venom, the merchant slipped all ten missiles into the crossbow's awkward vertical magazine.

Only then did he peer through the tent flap.

Vettius leaped sideways, kicking at the giant's knee. The ragged hobnails scored his opponent's calf, but the giant's deceptively swift hand closed on the Roman's outer tunic. For a heartsick instant the fabric held; then it ripped and Vettius tumbled free. The giant lunged after him. Vettius backpedaled and, as his enemy straightened, launched himself across the intervening space. The heel of his outstretched boot slammed into the pit of the giant's stomach. Again the iron nails made a bloody ruin of the skin. The titan's breath whooshed out, but its half-ton bulk did not falter at the blow. Vettius, thrown back by the futile impact, twisted away from the giant's unchecked rush. The creature's heels grazed past, thudded with mastodontic force. The soldier took a shuddering breath and lurched to his feet. A long arm clawed for his face. The Roman staggered back, barely clear of the spade-like talons. The monster pressed after him relentlessly, and Vettius was forced at last to recognize what should have been hopelessly obvious from the first: he could not possibly kill the giant with his bare hands.

A final strategem took shape. With desperate purpose Vettius began to circle and retreat before his adversary. He should have planned it, measured it, but now he could only trust to luck and the giant's incredible weight. Backed almost against a corner post, he crouched and waited. Arms wide, the giant hesitated—then rushed in for the kill. Vettius met him low, diving straight at his opponent instead of making a vain effort to get clear again. The Roman's arms locked about the great ankles and the giant wavered, then began to topple forward. As he fell his taloned fingers clamped crushingly on Vettius' ribs.

The unyielding basalt altar met the giant's skull with shattering force. Bone slammed dense rock with the sound of a maul on a wedge. Warm fluids spattered the snow while the Sarmatians moaned in disbelief. Hydaspes knelt screaming on the ground, his fists pummeling terror from a mind that had forgotten even the invocation it had just completed. The earth began pitching like an unmastered horse. It split in front of the wizard where the tooth had been planted. The crack raced jaggedly through the crowd and beyond.

"Lucius!" Dama cried, lifting the corner of the tent.

The soldier pulled his leg free from the giant's pinioning body and rolled toward the voice, spilling endwise the only Sarmatian alert enough to try to stop him. Dama dropped the tent wall and nodded toward the front, his hands full of crossbow. "There's horses waiting out there. I'll slow them up."

Vettius stamped on a hand that thrust into the tent.

"Get out, damn you!" the merchant screamed. "There aren't any more weapons in here."

A Sarmatian rolled under the furs with a feral grimace and a dagger in his hand. The soldier hefted a full case of books and hurled it at his chest. Wood and bone splintered loudly. Vettius turned and ran toward the horses.

The back flap ripped apart in the haste of the Sarmatians who had remembered its existence. The first died with a dart through his eye as Dama jerked the cocking handle of his weapon. The next missile fell into position. The merchant levered back the bow again. At full cock the sear released, snapped the dart out into the throat of the next man. The Sarmatian's life dissolved in a rush of red flame as the bolt pricked his carotid to speed its load of poison straight to the brain. The third man stumbled over his body, screamed. Two darts pinged off his mail before one caught the armpit he bared when he threw his hands over his face.

Relentless as a falling obelisk, Dama stroked out the full magazine of lethal missiles, shredding six screaming victims in the space of a short breath. The entrance was plugged by a clot of men dying in puling agony. Tossing his empty bow at the writhing chaos behind him, Dama ran through the front flap and vaulted onto his horse.

"We'll never get clear!" Vettius shouted as he whipped his mount. "They'll run us down in relays before we reach the Danube."

Wailing Sarmatians boiled around both ends of the tent, shedding helmets, weapons—any encumbrances. Their voices honed a narrow blade of terror.

"The control," Dama shouted back as the pair dodged among the crazy pattern of wagon tongues. "He used his own mind and a monkey's to control something not quite a man."

"So what?"

"That last tooth didn't come from a man. It didn't come from anything like a man."

Something scaly, savage and huge towered over the wreckage of the tent. It cocked its head to glare at the disappearing riders while scrabbling with one stubby foreleg to stuff a black-robed figure farther into its maw. Vettius twisted in his saddle to stare in amazement at the coffin-long jaws gaping twenty foot into the air and the spined backfin like that of no reptile of the past seventy million years.

The dragon hissed, leaving a scarlet mist of blood to hang in the air as it ducked for another victim.

COLD LIGHT

by Karl Edward Wagner

The assault on the ogres' stronghold had been brutal, reflected Gaethaa as he wearily looked over the ruins. Pulling off his silver-trimmed helmet, he ran a bleeding hand over his grimy face, pushing the sweat-soaked blond locks from his eyes. He squinted through the smoke that made red the sun. Inside the fortress walls all was one chaotic turmoil of smashed and burning buildings, seige engines—bodies of both his men and the ogres' retainers.

He pushed a corpse from an overturned cart and sprawled onto the vacated space. Wincing against the pain as he sucked in a deep breath—some bruised ribs there at best, but the cuirass had turned the sword—Gaethaa permitted himself the tired exultation befitting a man who has brilliantly conceived and executed a difficult task, one fully as honorable as it was dangerous.

Credit must be given to many others, to be certain. Had it not been for the genius of the young Tranodeli wizard, Cereb Ak-Cetee, the sorcerous flames that guarded the ogres' walls would not have been extinguished, nor their impenetrable obsidian gate blasted into splintered rubble. Mollyl had been magnificent as he led the first wave through the smouldering gap and into the full fury of the ogres' minions. And the Red Three had very nearly succeeded in overwhelming his soldiers, even with the failure of their spells and the rout of their servants. Many had been smashed and torn under the huge weapons of the seemingly invincible ogre brothers. Then Gesell, the middle brother, fell from the poisoned arrow which Anmuspi the Archer threaded through the visor of his helmet. And Omsell, the oldest, was grievously wounded from a swordthrust of the dying Malander, and as the ogre fell to his knees, Gaethaa himself had struck his hideous head from his shoulders. That left only Dasell, who had been knocked senseless when he tried to leap in escape from the fortress walls. Gaethaa had ordered him bound, and now the ogre's twelve-foot body swung in grotesque dance, as it dangled from a gibbet overlooking the valley that he and his brothers had so long held in terror.

Alidore approached him through the haze, his broken arm now roughly bandaged. You did that when you blocked Omsell's axe from splitting me, thought Gaethaa, and vowed to make his lieutenant a generous gift from his personal portion of the booty, although such bravery was truly a knight's duty to his lord.

"We've got it all about mopped up, milord." Alidore had started to salute with his other hand, but decided it would look foolish. "Looks like we've rounded together everyone still alive inside. Not too pretty—the Red Three must have ordered all captives slaughtered when it was obvious that we were about to break through the wall. So that leaves us with maybe twenty survivors that we're holding for your orders— the last of their soldiers and servants."

"Kill them."

Alidore paused, reluctant to dispute his leader. "Milord, most of them swear they were forced to serve the ogres. They either obeyed their commands or were eaten like the others."

A cold note crept into Gaethaa's voice and his face was hard. "Most are probably lying. The others deserve worse, for they stooped to save their own lives by becoming tools for the enslavement and destruction of their fellow men. No, Alidore, mercy is commendable to be sure, but when you seek to destroy an absolute evil, you must destroy it absolutely. Show mercy in expunging a blight, and you only leave seeds to spread it anew. Kill them all."

Alidore turned to give the order, but Mollyl had been listening and was already loping across the court to see it carried out. He would enjoy that, Alidore thought in distaste, then dismissed the Pellinite from his thoughts. He addressed Gaethaa sincerely.

"Milord, you have done a really magnificent thing here today! For years this land has lived in abject terror of the Red Three. Most of the countryside has been stripped bare by them, and no one can say how many captives have ended their lives as food on the ogres' table! With their death the area can return to life once more—its people can farm the lands and sell their wares in peace, and travellers can enter the valleys and pass without danger. And here—as before when I have followed you on your missions—you will accept nothing from the people but their gratitude!"

Gaethaa smiled tiredly and waved him to silence. "Please, Alidore! Save eulogies for my death. I can't bear them now. Many have died to help me in my crusade, otherwise I could have done nothing. They are the ones who deserve your praise.

"No," and his voice was dreamy, "my only desire is to destroy these agents of evil. It is my goal in life, and I ask nothing in return."

Admiration glowed on Alidore's battle-weary face. "And now that the Red Three are destroyed, what is to be our next mission?"

Gaethaa's voice was inspired. "As my next mission I will seek out and destroy one of the most dangerous agents of evil that history or legend knows. Tomorrow I will ride out for the death of a man called Kane!"

I. WHERE DEATH HAS LAIN

At times the awesome curse of immortality weighed on Kane beyond all endurance. Then he was overcome with long periods of black despair, during which he withdrew entirely from the world and spent his days in gloomy brooding. In such dark depression he would remain indefinitely, his mind wandering through the centuries it had watched, while within there cried unanswered a longing for peace. Ultimately some new diversion, some chance of fate, some abrupt reversal of spirit, would cut through his hopeless despair and send him forth once again into the world of men. Then cold despair would melt before the black heat of his defiance against the ancient god who had cursed him.

It happened that such a mood had seized Kane when he came to Sebbei. He had just fled the deserts of Lomarn, where his bandits had for a few months been plundering rich caravans and laying waste to the scattered oasis towns. An ingenious trap had cut down most of Kane's forces, and he had fled westward into the ghost land of Demornte. Here his enemies would not follow, for the plague which had annihilated this nation was still held in utmost dread, and although it had struck this desert locked land nearly two decades before, still no one entered and no one left silent Demornte.

Dead Demornte. Demornte whose towns lie empty, whose farms are slowly returning to forest. Demornte where death has lain and life will no more linger. Land of death where only shadows move in empty cities, where the living are but a handful to the countless dead. Demornte where ghosts stalk silent streets in step with the living, where the living walk side by side with their ghosts. And a man must look closely to tell one from the other.

When the great deserts of Lartroxia West and Lomarn to the east had been carved from the earth, some freak of nature had spared Demornte. Here, shouldered between two mighty deserts, green land had held out against scorched sand, and a considerable region of gently rolling hills and cool lakes had sheltered thousands of inhabitants under its low forests. It had been as a giant oasis, Demornte, and its people had lived pleasantly, working their many small farms and trading with the great caravans that crossed the deserts from east and west.

The plague had ridden with one such caravan, a plague such as these lands had never seen. Perhaps in the faraway land from which it had come, the people had formed a resistance to the disease. But here in fertile Demornte it sped like the wind throughout the green land, and thousands burned in its fevered delirium, screaming for water they could not swallow.

Desert locked Demornte. The plague could not cross the sands, so its fury fell on this peaceful world. And when it had run its course at last, peace returned to Demornte. The land became one vast tomb and knew the quiet of the tomb, for rarely were there enough survivors to bury the dead. Demornte, where ghosts stalk silent streets in step with the living, where the living walk side by side with their ghosts. And a man must look closely to tell one from the other.

Some few the plague had spared. Most of these gathered in Sebbei, the old capital, and here a few hundred dragged out their days where before 10,000 had bustled about their daily tasks. In Sebbei the remnants of a nation gathered together to await death.

To Sebbei Kane came seeking peace. A deathless man in a

land of the dead, he was drawn by the quiet peace of the city. Along overgrown roads his horse had carried him, past farms where the forest was ineluctably obliterating all signs of man's labors. He had ridden through debris strewn streets of deserted towns, watched only by empty windows and yawning doorways. Often he passed piles of bleached bones— pitiful relics of humanity—and sometimes a skeleton seemed to wink and smile knowingly, or rattle its bones in greeting. Welcome redhaired stranger! Welcome you with eyes of death! Welcome man who rides under a curse! Will you stay with us? Why do you ride by so fast?

But Kane only stopped when he came to Sebbei. Through gates left open—for who would enter? who would leave? —his horse plodded, past rows of empty buildings and down silent streets. But the streets were kept reasonably clear, and an occasional house showed occupants—sad faces that stared at him with little curiosity. None challenged him; no one asked him any question. This was Sebbei, where one lived amidst death, where one waited only for death. Sebbei with its few inhabitants living in its silent shell—mice rustling through a giant's skeleton. To Kane Sebbei seemed far more eerie than those towns peopled solely by the dead through which he had ridden.

At the town's one operating tavern he had halted. Assailed for a moment by the uncanny lifelessness of the city, he paused in his saddle and licked his cold lips with tongue dry from travel. Over his right shoulder protruded the hilt of the long sword he wore slung across his back, and its scabbard rattled when he shook the tightness from his corded muscles. Lightly he slid from the saddle and entered the tavern, gazing speculatively at the incurious eyes that greeted him. Eyes so dull, so lifeless, they seemed clouded with corpselike glaze.

I am Kane, he had told those who drank there. His voice had echoed loudly, for in Sebbei they speak in hushed whispers. I have grown tired in crossing this desert, and I plan to stay here in your land for a time, he had explained. A few had nodded and the rest returned to their thoughts. Kane shrugged and began to ask questions of some of the townsmen, who listlessly gave him the answers he sought.

At length someone pointed out a faded old man who sat at a table in one corner, his back straight but his face broken. Here was one called Gavein, who served as Lord

Mayor of Sebbei—a somewhat ironic dignity, for his duties were few in this town of ghosts, and prestige only a half-hearted echo of tradition. Gavein regarded Kane without comprehension when he attempted to explain his wishes to the mayor, but after a moment he seemed to awaken from his reverie. There are many empty houses, he told Kane. Take whatever you require—there are palaces or hovels, as you please. Most of our city has remained untenanted all these years since the plague, and only ghosts will take issue with your occupancy. Food you may purchase here at our market, or raise what you desire. Our needs are few these days, so you may soon grow tired of our monotonous fare. This tavern furnishes our amusements, if you feel inclined to such things. Stay with us then for as long as your spirit desires. Do as you wish, for no man will pry into your affairs. We are a dying people here in Sebbei. Our visitors are rare and few stay for long. Our thoughts and manner are our own, and we care not what chance brings you among us. It is our wish only to be left alone with our thoughts. We in turn leave you with yours. And Gavein tugged the worn folds of his cloak closer about his thin shoulders and returned to his dreams.

So Kane wandered through the deserted streets of Sebbei, watched by only an occasional pair of clouded eyes from the few inhabited dwellings. At length he took residence in an old merchant's villa, where the rich furnishings appealed to his taste for luxury, and whose neglected gardens along a small lake promised solace to his anguished spirit.

But he lived there not alone, for often there came to him a strange girl named Rehhaile, whom many called a sorceress. Only Rehhaile among those of Sebbei showed more than distracted aloofness to the stranger who had stopped in their city. An outsider herself, Rehhaile spent long hours in Kane's company, and she ministered to him in many ways.

Thus came Kane to Sebbei in Demornte. Demornte where death has lain, and life will not linger.

II. DEATH RETURNS TO DEMORNTE

Death came again to Demornte. Nine gaunt horses beat their hooves with hollow echo through the silent streets of Demornte, past the overgrown fields, past the empty, staring houses, past the mocking smiles of skeletons. Death had returned to Demornte flying varied standards—idealism, sa-

dism, duty, vengeance, adventure. New banners, but it was
death that marched beneath them, and the omniscient eyes
of the deserted houses, of the laughing skulls recognized
death and welcomed it home.

Only nine men. Many had started, seasoned mercenaries
hired with Gaethaa's wealth, adventurers drawn by the boldness of the mission, men of hate with festered scores to
settle with Kane. But the way had been hard, and some had
fallen on the trail, others had deserted when they thought
more about the man whom they were seeking. At Omlipttei
outlaws had mistaken them for a troop of the Lomarni
guard; their ambush had slain many. And when they at last
had reached Demornte, many had not trusted the triple spell
which Cereb Ak-Cetee swore would protect them from the
dreaded plague. They had tried to desert; Gaethaa had
pronounced them traitors and thus servants of evil, and he
had ordered all deserters executed. The fight had been short
and vicious, for these were hardencd warriors. At the end
there were left only Gaethaa and eight of his men to ride to
Sebbei, where Cereb Ak-Cetee's magic had shown Kane to
be staying.

We are enough, said Gaethaa. We must not give this
demon a chance to escape his doom. And so they had
followed him into the ghostland of Demornte.

Gaethaa—called also Gaethaa the Crusader, the Good,
the Avenger—had fallen heir to extensive baronial estates in
Kamathae. As a boy he had spent most of his time in the
company of his family's men-at-arms. He had grown to
despise the pampered luxury and wasteful existence of his
class, and to yearn for adventures like those the men talked
of by the fires. At manhood he had resolved to use his
wealth to fight the battles of the oppressed, to seek out and
destroy the creatures of evil who preyed upon mankind. He
was a fanatic in the cause of good, and once he had recognized a center of evil, he trampled over every obstacle that
would hinder him from burning it clean. For several years
he had marched forth against petty tyrants, evil wizards,
robber barons, outlaw packs, and monsters human and inhuman. Always he had vanquished evil in the name of good,
shackled chaos with law. And now he rode against Kane, a
name that had always fascinated him, but which he had half
regarded as legendary, until he began to realize the truth
that lay in the fantastic tales of this man. Kane would be a
magnificent challenge for Gaethaa the Crusader.

Alidore had followed him from the first. A younger son of impoverished Lartroxian gentry, he had left home early and had passed through Kamathae when Gaethaa was organizing his first mission. Gaethaa's idealism was mirrored in Alidore, and the young man had joined him with unfailing enthusiasm. Through all of Gaethaa's campaigns he had followed faithfully and fought bravely against all odds. Now he was Gaethaa's lieutenant and most trusted friend. Alidore would follow wherever his lord should lead and fight beside him with the same unfaltering zeal of idealism.

Cereb Ak-Cetee was a young wizard from the plains of Tranodeli. He looked like a gawking hayseed choirboy in his silken mage's cloak, but he was very far from harmless. Cereb needed wealth and experience before he could pursue his training to the not inconsiderable height of his ambitions. Gaethaa had noted the sorceror's skill in penetrating defenses and ferreting out fugitives, and he paid Cereb handsomely for his services.

Next in rank—although Cereb's position was ambiguous—came Mollyl from the ill-famed island of Pellin in the Thovnosian Empire. Mollyl was a dark man who smiled only when another screamed in agony. His total lack of fear—perhaps he lost it in the exultation of killing—made him indispensable to Gaethaa in battle. Mollyl took Gaethaa's wealth, but he would probably follow him without pay, so long as his lord offered him new fields of delight.

Also from the Thovnosian Empire, but from the island of Josten, came Jan. Ten years ago when Kane's pirate fleet had terrorized the island empire, Jan had seen his family butchered, and Kane himself had chopped off his right hand when Jan had tried to fight back against the raiders. Since then Jan had laced a padded base to the stump of his wrist, and from the base he could affix either a blunt hook or one with needle tip and razor-sharp inner curve. He had joined Gaethaa for vengeance.

Although aging, Anmuspi the Archer still boasted he could thread an axehead at hundred paces. Few who had seen the mercenary shoot would care to call his boast. Anmuspi's luck had run out in Nostoblet in Lartroxia South. A palace revolution had failed, his employers were crucified, and Anmuspi was put on the slave block. Gaethaa had bought him after hearing the auctioneer proclaim his skill as an archer. For Anmuspi it meant only another shift in employers, and he followed Gaethaa's every command faithfully. For Anmuspi right and wrong were not his to question; obedience was his code.

Dron Missa was a footloose adventurer from far Waldann. His people were a warrior race, and even among them Missa excelled as a swordsman. Gaethaa promised him adventure, so Dron Missa had exuberantly come along for the ride.

Two others sought vengeance. One was Bell, a peasant from the Myceum Mountains. Bell was fully as stupid as he was brutal and powerful. Five years before Kane had sacrificed two of Bell's sisters as part of an ill-fated sorcerous experiment. Bell never tired of telling people what he planned to do to Kane someday.

Sed tho'Dosso listened carefully to Bell's descriptions of torture, for like Jan and Bell he had a score to settle with Kane. Several months previous when Kane had been organizing the desert raiders of Lomarn, Sed tho'Dosso had offered resistance on the grounds that he should lead since his band was the largest. Kane had peremptorily smashed Sed tho'Dosso's forces and had left the bandit chieftain staked in the sun to die. By a freak chance he had escaped death, and when he heard of Gaethaa's mission in crossing the Lomarn, Sed tho'Dosso eagerly joined him.

So they rode through Demornte, each man silent with his own thoughts. Death rode nine gaunt horses through the familiar streets of Demornte, and dead Demornte bade Death welcome.

III. RIPPLES AND SHADOWS

The moon cast pale light upon Rehhaile's slender body, as she watched Kane moodily toss stones into the lake beneath their perch. Goose pimples rose on her tanned skin, and she wriggled over the velvet moss of the bank to press her shivering form against his. His body was warm, though his mind was distant, and she rested her head against his shoulder in contentment.

Rehhaile did not share the gloomy apathy, the bitter despair of her people. She loved the sunlight while the others generally kept to their shops and houses. As a result her lean figure was tanned an even brown that matched her unbound hair, and there was a strong hint of freckles across her face. Her features were somewhat boldly shaped, although not to the point of losing femininity. Her breasts were small and firm, her hips slim—making her appear a few years younger than her twenty years.

Bunching her long fingers over the massive muscles of Kane's shoulders and back, she began to massage them, trying to shape the knotted muscles to the pattern of the ripples on the lake. Kane seemed to ignore her, but she reached out with her mind and sensed that she was drawing him into lazy arousal.

For Rehhaile was blind, her wide eyes altogether sightless. Her mother had died from the plague while Rehhaile yet lay in her womb. Her father had sworn that death should not take all from him, and a physician had quickly torn her from the dead womb. Both father and physician died of the plague within the week, but somehow Rehhaile had survived while all about her Demornte was seared by the plague. Someone had taken care of her, for Demornte was a land of motherless children and childless mothers. Later she made a living by whatever way she could, for the most part hanging around Sebbei's sole tavern.

But Rehhaile had been blind since birth. And yet she had in place of sight an infinitely more precious power of vision. Her macabre birth, a genetic mutation, some whim of the gods—the reason was unknowable and unimportant. She was given a psychic talent that provided a far more wondrous sense of perception than any human eyes could afford.

Rehhaile could reach out to link her own mind with another. Through this psychic contact she could share the other person's perception of his surroundings, in effect see through another's eyes, hear through his ears, feel through his fingers. And along with this sharing of sensory impulses, Rehhaile could actually sense the feelings of another mind— not so much read the thoughts, but experience for herself the myriad emotions that drift through the corridors of the mind. Her incredible talent to see into another human mind established Rehhaile as a sorceress in the eyes of the townspeople of Sebbei, and in their despair they accepted this without concern or curiosity.

Because she could perceive the emotional turmoil of others, Rehhaile shared the distress of that soul she touched. If there was pain, she tried to soothe it in whatever way she could. For the people of Demornte nothing could be done. Theirs was an inconceivable, inconsolable grief, and their emotions were a burned out wasteland that could never be healed. The people of Sebbei largely ignored Rehhaile just as they ignored everything except their bitter memories. Rehhaile lived with them because there was nothing else she could do. And in sharing their thoughts, she shared their joyless depression, a steeping in gloom that almost overwhelmed her own soul.

The rare travellers whom chance brought to Sebbei were a marvel to her. She bathed in the exotic colors of their thoughts, finding a universe of unimagined interest and vitality even in the mind of a stray camel driver. She often tried to persuade these strangers to take her along with them across the desert, but inevitably the knowledge of Rehhaile's witch powers would turn them cold to her appeal.

Then Kane had come to Sebbei, and she had experienced worlds of sensation unlike any she had ever imagined a human mind could hold. Kane had been a whirling labyrinth to Rehhaile. Most of his emotions were altogether alien to her, and many frightened her with their strangeness. But she had recognized the awful need for rest that screamed within him—the unanswerable longing for peace. So she had gone to him to minister to his agony in the arts that only she knew, and through the months of companionship they had known, it seemed to Rehhaile that the pain had somewhat dimmed within Kane.

She tugged a shock of red hair playfully. "Hey! What do you see down there in the pool?"

His mind was cold, far away. "Ripples on the water like the passing of years. Man enters life and there is a splash. His life sends out ripples—small ripples for a little man, huge waves for a great man—waves that overwhelm the tiny ripples, wash them away or remold them. But in the end it is all the same, for the ripples go out into the lake of life and soon die away, to leave the lake smooth for new lives or stones."

She scratched lightly with her nails. "Make that up just now?"

"No. I heard that analogy from the sage Monpelloni whom I studied under in Churtannts." Rehhaile did not know that Churtannts had lain in ruins for over a century. "Only I don't fit the frame he proposed here. I'm something marooned on the surface of existence. Instead of a short splash, I keep floating there, struggling about and making an endless succession of waves."

"I can see you there. Like an old bat fallen in and flopping about the pool." She dug her nails in deeper. "Come back to me, Kane! Don't you love me?"

He rolled over so abruptly she nearly slipped off the bank. His cold blue eyes bored into her blind face. Those eyes—how they frightened her with the promise of death that lurked within! But now Rehhaile thought she sensed an even more haunted glare.

"No, Rehhaile!" He said with slow intensity. "Can't you understand! Your life is only a brief ripple across the pool, and mine is a constant flow of waves into infinity! Your ripple is only noted in passing and swept aside!"

She shivered with a coldness not of the wind.

"And do you love me?" he returned.

"No!" she answered him softly. "For you there can be no love. I can only pity you and try to soothe that which can never be healed."

"I think you begin to understand," Kane said with a bitter laugh. Then soon they lay together under the pale moon. And about them the ghosts of dead Demornte slipped by unheeded.

IV. THE CRUSADER IN SEBBEI

"Their faces are as empty as the skulls we've passed!" commented Dron Missa, craning his long neck to stare down a seated townsman who stolidly watched them ride by. "Bunch of fish faces! I've eaten baked fish that had more intelligence in their boiled eyes than these cretins."

"Thought they ate only flesh in Waldann—raw flesh at that," scoffed Cereb Ak-Cetee.

Missa laughed unappreciatively. "Nothing wrong with raw flesh. Tastes good with a little salt. Once ate a squirrel raw on a bet—whiskers to tail with the thing still kicking. I've hated the little furry bastards ever since."

"How about keeping your mind on finding that tavern," interrupted Gaethaa caustically. His nerves had been on edge since entering Sebbei. Ruined cities were no novelty to him. But the utter lack of curiosity shown by the people was unnerving. Their indifference upon seeing a band of heavily armed stranges ride into their city was unsettling—and something of a subtle insult.

The first person they encountered in this city of ghosts had been a disheveled fat man with a yellow streaked beard.

He was sitting loosely before a stagnant fountain near the unguarded city gates. With a vapid expression he had watched their approach, then scurried off giggling when Alidore stopped to question him. It was not an auspicious welcome.

Several others that they met had turned away or closed their doors when hailed, and Gaethaa had grimly recalled the stories heard while crossing the Lomarn that in Sebbei there dwelled only ghosts and madmen. Still it seemed evident now that they would confront no organized opposition from the townspeople. This would make their mission one of more direct attack—Gaethaa had been prepared to use more subtle tactics should it have developed that Kane had established himself as ruler of the dead city.

Finally, persistent questioning of those they met indicated that someone named Gavein, who held the office of Lord Mayor, was more or less responsible for central authority in Sebbei. This Gavein could likely be found at Jethrann's tavern. Directions to Jethrann's tavern had been given with the provincial assumption that a stranger knew his way through the city to begin with. Sebbei was an old city, laid out in chaotic growth, and its narrow streets were disturbingly labyrinthian.

After several wrong turns and unenlightening inquiries, they came upon a brown haired girl seated under a tree. She seemed to be asleep, for she failed to notice them until the riders drew close. Then her head snapped toward their approach, face wild in an uncanny wide-eyed look of fright.

"By Thoem—at least here's somebody that doesn't have both feet in the grave!" smiled Dron Missa appreciatively. "Hey, Miss! Care to help some bone dry travellers find a cool place to rest? We're looking for a tavern—Jethrann's place."

The girl rose to her feet and began to back away from them, her face oddly contorted in fear. Gaethaa spoke quietly in reassuring tones, explaining that he and his men were strangers passing through Sebbei, that they . . .

She turned from them and broke into a run. As she dashed from the shade, sunlight caught the flash of tanned limbs beneath her short dress of green trimmed brown suede. Hooves struck the earth in faster rhythm. Mocking laughter overtook her. Defiance edging her squeal of fright, the girl was jerked from the street by a bronzed arm and swung onto a saddle.

Mollyl laughed as he pinioned her lashing arms against

her side. "Cut it, sweetheart!" he grinned. "Young girl like you must be real lonely here with all these dried up old scarecrows! Is that why you shy away when you see a real man, sweetheart? Maybe I could teach you the right way to say hello to a stranger."

"All right, Mollyl! We don't want to frighten her any more than we have already!" Gaethaa growled. "Stop squirming, child! We're only trying to get directions to Jethrann's tavern. Please forgive my men's lapse of breeding—we meant no harm to you. Now can you please tell us the way?"

Fear still lined her features, but her struggles grew less. Helplessly she perched on the saddle edge, crushed against Mollyl's hard chest. "It isn't far," she answered haltingly. "Keep on down this street maybe half a mile. You can begin to see the market square on down to your left then. The tavern is on the square."

"My thanks, child," Gaethaa returned. "We were on the right track at least. Guess our preconception of a market square doesn't fit this ghost town."

The girl wriggled hopefully, seeking to slip away. The expression of unaccountable fear still marred her face. Cereb Ak-Cetee grunted curiously and leaned toward her, peering at her face. Frowning in puzzlement he moved his long fingers before her eyes. She drew away with a shudder when his hand brushed her flesh. The wizard examined her speculatively.

Gaethaa spoke in command, and Mollyl reluctantly permitted his captive to slip to the ground. Shaking herself as if to shed some taint, the girl stepped back, still staring at them in dread fascination. Abruptly she whirled and disappeared into an alley.

"She's blind," observed Cereb Ak-Cetee as they rode away. "Did you notice? No focus. Her eyes are sightless."

"What do you mean—blind?" Alidore exploded. "She damn well acted like she could see good enough. Had a strange look to her eyes, granted. But she can't have been blind."

"I said she was blind," the wizard persisted tight lipped. "I'm not at all sure how she perceives things, but I know enough to recognize blind eyes when they present themselves to me."

"Yeah—Ok!" Alidore answered in dismissal. He was not about to provoke the wizard's petulance.

"Hey, Bell!" Dron Missa whispered. "Cereb says we just

took directions from a blind girl. Doesn't that ring a bell even in your thick skull?"

"You're funny, Missa," Bell rumbled. "Real funny. Yeah, you're a scream. You ought to become a jester. You'd be good. You're really a riot."

Alidore wondered how long it would take Dron Missa to push Bell too far—or vice versa. The Waldann's sword arm was among the deadliest Alidore had witnessed, but Bell could tear him into quarters if he ever got the drop on him.

"That's it!" Jan pointed with his hook. "Hell, man! I can smell that wine from across the square!"

"Good!" Gaethaa exclaimed. "And this part of town is as stagnant as the rest of the place. Doesn't look like there's any kind of organized force here, but we can't be sure what Kane will have done. Looks like he's just lying low so far though. So we'll play it by ear until we know the set up. Stroll on into the tavern just like we were on our way across Demornte and stopped to rest. Alidore and I will start talking with this Gavein—assuming he's here—and sound him out. Then we'll take it from there. But no mention of Kane by any of you until I make the move. And easy on the wine—things might happen fast."

Tethering their mounts before the three-storied stone structure, Gaethaa and his band entered the open doorway. Inside the air was cool, albeit somewhat stale. A small number of men stood at the bar and sat at small tables occupied with their drinks. Low-voiced conversation broke off as the riders sauntered across the smoky room to the bar—a conspicuous entrance even had strangers been commonplace in Sebbei. Still the townspeople returned to their incurious aloofness once the initial stir had settled, and the murmur of quiet voices began again.

Jethrann, the scar-faced innkeeper, took their coin with an empty smile and brought them wine. In response to Gaethaa's guarded inquiry he indicated the Lord Mayor, who sat alone and half asleep at his usual table.

Wiping the wine from his mustache, Gaethaa carried his mug across to Gavein's table, followed by Alidore who brought along the bottle. "Mind if I join you?" he asked.

Gavein shrugged. "Suit yourself."

"Have a drink with us?" suggested Alidore, already filling the mayor's empty mug.

"Thoughtful of you," Gavein observed. "Bunch of well armed toughs comes stomping into the place when we see maybe a dozen strangers in a year, and right away they want to share a bottle with the mayor. Maybe mercenaries are better mannered now than in the old days, but I doubt it. So thanks for the drink, and what do you want?"

"My name is Gaethaa," he introduced himself, deciding to come directly to the point. This gambit fizzled when Gavein made no show of recognition at the name. But Gaethaa was not a vain man, and he realized that it was unlikely tales of his exploits had penetrated empty Demornte.

He shifted to another approach. "I see my name is not known here in Sebbei—but then there are many names known far wider than Gaethaa. Take the name *Kane* for instance— there's a man whose fame has reached across our world. I seem to have heard that Kane came through Demornte once—perhaps you've met him?"

"I know a man of that name," Gavein admitted.

Gaethaa caught Alidore's eyes significantly. "Perhaps this isn't the same man. The Kane I have in mind is a giant of a man—stands about six feet and is built like he had the muscles of three strong men stretched upon a single frame. He has sort of a coarse face, has red hair and often a short beard. Generally carries his sword slung across his back in the Carsultyal fashion. Left-handed—although he's a deadly swordsman with either arm. His eyes though—people remember his eyes. Has blue eyes with some sort of insane menace in their gaze . . ."

"We're talking about the same Kane," Gavein grudgingly acknowledged. "What about him?"

Gaethaa forced himself to speak noncommittally. "So Kane is in Sebbei, is he?"

The mayor considered his wine cup. "Yeah, Kane's here in our city—Thoem knows why he stays. Lives out in the Nandai's old villa. Keeps to himself—Rehhaile's the only one who sees much of him. You some friend of his?"

Gaethaa laughed and rose to his feet. His men along the bar wavered hands near weapon hilts at the movement, but halted when they saw the eager triumph lighting the Crusader's long face. "No—Kane is no friend of mine! Far from it!" he intoned loudly. The townspeople gaped at him in startled amazement.

"In the world outside your ghostland men know me as Gaethaa the Avenger!" he announced. "I have made it my mission in life to hunt down and destroy the agents of evil who bring death and deprivation to the helpless! Too long has evil held sway over our lives—too long have the creatures of evil run unchecked among mankind! Evil has ruled the lives of men with the consuming might of merciless force—and mankind has had to bow to its terror or else be destroyed! But I have sworn to destroy the servants of evil wherever they hold mankind in thrall! I have time and again done battle with the forces of evil, and each time I have triumphed and destroyed with the greater strength of good! Order has mastered chaos—because I have fought evil on its own ground, and with the superior power of good I have conquered! Conquered because I have had the courage to confront evil face to face—because I have turned against evil the very violence with which it holds mankind under its heel—because I have met force with force and destroyed brute power with brute power!"

Gaethaa's face was bathed in demonic transfiguration as he breathed fierce sincerity into his explosive diatribe. His listeners watched him with the awestricken attention commanded by saints and madmen, and even here in Demornte none dared to break into the spell of ferocious fanaticism he spun for them.

Seeming to recollect himself, Gaethaa paused in his harangue and gestured toward his men. "These are my followers," he explained hoarsely. "A small army at the moment, but they're picked fighters and every man a seasoned and fearless warrior! Many have followed my command through other hard fought campaigns, and in all have endured sufficient hardships and danger just in winning through to Sebbei to put old sagas to shame! For I have come to Sebbei with my men to seek out this creature who calls himself Kane! I am here to deliver your city from Kane!"

Gavein shrugged uneasily, uncertain how all this was going to involve him and his townspeople. "But Kane does nothing to us here in Sebbei. He keeps to himself in a villa at the edge of our city, as I've said. We don't even see him except when he comes by from time to time to buy provisions. Why don't you take your quarrel elsewhere?"

Gaethaa was aghast. Stunned by the mayor's indifference, he turned to Alidore to see if madness had claimed all present. Alidore cleared his throat and suggested in Kamathaen, "It may well be, milord, that we underestimated the parochial isolation of these people. Incredible as it seems, I don't think they have any idea who Kane might be. Why else would they have permitted him to remain in their city?"

Once more assured, the Avenger addressed his nervous audience. "Obviously then you people don't realize what manner of fiend is living here in your city! It seems incredible in view of his dark history that he hasn't already turned on you—Tloluvin only knows what demonic scheme he has in mind for you and your land! I've pitted myself against some utterly ruthless black hearted monsters in human guise in the past, but this Kane could be the most evil man ever to walk the earth! His crimes are so numerous, so colossal in infamy that most people believe Kane nothing more than wild legend! I once thought him legendary myself—until in my far searching crusade against the forces of evil, I began to cut across his blood stained trail too often for me to doubt his existence among us!

"Legends—there are countless legends if you travel far enough to hear them! It's astonishing how far back these tales go in man's history. A lot of these things may well be spurious or latter day reinterpretations, but there are enough common themes to make me give serious consideration to many points. These legends tell that Kane is immortal—further that he was one of the first true men! They say Kane rebelled against his creator—some forgotten god who had attempted to create in mankind a perfect race modeled according to his own warped ideal. This god had failed many times before he finally created a golden race that he kept in a sheltered paradise for his own amusement. It's not clear how, but evidently Kane provoked this golden race of men to revolt from their paradise existence—even killed his own brother when he tried to prevent this. Kane's defiance and murderous violence resulted in the destruction of the golden age, with the subsequent scattering of humanity across the ancient earth. Kane himself was doomed by this god with the curse of immortality! A curse of eternal wandering, never to know peace, haunted by the spectre of the violence he introduced to mankind—marked an outcast from humanity by the brand of his eyes, a killer's eyes! Only through violence such as he engendered can he die, but throughout the centuries no man has been able to destroy Kane in this his own element!

"Well, that's the gist of the oldest legends, and of course you can't tell where to draw the line with these old tales. But there are too many other legends and sagas over the centuries in which the name of Kane appears to lay this entirely to chance or to recurrent poetic theme! A few facts appear certain. Kane has lived for at least a few centuries—he is not the first agent of evil endowed with preternatural longevity by any means—and during this time he has brought nothing but death and destruction wherever he has wandered! Catastrophic violence seems to slither behind him like a shadow! And Kane has generally been the author of this bloodshed and ruin! He has engaged in the most hideous acts of black sorcery—the wizards of Carsultyal even drove him from their land in abhorrence at one time! He has been a pirate, a bandit, an assassin—committed countless numbers of violent deeds! He has gathered and led gigantic armies and navies against peaceful lands for purpose of conquest and pillage! He has ruled nations as the blackest of tyrants! He has been involved with—often instigated—numberless conspiracies to overthrow lawful governments! His name has become a byword for treachery over the centuries!

"I'm not just rehashing a bunch of fantastic legends for you to hear! Men who are with me today will attest to his guilt—they have seen Kane's insane deeds with their own eyes!" It was essential to Gaethaa that Gavein and his people recognize the justice of his mission—fully appreciate the infamy of Kane. "Talk to them! Just ask either Jan or Mollyl there what the name of Kane means to their fellows in the Thovnosian Empire! Ask Bell what Kane did to the people of his native Myceum Mountains! Ask Sed tho'Dosso to describe for you the murderous attacks Kane and his bandits made upon caravans crossing the Lomarn here at your doorsteps only a few months ago! I've talked enough now—go on and question these men!"

Gaethaa looked about him, earnest eyes seeking the faces of the townspeople—faces that turned away in frightened confusion. Finally Gavein essayed to speak, blinking at the Avenger as if hoping he and his men would suddenly fade off into the late afternoon shadows. His response gave Gaethaa his greatest shock of the long, trying day.

"Please! I don't really care to hear your tales of ancient legends and black evil run rampant in the world beyond our land. We of Demornte have quite enough to consider in our own sorrows. You speak to us of murder and destruction—but we have watched the death of our entire land and its people. Kane's crimes mean nothing to us here; we care nothing and ask nothing of the outside world. What happens or has happened there does not concern us."

The paleness of his face made his lips a red wound. Checking his hand that longed to seize sword hilt, Gaethaa thundered incredulously, "Do you mean to say that you intend to protect Kane!"

Gavein looked at him with a touch of almost pity in his tired face. "You misunderstand. We care nothing of your quarrel. If it is between you and Kane, then go to him with it. The two of you settle it according to whatever laws seem best to you. In Sebbei we ask only to be left alone with our sorrow. As regards your 'mission,' we will neither help you nor hinder you in any manner whatsoever. It's your fight—do what you wish. But leave us alone!"

Shaking his head in astonishment, Gaethaa turned to Alidore for counsel. "They're obsessed, you know!" he exclaimed in sick pity. "The whole land is like this it seems. So obsessed with this one thing that they've lost all perspective! I don't think a man here really understands anything I've tried to tell them!"

"I'll agree it looks hopeless for them. At any rate they'll pose no threat to us," Alidore observed. "Kane's backed himself into a corner this time, and it appears that he has only himself to turn to for help. Ask the old man to tell us where Kane's villa is."

"And get lost again?" Gaethaa growled. "Got a better idea. We'll let him lead us there in person."

Invited to accompany them, Gavein protested that it was not his affair. But when Bell and Sed tho'Dosso eagerly stepped toward him at Gaethaa's nod, the Lord Mayor gloomily rose to his feet and was escorted into the street outside.

V. TO TRAP A TIGER IN HIS LAIR

Rehhaile frantically hurried through the narrow streets of Sebbei, her mind still crawling with fear and loathing. The shock of confronting Gaethaa and his men had been brutal; and her concern for Kane was obscured by the pall of revulsion she had felt on touching their thoughts. Her soul felt outraged at the contact. Never had she experienced such a barrage of depraved, bestial images and cravings. Kane's mind was altogether alien to her, and she took care never to reach too deep within its tortuous depths. But among the thoughts of Gaethaa's band outright cruelty reveled alongside demented lusting, and Rehhaile's mind still cringed in memory, sick and soiled by the touch.

She ran along recklessly, stumbling in her haste, avoiding jarring collision time and again by the closest margins. To her sightless mind the twisting alleys of Sebbei assumed à bewildering pattern of clarity and darkness. Wherever possible Rehhaile cast out her mind to draw sight from another. At fortunate moments she made contact with one of the townspeople who was in the vicinity and through whose eyes she could see a portion of the course she followed. But in deserted Sebbei such chance encounters were too few, and more often Rehhaile found her path blotted out in darkness. Where there were no other's eyes through which she could see, she attempted to make a detour by reaching out to touch another nearby mind and follow a circuitous route along this region of light. But this wasted too many invaluable minutes, and Rehhaile was forced to plunge into the darkened segments of the labyrinth frequently—there to rely on shadowy hints from distant minds, or to feel her way along blindly. Although she knew the streets of Sebbei well, these passages of absolute blindness placed deadly obstacles in her search for Kane.

As she had felt certain she would, Rehhaile found Kane at the abandoned Nandai villa. Gasping for breath she ran through the walled gardens, her remaining steps made certain as Kane watched her disheveled approach. Kane had been half asleep, moodily contemplating the late afternoon sun from the shade of a densely laced roof of floral vine. A nearly drained amphora of thin Demornte wine leaned beside him, still damp from the cool waters of the lake. Alongside rested a bowl of strawberry domes.

"Hello, Rehhaile," he greeted her thickly, rising to his feet at the panic that lined her face. "Hey, what the hell's the matter? Somebody chasing you?"

"Kane!" Exhaustion forced her words out in strangled bursts. "Kane! You're in danger here! There're some men in Sebbei! They've come to kill you! They've been searching for you for weeks! They know you're in Sebbei! They'll be coming here to kill you as soon as they find out where you are! They'll be here any minute! They're going to kill you!"

Desperately Kane fought to command his semi-drunken faculties. "Men in Sebbei looking for me!" he exploded. "How many? Who are they? How are they armed? How do you know they're on my trail?"

Rehhaile poured out an incoherent account of her accostal by Gaethaa and his men, babbling frenziedly of strange men with harsh minds and thoughts of violence and death. Her words were disjointed, attempting to convey sensations for which language failed to accommodate—but Kane immediately understood the imminent danger of his position. Cursing bitterly the monumental carelessness into which his despair had lulled him, Kane questioned her sharply for details. She followed him into the villa as he dashed about buckling on his sword and searching for an extra quiver of bolts for his crossbow.

"Kane—what are you going to do?" Rehhaile moaned. "Are you going to try to stand them off from the villa?"

Kane's boot caught the edge of a bench, and he reeled away clumsily, slapping at his shin and snarling angrily. "I'm not sure what I'll do! Nine seasoned professionals make tough odds in an open fight! And they must be damned good to have trailed me to Sebbei—Tloluvin knows why, although that's beside the point at the moment! If I wait for them here, they can bottle me up like a bear in his cave! I can run for it, but if they've followed me this far, there's no reason to hope they won't hunt me down elsewhere in Demornte or the desert beyond!"

With practiced hands Kane worked the action of his crossbow. He felt grim satisfaction that he had permitted no rust or dirt to collect on his weapons—at least he had not fallen altogether under the spell of dead Demornte! "The best chance is going to be for me to get out of this villa, but to stay here in Sebbei. I can use the empty buildings for cover, and strike back at them on my own terms! These bastards won't be the first hunters to make the mistake of daring their prey within its lair!"

He started for the garden gate, when Rehhaile abruptly cried out a warning. "Kane! Get back! Those men are almost here! You'll never make it to cover!"

"That tears it!" growled Kane. Wheeling about he darted back into the villa—cursing vehemently in several languages. Quickly he gained the second floor of the dwelling and glanced through a window in the direction Rehhaile indicated. The sun cast long shadows away from the group of riders who stood near the edge of Sebbei watching the villa expectantly.

"You can see them now," Rehhaile observed.

"Yeah, I see them!" Kane rasped. "And they seem to

know just where to find me! Is that Gavein with them? Wonder what's holding them back now!"

At the outskirts of Sebbei Gaethaa halted with his men to consider the villa before them. The inner wall of Sebbei stood behind them. Beyond the old wall extended a periphery of newer structures—shops, inns, estates of the wealthy—a scattered suburban area outside the dirt, noise and stench of the crowded old city, but still within the confines of Sebbei's widely flung outer wall. Only now the outer wall guarded a ghost city from nonexistent raiders, and the forest was seeking to reclaim the outer city unchallenged by any hand.

The old Nandai villa had been situated somewhat apart from neighboring structures. It stood against a small lake on one side, a lake which curved back upon the inner wall in one direction and extended toward the low outer wall in the other. Rotted piers tenanted by half-sunken vessels reached out across its quiet surface, and the lake shore was overgrown with tall reeds and low shrubs. The over-grown gardens encircled the old villa, and outside the garden wall there had once been tilled fields. These fields were now in weeds with a sparse growth of young palms and pine trees, but there was little or no cover afforded here, and the villa was in effect surrounded by a clearing.

"No chance of riding up on him unobserved," Alidore commented.

Gaethaa grunted acknowledgment. Turning to Cereb Ak-Cetee, he asked, "Gavein still swears he knows of no protective magic that Kane has invoked to guard his lair. How about it?"

The wizard absent-mindedly picked at his nose and stared at the villa. "Well, there's no immediate evidence that we'll be dealing with sorcery here. I think we've caught Kane totally off guard. Give you odds we could ride in on him right now and take him."

Mollyl looked at Gavein knowingly and whispered something to Jan, who laughed and stropped his gleaming hook across his leather pants. "Now, Gavein," Mollyl grinned, "I just know you're telling us the truth about old Kane living out here all alone and all. But Jan here thinks maybe you might be holding back something on us—maybe that Kane keeps some men around as bodyguards, or maybe Kane has some little sorcerous devices waiting for his enemies. You sure you got your story straight, Gavein? You're not going to let Jan change your mind for you now, are you?" Gavein shuddered, eying the razor-edged hook in fascination.

"Cut it out, Mollyl," Gaethaa commanded. "I believe him. These people are too gutless to lie to us.

"Cereb, make damn sure Kane doesn't have anything in store for us we aren't expecting! The black hearted devil didn't live this long on the strength of his reputation alone. Others have been destroyed by Kane when they thought he was helpless, and I'm not about to believe we'll walk in and find him snoring away on a pile of empty wine jugs!"

The wizard slipped to the ground and began to remove a number of items from his voluminous packs. "Let you know for certain in a minute. But we'll end up wasting our advantage of surprise at this rate."

"Kane has no reason to expect us," Alidore pointed out.

"No, we don't look too suspicious, do we now." Cereb Ak-Cetee shrugged and bent to his work. His movements were certain, and his slender fingers arranged his paraphernalia with professional confidence. For all his youth, the Tranodeli was well on his way to becoming a powerful wizard. In his own mind, Cereb had decided to seek tutelage from one of the old Carsultyal masters after he had gained the experience and wealth of a few more of Gaethaa's missions.

Carefully he filled a copper bowl with water from a canteen, poured a few droplets of oily fluid from three vials, then dusted the opalescent surface with tiny pinches of powdered substance from other containers taken from his kit. He squatted over the bowl, his bony knees poking tightly against his robe, and began to chant into the bowl, but its surface remained clouded. Abruptly a tiny mote of red fire seemed to dance upon the center of the bowl. The surface shimmered faintly for a moment, then vaporized with a rush of thick fumes. The red flame lingered sullenly for a second, then winked out.

Dusting his hands on his cloak, Cereb straightened and began to collect his accoutrements. "As I said, nothing," he explained. "Any forces of magic connected with the villa before us would have been reflected on the surface of my bowl. As you observed, the only response was a flicker of crimson. This I interpret as representing Kane himself, who if all tales are true has sufficient sorcerous influences about him to elicit a reflection."

He chuckled affably. "I'd say we've caught Kane completely by surprise. They claim he's a good enough wizard in his own right, but so far as I know Kane's never made a sorceror's pact with any god or demon. That means he has no powers to turn to for immediate assistance. Without some form of patron deity to call upon, a sorceror—no matter how adept he may be—requires a lot of time, effort and materials to cast any sort of effective spell. Black magic isn't some cheap charlatan's trick you can perform with a finger snap and a puff of smoke, after all. Well, Kane hasn't had any time, and I doubt if he has any sorcerous materials at hand either. He's all yours, Milord Gaethaa."

"Well done, Cereb," Gaethaa returned with a thin smile. "We'll put your words to a test then. All right men, we'll play it like Kane doesn't know we're searching for him yet. The road to the outer wall leads straight past the entrance to the villa. We'll ride along it like we were headed on out of Sebbei minding our own business. Then once we get abreast of the villa, we'll rush the place. With luck he won't suspect anything until that moment. The garden gate will pose no problem, and once through, Mollyl, Jan, Bell take the front with me; Sed and Missa take the back with Alidore; Anmuspi and Cereb hold back to see if he gets past us. Cereb, I'm counting on you to be alert for any sorcerous defenses. Gavein, you can go now. So act nonchalant then, and let's get him!"

Released, Gavein gloomily watched them ride away toward the villa. He ran damp fingers across his throat, as if to convince himself it was yet intact, then shuffled back through the streets of Sebbei muttering under his breath.

Gaethaa led his men at a slow pace along the road, offering only casual attention to the villa they approached. Dron Missa argued with Mollyl over an imaginary dice game, and Jan loudly complained that both men had cheated him of his share of the pot.

They drew closer to the villa. Still there appeared no threatening movement from inside. Yet it seemed impossible that Kane was not watching their approach. Did he suspect?

At about two-hundred yards there sounded a sudden deadly hiss! Bell screamed and fell back on his saddle, reddened fingers clutching at the crossbow bolt that had abruptly sprouted from his left shoulder! His horse reared in alarm at the scent of fear and pain.

So Kane had been waiting! Gaethaa whirled in his saddle

to shout an order, and a second bolt screamed through the space he had just turned from! Alarmed at the accuracy and speed of Kane's marksmanship, Gaethaa again realized there was no cover for them until they could reach the villa.

"Get back!" he bellowed, as his men started to spread apart to ride in low. "Get back out of range! Hurry!"

A third bolt glanced across the back of Alidore's mail as the men wheeled on his command. Alidore cursed and bent low over his horse's neck. Luckily the shaft had struck him as he was turning and merely glanced on past him. Even at this range a direct hit from a powerful crossbow would slice through chain mail such as he wore. A fourth bolt narrowly missed Dron Missa before they galloped beyond range.

Bell held his saddle until they returned to the shelter of a grove of palms. There he slumped to the earth and sat against a palm trunk while Sed tho'Dosso examined the wound.

"Can't be fatal if he can still cuss like that," Missa offered thoughtfully. "A few inches off the heart, but not bad for the range. Why call us back here, milord?"

Gaethaa scowled at the villa in reappraisal. "Don't want to risk any further casualties. Too little cover around the place, damn it! Fast as he was firing, Kane must be working the cocking lever by hand. He'd be sure to get off a few more shots before we reached him, and at the range he hit Bell he must be as good a marksman as they claim! Damn near finished a few others of us anyway—he waited till we were well in his range before attacking! Not worth the risk to rush him now. We'll have darkness shortly. So we'll hit him again when the light's too poor for archery, but still too bright for Kane to slip away—if we watch carefully!"

"That's cutting it close," Alidore commented.

"Don't tell me what I already know!" Gaethaa retorted. "Anmuspi! Think you can get a fire arrow in where it can smoke him out? If we drive him from the villa, then Kane will be the one caught in the open!"

The archer smiled deliberately, his lined face asymmetrical with the sword scar that flashed white in rare moments of anger. "Roof of that place is timber, of course. I can ride a bit closer and pepper it with as many fire arrows as you want. It's an easy target that size, and I'll still be out of Kane's range. No crossbow can shoot as far as a heavy horn bow—unless you count those stupid-looking contraptions that take five minutes for a strong man to wind to a cock."

"Great! We'll burn him out then!" Gaethaa declared.

So Anmuspi the Archer rode back toward the villa. Dismounting beside a clump of young palms, he kindled a small fire and wrapped the ends of several shafts with resinous material. Lighting these from the fire, Anmuspi stepped into the open to draw his bow. He sank his first arrow into the roof of the villa, and his second shot struck about two feet from the other. They burned dismally, evidently unable to fire the timbers. The third arrow was snuffed out in flight and fell without effect upon the roof.

"Try for a window, Anmuspi!" Alidore called.

The archer nodded and shifted his target. Without apparent effort, he fired two more arrows through one window and embedded another in the wall beside the opening. This time he was rewarded with billows of smoke from within. Dron Missa applauded loudly.

Anmuspi was drawing a seventh arrow then, when a crossbow bolt tore straight through his heart. Released, the last arrow shot into the sky and made a burning arc through the gathering night before it plunged into the lake.

"Damn!" exclaimed Gaethaa in amazement, staring at the archer's body on the ground. "There died a good man! Chalk up one more point on Kane's tally—he'll make an accounting soon!"

"Looks like he's put the fire out too," observed Alidore glumly after a pause. "See—the smoke has just about cleared away. Bell will live, but he's useless for the moment. That leaves seven of us to deal with Kane now, milord."

"Seven to rush him, it seems," Gaethaa mused. "Still that looks like our best strategy. Once it gets a little darker we'll charge the villa. Spread out and move fast in the bad light— all of us ought to make it to him. One man isn't going to prevail against seven like us. Kane may get a few of us before he's taken, but take him we will!"

Cereb Ak-Cetee had been rubbing his narrow jaw in thought for several minutes. Now he smiled like a schoolboy with the solution to an examination question and announced brightly, "It may be that Kane will offer us no further resistance, milord. I know of one spell that has a fair chance of drawing his fangs, and I should have enough time to cast it before the light grows too dim to keep watch!"

"You picked a fine time to remember it, wizard!" Alidore exploded. "What kept you from mentioning this spell earlier!"

"Just remember that you're Gaethaa's lieutenant, Alidore,

and leave the science of magic to me!" Cereb snarled. "In simple words for simple minds to grasp, I'll remind you that sorcery has its laws and limitations. As you know, I've made no pact as yet with any patron god—if I had I wouldn't be wasting my time riding around with your sort!

"Without direct demonic aid, I have to resort to the pure science of sorcery. That means in general that I require lengthy and arduous preparations to weave any powerful spell. The fact that I have no bit of hair, piece of nail, any fragment of Kane's body—not even an item intimate to his person for that matter—to serve as a focus for my magic eliminates most possibilities for any sort of really potent spell. I've never even seen Kane, and we're no more than reasonably certain that he's the man inside the old villa. Add to this the fact that Kane is himself a sorceror of considerable ability—a man who can probably block most of my spells through his own knowledge. Now then, tell me where that leaves me!"

"All right! I apologize," conceded Alidore with little grace. "So where does that leave us? What do you have in mind?"

Cereb Ak-Cetee went on with a sneer in his eyes. "I know a fairly simple spell to induce stupor. I can diffuse it to include anyone within the villa, which will seriously weaken its influence. And Kane may bear some counter-charm against such minor sorceries for all I know. In fact, he can probably resist its effects to an extent purely through force of will, granting he's had extensive occult training. But regardless of whether he can resist it or not, unless he's completely protected the spell is going to slow him down considerably, even if it doesn't lay him out altogether. I didn't mention this spell earlier, because I had assumed he would be too great an adept to fall under its influence. Now I'm not so sure—I doubt if he's made any sort of preparations to guard against attack, in fact. Anyway the spell can soon be cast, and if it doesn't work we're no worse off than before."

"Cast your spell, Cereb," Gaethaa ordered eagerly. "If it can silence that crossbow and nothing more, it can drop Kane right into my hands!"

Kane watched the spot where his attackers had taken cover carefully, the closing darkness limiting his vision far less than for another man. "They seem to have given up the fire arrow idea for now. Guess that means a concerted attack before long. Anyway we seem to have all the fires put out."

He caressed the crossbow stock appreciatively. Kane had had it crafted according to his design, and he prized it highly. "There's a good weapon, though I doubt if many men could draw it with nothing more than this lever. Still the thing takes too long to cock and fire—though that last shot proved its worth once again. Thoem! If I just had that archer's bow, I could pick off every last one of them before they could cross the clearing!"

He addressed Rehhaile. "What are they doing now?"

Rehhaile's face was tight with concern under the soot— she had helped Kane put out the fires—working through the vision his eyes had given the scene. Cautiously she reached out with her mind to link with the attackers. Avoiding the touch of those whose contact so distressed her, she felt for Alidore. At that distance she could appreciate only dimly the sensory impulses his mind emanated.

"It's hard to say, Kane. The one you shot first is still moving. They don't seem to be getting ready to charge just yet. Some are watching us, and the others are watching someone who seems to be working at something on the ground—I can't tell what. Kane—he's the one that scared me worst—the one who knew I was blind! I think he must be a sorcerer from bits of their thoughts. I could never touch that demented mind of his again!"

"A sorceror! As if a simple attack by a band of professionals wasn't enough!" Kane swore. "I wonder though— I've heard of some madman called Gaethaa the Avenger who travels with a wizard in his band. A savior of the oppressed, they call him. Maybe this is Gaethaa then who's gone to all the trouble to trail me here—he's fanatical enough to pull the stunt from all I hear! Thought he usually kept a small army with him though."

Anxiously he gauged the amount of daylight left. "Suppose there's no chance they'll let it grow dark enough for us to make a break. They'll rush as soon as it's too dark for me to pick them off in the open. Break through the garden without any problem and be at the door. I'll try to take them one by one in the entrance hall—maybe get a few shots off first. No, they'll expect that and enter in groups from both sides to surround me. Damn! Wish I knew what that wizard or whatever they have can do! Rehhaile, can you maybe try to enter his mind long enough to . . ."

Rehhaile cried out in terror. "Kane! Something's wrong! I can't stay awake! Kane! I feel like I . . ." Her frightened voice trailed off. Like a collapsing puppet, she slumped to the floor. Arms pushed out to hold back the lethargy gave way brokenly, dropping her body to the planks with a soft thump. A tremor shook her as she struggled to rise, then her face fell back, unconsciousness preserving a mask of fear.

Kane struggled to keep to his feet! Blackness slashed through his mind, and his limbs were cased in lead! His strength slipping from him, Kane grimly recognized the cold touch of a spell of paralysis! A simple spell, but one for which he was totally unprotected. No time even to work the counterspell that almost any third-rate conjurer could command.

Desperately he fought the spell. It was a weak one, or he too would lie stretched out on the floor. Still he knew he was helpless to fight off an attack unless he could break free. Sweat dripping from his frame, Kane forced wooden muscles to move limbs of stone. There was a chance for him if he could only move outside the spell's range.

He tottered to the stairway, commanding his body to resist the spell with every atom of his will. On the first step he lost balance and slid drunkenly down the entire flight, rolling to a painful stop at the bottom. Setting his teeth in a death head grin, Kane crawled to the rear door. Already he could hear the hoofbeats of his enemies closing in for the kill. Somehow he pushed through the doorway and kicked it closed behind him. The lake offered an avenue of escape—or a death trap if he could not swim. Still it was his only chance.

Staggering, lurching, crawling, writhing on his belly—frantically Kane forced his body to cross the twilit garden. The sound of riders was closer now, and Kane had no way of knowing whether they had spotted him in the semi-darkness. Hunching forward, he gained the bank of the lake at last. Now he could hear them pounding against the front gate. A final few yards remained. Kane rolled weakly down the slope of the bank and slid off into the lake.

He floundered for a moment, trying to reach deeper water. The cool water closed over his body, and the weight of the sword on his back drew him down. Grimly holding his breath, Kane kicked against the bottom in an effort to get farther from shore. If the water were deep enough, he hoped to be able to float. But although Kane was a strong swimmer, he knew his massive bulk permitted him to float with difficulty in the best of circumstances.

His breath was growing short. With a major effort he wrenched his head above the surface to draw a gasping breath. He had progressed a good many yards from shore, he saw with relief, and as yet his attackers were too busy breaking into the villa to search for him in the lake.

The spell seemed to be lifting! Each movement seemed easier now; no longer did blackness seek so ineluctably to overwhelm his consciousness. The water, the distance he had moved from its focus had stolen power from the spell. The wizard must have ceased to send it against the villa now that his fellows were within. Whatever the reasons, Kane felt his strength begin to return to him.

With silent, powerful strokes Kane swam away underwater across the darkened lake. Behind him his baffled enemies were angrily searching through the silent villa and its gardens for their prey. But it would be too late to act by the time they realized how their quarry had escaped.

VI. SWORD OF COLD LIGHT

Gaethaa had been furious once it was obvious that Kane had somehow escaped him. A careful search of the villa had turned up no one other than Rehhaile, still unconscious from the wizard's spell. A search of the gardens had disclosed a trail such as a crawling man might make that led into the lake. Reconstructing Kane's probable actions, Gaethaa had ordered his men to circle the lake shore. But by this time darkness had settled, and it was a hopeless task to search along the overgrown shoreline. Of Kane there was no sign.

In baffled disgust they finally returned to Jethrann's tavern in Sebbei. Rehhaile they bound and brought with them, for Gaethaa had hopes of learning something of value from her.

"Maybe he drowned," Dron Missa offered. "If Cereb's spell was so efficacious, he shouldn't have been able to swim. But then he shouldn't have been able to crawl off either."

"Don't make any bets on it," Gaethaa growled. The Avenger frowned and tugged at his mustache in frustration. "Missa! Damn it all—stop the racket! I'm trying to think!"

Dron Missa started and laid aside his dirk. He had been nervously tapping the horn handle against the table.

"What now?" Jan wanted to know.

"Good question," Gaethaa cursed. "We do nothing now—nothing we can do until morning! By then Kane will be half way across Demornte, no doubt! And for the moment we can't stop him. All we can do is patch up Bell and try to pick up Kane's trail when it gets light.

"Well, what's the story with this girl we captured?" he asked, as Alidore took a seat beside him.

"Got kind of a crazy story on her, but they all say about the same," Alidore explained. "Her name's Rehhaile, and she's the one Gavein mentioned earlier as spending a lot of time with Kane. Seems she's his mistress, although I gather she's pretty much anybody's who wants her. Lived in Sehhei all her life—family died in the plague—and makes a living anyway she can. Seemed fascinated with Kane when he showed up, so she's been living with him mostly since then.

"The townspeople consider her to be a sort of witch. They say she's been blind since birth—and that bears out—but she seems to have some type of second sight. It's claimed she can look into your mind and see through your eyes so to speak. They say she can read your thoughts—can tell exactly what your feelings are and what you're thinking. I tried her and the story seems to be true."

Gaethaa nodded solemnly. "A witch with psychic powers. Cereb has been telling me of such—he noticed her from the first. Just the sort of creature to be in league with Kane! Obviously she sensed our intentions when we met her on the street and ran off to warn Kane while we were wasting time here with Gavein. Damn the luck!"

"What are you going to do with her?" Jan persisted.

"I'll decide what to do with her tomorrow. She may be of some use to us yet, so we'll hold her for now. As an accomplice of that devil, she deserves death."

"No objections to our having some fun then?" murmured Mollyl, winking at Jan.

"She cost us our quarry," Gaethaa said coldly. "But don't you guys rough her up so she won't be of use to me later. Doesn't look like she knows anything important about Kane, but maybe there'll be something."

"Even if we must execute her," Alidore protested, "is it right for the men to rape her? This seems like pointless torture."

"Can't rape a whore, Alidore!" laughed Dron Missa, joining the other men in a squabble over seniority.

After the others moved away, Alidore remained at the table beside Gaethaa, a frown still troubling his tanned face. His wine cup stood before him untasted. An occasional twitch flickered along the square line of his jaw, as if there were words that must be uttered, but that he kept to himself.

Gaethaa noticed his lieutenant's mood and turned to him in concern. The Kamathaen lord prized Alidore's comradeship highly. He had admired the Lartroxian youth's tough courage and intelligent zeal when Alidore had first joined his band nearly two years ago. Alidore had been in his late teens then, and Gaethaa, about a dozen years his senior, had grown to consider him a younger brother. He knew he could count on Alidore to stand beside him in any battle and he relied on his counsel in deciding many points of strategy. While most of his followers over the years rode behind his banner for gold, adventure, revenge or other personal motivations, Gaethaa recognized that Alidore more than any of the others was drawn by the same idealism he felt. His present mood puzzled Gaethaa.

"All right, Alidore," he said quietly. "What is it? Something has been gnawing away at you for a good while now. I've watched it building up inside you bit by bit. Out with it—what's bothering you? You know you don't need to hold it back from me if you don't feel right about the way something is going."

Alidore bit his lip and raised his wine cup, not yet meeting Gaethaa's eyes. "It's nothing worth . . . It's vague . . ." he began uneasily. "Just something that's been getting to me more and more as it keeps showing up. I don't know, maybe I'm getting battle fatigue after too many campaigns. I just notice it more. Nothing definite I like to bring up, but . . ."

Gaethaa watched him anxiously, knowing that in time his lieutenant would speak his mind. This much reticence was out of character for him.

"It's this girl Rehhaile . . ."

"Rehhaile?" Gaethaa's hawk-like face twisted in surprise. "Rehhaile? What's there about the witch that bothers you?"

"Well, it's not just her, it's a lot of things that keep hanging in my mind. She's an example is all," Alidore continued. "The mutiny we had at the border of Demornte. The execution of the prisoners when we destroyed the Red Three. The way we took the town apart last year in Burwhet when we took on Olidi and his gang of raiders. Those men you let Mollyl torture to tell us where Recom Launt would attack next. The hostages you let him butcher when you refused to lift the siege of his fortress. . . ."

"The alternative was to withdraw—to turn tail and let that murderous robber baron regain his stranglehold on the trade routes. And I had to know when and where to strike for that first battle with him. The lives of his henchmen and of some hostages were unimportant weighed against the greater good I accomplished there by destroying Launt and permitting thousands to cross his domain in peace. Perhaps the men were a bit out of hand in Burwhet, but regardless of the destruction we caused there, Olidi and every last one of his cutthroats died in the fighting. Burwhet could rebuild and prosper with that gang of renegade bandits finally scoured from the land. Those weren't prisoners we executed—they were accomplices of the Red Three and tainted with the ogres' inhuman crimes. As for the men who turned traitor to me in the shadow of Demornte, any man who's ever carried a sword in his lord's army knows that mutiny is punishable by death. No leader could ever command respect and discipline of his men if he ignored blatant desertion. We've been through this before, Alidore.

"This sorceress Rehhaile—in view of her youth and ignorance I could have overlooked her living with Kane. But she deliberately gave him warning of our presence here, and for that crime she must pay the price. If we had taken Kane by complete surprise—as it seems likely now we would have—our mission here would be completed. Anmuspi might well be alive still, although it's foolish to think we could have taken Kane without some casualties. Foolish to speculate over what would have happened anyway."

A woman's moan of pain broke from the upstairs of the tavern, accompanied by thick laughter.

Alidore winced. "Why not give her a clean death then? Why torture her like this?"

"She's a wanton—you told me as much yourself." Gaethaa shrugged. "She's not getting anything such a woman isn't used to. Besides the men need a break—they've ridden long and hard without any sport. Let them have their fun—I'll deal with Rehhaile tomorrow maybe."

Alidore still seemed troubled. "It's all logical when you explain it. I'm not implying we've ever stooped to senseless brutality, of course. I don't know, maybe my backbone's getting soft. It seems like there could be a little room for mercy. . . ."

Drawing a hand across his high forehead to push back the blond locks that drifted down, Gaethaa drew a deep breath and leaned back in his chair. His blue-gray eyes grew bitter in memory. "Sure, mercy. Remember the time years ago when Reanist talked me into sparing that girl we found chained in the sorceror's tower? The people of the region protested, but Reanist had an eye for beauty and insisted she was only a prisoner. That night her kisses killed Reanist and five other good men before my sword ended her inhuman thirst, and even Cereb Ak-Cetee wasn't certain what manner of demon we had harbored. Or earlier when we spared Tirli-Selan's family, then had to return later and fight a far more costly battle when we learned that they were bloodier despots than their uncle.

"Alidore, it doesn't work out like you'd hope for it to. I've let too many men die from blood poisoning still begging my surgeon not to amputate all of a gangrenous limb. Poison spreads. A tiny cancer will ultimately corrupt and destroy the strongest organism. Let a fragment of evil evade your exorcism, and it will inevitably flourish to cause even more death and suffering to humanity. False mercy is worse than ill-advised in my struggle against the forces of evil. Its consequences can completely pervert and destroy all the goals for which I fight."

Gaethaa's face grew pale with emotion. His eyes glowed with vision, and sweat glistened over his forehead. A tremor passed through his clenched hands, as his voice shook with intensity.

"I am called Gaethaa the Crusader, and the name is one I hope to be worthy of always. I have made my life a crusade against evil, and it is a crusade that will end only when the last spark of life fails me. When I was a child I listened to the great sagas told by my father's soldiers around the fires—and I listened to the darker tales they whispered of the strange lands where forces of evil held power over all who dwelt therein. Even then I vowed to myself that when I became a man I would not waste my life among the perfumed sycophants of Kamathaen nobility. I turned my back on indolent court life, and chose instead a life of riding against the cold wind with a war cry on my lips and a sword raised in my hand. I worked from childhood to prepare myself for this life. For tutors I drew upon the best tacticians available to teach me military strategy; my training at arms was at the hands of masters of their chosen weapon. I learned to read and converse in a dozen languages, and the wisest scholars of our age instructed me in logic and philosophy—for I knew it was not sufficient that I learn to wield a sword untempered by reason, nor allow other men to be my ears and tongue.

"Alidore, I have seen the cold light of good! The cold light shed by truth, righteousness, justice. The cold light that dispels the darkness of evil! The universe is structured on these two forces—the power of good shining as a beacon of cold, clear light against the smothering blackness of evil! And as surely as sunlight drives away the night, the cold light of good annihilates the darkness of evil!

"And I have vowed to serve the cold light! To destroy with a sword of cold light the shadow of evil that darkens our world! Darkness is vanquished by light, and the forces of evil fall before the powers of good! But in the battle of light against darkness there can be no intermediate shades—no twilight powers! Those who do not follow the cold light are children of darkness, and they must and shall be destroyed by the cold, clear light of good!

"And if my crusade at times strikes you as without mercy, it is because there can be no mercy, no uncertainty in this struggle! The cold light shall burn away the darkness of evil, even if a thousand must die to drive back the shadows! Their suffering is a petty price to pay for the ultimate victory!"

Totally swept up in the spell of Gaethaa's exhortation, Alidore listened with mind awhirl—uncertain at times whether he served a saint or madman.

Gaethaa had been silent for several minutes before Alidore broke from his near trance. "I'm sorry to have sounded unworthy of the confidence you place in me, milord," he spoke dazedly, not certain how the Crusader had interpreted his misgivings.

A quiet smile crossed Gaethaa's face, and he rose to brush his fist against his lieutenant's shoulder. "Why are you apologizing, Alidore? Your concern is understandable, and mercy is an invaluable principle when it is called for. Your feelings are misplaced, that's all, and I hope I've done a little toward clearing away the confusion in your mind. You need to remember that we're only a badly outnumbered few aligned in a cosmic struggle between diametrically opposed forces. Softness in this struggle isn't mercy, but unforgivable stupidity.

"Look, it's getting late, and we'll be up and after Kane as soon as there's daylight outside. I'm going to get some sleep now, and why don't you turn in yourself. You're exhausted now, and a lot of things will be clearer to you in the morning."

Alidore watched his leader depart. Things were a lot clearer after listening to Gaethaa, he realized. Still he did not feel like turning in. A strange restlessness still haunted him, and he sat up mulling over his thoughts and slowly sipping his wine. Sleep did not come, perhaps because every time his eyes started to close he caught the sound of choked cries from the room above.

At length when the others lost interest, Alidore went to Rehhaile also.

It was near dawn when Alidore left Rehhaile and started to pull shirt and trousers over his lean body. She was not asleep, but turned toward him on the bed, her uncanny blind eyes red from tears. There were many sullen purple bruises marring her tan skin, and her back was crossed with livid welts. Compared with other women whom Mollyl had amused himself with, she hadn't been badly messed up, Alidore thought.

She looked so forlorn there on the rumpled bed, and Alidore felt remorse for what they had done to her. She hadn't been like a whore at all—there had been no hardness, no professionalism. In a way it made him feel like he had raped one who loved him, and Alidore couldn't shake the awful feeling of betrayal.

Rehhaile ran a tongue over swollen lips, sensing his guilt. "Don't feel too bad. You were kinder than the others at least." Alidore muttered something and offered her a cup of wine. "What is to happen to me now?" she asked, and he felt uncomfortable and told her noncommittally that this was for Gaethaa to decide. Weakly she sat up and touched her bruised abdomen tenderly, a whimper hovering on her lips. "Why are you doing this to me?"

Alidore looked away. He could tell her that she deserved no better because she had chosen to align herself with evil, but somehow the words seemed unreal now. "You did a foolish thing when you helped Kane escape. In doing so you have thwarted the cause of justice, and punishment must be carried out."

"Was raping me an act of justice? Do you think I deserve what is being done to me?" Rehhaile responded illogically.

Alidore was fumbling for a reply, when a shriek echoed from the stables!

VII. A WOUNDED TIGER

Kane had not fled Sebbei.

Regaining his strength, he had crossed the small lake in the darkness. Reaching the inner wall of the city, Kane had lain hidden among the tall reeds while Gaethaa and his men floundered about in a futile search for him. Silently he had watched from the shadows as Gaethaa returned to Sebbei. With noiseless step he had followed his enemies back to Jethrann's tavern.

Like a phantom he had stalked them through the ghostly streets of Sebbei, and in his killer's eyes there gleamed the cold fires of death. For Kane had no thought of fleeing from his pursuers. Their attack had made a fool of him— nearly succeeding because of the apathy into which he had drifted. Now only blood would shake the fury that drove him after those who hunted him.

Crouched in the darkness outside the tavern, Kane watched and listened, striving to learn more of his assailants. Among them Sed tho'Dosso was the only man he recognized. But once he heard spoken the name *Gaethaa*, Kane understood the reason for the attack.

Gaethaa the Avenger—so the Kamathaen lord had at last determined to include Kane in his crusade. Kane worked to recall all the scraps of information he had come across concerning Gaethaa. The prospect was not pleasing. Gaethaa was a dangerous opponent—a man of tenacious courage who was reputedly a deadly warrior as well as brilliant strategist. His mercenaries were one of the best private armies in the civilized world, it was said. From their numbers they must have had a few setbacks in finding him though, Kane mused.

Eight men—all professional fighters—plus the unknown factor represented in the wizard. The wizard would be that young Tranodeli he had heard a little about—one of the Cetee clan whose talents had run toward sorcery. And he was supposed to be as brilliant a mind to study the black arts since the strange fall of Carsultyal. The odds were clearly too great for direct attack. The game would have to be played by more subtle rules.

And so Kane waited in the darkness, waited for a chance to kill, and to his ears there came at times a girl's cry of pain.

Toward the approach of dawn Kane crept into the shelter of the tavern stable. He had hoped for a chance to attack Gaethaa's band while they slept, but several of the men had been up throughout the night—not so much standing guard as raising hell. Abandoning the idea, Kane stealthily climbed into the darkened loft to wait for events to unfold. Evidently Gaethaa's confidence in his own power was sufficient that he assumed Kane would spend the night hours in full flight. Lurking in his very shadow was as safe a position as any. Besides the night was cold, and Kane was still damp and caked with mud from the lake. Shivering from the chill, he helped himself to a pile of horse blankets and snuggled into the straw of the loft. There were fleas crawling through the blankets, but they were warm.

In the last quiet moments before dawn his vigilance was rewarded. A man now stumbled through the door—Sed tho'Dosso, Kane recognized with grim delight. The desert bandit had been awake most of the night, and now he sleepily cursed Gaethaa for sending him to look after the horses. With groggy movements he passed from stall to stall, checking to see that each mount had all the grain and water it required. Completing his rounds, Sed rested his lantern on a barrel and sullenly contemplated the pile of saddles and equipment that would have to be harnessed to the horses before long. There was time enough for a nap, he decided. With a groan he sank down against a stall and closed his eyes.

Kane watched the Lomarni bandit chieftain intently. Here was an excellent chance to rid himself of one of his enemies, but there were a few problems. Kane still carried his sword and dagger, but neither weapon was useful at the moment. With Sed tho'Dosso below him, he would have to descend the loft ladder to reach him—and that meant too much noise to hope to take the other unawares. In his huddled position, the bandit presented a difficult target for a dagger throw. There was no chance for a quick, clean kill, and Kane knew he would have to strike silently. At the first shout of danger, Gaethaa's men would come swarming over the stable, and Kane would again be trapped.

Slowly Kane slipped free of the blankets. A coil of rope lay at hand in the loft, suggesting a possibility. Cautiously he crawled across the loft, watching the sleeping bandit for the first sign of alarm. The loft was laid with thick beams, and they held his weight without creaking. Still the boards were widely spaced, and a thin trickle of dust and straw sifted down from the loft as he passed. The stream was not noticeable in the darkness, but as it drifted closer to Sed tho'Dosso, there was danger that he might feel the dust brushing his face.

The desert man snored softly. Gingerly Kane rose to his feet and reached for the rope. The sky was starting to gray, but the loft was still hidden in shadow. At any moment another of the Crusader's men might enter the stable to help Sed with the horses, and Kane knew his time was running out. A chance entrance, a flash of lantern light, and he would be silhouetted against the rafters.

Quickly he worked one end of the rope into a sliding noose. Playing the hemp through his hands, he coiled it into a throwing lariat that he felt he could count on. Poising himself on the open edge of the loft, Kane looked down at the sleeping bandit. Grimly he readied the noose in his hands.

"Sed! Sed tho'Dosso!" he called softly. "Wake up, Sed!"

With a guilty start the Lomarni roused himself. Still groggy, he raised his head and looked about him stupidly. "Huh?"

Kane cast his lariat the instant Sed lifted his head. Perfectly aimed, the noose dropped over the bandit's head, and with a jerk Kane snugged it tight against his neck. Sed had time for one thick shriek as terror slashed through the curtain of sleep, then th biting noose cut off his breath! Even as his frenzied fingers tore at the choking coil, the Lomarni was violently yanked from the stable floor and swung into the air!

Kane swore in anger, the muscles bunched along his shoulders and back as he hauled the bandit free of the earth. His cast had been on target, but he had meant to draw tight the noose before his startled victim could cry out. Now a warning had been sounded. Helplessly twisting like a fly in a spider's wed, the wiry desert man kicked and contorted in Kane's grasp.

Holding the writhing bandit chieftain suspended with one hand, Kane hurriedly tossed the free end of the rope over a rafter. Then he seized the loose end and leapt from the loft.

Sed tho'Dosso jerked and shot relentlessly toward the roof, as Kane's greater weight bore his end downward to the floor. Lightly he landed and knotted the rope over a stall. The entire episode had taken seconds.

Eyes bulging horribly, Sed tho'Dosso watched his laughing enemy wave a derisive farewell as he stepped through the rear door to vanish into the dawn.

Seconds later Gaethaa and his men pounded into the stable. They glared about without comprehension until Jan pointed his hook upward, and then they cut him down. But the Lomarni's neck was broken, and even as his lips formed the name "Kane," his body shuddered in death.

"Kane!" shouted Gaethaa in exultation. "Then he came back! By Thoem! I was a fool to think that he would flee us! Like a wounded tiger, he's turned on his hunters! Well, he's the fool this time, because now we don't have to ride off after his trail! We have him trapped!

"How about it Cereb—can you flush him out for me?"

The wizard tossed his bony shoulders beneath his cloak. "Just watch," he replied lazily.

Shortly thereafter Kane was not overly surprised to see the walls of Sebbei suddenly burst into blue flame. From his vantage point on the flat roof of an empty house, he watched the fires blaze with undiminished heat, despite the fact that they were fed by nothing visible, and that within them the wall stood undisturbed. But anything living would be instantly consumed he knew, for he recognized the spell.

He drew back his lips in a savage grin. Yes, it was a powerful spell, one which he had no hope of breaking in his present position. He was trapped in Sebbei. But then, he had no intention of fleeing the city until the game was played out. Gaethaa probably sensed this now, so perhaps he and his pet wizard had something in mind that might shake his resolve.

Something had to be done about the sorceror, and Kane searched through his fantastic stores of black knowledge for something that he could use to retaliate. Finally in utter frustration he realized that his opponent was certain to be protected against any spell available to him under present circumstances. Gaethaa would keep his wizard well guarded from physical danger as well. An arrow might do it, and Kane again regretted the loss of his crossbow. So far the only serviceable long range weapon he had found in the deserted buildings was a thick spear—designed only for stabbing and short casts.

Disgusted, Kane slipped away to see why his enemies had not yet followed.

In the square before the tavern he found them. Fascinated, Gaethaa and his men observed while Cereb Ak-Cetee performed a long incantation over an intricately designed pentagram. Abruptly the incense-choked air within the pentacle wavered, and then within the smoke crouched a demon with checkered, reptilian scales—summoned from some unguessable plane.

Pleased with the success of his invocation, Cereb's flushed face broke into a boyish grin. Trapped within the pentagram, the demon glowered back wrathfully and champed its reeking fangs. Suddenly its hunched shoulder heaved and the demon's crusted talons ripped out for the wizard—only to strike crimson sparks as they encountered the magic barrier! Cereb Ak-Cetee chuckled at the monster's howl of agonized rage. "Fight all you want to, slave! The pentagram will hold you fast until I grant you release! And that I won't do until you first swear to perform a service for me!"

The demon spat out a mockery of human speech. "You have summoned the wrong servant then! In my sphere I hold only very minor powers. Release me now, and summon one greater than I to do your bidding!"

"Modest, aren't you now. No—I'm not about to call any of your brothers! A bigger fish might prove too strong for my net to hold. You can do what I require of you well enough though. We have a man who hides from us here, and I command you to bring him to us. He's trapped here—I've enclosed the town within a ring of fire. And my spell will make it possible for you to move within the ring of fire, despite the disparity of your universe and this one. All you need do is ferret him out, and to help you we've procured this . . ."

"Watch out!" shouted Jan. "It's Kane! Making a rush!"

They all whirled at the shout to see Kane dashing toward them with spear poised!

"Cover Cereb!" Gaethaa ordered. "We've got . . ."

And Kane hurled the spear! Wobbling, the clumsy missile curved across the square—easily dodged even in the short space. But Kane had not thrown at the sorceror, nor at any of the men; such an effort would have been wasted at this range. Instead he cast the spear for the pentagram!

The iron spearpoint skittered upon the packed ground and ripped into the earth, cutting through the border of the pentagram!

The demon howled in unearthly laughter as it catapulted from its shattered prison! Cereb Ak-Cetee uttered one great scream of inexpressible horror as the vengeful creature swept him up in its awful embrace! "Now who commands his slave!" roared the demon in triumph.

Shuddering roar as the cosmic portal swung open, then shut—cutting off hopeless shriek and mocking laughter in mid-peal! Then only a trailing puff of sulfurous mist marked the spot where wizard and demon had disappeared.

Nor—when they at last broke from their shock to look—was there any sign of Kane.

VIII. TO DESTROY THE SERVANT OF EVIL

Glumly Gaethaa considered the fate of his wizard. So now it was just the six of them against Kane.

"The flame barrier has fallen, milord," Alidore observed. The spell had broken with the wizard's death.

Gaethaa pensively scratched his long jaw. "Doesn't matter. Pretty obvious by now that Kane means to finish the chase right here. Looks like Kane has lived up to his legend— easily the most deadly and resourceful agent of evil I've set out to destroy." There was grim satisfaction in his face.

He turned for the tavern, and his men followed willingly. Dron Missa rummaged around frantically for an unopened flask of wine among the wreckage of last night; a delighted cry marked his success.

"Question is, how do we find him in all this maze," continued Gaethaa. "Damn it! Quit fighting over that wine and let me think! Jan—tell that spineless host of ours to bring up some more on the double! After what we've just seen, a drink is damn well called for!" He frowned and pulled at his mustache in thought.

Mollyl glanced towards Rehhaile, who slumped bound against a pillar. "Kane seemed hot for the bitch there. Maybe if we took her outside and started to tickle her a bit, Kane would make a rush to get her. If she can't tell us anything, she'd still be good bait."

Gaethaa considered the suggestion carefully, staring blankly at Rehhaile, mindless of the girl's terror. "Could be," he concluded.

A sick feeling was growing in Alidore's stomach. Witch, whore, whatever her crimes might be—it was too much to turn this girl over to Mollyl's twisted amusements. "Milord," he said hastily, "it seems altogether unlikely to me that a demon like Kane would give a second thought to the sufferings of another person—regardless of the fact she saved his life with her warning. Mollyl's suggestion would only give Kane valuable time either to escape or hatch further schemes."

Gaethaa nodded at his logic, and Alidore felt unreasonably relieved. And in noting the expression of gratitude flashed him by Rehhaile, he missed the glare of hatred on Mollyl's face.

"Nothing for it but a house to house search," concluded Gaethaa. He rose to his feet. "Only six of us. That means we'll need the help of the townspeople.

"Gavein! I want you to call together all available men who can carry a weapon! We'll initiate a systematic sweep of the town until we can uncover that devil!"

His face was tired beyond human endurance, but his rusty voice rasped in weary determination. "Please, milord. I have already told you that we of Sebbei will have nothing to do with your fight with this Kane. We wish only . . ."

"I know—only to sit around and slowly die. Thoem! You people take longer to die than anyone has a right to! Well, you can go on with your merry little moldering lives as soon as we finish with Kane! Until then I'll demand that your people give me full co-operation!"

Gavein set his stubbled jaw. "Demand all you want then. But no one in Sebbei will bother to obey your ranting!"

Gaethaa uttered a curse of baffled anger. "Mollyl! You and Jan talk to this fool outside where they can all see we mean business! If I have to bully them into helping us look for Kane I will! It's plain this bunch of gutless slugs won't lift a hand against us!"

With a thin smile Mollyl grabbed the scrawny mayor, while Jan painstakingly rescrewed the hook to the stump of his wrist. "Gaethaa—you can't be going to torture this man because he refuses to help us!" Alidore protested.

The Crusader's face was grave. "Regrettable I know, Alidore. But desperate measures are called for. I am prepared to sacrifice any number of lives to destroy this madman Kane—because in the end many more lives will be spared from his monstrous schemes! Anyway, in refusing to help, Gavein and his people are giving direct aid to the cause of evil! They've brought this all upon themselves!" He stalked resolutely from the room.

"Stay here with the bitch if you're squeamish," suggested Mollyl with a smile. "Jan, you and Bell give me a hand. Go call the people together, Missa."

Alidore frowned irritably and started to follow, but Rehhaile called his name. So he stopped, mind in indecisive turmoil, and hesitantly approached their captive. From the square outside came a howl of agony and an inspired laugh.

"Is that what's going to happen to me?" she asked him.

He felt a sharp nausea of unreasonable guilt. "I'll see that you'll feel no pain," he declared, then cursed his callousness as he saw her frightened tears. Damn! He had no business permitting personal feelings to intrude on a clear-cut matter like this. What difference did the fate of this devil's whore make to him? She mattered nothing weighed against the rightfulness of their mission. Uneasily Alidore realized that despite her guilt, her own fate meant a great deal to Rehhaile.

He drew his knife. "Look. You don't really belong in this mess. Your crimes aren't that important to us." He mumbled on clumsily, unable to say anything that did not sound foolish in his own ears, still unable to shut up. The knife sliced her bonds as he talked.

Unsteadily she rose to her feet. "You're letting me go," she said needlessly.

Alidore gave a tight lipped nod. "I can slip you through the rear door—I can see everyone else is out front." She shuddered, her face frightened and pale. Alidore thought of her uncanny second sight and realized she could sense every detail of the beating going on outside.

"Get away from them!" she whispered fiercely. "You don't belong with them! In your soul there is still some human feeling! All but burned out!"

"What do you mean!" Alidore protested. "These men are my fellow soldiers on a mission of good! We may be forced to resort to savage methods, but our goal is to help mankind! I'd die for Gaethaa willingly! He's the greatest man of this age!"

She laughed then—or maybe it was a sob. Alidore could not be certain. Her sightless face held him as she spat back in scornful pity. "Do you call me blind, Alidore! Gaethaa a great man! A Crusader battling the forces of evil! While

Kane has lived here he has harmed no one. Since you came yesterday, your great man and your fellow soldiers have terrorized the town, raped me and threatened worse, demolished this tavern, bullied Gavein—and now you're beating him to death to force the people of Sebbei to obey commands meaningless to them!"

Alidore protested hotly. "But it's for the good of all! The man we're after is one of the most villainous . . ."

"Are you so much better then? Is Gaethaa a saint who has brought all this upon us? Are men like Mollyl, Jan, Bell and the others heroes? Perverted killers! Animals! Mercenaries who kill for profit and pleasure!

"Alidore! Please leave them now!"

"Get out of here! Right now!" he snarled. "I'll not desert Gaethaa!" His mind a whirl of confusion, he buried his head in his arms upon the table. Her steps moved away hurriedly, but he no longer listened.

A thousand years passed before Gaethaa called him, and he dazedly went outside. "Well, the old fool's dead!" the Crusader snapped in annoyance. "Completely useless too. These walking dead men only ran off when we tried to show them a lesson! Locked in their houses! They'll all die in their shadows before breaking out of their apathy! Never mind though! Their cowardice makes them worthless to us. We'll find Kane ourselves one way or another!"

Hoping that Rehhaile would have time to reach some place of safety before the others noticed her absence, Alidore joined Gaethaa in the square. The twisted body of Gavein lay sprawled in the dust, a patch of dampness growing in the late morning sunlight. His veins should have contained only dust, Alidore mused, avoiding the ruined face that tilted upward toward the sky. Jan caught his eye and grinned, fastidiously polishing his hook across his thigh.

"Shall I bring out the girl?" Mollyl smiled, his pale face a tight mask. "Anything's worth trying now."

Gaethaa shrugged. "Might as well. We'll stake her out in the sun and leave her. It might draw Kane's attention and keep him close by, even if he won't risk getting to her."

Alidore casually watched as Mollyl and Bell entered the tavern. No longer did he have second thoughts on his decision to release her. He almost smiled at the angry shout from within, as Mollyl discovered her escape.

"Hey, she's gone!" Mollyl bellowed from the doorway.

"Her bonds were cut! Damn you, Alidore! You turned the witch loose!"

Bristling in defense of himself, Alidore snarled back, "The hell I did! She was tied up when I left her a minute ago! One of the townspeople must have done it! Maybe Kane came back! Hell, there's broken glass all over the tavern—she might have cut herself free while you were playing with Gavein!"

"All right! Let it pass! She's gone!" Gaethaa shouted to halt the dispute. He looked at his lieutenant narrowly, but decided it was not worth an inquest. Maybe Alidore would be less moody now.

"She wasn't of any real use to us anyway," he continued. "If she's with Kane now, that's fine for us. She'll only hinder his movements, and the two should be ten times easier to find than Kane alone.

"We'll divide our forces and start searching from house to house. That will make it three to one when we find Kane, and I'd rather the odds were greater after what we've learned of him. Still it's the best we can do. If we stuck together, we'd only chase around in circles through this ghost town. And if we spread out any more he might pick us off one by one. So don't underestimate our quarry. Remember he has untold centuries of cunning to direct his every move. When you find him don't give him a chance. Call for the rest of us when you get close to him, and be ready for anything.

"Ok then. Mollyl and Jan come with me—we'll start to the west from the square. Alidore, you take Missa and Bell and search east. Good hunting!"

Dron Missa critically eyed Bell, whose left shoulder was wrapped in thick bandages. "Too bad you can't trade that sling for a hook like Jan's," he commented. "Then you'd maybe be worth something in a fight."

Bell's coarse face grew scarlet in anger. "Anytime you want to find out, kid! Anytime—you don't even need to ask! I'll push in your smirking little face just as sure with my right arm as with both! Want to try it right now?"

"All right! Save it for Kane when we find him!" Alidore ordered.

Eyes alert for the first sign of danger, the hunters strode across the square and into the silent streets. Somewhere in this city of ghosts lurked the man they had come to destroy. This mission that had already cost so much hardship and death must soon be completed.

"By the way, Alidore," Dron Missa whispered as they moved away. "That was a good move with Rehhaile."

Alidore looked at the Waldann curiously, then answered his grin.

IX. DEATH IN THE SHADOWS

Kane edged along the rooftop cautiously, keeping in view the three men who walked through the street below. The morning had faded into afternoon, and now the shadows again were stretching out across the empty streets. Soon they would reach all the way across, then the shadows would soften and begin to creep over the entire city. And darkness would return to Sebbei.

Kane was waiting for the night. Throughout the day he had assiduously avoided his pursuers, moving always just a little ahead of their search. This way he could keep them in view at all times, and thereby preclude a chance confrontation. He had considerable confidence in his own prowess, but he recognized that his opponents were hardened fighters as well. At present it seemed pointless to meet his enemies on their own terms. Three of them might well hold him at bay long enough for the others to arrive. Kane did not care to be caught in a trap again.

So he waited for darkness to come. Night would be to his advantage, and in the interim Gaethaa and his men could grow exhausted and careless.

The roof was hot. Exposed on the glossy slate surface, Kane was reminded most emphatically that it was a desert sun shining down over Demornte. The tiles stung his bare flesh as he crept over them—slabs of green- and gray-hued black, whose relative darkness Kane could judge from the heat that met his touch. Sweat trickled across his body, leaving damp patches wherever he rested, making his hands slip against the slate as he climbed the sloping roof.

It was easier to steal through the streets, keeping to the alleys and slipping through the empty buildings. The few townspeople that Kane encountered slunk away from him with faces averted, all but squeezing shut their eyes to avoid any contact with him. So did they creep away from his pursuers, Kane had observed, scuttling for their burrows when the strangers demanded information of them. They would not betray him, Kane felt assured. They only stood wretchedly by while his hunters searched suspiciously through their shops and houses, or pointed blindly when impatient threats demanded an indication of Kane's hiding place. At length Gaethaa's men too dismissed the townspeople as participants or even witnesses in this hunt.

But Kane made it a point to leave the maze of narrow streets and empty buildings at frequent intervals. Their cover masked his enemies' movements as well as his own, and such apparent sanctuary could too easily become a cul-de-sac. Climbing along the rooftops he could follow their progress and alter his own course as their movements dictated.

A rustling scrape alerted him and he spun about with knife poised. It was a long, gray lizard, crawling across the tiles away from him. The reptile halted, settled against the sun steeped slates, and regarded the human with a glassy, inscrutable stare. Kane licked his dry lips, tasting salt, and wiped his sticky face with a grimy arm. His sword belt chafed his back, and sweat dripped across his chest to soak the harness. He had rolled the sleeves and opened the front of his shirt, but his leather vest and pants offset any help this afforded toward cooling him off. With darkness the air would soon grow chill again.

The inner wall of Sebbei was growing close again, so the search had now completed half of its second circuit—once already Gaethaa's men had worked their way from the square to the wall and back again, and now they had returned to the wall a second time. Tempers were as burning hot as the slate tiles he rested upon, and Kane caught shreds of argument that he probably had left the old city altogether. Vigilance had relaxed as frustration piled up, and Kane decided it was an opportune point for him to strike.

Kane had always been careful to stay well ahead of his pursuers while he climbed across the rooftops. His boots made a soft scuffling upon the slates no matter how gingerly he moved about. In each group of searchers, one man always held an arrow ready to draw, and no building was entered until they made a close scrutiny for evidence of their quarry lurking somewhere above them. Now as he saw them approaching the empty apartment house on whose roof he lay hidden, Kane held his position.

Huddled against the stone cornice, he watched through a chink in the blocks as the three halted before the structure and looked it over. Alidore stood back with an arrow nocked and ready, his eyes scanning the building front for any sign of danger. Swords drawn, Dron Missa and Bell entered the tenement ahead of him. Once they called out to him, Alidore hurriedly stepped inside as well.

His ear pressed to the roof, Kane could hear an occasional faint crash from within, as they carried out the tedious business of examining each room of the crumbling apartment. There was no access to the roof from within, so Kane knew they could not reach him at the moment. This particular tenement had obviously been in disrepair even before the plague, and the intervening years were not far short of bringing it to total ruin. Earlier in the day Kane had almost lost his balance when a cornice stone had shifted beneath his weight, and the decrepit state of the entire building front had suggested a possibility.

Now while his enemies searched through the rotting apartments, Kane busily attacked the cornice with his knife. The dagger point dug into the crumbling mortar as if it were mud. A growing pile of grit and dirt spread about his knees as he worked, hoping that the soft grating of metal on stone would not be heard below.

The sound of voices reached the street again, and Kane sheathed his blade quickly. Rising to his feet he tried to peer through the cracks to see when the men would step out into the street. Luck was still with him—they had not attempted the rotted stairs leading from the tenement's rear exit. But his vision was limited by the position, so the best he could do would be to estimate by the sound of their voices the approximate moment they would walk beneath the cornice.

It was time to take the risk. If his timing were off this might prove catastrophic. His feet set against the slates, Kane braced his shoulder against the cornice and slowly heaved, hoping that the entire building front would not collapse as well. The cornice resisted his pressure at first, so he threw against it the full strength of his massive frame. With a sudden treacherous release of tension, the stone facade buckled outward and collapsed! Thrown off balance, Kane waved his arms wildly and tottered on the brink, about to topple after the plummeting stonework!

The three were just emerging from the doorway in chagrin, when Dron Missa felt a trickle of grit sift past his face. "Look out!" he howled, his fighter's reflexes reacting faster than thought to the cold breath of death he sensed. With the blinding agility of an acrobat, Missa sprang into the street and rolled in a somersault across to the opposite side! Still in the doorway, Alidore leapt back into the hallway at the Waldann's cry of warning!

Bell's dull mind was slower to react. Not comprehending the cause for Missa's shout, he wasted a scant second to glare upward. His eyes had barely time to register the terror that started within him as Bell saw the wall of rock hurtling down upon him! His scream had scarcely reached his lips before it was swallowed in the thunderous shock of the facade slamming against the street!

Alidore glanced in horror at the scarlet splotched heap of rubble strewn before the doorway. Only the barest fragment of time had separated him from such a death.

"There he is!" shouted Missa, recovering from the shock in time to see Kane regain his balance and dart back from the roof's edge. "Quick, Alidore! Bring the bow! Kane's on the roof!"

Scrambling over the roofing tiles like an ape, Kane dashed for the neighboring building. Not so distant shouts were answering the alarm in the street below, and Kane had no desire to be caught in the open. Another building stood adjacent to the tenement. Kane threw himself upward to clear the few feet discrepancy between the two structures and started across the steeper sloping roof.

A tile broke loose under his feet halfway up, and Kane skidded dizzily downward, hands clawing to secure a grip! But there was no purchase! Helpless to halt his slide, Kane floundered over the edge and dropped back to the tenement roof. His heart racing, Kane leapt up and began his climb again, thankful that his fall had been only a few feet rather than all the way to the street below. An arrow grazed past to shatter a tile under his fingers. Then Kane gained the crest of the roof and slid down the other side, protected for the moment.

This side abutted upon a building one floor less in height. Catching the gutter as he reached the edge, he lowered himself over the side and dropped lightly to this next rooftop. Angry shouts sounded closer now as his pursuers sought to close in, but Kane felt more confident. A stairway at the far end of this structure led him down to an alley in back.

On reaching the alley, he pushed through a door in an opposite building and vanished before Gaethaa's men could circle from the other street. While they frenziedly sought to retrace his movements, Kane ducked through several empty buildings and finally re-emerged some distance away. The darkening streets cloaked his escape.

The twilight deepened and was swallowed by the night. Across dead Demornte settled the blackness of the tomb. No lights shone in the empty towns and abandoned homes, and a velvet curtain was drawn over the plague scarred corpse of the stricken land. Starlight and gibbous moon looked down on dead Demornte, their soft illumination no more than shading the night to gray. Their glow was like candles burning at a wake, sculpturing the face of the deceased with stark angles and shadowed hollows. Among the bones of a nation crept the creatures of night, stepping solemnly as mourners through the spectral silence.

In Sebbei only a few houses showed light, and this through cracks in bolted shutters and doors. For death again stalked the streets of Sebbei, and even in their despair the townspeople trembled at the familiar sound of his step. In the darkened streets even the phantoms who nightly walked the stones seemed aware that death had returned to Demornte, and the wraiths melted into the silent shadows, abandoning the night to the spectre of death with his bared sword.

Half a dozen torches blazed yellow in the deserted streets, driving back the shadows as they passed. Grim-faced men cast suspicious eyes over each segment of nighted city laid bare by the torch flames. Warily they searched for some new evidence of their quarry's presence.

Determined to put an end to this deadly match of cat and mouse, Gaethaa grouped his remaining men together and ordered an all night search. Now by torchlight he and his band relentlessly pushed through the city of ghosts, stalking their prey through the now familiar streets and deserted buildings. If this was to be a contest of endurance, Gaethaa meant to give his enemy no chance to rest. Not even Kane could hold up against the strain of ceaseless skulking from place to place, never gaining more than a few steps on his pursuers. And if Kane's role as fox were any less taxing than that of hound, the hounds out-numbered him and could hunt in shifts if need be. Eventually Kane would grow weary and then careless. They would trap him and learn how well an exhausted fox could fight as the pack closed in to kill.

"Hell, I'll lay you odds Kane's clear out of Sebbei right now!" Jan growled, his surly temper worn thin from the hours of tedious search. "Probably sleeping somewhere out beyond the wall—while we're here wearing ruts down the streets. He'd be a fool to stay here inside the walls dodging us all night."

"That's true enough—assuming Kane is running from us," Dron Missa pointed out, an unaccustomed note of unease in his voice. "But that isn't the case here. It seems to me Kane is stalking us just as we're hunting him. We've thought we were hounds chasing down a fox, but I think it's more realistic to consider this a tiger hunt. I was on one once far south of here, and I remember the crawling sense of danger that haunted each step through that shadowy jungle. We were stalking the beast in his own element, and no one had convinced the tiger that he was supposed to be the quarry. Three of us died in the shadows before we finally brought him down."

"Well, it's obvious enough by now that Kane isn't exactly in full flight," Gaethaa broke in brusquely. "We've known that ever since he followed us back to the tavern and murdered Sed tho'Dosso. He's still with us—staying just out of sight like a cobra, waiting for a chance to strike at us. But his boldness will be his undoing eventually—we'll wear him out before he does us. So keep your eyes open, damn it! Remember he's waiting desperately for us to give him an opening!"

Doggedly the Avenger and his men concentrated on their search. Alidore worked his way close to Dron Missa and studied the normally flippant Waldann. "What's the trouble, Missa?" he asked quietly. "I don't recall seeing you in so gloomy a mood before. Is this place getting to you?"

The other man glanced at him edgily, somewhat ashamed at broadcasting his ill ease. "I'm all right. Been a long day, that's all." He paused, "No, that's not all of it. Kane, this place, these people . . . Something's getting to me. My nerves are all sort of . . . Well, like on that tiger hunt—right before that striped devil came bounding out of the brush and tore apart the guy three steps back of me. Only I've got the same feeling worse this time . . . thinking maybe I'll be the one the tiger picks to spring upon this time . . ."

His voice trailed off uncertainly. Then he smiled and punched at Alidore's shoulder, his old smile returning. "Look—don't let me pass my bad nerves on to you. I'll be in fine form once we drive Kane out into the open. This monotonous game of poking through a ghost town trying to flush a cobra is not my style, that's all. Give me an open fight, and I'll shake off my depression soon enough."

"Hell, I'm not worried about your nerves, Missa," Alidore assured him. "All of us are on edge by now—who wouldn't be! Kane is feeling it worse than we are though, and my guess is he'll either make a stand or break and run before much longer. Dawn can't be more than a few hours off."

Death waited in the shadows.

Stealthily Kane raised the heavy trapdoor. Its dry hinges rasped in loud complaint, and Kane uneasily peered about the darkened warehouse. Satisfied that no one was near enough to catch the sound, he grimly inspected the dank smelling subcellar below, then replaced the trap over the opening. Whether the old tunnel still lay open was impossible to say without light, but at least the trapdoor would open for him. Silence. His pursuers had not yet reached the warehouse, although their torches had been drawing close to the seemingly abandoned structure when last Kane had looked outside.

The warehouse was a looming structure of unyielding stone walls, stoutly built to protect costly merchandise from thieves and the elements alike. It stood somewhat apart from neighboring buildings, with only a short open space intervening between its rear wall and the inner wall of the old city. At some time in the past, evidently before the outer wall had been raised, the merchant owners had found it expedient to drive a tunnel beneath the city walls—and thereby link the warehouse with the cellars of another establishment located a short distance beyond the inner city. In those days caravans with trade goods had stopped by the outlying inn to rest and partake of pleasures offered there. It had been profitable to bring certain goods directly to the warehouse from the inn by way of the tunnel, an artifice which avoided the needless expense of custom duties, as well as suspicious eyes of city officials who might scruple over legal ownership of some items.

The tunnel had fallen into disuse in later times, abandoned altogether after the plague. Kane had discovered it one day while prowling through the deserted city in search of nothing in particular. Despite its advanced state of disrepair, curiosity drove Kane to risk one trip through the tunnel with its rotting timber braces and settling walls. Now he remembered the old warehouse with its smuggler's tunnel, and centered upon this he had planned a rather dangerous attack upon his pursuers—a trap that could strike either way.

As Gaethaa and his men drew close to the deserted warehouse, Kane moved on ahead of them, certain that they would again enter to search among the dust laden stacks and bales. There was no evidence that the trapdoor had been discovered—it was well concealed, and Kane himself had originally come upon the tunnel from its other end. This would leave him an exit from the warehouse once they knew he was inside. There was no way they could trap him inside—assuming the tunnel had not collapsed since he passed through many weeks before. That was a risk he could not escape at this point, though.

With soft steps Kane ascended the cellar stairs and crossed the darkened warehouse. At the side and rear doors he paused to make certain their heavy bars were in place. A smaller front door was similarly bolted. There remained only the massive main door through which to enter the warehouse. All doors were of thick, iron-bound timber, windows there were none, and the walls built from heavy sandstone blocks. Once the main door too was locked, long hard work with axes and prybars would be needed before entrance could be forced.

About him in the darkness lay boxes and piles of costly merchandise, waiting under a wrapping of dust and spider webbing for buyers who would never come. They formed fantastic shapes in the darkness, crouching patches of blackness against the night—all but invisible until they were brushed upon. Mounds of moldering rugs, rotting heaps of cloth and furs, shelves of tarnished metalwork, pieces of furniture standing in musty aloofness, broken boxes of spices imparting a sick pungency to the odor of decay. Wealth lay crumbling beneath the cold caress of time, and the same vermin now crawled alike over the bones of merchant and buyer and the corpse of their wares.

The warehouse ceiling stretched high, and the door which closed its main entrance was immense. A system of chain and pulleys lifted the main door vertically along grooves cut into the jamb, sliding the heavy barrier upward and down by means of a capstan. Entire wagons could be driven through the doorway when open; once closed it would require a powerful battering ram to smash through. For years the door had stood open, raised upward to the ceiling—the warehouse abandoned to the plague when death claimed its owners.

The capstan mechanism was mounted alongside the front

wall. A thick iron chain strained from the winch, ran along heavy pulleys jutting from the stones, and fastened to the massive door. Kane had inspected the fittings on earlier occasions and was familiar with their operation. Now he drew his long sword from across his shoulder and crept into the shadow of some bales piled against the wall close to the capstan. A rat darted away from his boot and scurried off cursing into the darkness. Kane's lips pressed in a thin smile as he saw first flickers of torchlight streak the entranceway, heard shuffle of approaching steps, low mutter of voices. Tightness of anticipation slipped from him. Cunning or foolhardy, he was committed now.

Closer came the light, the sound—spilling echoes across the deserted darkness within. Light brighter. Figures appeared at the doorway. Entered.

They stood just inside the door, torches raised, eyes narrowly scrutinizing the shadows beyond. Kane mashed himself against the wall, unseen in the cover of the bales. Two had entered. The rest would hold back a moment.

"See anything, Mollyl?" came the call from outside.

"No. There's nothing here—as usual!" came the grumbling reply from the one who bore a hook for a right hand. Jan belligerently pushed his way into the warehouse, Mollyl beside him. They turned to inspect the wall behind them, just as the others moved to follow them inside.

Kane leapt from the shadows and reached the capstan in a bound! Framed against the darkness by yellow torchlight, his blade flashed a menacing gleam, reflected in his eyes!

"Kane! Here he is! Watch out!" Mollyl shouted in warning. From outside Gaethaa swore in triumph.

Only seconds were left to close the trap—or to be crushed in it jaws himself! Kane's right hand lashed out as he gained the capstan—seizing the brake lever and hauling it free! The lever snapped back in his grasp and ripped loose from its fitting! The winch now stood free from its pinion—no brake locked its mechanism to hold the main door suspended!

The door should have fallen. It remained in its place.

Dismayed by the failure of his strategy, Kane wasted a few seconds in sick conjecture. Had he miscalculated the capstan's operation then? Was the mechanism frozen after years of stressed immobility?

Snarling in rage, Kane threw himself against the horizontal crossbars, straining his massive bulk against the capstan handles! Another few seconds and he would be hemmed in by his enemies! Even now Jan and Mollyl were recovering from initial surprise to attack! Excited shouts, cold death knell of iron, boots pounding for the doorway!

Kane's shoulder struck the crossbar, and seasoned wood cracked. Muscle and timber rebounded. Jolted by the terrific impact, the capstan shuddered and recoiled in submission. With a dry, grinding snarl the mechanism began to rotate! Rusted chain groaned and cracked in protest! The immense overhead door shook itself in angry arousal and broke free of its bed of dust! Debris fell in a trickle—then exploded through the night. An inch . . . three . . . ten . . .

Thunder roared in fury as the tons heavy door tore loose and hurled itself down across the entranceway—momentum building to blinding acceleration! The capstan shrieked on its pivot, spun like a gigantic top by the streaking chain. Crossbars whirled a vortex, the wooden arms driving Mollyl and Jan back in alarm. As he darted back from the berserk mechanism, a handle struck Kane across the side and sent him reeling against the wall.

The entire warehouse rocked as the door crashed against its sill with the finality of the gate of hell. Caught by the inertia of its fall, the chain snapped short on the spindle and ripped the spinning capstan free of its smoking mounting. Wooden drum and iron chain lashed across the warehouse like a beheaded python, sending all three men flat behind cover. The mammoth scourge cracked against a pile of crates and exploded into a storm of splintered wood and glassware.

Chips of stone pelted Gaethaa and the other two as they frantically drew back from the downrushing barrier. Clouds of dust blasted their faces, whipped the torches as the door thundered shut. Baffled rage again cut through the chill of death's brush, as Gaethaa howled orders. "Alidore, Missa! Left and right fast! Find an entrance! If they're all locked, we'll break through the weakest! Damn his cunning! Kane's split us up again, and we've got to get in there fast! Move!"

Within the warehouse silence droned as the dust and echoes fell away. Picking themselves up warily, three killers moved to renew the attack. Mollyl and Jan still held torches, giving light across the interior.

The crossbar had struck only a glancing blow, but Kane's side throbbed agonizingly as he straightened. He shifted weight experimentally, judging from the ache that no ribs had broken. With his right hand he drew his dirk.

"Kane!" Jan hissed. "Remember me? It's been over ten years though—ten years ago when I still had a right hand—and a home and family! But you and your Black Fleet saw to that—didn't you, Kane! Should have cut off my head then, Kane—instead of just a hand! I've hunted you since then, Kane! Missed you at Montes—they said you died there! But I knew you were still alive—still playing your devil's games in other lands! I knew we'd finally cross swords again! Fate ordained this—just as Fate ordained your heart should dangle from Jan's hook!"

"So you know me, Hook?" sneered Kane. "Sorry, but I've forgotten your name as well as your face. I ought to remember anyone fool enough to cross blades twice with me!"

From the side door came the shock of muffled pounding. But Kane knew the timber was sound.

With a snarl Jan hurled his torch at Kane's face! Several yards yet separated them, and Kane easily dodged the missile. Its flames fanned his red beard and smoke stung his eyes, as the torch shot past him to thud against some bales of cloth. Oil soaked fragments spattered across the bales, and the torch spread its flame over musty rolls of fabric.

"Don't lose our light!" cursed Mollyl, lodging his torch between two crates. "I know you for a black hearted pirate as well, Kane! Surprised to find two of the Island Empire dogging your twisted path even across the sands of Lomarn?"

"Spread out, Jan! We'll find out for ourselves how Kane can fight without his men behind him—see if the serpent can strike when he's chased out of hiding!"

Jan's sword was in his good hand now, and the torchlight caught the razor edge of his hook's inside curve. Dagger replaced torch in Mollyl's grasp, and the Pellinite rushed for Kane with sword thrusting. Jan slid off to the side to press Kane's flank. Behind Kane, flames streaked across the bales of cloth like sparks through tinder.

Crackling heat against his back, Kane's sword sprang across Mollyl's, driving the other man back in a powerful followthrough. His dirk rose to block Jan's blade at the same instant, sparks shooting as the hilt turned the heavier weapon. Desperately Kane backed to the burning mound, preventing his assailants from circling behind. Again and again their blades clashed together, Kane's blinding defense turning aside the attack of two skilled swordsmen. At the side entrance heavy blows shuddered the door against its bolt and hinges, but the thick barrier held. It would take some time for Gaethaa and his men to break through. Neither Kane nor his assailants fought with armor or mail— their duel would be a short one.

The fire at his back spread rapidly, licking across to ignite closely piled heaps of rugs, crates, furniture. Heat became scorching, forcing Kane away from the flames. Smoke stung their eyes and nostrils. Swinging his blade in a whirlwind of death, Kane drove back his opponents' attack and leapt between them. Jan's sword dashed past his shoulder by a finger's width.

Into the open now they fought, Kane pressing more on the offensive as he heard axes bite into the side door. The warehouse was brightly lit now, as the fire spread across one end. Sheets of smoke poured over the interior, shading the firelight to dark yellow. The countless piles of merchandise threw long, grotesque shadows across the floor and far wall—twisted shapes that drew away in fear from the destroying flames.

With a powerful effort, Kane forced his opponents apart. Before Jan could recover, Kane lunged at Mollyl. The Pellinite lacked the strength to match Kane blow for blow. Frantically he retreated, only barely parrying Kane's thrusts. The flames seared his back now, and his pale face twisted in fear and pain. His defense wavered an instant. Kane's blade slashed downward faster than Mollyl could turn, its tip slicing across the flesh of his sword arm. Dropping his sword with a howl of terror, Mollyl jumped back to avoid Kane's lunge. His impetus carried him over a low crate at the fire's advancing edge! Arms flailing wildly, Mollyl tumbled backwards into a blazing mound of furniture! Flames wrapped about him as he fell, smashing through a red hot jumble of carven wood and padded leather.

Screaming in agony, Mollyl lurched to his feet and stumbled from the blaze, tongues of fire dancing over his hair and clothing! Blinded by the flames, flesh seared and blackened, he flopped across the warehouse floor, smashing into objects in hopeless effort to escape the unendurable pain. Kane ignored him as he crumpled into a writhing, mewing smouldering mass.

Kane's concentration on Mollyl gave Jan sufficient time to renew his onslaught. In the seconds it took for Kane to drive Mollyl into the fire, Jan rushed his hated enemy from behind—his sword darting for Kane's back even as Mollyl tumbled onto his pyre. But Kane had not forgotten the other man, and sensing the danger as he heard the scuffle of boots, he twisted sideways to avoid the striking sword tip. Jan's blade shot past him narrowly, but a flash of pain stabbed across his right shoulder as he turned. Jan's hook slashed through leather vest and tore the flesh of his shoulder, but failed to lodge.

Reeling back, Kane thrust his dirk for the other's side. The agony in his shoulder slowed his movements though, and with a wild laugh Jan jerked his reddened hook against the dagger, skittering down the blade and meshing it into the hilt. The hook's tip gashed Kane's hand, and jerking back Jan tore the dagger from his weakened grasp. Jan yelled in triumph and slashed out with his sword. In red fury Kane beat back his attack and hammered his blade against his assailant's guard. The fire was spreading, and the side door was beginning to splinter. A brutal stroke stunned Jan's sword arm for an instant, and Kane struck before he could parry effectively. His blade tore through the other's side, shearing through ribs and lung! Jan toppled to the floor, eyes brimming hatred through death agony. His sword had fallen, but he crawled on his belly toward Kane, hook outstretched, its razor tip scoring the planks as he dragged his broken body onward. He died as his hook stabbed inches from Kane's boot.

Heat from the fire beat at Kane's face. He stepped back. Already the flames had engulfed the section where Mollyl's body had lain. The side door still held against Gaethaa's assault, but the warehouse was ablaze. Flames now had leapt over half the floor, and in places the planks had given way to collapse into the cellar. It was hard to breathe, even to see with the rapidly building smoke and heat. Hurriedly Kane retrieved his dirk and started for the cellar stairs. His enemies were outside waiting—the tunnel was his only escape now. But if the blazing floor collapsed over the cellar trapdoor before he reached it . . .

The trapdoor was still clear of flaming wreckage. Seizing a rough torch from the edge of the fire, Kane heaved open the trapdoor and descended the steps into the tunnel. Here the musty dampness of the earth was undisturbed by the holocaust above. Though stale, the dank air was relief from the burning smoke that choked the warehouse.

Rapidly as he dared, Kane passed through the tunnel. His

torch offered poor light, but sufficient to pick out his way. Rotting timbers sagged overhead, bowed out from the walls. Dirt had trickled through to make soft ridges along the floor, and in a few places mounds of debris almost occluded the passage. Gingerly Kane crawled over these crumbling heaps of dirt and shoring, torch out-thrust to give light. Clods and sand fell over his back and legs, making a dark paste with the blood that flowed from his cuts.

At any second Kane knew the tunnel might give way altogether, sealing him in this tomb beneath the city of the dead. At one point a dull shock echoed through the tunnel, along with a muffled crash from behind him. The warehouse roof must have fallen, Kane guessed, nervously eyeing the tunnel walls. But by now he had come a good distance beneath the earth, and the tunnel seemed somewhat more solid as he approached its far end.

The floor rose, and a flight of steps appeared before his dying torch. Eagerly Kane ascended them and pushed open the concealed door in the inn's cellars. Moving confidently through the deserted inn, Kane found a door and stepped outside. Within the walls of Sebbei the blazing warehouse threw a glow against black skies soon to gray with dawn.

For the moment his enemies must believe him dead. Wincing at the pain, Kane paused by the inn's wall to wash his scorched, bleeding body and bind his wounds. Three yet lived of those who had hounded him, and neither injuries nor fatigue had abated Kane's fury.

X. LAND OF THE DEAD

When smoke began streaming from cracks and openings throughout the warehouse, and the splintering door began to emanate heat from the inferno within, Gaethaa called a halt to their frantic efforts to break in.

"This place is doomed!" he pronounced, laying aside his axe. "Anyone still alive in there has to get out in a hurry, or the smoke will kill them if the flames don't! Jan or Mollyl will open up if Kane hasn't finished them—and if he has, then we'll give Kane the choice of roasting inside or coming out to meet our swords! Either way he'll be burning in hell before dawn breaks! Spread out and watch the doors."

His men did as ordered. One man had always kept watch on the warehouse doors while the other two had attacked the side entrance. Clearly no one had escaped from within while they fruitlessly attempted to break down the door. Swords ready for instant use, they watched vigilantly for one of the doors to swing open, for a figure to stumble out in a shroud of smoke and flame, blinded and coughing. If it should be Kane who emerged, Gaethaa meant to give him scant time to draw clean air into his lungs.

But no door was flung open. No scorched figure stepped out. Crashes from within indicated the floor was giving way, and then came a ripping concussion as the warehouse roof collapsed ponderously upon the wreckage within. A cataclysmic blast of flame and cinders leapt into the night skies, transforming the yet standing walls of the warehouse into the cone of a volcano. Soon the doors crumpled from the heat, falling inward to reveal a blazing holocaust. Still stood the thick stone walls, red hot now from the furnace that raged within. But long before this, the watchers had ceased to guard the exits.

"Kane's funeral pyre!" observed Gaethaa triumphantly. "He took two more good men with him, but they died as heroes." He turned to accept Alidore's congratulations. "Only three of us left. It's been a costly campaign—the most dangerous of my career clearly. But our goal was a great one, and we have at last met success. History's blackest monster has finally met the death that for centuries he had cheated. Mankind will be greatful for this work we have done. Once again I have cleansed a dark shadow of evil with the cold light of good."

A rustle from the alley behind them abruptly drew attention. "Why, it's the witch," Gaethaa announced, catching sight of her in the light from the blaze.

Rehhaile hung poised at the alley's entrance, almost concealed in the shadow of a building. Firelight shone across her face and limbs, as her blind eyes stared beyond them. She seemed to be summoning the courage to approach them, yet remained on the verge of flight.

Why had she come back? Alidore wondered. Surely her second sight told her she had been seen. Had Kane meant so much to her that she had thrown away all caution just to be present at his death? Alidore sensed a note of jealousy in his musing. "Milord," he began, "can't we forget about her . . . ?"

Gaethaa shrugged. He was in a jubilant mood, and if his lieutenant felt concern for this creature, he could easily grant him his whim. "Sure, Alidore, if this will assuage your misgivings. Kane is dead, and she was only his whore and dupe. She was punished for her tiny part in his crimes.

"Come on out of the shadows, witch," he called magnanimously. "We have decided to grant clemency. You need have no further fear of our justice. Come see the fate of the monster you served."

Sensing the leniency of the Avenger's disposition, Rehhaile stepped forward to join them. "Kane's dead," she informed them dully. "I knew when you at last cornered him, so I came to be in on the finish, however it turned out. But Kane was trapped within the burning warehouse. He died in the flames—I felt his death in my mind. You destroyed Kane as you had intended; your mission is complete now. Will you leave Sebbei at dawn?"

"So your witch's sight showed you Kane's death," Gaethaa smiled. "I envy you—that was a vision I would have given much to have shared. But see, Alidore—despite your concern for her, she only desires our departure. Well, my men and I will ride on as soon as we've rested and reprovisioned. I never care to wait around for the fulsome praise of those whom I have served—and Sebbei holds little attraction for me. But for now I'll soothe the strain of this mission by basking in the glow of my enemy's death pyre."

"I'll take some fresh air instead," Dron Missa yawned. "The smoke from this pyre is as redolent as a burning dump. Thoem! What kind of junk did they have stuffed away in there!" The Waldann strolled toward the city wall and climbed the steps to the parapet. His lean figure could be seen silhouetted against the graying skies as he leisurely paced alongside ghost guardsmen of dead Sebbei.

Gaethaa the Crusader settled himself against a wall and stretched his long legs out before him. Dreamily he smiled into the dying flames of the warehouse, reliving the excitement of the past days and wondering where the cold light would lead him next. First to Kamathae for new men and equipment. The death of Kane could occupy the court poets, but elsewhere there were others who needed the help of the Avenger.

Alidore and Rehhaile wandered on down the street. The witch was eager to draw away his lieutenant, Gaethaa mused. Still Alidore seemed fascinated with her, and he was entitled to the diversion.

The lake lay below him, its gray mist rising in the predawn darkness. Idly Dron Missa leaned against the parapet and felt the tight muscles of his back slowly loosen. A scrape of boot on stone met his ear, and he looked up, wondering who had joined him.

A figure approached him along the wall, striding through the mist as ominously as the angel of death. Menace radiated from the fog wrapped figure, shone in his killer's eyes, gleamed along his drawn sword, "Kane!" gasped Missa, recognizing the singed and bandaged swordsman. Only a second did he waste on amazed confoundment. Missa's own blade leapt from scabbard to answer Kane's challenge!

Kane rushed upon the Waldann, his sword hissing through the fog. Missa's blade moved in swift parry, then thrust past in a sudden lunge. Slipping away from the razor point, Kane swore and renewed the fight with more cautious tactics. His opponent was an excellent swordsman, and Kane's stiff right arm could wield his dirk only clumsily. Carefully he pressed his attack, Missa's darting blade baffling his own efforts to overwhelm his guard.

Left-handed opponents Missa had fought before, and he had no difficulty adjusting to the other's stance. Kane's speed amazed him though—astonishing agility for a man of his bulk. And as Kane continued to batter him relentlessly, Missa became conscious of the vast power that underlay his speed. Here was as skillful and deadly an opponent as he had ever confronted, and only Missa's own brilliant swordplay saved him from Kane's blade time and again. With growing concern, Missa coldly remembered the tales he had heard of Kane—recalled the spectre of violent death that had haunted them ever since Gaethaa began his mission to destroy Kane.

A twinge of pain shot along Missa's right thigh as Kane's partially deflected blade turned to slice shallowly across his leg. Ignoring the wound, Missa fell back a pace as if to stagger. As Kane stepped forward to follow his advantage, Missa raised his sword to parry and lashed out with the dagger in his left hand. Kane's recovery with his own dirk was too slow, and Missa's blade gashed across his ribs fleetingly as Kane twisted away.

Cursing in anger Kane recklessly hurled his dirk at the Waldann. Badly thrown, the blade cleanly missed the other. But as Dron Missa dodged to avoid the streaking knife, his guard fell for an instant. Kane's sword flashed down, slashing Missa's swordarm to the bone—only its downward course spared his arm from amputation. A return flick of Kane's weapon sent his opponent's blade spinning into the dawn mists. Badly wounded and armed with only his dagger, Missa saw Kane's killing stroke slash toward him with dream-like slowness, nightmare inexorability.

In the split second of life that remained to him, Missa reacted with desperate speed. Darting back from the search-ing blade, he threw himself from the parapet and dived into the lake below. The darkness, the cold water, received him in a stunning embrace.

Surfacing quickly, Missa paddled away clumsily. His wounds were bleeding freely and stung even more fiercely as the water bathed them. Still they were not of themselves fatal, although disabling. Once he could bind them, stop the bleeding—with proper care they would heal, and not too many months would pass before he could wield a sword as expertly as before. But that would be for another lord and another cause. Gaethaa's insane missions had paid him well, yet the Crusader had not bought his life. Missa understood concepts of loyalty and duty of mercenary to his lord, but only within reason. Gaethaa's mission to destroy Kane had been cursed with dark fortune from the beginning, and Dron Missa decided it was time for discreet withdrawal. The gods plainly had given him this chance; it would be sacrilege to ignore their intercession.

He looked back at the hulking figure leaning against the parapet in the dawn light. "Go to hell, Kane!" he shouted back, then disappeared into the mists.

When Gaethaa had first heard Missa's shout and the clash of arms, he stared at the scene of combat in disbelief. Then through his astonished mind filtered the incredible truth—Kane still lived! The devil had not died in the flames—by some sorcery he had escaped! The witch had lied to com-plete the collapse of their vigilance! Now Kane had again returned to strike from the shadows! How many more times could the demon cheat death!

"Alidore! Alidore! Kill that damned witch and get over here quick!" He bellowed shrilly, watching the parapet duel. "Alidore! Run, damn you! Kane's still alive! He's attacked Missa on the wall!"

Forgetting Rehhaile for the moment, Alidore dashed to his lord's call. Against graying skies could be seen the deadly display of swordplay atop the wall. Swords in hand, they rushed to the steps that ascended the wall in this quarter.

But the distance was considerable, and as they reached the stairs, they saw the fight's abrupt climax, watched Dron Missa plunge from the parapet into the lake.

"Missa too!" Gaethaa swore in rage. "Now he's killed Missa! I think we fight Lord Tloluvin himself! But we two have not fallen! We'll let Kane taste our iron before this sun has risen!"

Yet when they reached the top, Kane had stolen away into the mists of dawn, eluding them once again.

"He runs from us, milord!" Alidore exclaimed bewilderedly. "Strange Kane should slink off with only two to face. He won't face an opponent in the open it seems."

"No!" hissed Gaethaa, his eyes aflame. "See there on the stones! Blood! A blood trail! Kane's been wounded! Missa died not without giving account! No telling how badly wounded Kane might be! We've put him to flight now though—and here's the trail to lead us to him!"

But the trail of blood dwindled and vanished altogether after they had followed it for only a short distance through the streets of Sebbei, where now the rising sun was cutting through the concealing night. Grimly Gaethaa realized that Kane's wounds had not been as severe as he had hoped. However seriously he might be disabled, at least he had been able to staunch the bleeding. And now Kane had again hidden himself in the maze of dead Sebbei.

"The game continues," intoned Gaethaa heavily. "We have gained nothing. Again we must search for Kane through this damned labyrinthian ghost city, stalking him through his lair. Except today there are only you and I to hunt the tiger, Alidore. We can never destroy Kane like this."

Alidore looked at his lord in concern. There was a sharp cry of despair in Gaethaa's voice that his lieutenant had never heard before. But though the Crusader's lanky figure was slumped and his chin propped against fist, his eyes were lost in thought. His long face bore twisting lines of raw emotion as his keen mind sorted through and rejected dozens of strategems from past campaigns.

Abruptly his face broke into inspired smile, and a triumphant laugh barked from his lips. "We're not done yet, Alidore!" he cried wildly. "We'll burn this accursed city to the ground!"

"Burn Sebbei!" Alidore exploded incredulously.

"Right! Burn it all! Let it all burn to the ground! Kane's using these deserted buildings for cover—we'll smoke him out into the open. Thoem knows how he escaped that warehouse without our knowledge, but his cunning won't help him when all Sebbei is in flames! He'll burn with the town, or he'll head for open country. Even if we miss him at first, picking up his trail will be child's play in this ghost land. We'll run him to earth even if he tries to cross the Lomarn— wounded as he is, he won't get that far! No more playing into his traps!"

"Milord Gaethaa!" Alidore protested. "You can't be serious! Burn down the entire city to kill one man! What of the townspeople?"

"Their backbones have dryrot! Don't worry about them. We'll fire a few buildings across the city—enough for the wind to spread the flames over the rest! It will be done before they can lift a hand—not that I believe any man of them has the guts to stop us! Maybe we can tell some that Kane started the fires—might jolt them out of their cowering lassitude to the point they'll tell us where Kane is, though I doubt if they're worth even that!"

"No! I mean, we can't raze an entire city just to destroy Kane! These people will be killed—at best they'll lose everything they possess!"

Gaethaa shrugged impatiently. "The town has no more than a few hundred. Most should escape easily enough, and there's any number of empty towns and villages they can move into. And don't waste pity on them! Had they done their duty to mankind, they would have pitched in and helped us destroy Kane! By their cowardly negligence they're responsible for the deaths of all my men—as well as being traitors to the cause of good! Burning these whining rats from their rotten dens is a fitting punishment for their complicity! Come on Alidore, we're wasting time!"

Alidore's voice was strained, as he grasped Gaethaa's shoulder and turned him half around. "But to burn an entire city for one man! Kane isn't worth it!"

Face white with rage, Gaethaa threw off his lieutenant's hand. "Kane not worth it!" he roared. "Alidore, have you lost your mind! We've crossed half a continent to destroy this demon! All of your comrades have given their lives for this mission! And after all this effort, this sacrifice, the man I came to destroy still mocks me! I'll raze a hundred towns if need be to destroy Kane! Yes, and consider the price a cheap one balanced against the evil this man has committed— evil he will continue to bring upon mankind until he is hunted down and slain! What's the worth of this city of ghosts opposed to the greater good of mankind!"

The logic was inescapable, but Alidore still balked. "But the strategy may be entirely in vain!" he argued weakly. "Kane won't be trapped in the flames! He'll escape the city easily—we can't begin to guard the gates, let alone the entire wall! He'll flee Sebbei, and we'll never pick up his trail in the confusion!"

"A general who believes his plan of attack infallible is a fool!" Gaethaa snapped. "Tell me a better one, and I'll accept your counsel. The plain truth is that Kane has beaten us at this damnable game of cat and mouse! He knows Sebbei better than we do, so he has only to lie in wait for us to enter his traps! We failed yesterday with six men—it's hopeless to try again with two! We have to force him into the open—make him run instead of spin webs to ensnare us! Damn it, Alidore—what's wrong with you! Have you lost your ideals and your nerve together!"

The Lartroxian wavered, thoughts spinning in soul wrenching tumult.

A voice cried out from behind them. "Alidore! What are you doing? Have you completely sold your soul to Gaethaa? That madman and his band of killers have done more evil than Kane has ever been responsible for! Will you help him now to destroy Sebbei and its wretched people on the chance you might kill Kane with this atrocity! Alidore, if you have anything but iron left to your soul, leave Gaethaa! Stop him before he sacrifices more lives to his merciless gods!"

"Ah! I hear a witch!" Gaethaa whispered in knifelike tones. "The same lying voice that told me of Kane's death. Now we see the harvest of false mercy! But it's all apparent. The witch has perverted my lieutenant's soul—twisted his spirit with her sorcery—seduced him to serve the black powers of evil!"

He drew his sword and stepped toward her slowly, blade held low. "Come embrace me, witch!" he hissed. "I think this time you have overestimated my blind stupidity and your own dark glamour as well!"

Alidore leapt in front of him. "Stop, milord!" he pleaded. "She means nothing by her words—she has no sorcery!"

There was pity in Gaethaa's voice as he moved to push Alidore aside. "You're bewitched, Alidore—your reason no longer serves you. Stand back now while my blade severs her spell over you, and sends this witch back to the darkness she serves."

Resolution hardened Alidore's face as he planted himself firmly and drew his own sword. "It's not madness, milord—nor is it Rehhaile's sorcery! I recognize the truth in her words, understand the misgivings that have plagued my spirit these last months! I can't let you kill an innocent girl . . ."

"Innocent girl! She's a witch! She's lied to you! She's helped Kane strike at us from the first moment we entered Sebbei!"

". . . Nor can I permit you to burn this city just to destroy Kane!" Alidore rushed on. "Come on, Gaethaa," he begged. "Let's get out of this land of the dead! We'll return to Kamathae, raise a new army, and return with sufficient strength to destroy Kane!"

"Out of the question! Now Kane knows I intend to kill him! He'll hide where no man could find him—use his evil powers to build up defenses I could never hope to overcome! Stand aside, Alidore, and I'll forget your insane insubordination!"

"I'm sorry, milord Gaethaa," he returned slowly. "You'll kill Rehhaile and raze this city by yourself—but first you'll have to kill me!"

Sudden rage claimed Gaethaa. "Betrayal is it—and from you, Alidore! Damn you—if you stand among the forces of evil, stand against the cold light of good, then by the cold light you shall be destroyed! Get out of my way!"

"Don't force me to cross blades with you, milord!" Alidore's plea was a warning as well.

Gaethaa's face broke into a pale mask of vengeful fury. "You're a fool, Alidore!" he screamed. His sword streaked outward, all but tearing Alidore's weapon from his grip.

Alidore jumped back, blade weaving a defensive pattern. His soul was close to shattering with the conflicting emotions that raged through him. His entire universe had suddenly collapsed about him, so that now he found himself locked in deadly combat with the man for whom an hour ago he would have willingly given his life. Suddenly he was pitted against the beliefs and ideals he had sworn allegiance to all his life. Spurred out of his emotional maelstrom only by the instincts of self-preservation, he desperately parried Gaethaa's maddened attack.

It was not the state of mind to offer a chance against an opponent of Gaethaa's prowess. Rapidly, easily the Crusader wore down his guard. A sudden thrust lay open Alidore's side, and as he recoiled in pain, a glancing stroke tore off his helmet. Alidore was driven to the ground, blackness flashing through his skull, while his eyes were blinded by blood pouring from his gashed brow. A thousand miles away echoed a girl's scream.

Gaethaa surveyed his fallen lieutenant, madness still in his eyes. "I'm sorry, Alidore," he intoned with heavy regret. "You were a brother to me—a friend through many battles. Though I must kill you now to purge this evil spell that has stolen you from me, I'll always remember you as the loyal and courageous lieutenant you once were to me." He raised his sword for the *coup de grâce*. "The tales spoke of the evil curse that follows Kane—evil that destroys those who cross his twisted path. Now I understand the truth behind those legends. Good-by, Alidore—Kane has destroyed you, but die assured that you will be avenged!"

"Hell, kill him if you're going to—but don't give me credit for it. It bothers me to accept favors from a man I'm going to kill in another minute." The mocking voice grated from the street behind Gaethaa. "Or if you're embarrassed to kill a friend, let him lie there and I'll finish him after I've carved out your heart."

Gaethaa whirled to face Kane. His enemy stepped from out of the fog and smoke and casually strode toward him, sword poised. Rough bandages were bound across his ribs; others made crimson bands across his right shoulder. A murderous light shone from his blue eyes, brutal face drawn in a savage snarl.

"So the tiger has come out of hiding!" Gaethaa purred. "I had thought I'd be forced to smoke you from your lair! But now comes the final cast of dice in this game we've played, and it's only fitting that the principal players should meet at last. You've cost me every man in my command, Kane—it's for their lives you now must answer—and for the centuries of crimes that lie behind you like an accusing shadow!"

"You've achieved a fair number of atrocities in your own short career—soon to be lamented!" sneered Kane, raising his sword.

Gaethaa's silent lunge brought them together. Their swords clashed and locked, then Kane hurled the lighter man back. The knife in Gaethaa's other hand sliced empty air. Blow upon blow hammered a vicious cacophony to death. Kane's right arm was all but useless to him, but the dazzling speed of his sword arm made the loss seem minor.

"Call upon the forces of evil to aid you, Kane!" jeered Gaethaa, observing the crimson stigma of fresh blood spread over Kane's bandages. The wounds were opening, and soon his strength would waver. "Or have your dark gods left you in fear, just as evil must always flee before the invincible sword of good!"

"I serve neither gods nor fool's causes!" Kane growled. "And don't delude yourself into terming invincible principles that are meaningless except to the relative viewpoint of the beholder!" His apparent feint twisted into a sudden lunge that sliced across Gaethaa's cheek. "First blood!" he laughed.

The men struggled on in silence then, voiceless save for panting breath and animal grunts. Gaethaa was a deadly opponent—a shrewd and skillful swordsman with wiry strength driving his long frame. In addition he was relatively fresh, while Kane was fatigued and bleeding from wounds suffered in recent combat. Still his endurance did not falter before the Avenger's fanatical attack, not did the lethal beauty of his swordplay grow strained. Relentlessly the two men slashed and thrust, parried and feinted—each confident that his attack would exhaust the other and soon bring an end to the stalemate.

Again their swords locked hilts. They strained against one another, man to man, blade to blade—a split second would see them thrown apart again! Gaethaa's dagger slipped past Kane's guard and slithered for his side. Heaving against the other blade, Kane threw Gaethaa back a step, dropping his own knife at the same instant. As Gaethaa fell away, Kane seized his left wrist in passing. Forcing the thick muscles of his injured arm to respond, Kane crushed the wrist in his grip and bent it back as his enemy lunged away. Gaethaa's dagger stabbed around to gash his arm. Then with a grating snap, the forearm bones cracked under the twisting pressure.

Gaethaa gasped and swung his sword wildly at Kane's arm, frantic to relieve the crushing agony. Kane released his grip and jerked his arm clear. At the same moment his sword flashed out at Gaethaa's unprotected trunk, before the other could recover his guard. The powerful blow clove down through Gaethaa's right shoulder, all but severing arm from trunk! Kane's reddened blade gleamed and slashed out again, catching his opponent as he spun about and sundering head from body! The head bounced twice with a hollow tolling.

Kane stood before the grotesquely strewn corpse of Gaethaa the Crusader, sucking great gasps of air into his hammering chest. In the crisp dawn chill tiny tendrils of smoke seemed to writhe from the scarlet splashed stones, from his dripping sword, from his torn flesh. It blended with his steaming breath and vanished into the morning mist.

Shaking himself wearily, Kane frowned at Alidore's fallen form, stretched out across the deserted street, his head staining Rehhaile's skirt. Kane strode toward him purposefully.

"Don't, Kane!" Rehhaile pleaded. "Please don't kill this one! Alidore saved my life several times from those killers! Spare him now for me! Please, Kane! Alidore can't harm you now!"

Kane swayed before them, sword raised, murder lust still twisting his face. Alidore stared up at him blankly, face an expressionless mask. No move did he offer in defense or in flight; his eyes met Kane's in uncaring gaze. With a shrug Kane lowered his blade, blood fury slipping from his face—only to remain smoldering in his eyes, where its fires never slaked.

"All right, Rehhaile," he said. "I give him to you. But I doubt that your pity will be of much use to him. It seems that Gaethaa's blow knocked loose his brain inside that thick skull."

"No, Kane! It's his soul that's torn loose within him! I can heal his spirit's torment in time."

"So that's it," Kane laughed mirthlessly. "No point in asking you to come with me then, I see. Just as well. I'm leaving now, Rehhaile. I've had my fill of living among ghosts. I'm sick of morbid brooding—there's still adventure to amuse me in the world outside. Your companionship here has been interesting—soothing. I'm grateful."

"Good-by, Kane," said Rehhaile softly, turning her mind from the winter of his thoughts and spirit.

Kane muttered something she did not quite hear, then turned and stalked away down the empty streets. The ghosts of dead Demornte watched him depart. Go from Demornte, land of the dead, world of shadows, where death has lain and life cannot linger.

Alidore stirred. Sitting up dizzily he reached for his fallen sword. With shaking hands he placed its point against his chest. His universe had toppled, pinning him in the wreckage of his unshakable beliefs, unassailable truths. What use to survive the death of his gods?

"Alidore! Don't!" screamed Rehhaile, sensing what he was about to do. "For my sake—don't! I want you to live! Together we can leave this land of the dead—we can go out into the world of life!"

"I thought I followed the cold clear light of right, of good," Alidore spoke in agony. "Instead I served the cold light of death!"

The swordpoint wavered against his chest. The soothing oblivion of death? Or try to return to life with Rehhaile? His soul was too wounded to decide.

A DIFFICULT
UNDERTAKING

by Harry Turtledove

Ulror Raska's son stood in the topmost chamber of the tall watchtower, staring out to sea. Like most Halogai, he was tall and fair. His shining hair hung in a neat braid that reached the small of his back, but there was nothing effeminate about him. His face, hard-featured to begin with, had been battered further by close to half a century of carousing and war. His shoulders were wide as a bear's. Until a few weeks ago, his belly had bulged over his belt. It did not bulge anymore. No one inside the fortress of Sotevag was fat anymore.

Staring out to sea kept Ulror from thinking about the Videssian army that sat outside the walls of the fortress. The sea ran east forever from Sotevag. Looking at it, Ulror could feel free for a while, even if these southern waters were warm and blue, not like the chill, whitecap-flecked Bay of Haloga he had watched so often from the battlements of his keep.

Of course, in the north the harvest failed one year in three. Even when it did not, there was never enough, or enough land, not with every family running to three, five, seven sons. And so the Halogai hired on as mercenaries in Videssos and the lesser kingdoms, and manned ships and raided when they saw the chance.

Ulror smacked a big fist into his open palm in frustrated rage. By the gods, this chance had looked so good! With Videssos convulsed as two rival emperors battled, the island of Kalavria, far from the Empire's heartland, should have been easy to seize, to make a place where Halogai could settle freely, could live without fear of starving—it even reminded Ulror of his own district of Namdalen, if one could imagine Namdalen without snow. Chieftains whose clans had hated each other for generations joined in building and crewing the fleet.

The really agonizing thing was that, over much of the island, the men from the far north had managed to establish themselves. And here sat Ulror, under siege. He would not have admitted it to any of his warriors, but he expected Sotevag to fall. If it did, the Videssians would probably mop up the rest of the Halogai, one band at a time.

Damn Kypros Zigabenos anyway!

Kypros Zigabenos stood staring up at the walls of Sotevag, wondering how he was ever going to take the stronghold. His agile mind leapt from one stratagem to another, and unfailingly found flaws in each. From where he stood, the fortress looked impregnable. That was unfortunate, for he was all too likely to lose his head if it held.

An eyebrow quirked in wry amusement. Zigabenos had a long, narrow, mobile face, the kind that made him look younger than his forty-five years. Hardly any gray showed in dark hair or in the aristocratic fringe of beard tracing the angle of his jaw.

He brushed a speck of lint from the sleeve of his brocaded robe. To wear the rich samite in the field was the mark of a fop, but he did not care. What was the point to civilization, if not the luxuries it made possible?

That they destroyed the opportunity to create such things was to him reason enough to oppose the Halogai. As individuals he valued highly many of the northerners, Ulror not least among them. Certainly Ulror was a better man than the fool and the butcher who both claimed to be rightful Avtokrator of the Videssians.

Both those men had called on him for aid. In a way, he thanked the good god Phos for the arrival of the Halogai. Their attack gave him the perfect excuse to refuse to remove men from Kalavria to take part in internecine strife. He would have done the same, though, if the invaders had not come.

But either the butcher or the fool would be able to rule Videssos, once the internal foe was vanquished. The Empire had survived for close to a thousand years; it had seen bad emperors before. The eternal bureaucracy, of which Zigabenos was proud to be a part, held Videssos together when leadership faltered.

And that the Halogai, were their chieftains the best leaders in the world—and some came close—could never do. They knew nothing of the fine art of shearing a flock without flaying it. Like any barbarians, if they wanted something they took it, never caring whether the taking ruined in a moment years of patient labor.

For that Zigabenos would fight them, all the while recognizing and admiring their courage, their steadiness, aye, even their wit. When Ulror had sensibly decided to stand siege at Sotevag rather than risk his outnumbered, harried troops in a last desperate battle, Zigabenos had shouted to him up there on the battlements: "If you are so great a general, come out and fight!"

Ulror had laughed like one of his heathen gods. "If you're so great a general, Videssian, make me!"

The taunt still rankled. Zigabenos had surrounded the fortress, had even succeeded in cutting it off from the sea. The Halogai would not escape that way, or gain fresh supplies. But the storerooms and cisterns of Sotevag were full, thanks in no small measure to Zigabenos' own exertions the year before. Now he could not afford to wait and starve Ulror out. While he sat in front of Sotevag with forces he had scraped together from all over Kalavria, the northerners could do as they would though the rest of the island. Yet trying to storm the fortress would be hellishly expensive in men and materiel.

Damn Ulror Raska's son, anyway!

"They're stirring around down there," said Flosi Wolf's-Pelt, brushing back from his eyes the thick locks of gray hair that gave him his sobriquet.

"Aye." Ulror's eyes narrowed in suspicion. Till now, Zigabenos had been content to let hunger do his work for him. Like many Videssian generals, he played at war as if it were a game where the object was to win while losing as few pieces as possible. Ulror despised that style of fighting; he craved the hot, clean certainty of battle.

But there was no denying that what Zigabenos did, he did very well. He had chivvied Ulror's Halogai halfway across Kalavria, never offering combat unless the odds were all in his favor. He had even forced Ulror to dance to his tune and go to earth here like a hunted fox.

So why was he changing his way of doing things when it had worked so well for him up to now?

Ulror pondered that as he watched the Videssians deploy. They moved smartly and in unison, as if they were puppets animated by Zigabenos' will alone. The Halogai lacked that kind of discipline. Even as the horns called them to their places on the battlements of Sotevag castle, they came out of the great hall in straggling groups of different sizes, getting in each other's way as they went to their assigned sections of the wall.

A single man rode past the palisade the Videssians had thrown up around Sotevag. He came within easy bowshot of the walls, his head bare so the defenders could recognize him. Ulror's lip twisted. Zigabenos might favor a spineless kind of warfare, but he was no coward.

"Your last chance, northerners," the Videssian general called, speaking the Haloga tongue badly but understandably. He did not bellow, as Ulror would have; still, his voice carried. "Surrender the fortress and yield up your commander, and you common soldiers will not be harmed. By Phos I swear it." Zigabenos drew a circle over his breast— the sun sign, symbol of the Videssian god of good. "May Skotos drag me down to hell's ice if I lie."

Ulror and Flosi looked at each other. Zigabenos had offered those same terms at the start of the siege, and been answered with jeers. No commander, though, could be sure how his troops would stand up under privation. . . .

An arrow buried itself in the ground a couple of strides in front of Zigabenos' horse. The beast snorted and sidestepped. The Videssian general, a fine rider, brought it back under control. Even then he did not retreat. Instead he asked, "Is that your final reply?"

"Aye!" the Halogai yelled, shaking their fists and brandishing weapons in defiance.

"No!" Ulror's great shout overrode the cries of his men. "I have another."

Zigabenos looked his way, suddenly alert. The northern chieftain understood that look, and knew the Videssian thought he was about to turn his coat. Rage ripped through him. "The gods curse you, Zigabenos!" he roared. "The only way you'll get me out of Sotevag is stinking in my coffin!"

His men raised a cheer; the more bravado a Haloga showed in the face of danger, the more his fellows esteemed him. Zigabenos sat impassive until quiet returned. He gave Ulror the Videssian salute, his clenched fist over his heart.

"That can be arranged," he said. He wheeled his horse, showing the northerners his back.

Ulror bit his lip. In his own cold-blooded way, Zigabenos had style.

The palisade drew near. The space between Zigabenos' shoulder blades stopped itching. If that had been he in the fortress, no enemy commander who exposed himself would have lived to return to his troops. The Haloga notion of honor struck him as singularly naive.

Yet the trip up to the walls had been worth making. When the northerners once fell into corruption, they wallowed in it. They reminded the Videssian general of a man never exposed to some childhood illness who would die if he caught it as an adult. His own troops, no more brave or honorable than they had to be, would never sink to the depths of a Haloga who abandoned his code of conduct.

No time for such reverie now, he told himself reproachfully. The trumpeters and fifemen were waiting for his signal. He nodded. As the martial music rang out, his command echoed it: "Forward the palisade!"

Half the Videssian soldiers picked up the stakes and brush surrounding the castle of Sotevag and moved ahead, toward the fortress' walls. The rest of the men—the better archers in the army—followed close behind, their bows drawn.

The Halogai began shooting to harass the advance. The range was long and the stuff of the palisade gave some protection. Nevertheless, here and there a man dropped. The dead lay where they had fallen; the wounded were dragged to the rear, where the priests would tend them with healing magic.

Zigabenos gave a quiet order. The musicians sent it to the troops, who halted and began emplacing the palisade once more. "Give them a volley!" the general said. "From now on, they keep their heads down!"

The thrum of hundreds of bowstrings released together was the only pleasant note in the cacophony of war. Arrows hissed toward Sotevag. The Halogai dove for cover. Shouts of fury and screams showed that not all reached it.

One by one the northerners reappeared, some standing tall and proud, others peering over the top of the battlements. Zigabenos gauged the moment. "Another!" he shouted.

The Halogai vanished again. "Marksmen only, from now

on," the general commanded. "If you see a good target, shoot at it. Try not to waste arrows, though."

He had expected a furious answering fire from the besieged warriors, but it did not come. They were shooting back, but picking their marks as carefully as their foes. That made him want to grind his teeth. Ulror had learned too much, fighting against Videssians. Most of his countrymen would never have thought about saving arrows for a later need.

Zigabenos shook his head in reluctant admiration. He sighed, regretting the need to kill such a man. A race with the restless energy of the Halogai might go far, allied to Videssian canniness. Unfortunately, he knew the first place it would head for: Videssos the city, the great imperial capital. No lesser goal could sate such a folk. And so he would do his duty, and try to make sure it never came into being.

He waved. An aide appeared at his elbow. "Sir?"

"Muster the woodworkers. The time has come to build engines."

"I grow to hate the sounds of carpentry," Ulror said. The Videssian artisans were a quarter mile away, out of reach of any weapons from inside Sotevag, but there were so many of them and they were chewing up so much timber that the noise of saw, hammer, axe, and adze was always present in the fortress.

"Not I," Flosi Wolf's-Pelt said.

"Eh? Why not?" Ulror looked at his companion in surprise.

"When the building noises stop, they'll be finished. Then they'll start using their toys."

"Oh. Aye." Ulror managed a laugh, as any northerner should in the face of danger, but even he could hear how grim it sounded. Frustrated, he shook his head until his braid switched like a horse's tail. "By the gods, I'd give two thumb's-widths off my prong for a way to strike at those accursed siege engines."

"A sally?" Flosi's eyes lit at the prospect; his hand went to the hilt of his sword.

"No," Ulror said reluctantly. "Look how openly the carpenters are working out there. See the cover off to the flanks? Zigabenos wants to tempt us into the open, so he can slaughter us at his leisure. I'll not give him his triumph so cheap."

Flosi grunted. "There's no honor in such tricks."

"True, but they work all the same." Ulror had lost too many men to ambushes to doubt that. Such tactics were of a piece with the rest of the way the Videssians made war, seeking victory at the least cost to themselves. To counter them, a man had to fight the same way, regardless of how much it went against his grain.

Flosi, though, still wanted to strike a blow at the enemy. "What of using sorcery on their engines?"

That had not occurred to Ulror. Battle magic almost always failed; in the heat of combat, men's emotions flamed strong enough to weaken the bite of spells. Only the most powerful wizards went to war, save as healers or diviners. And the one Haloga with Ulror who knew something of magic, Kolskegg Cheese-Curd, had a better reputation as tosspot than sorcerer.

When Ulror said as much to Flosi, his comrade snorted in disgust. "What do we lose by trying? If you don't aim to fight, why not throw yourself off the wall and have done?"

"I aim to fight," Ulror growled, pointing down into the outer ward, where men chopped logs and filled barrels with earth to build makeshift barriers if the walls should be breached.

"Defense," Flosi said scornfully.

Nettled, Ulror opened his mouth to snarl back, but stopped with his angry words still unspoken. How could he blame Flosi for wanting to hurt the Videssians? He wanted to himself. And who could say? Maybe Kolskegg could take the imperials by surprise. Ulror made for the stairwell to track down the wizard. Behind him, Flosi nodded in satisfaction.

Kolskegg Cheese-Curd was a big, pockmarked man who, like Ulror, had been fat before the siege of Sotevag began. Now his skin was limp and saggy, like a deflated bladder. Something seemed to have gone out of his spirit, too, when the castle's ale casks ran dry. Living on well water was torment for him.

His eyes widened in alarm as Ulror explained what he required. "You must be mad!" he burst out. "A hundredth part of such a magic would burn out my brain!"

"No great loss, that," Ulror growled. "How do you have the nerve to call yourself a wizard? What *are* you good for, anyway?"

"My skill at divination is not of the worst." Kolskegg

eyed Ulror warily, as if wondering how much trouble that admission would get him into.

"The very thing!" the Haloga chieftain said, slapping him on the back. Kolskegg beamed until Ulror went on, "Divine me a way to slip out of Zigabenos' clutches."

"But—my art is tyromancy," Kolskegg quavered, "reading the future in the patterns curds make as they separate out in new cheese. Where can I get milk?"

"One of the last two jennies foaled the other day. The colt went into the stewpot, of course, but we still need the mother for hauling wood and earth. She may not have dried up yet."

"Ass' milk?" Kolskegg's lip curled. Even poor sorcerers had standards.

"What better, for you?" Ulror said brutally. Losing patience, he grabbed Kolskegg by the arm and half-led, half-dragged him down to the ward, where the donkey was dragging a log up to the wall. The beast's ribs showed through its mangy coat; it was plainly on its last legs. It gave a sad bray as Kolskegg squeezed a few squirts of milk into a bowl.

"Butcher it," Ulror told his men; if they waited any longer, no meat would be left on those sad bones.

Seeming more confident once he had sniffed and tasted the milk, Kolskegg took Ulror back to his pack, which lay on top of his straw pallet. He rummaged in it until he found a small packet of whitish powder. "Rennet," he explained, "made from the stomach lining of young calves."

"Just get on with it," Ulror said, faintly revolted.

Kolskegg sat cross-legged in the dry rushes on the floor. He began a low, whining chant, repeating the same phrase over and over. Ulror had seen other wizards act thus to heighten their concentration. His regard for Kolskegg went up a notch.

He noticed Kolskegg was not blinking. All the sorcerer's attention focused on the chipped earthenware bowl in front of him. Ulror tried to find meaning in the swirling pattern of emerging curds as the rennet coagulated the milk, but saw nothing there he could read.

Kolskegg stiffened. White showed around the irises of his staring blue eyes. "A coffin!" he said hoarsely. "A coffin and the stench of the grave. Only through a death is there escape." His eyes rolled up altogether and he slumped over in a faint.

Ulror's lips skinned back from his teeth in a humorless grin. Too well he remembered his roar of defiance to Zigabenos. The gods had a habit of listening to a man when he least wanted them to.

"I wish Skotos would drag that heathen down to the ice of hell now, instead of waiting for him to live out his span of days," Kypros Zigabenos said furiously, watching from the Videssian lines as Ulror dashed along the battlements of Sotevag, his blond braid flapping behind him. The barbarian ignored the hail of stones and darts with which the imperials were pounding the fortress. Buoyed by his spirit, the defenders stayed on the walls, shooting back with what they had and rushing to repair the damage from the bombardment.

Then, because he was an honest man—not always an advantage in Videssian service—Zigabenos felt he had to add, "But oh, he is a brave one."

"Sir?" said the servant who fetched him a cup of wine.

"Eh? Nothing." Zigabenos was irritated that anyone should have heard his mumblings. Still, he wished with all his heart for one of the Videssian missiles to dash out Ulror's brains.

Quite simply, the man was too good. Aye, he had let himself be penned here, but only as an alternative to worse. If ever he escaped, he might yet find a way to rally the Halogai and rape Kalavria away from the Empire. He was worth an army to the northerners, just as Zigabenos, without false modesty, assessed his own similar value to Videssos.

He snapped his fingers in happy inspiration. At his shout a runner came trotting up. He sent the man over to the stone throwers and ballistae. One by one the siege engines stopped. Zigabenos took up a white-painted shield—a badge of truce or parley—and walked toward Sotevag's battered walls.

"Ulror!" he called. "Ulror, will you speak with me?"

After a minute or so, the northern chieftain shouted back, "Aye, if you'll talk so my men understand us."

"As you wish," Zigabenos said in the Haloga tongue. Another ploy wasted; he had deliberately used Videssian before to try to make Ulror's warriors doubt their leader. Very well, let them hear: "Come out of the fortress and I will still guarantee all your lives. And I pledge better for you, Ulror: a fine mansion, with a stipend to support a large band of retainers."

"And where will this fine mansion be? Here on the island?"

"You deserve better than this backwater, Ulror. What do you say to a residence at the capital, Videssos the city?"

Ulror was silent so long, Zigabenos' hopes began to rise. At last the northerner asked, "Will you give me a day's leave to think on it?"

"No," Zigabenos said at once. "You'll only use it to strengthen your defenses. Give me your answer."

Ulror boomed laughter. "Oh, how I wish you were a fool. I think I will decline your gracious invitation. With civil war in the Empire, even if by some mischance I reached the capital alive, I'd last about as long as a lobster's green shell when you throw him in the boiling pot."

The Videssian general felt like snarling, but his face never showed it. "You have my personal guarantee of your safety," he said.

"Aye, and that's good as silver so long as I'm on the island, and worth nothing soon as I sail west, since both emperors hate you for not sending 'em men."

Too good by half, Zigabenos thought. Without another word he turned and walked away. But Ulror was still in the lobster pot. It remained only to bring him to the boil.

The cat crawled forward, its timber sides and roof covered with green hides to keep them from being burnt. Fire arrows streaked from the Videssian archers toward bales of straw the Halogai had hung on the side of the wall to deaden the impact of the battering ram the cat protected. The northerners dumped pails of water and sewage, snuffing out the flames before they took hold.

Then the imperials manhandled their shed up to the base of the wall. The Halogai pelted it with boulders and spears, trying to create rifts in the hide covering through which boiling water and red-hot sand might find their way.

"There!" Ulror cried, pointing, and another stone thudded home. The din was indescribable. Through it all, though, Ulror heard the commands of the Videssian underofficer in the cat, each order delivered as calmly as if on parade.

He could not fathom that kind of courage. The hazards of the field—aye, he had their measure. This siege was harder, but here he had had no good choice. But how men could hold their wits about them advancing turtle-fashion into danger, knowing they would die if their shell was broken, was beyond him.

Like so many Halogai he scorned the discipline Videssos

imposed on her troops; no free man would let himself be used so. Now he saw what such training was worth. His own men, he knew, would have broken under the punishment the imperials were taking. Yet they stolidly labored on.

Rather than hearing the ram strike the wall, Ulror felt it through the soles of his feet. Chains rattled in the cat below as the Videssians drew their great iron-faced log back for another stroke. The wall shook again. Ulror could see the spirit oozing out of his warriors. They had gaily faced the chance of arrow or flying stone, but this methodical pounding stole the manhood from them. He wondered if he could make them fight in the breach. He had no great hope of it.

Just when he was telling himself he should have made what terms he could with Zigabenos, shrieks replaced the stream of orders coming from the cat. One of the smoking cauldrons the Halogai tipped down on it had found a breach of its own.

When the ram's rhythm missed a beat, the northerners above seemed to realize their doom was not inevitable after all. Ulror bellowed encouragement to them. They redoubled their efforts, working like men possessed.

Three soldiers grunted to lift a huge stone to a crenelation, then shoved it out and down onto the cat. The shed's sloping roof and thick sides had sent other boulders bouncing aside, but this one struck square on the midline. Along with the crash, Ulror heard a metallic snap as a chain holding the ram to the roof of the cat broke. Shouts of pain from the imperials it injured in its fall and curses from the rest were as sweet music in his ears.

Like a wounded animal, the shed began to limp away. Videssian shieldsmen stood at its open front, where the ram had swung. They protected their comrades from the missiles the Halogai rained on them. Whenever one was shot, another took his place. That was bravery Ulror could grasp. Even as he let fly at them, he hoped they would safely reach their own line. Zigabenos, he thought, would want them to fall to the arrows like so many quail. That was sensible, but he did not have the stomach for it.

The Halogai danced with joy as the cat withdrew, their heavy boots clumping on the stone walkways and stairs. "A victory," Flosi Wolf's-Pelt said.

"Aye, or so the lads think, anyway," Ulror answered quietly. "Well, that's worth something of itself, I suppose. It'll take their hands off the stale donkey tripes—the last of them left— and the handful of barley meal they'll be eating tonight."

"We hurt the cat," Flosi protested.

"So we did, and they hurt the wall. Which do you think the easier to repair?"

Flosi grimaced and turned away.

High overhead, a seagull screeched. Ulror envied the bird its freedom. Not too many gulls came near Sotevag any more. If they did, the Halogai shot them and ate them. Their flesh was tough and salty and tasted strongly of fish, but hungry men did not care. Ulror had stopped asking about the meat that went into the stewpots. He did know he had seen fewer rats lately.

Watching the gull wheel in the sky and glide away was suddenly more than Ulror could bear. He slammed his fist against the stone of the battlement, cursed at the pain. Ignoring Flosi's startled look, he rushed down the stairs and into the outer ward.

Kolskegg Cheese-Curd had been making what looked like a mousetrap out of sticks and leather thongs. He put the contraption aside as his chieftain bore down on him, asked warily, "Is there something I might do for you?"

"Aye, there is." Ulror hauled his reluctant wizard to his feet; his belly might be gone, but he still kept his bull strength. Paying no attention to the protests Kolskegg yammered, he dragged him through the gatehouse into the keep, and on into the chamber he had taken for himself.

The goosefeather mattress had belonged to the Videssian who once commanded here. So did the silk coverlet atop it, now sadly stained. Ulror flopped down on the bed with a sigh of relief, waved Kolskegg to a chair whose delicacy proclaimed it also to be imperial work.

Once Kolskegg had made himself comfortable, Ulror came to the point with his usual directness. "That was a true divination you gave me—that the only way I would leave Sotevag would be in my coffin?"

The wizard licked his lips, but had to answer, "Aye, it was."

To his surprise his chieftain grunted in satisfaction. "Good. If Zigabenos' priests read the omens, they should learn the same, not so?"

"Aye." Kolskegg had been a warrior long enough to know not to volunteer more than he was asked.

"All right, then," Ulror said. "Give me a spell to turn me

to the seeming of a corpse, stench and all, to let me get away. Then when I'm outside, you can take it off, or arrange in the first place for it to last only so long, or whatever you think best." He nodded, pleased at his own ingenuity.

The wizard's face, though, went chalky white. "Have mercy!" he cried. "I am nothing but a miserable diviner. Why do you set me tasks to strain the powers of the greatest adepts? I cannot do this: he who trifles with death in magic courts it."

"You are the only sorcerer I have," Ulror said implacably. "And you will do it."

"I cannot." As a weak man will, Kolskegg sounded querulous in his insistence.

"You will," Ulror told him. "If you do not, Sotevag will surely fall. And if the Videssians take me alive, I will tell them you worked your charms through their dark god Skotos. Once they believe that, you will wish you died fighting. No demon could serve you worse than their inquisitors."

Kolskegg shivered, for Ulror was right. As dualists, the imperials hated their deity's evil rival and dealt with legendary savagery with anyone who dared revere him. "You would not—" the wizard began, and stopped in despair. Ulror would.

The Haloga commander said nothing more. He waited, bending Kolskegg to his will with silence. Under his unwinking stare the wizard's resolve melted like snow in springtime. "I will try," he said at last, very low. "Maybe at midnight, a spell I know might serve. It is, after all, only a seeming you seek."

He spoke more to reassure himself than for any other reason, Ulror judged. That was all right. "Midnight it is," Ulror said briskly. "I'll see you here then." He did not put any special warning in his voice. He had done his job properly and did not need to.

The wizard returned at the hour he had set, stumbling in the darkness as he approached Ulror's door. Inside, the chieftain had a tallow dip lit. Not many lights burned in Sotevag at night; tallow and olive oil could be eaten if a man was hungry enough.

Even in the red, flickering light, Kolskegg looked pale. "I wish I had a beaker of ale," he muttered under his breath. He fumbled in his pouch, finally digging out a chain that held a black stone with white veins. "An onyx," he said, hanging it around Ulror's neck. "The stone for stirring up terrible fantasms."

"Get on with it," Ulror said. He spoke more harshly than he had intended; Kolskegg's nervousness was catching.

The wizard cast a powder into the flame of the tallow dip, which flared a ghastly green. Kolskegg began a slow, rhymeless chant full of assonances. The stone he had set on Ulror's breast grew so cold he could feel its chill through his tunic. He could also feel the little hairs at the nape of his neck prickling upright.

The chant droned on. Kolskegg began singing faster and faster, as if he wanted to get through the incantation as quickly as he could. In the end, his own fear of what he was doing undid him. His tongue slipped, so that when he meant to intone "thee," "me" came out instead.

Had he been wearing the onyx, the spell might have possessed him as he intended it to possess Ulror: as an unpleasant but impermanent illusion. But the Holga chieftain had the magical focus, not his wizard. Before Kolskegg could do more than gasp in horror at his blunder, the transformation struck him.

Ulror gagged on the stench that filled his chamber. He staggered outside and was sick against the wall of the keep. Several of his warriors rushed over, asking if he was all right.

One had the wit to offer a bucket of water. He rinsed his mouth, spat, rinsed again. The sour taste remained. His men began exclaiming over the graveyard reek that followed him into the inner ward.

"You will find a lich—not a fresh one—inside," he told them. "Treat poor Kolskegg with respect; he showed more courage dying at my order than ever he did in life."

As was his privilege, even after midnight, the blue-robed priest burst past Zigabenos' bodyguard and into the tent of the Videssian general. "Sorcery!" he cried, the firelight gleaming from his shaved pate. "Sorcery most foul!"

"Huh?" Zigabenos sat up with a start. He was glad he'd sent the kitchen wench back to her tavern instead of keeping her for the night. He enjoyed his vices, but had learned long since not to flaunt them.

His wits returned with their usual rapidity. "Say what you mean, Bonosos. Are the Halogai assailing us with magic?"

"Eh? No, your illustriousness. But they play at wizardry

even so, a wizardry that stinks of Skotos." The priest spat on the ground in rejection of the wicked god, his faith's eternal enemy.

"The conjuration was not aimed against us? You are certain of that?"

"I am," Bonosos said reluctantly. "Yet it was strong, and of a malefic nature. It was not undertaken to curry favor with us."

"I hardly expected it would be," Zigabenos said; he had no intention of letting a priest outdo him in irony. "Still, so long as they do not send a blast our way, the Halogai are welcome to play at whatever they wish. Maybe it will go awry and eat them up, and save us the trouble."

"May the lord of the great and good mind hear and heed your prayer," Bonosos said, drawing Phos' sun sign on his breast.

Zigabenos did the same; his own piety, though he did not let it interfere with whatever he had to do, ran deep. After a moment he said, "Bonosos, I hope you had a reason for disturbing my rest other than merely to tell me the Halogai have some fribbling spell afoot."

"Hardly fribbling." Bonosos' glare was wasted; to Zigabenos he was only a silhouette in the doorway. But there was no mistaking the abhorrence in the priest's voice as he went on, "The conjuration smacked of necromancy."

"Necromancy!" Zigabenos exclaimed, startled. "You must be mistaken."

Bonosos bowed. "Good evening, sir. I tell the truth. If you do not care to hear it, that is none of my affair." He spun on his heel and stalked away.

Stiff-necked old bastard, the Videssian general thought as he settled back under his silk coverlet, and mad as a loon besides. The Halogai inside Sotevag had too many other things to worry about to bother with corpse-raising or anything like it.

Or did they? Zigabenos suddenly remembered Ulror's howl of defiance from the battlements. The northerner must have taken that for prophecy as well as brag. Zigabenos laughed out loud, admiring Ulror's ingenuity in trying to get around his own oath. Unfortunately for the Haloga, he thought, there was no way around it. The northerners fought bravely and, under Ulror's command, resourcefully. Against siege engines, however, bravery and resource only counted for so much. In a week, maybe less, maybe a day or two more, he would be inside Sotevag. And then Ulror's boast would be fulfilled in the most literal way imaginable.

Still chuckling, Zigabenos rolled over and went back to sleep.

After a sleepless night, Ulror stared out to sea, watching the rising sun turn the water to a flaming sheet of molten gold and silver. He regretted Kolskegg's death, and regretted even more that it had been in vain. Now, impaled on his own rash words, he found nothing else to do but face the prospect of dying.

He did not fear death. Few Halogai did; they lived too close to it, both at home and in battle on distant shores. But he bitterly regretted the waste. If only he could get free, rally the Halogai all across Kalavria. In pursuing him, Zigabenos really had concentrated his own forces too much—provided the northerners moved against him in unison. If not, he would go on dealing with them piecemeal, methodical as a cordwainer turning out boots.

Ulror ground his teeth. All he, all any of the Halogai, wanted was a steading big enough for a free man to live on and to pass down to his sons; a good northern woman to wife, with perhaps two or three of these island wenches to keep a bed warm of nights; a chance to enjoy the luxuries the imperials took for granted: wine grown on a man's own holding, a bathtub, wheat bread instead of loaves of rye or oats. If the Empire's god would grant him so much, he might even give worship to Phos along with his own somber deities.

Unless Zigabenos made a mistake, though, none of that would happen. And Zigabenos was not in the habit of making mistakes.

As had happened a few days before, a gull gave its raucous call high over Sotevag. This time the frustration was more than the Haloga chieftain could bear. Without conscious thought, in one smooth motion he reached over his shoulder for an arrow, set it to his bow, and let fly. His rage lent power to the shot. The bird's cry abruptly cut off. It fell with a thud to the dirt of the outer ward. Ulror stared malevolently at the dead gull—miserable, stinking thing, he thought.

"Good shooting," one of his warriors called, ambling over to pick up the bird and carry it off to be cooked.

"Hold!" Ulror shouted suddenly, rushing for a stairway.

"That seagull's mine!" The warrior gaped at him, certain he had lost his mind.

An orderly came dashing into the tent, interrupting Zigabenos' breakfast. Paying no attention to the Videssian general's glare, he said breathlessly, "Sir, there's sign of truce over the main gatehouse of Sotevag!"

Zigabenos stood up so quickly that he upset the folding table in front of him. He ignored his valet's squawk of distress and hurried out after the orderly to see this wonder for himself.

It was true. Above the gate a white shield hung on a spear. "They turned coward at the end," the orderly said, "when they saw what our engines were about to do to them."

"I wonder," Zigabenos said. It was not like Ulror to give in so tamely. What sort of scheme could the Haloga chieftain have come up with? No one had spied him on the walls for several days now. Was he planning a last desperate sally, hoping to slay Zigabenos and throw the Videssian army into confusion?

To forestall that, the general approached the fortress in the midst of a squadron of shieldsmen, enough to get him out of danger no matter what the Halogai tried. When he was within hailing distance, he called, "Well, Ulror? What have you to say to me?"

But it was not Ulror who came to stand by the northerners' truce shield. A rawboned Haloga with gray hair took that place instead. He stared down at Zigabenos in silence for a long moment, then asked, "Have you honor, imperial?"

Zigabenos shrugged. "If you need the question, would you trust the answer?"

A harsh chuckle. "Summat to that. All right, be it so. You'll do what you promised before, let the rest of us go if we yield you Sotevag and bring out Ulror?"

The Videssian general had all he could do not to cry out for joy. In exchange for Ulror, he was willing, nay eager, to let a few hundred barbarians of no special importance keep their lives. He was too old a hand, however, to let his excitement show. After a suitable pause he demanded, "Show me Ulror now, so I may see you have him prisoner."

"I cannot," the Haloga said.

Zigabenos turned to leave. "I am not a child for you to play tricks on."

"He is dead," the northerner replied, and Zigabenos stopped. The northerner went on, "He took a fever a week ago, but fought on with it, as any true man would. He died four nights past. Now that he is gone, we ask ourselves why we must sell our lives dear, and find no answer."

"You need not, of course," Zigabenos said at once. No wonder the Halogai had tried necromancy, he thought. But Ulror was tricksy, and who knew how far he would go to lend verisimilitude to a ploy? The Videssian general declared, "I will abide by my terms, save that I add one condition: as each man of yours leaves Sotevag, my wizards will examine him, to be sure he is not Ulror in sorcerous disguise."

The Haloga spokesman spat. "Do what you please. Victors always do. But I have told you you will not find him among them."

They haggled over details for the next hour. Zigabenos was lenient. Why not, with the one great northern chieftain gone and Sotevag about to return to imperial hands?

When noon came, the long-shut fortress gates swung open. As had been agreed, the Halogai came out two by two, in armor and carrying their weapons. They were all skinny, and many wounded. They could not help looking out toward the imperial lines; if Zigabenos wanted to betray them, he could. He did not want to. He expected to fight their countrymen again, and fear of a broken truce would only lead the Halogai to fight to the end from then on.

The Videssian general stood outside the gates with a pair of priests. The blue-robes had anointed their eyes with a paste made from the gall of a male cat and the fat of a pure white hen, an ointment that let them pierce illusion. They examined each emerging northerner, ready to cry out if they spied Ulror behind a veil of magic.

The gray-haired Haloga with whom Zigabenos had dickered came limping out. The general gave him a formal salute. He had developed some respect for this Flosi Wolf's-Pelt, for his spirit, his courage, and his blunt honesty. What sprang from those, though, was easy to anticipate. When the time came, he knew he would beat Flosi. With Ulror he had never been sure.

Flosi looked through him as if he did not exist.

The moment Zigabenos had been waiting for finally came. A dozen Halogai dragged a rough-built coffin behind them on a sledge. "Ulror is inside?" the general asked one of them.

"Aye," the man said.

"Check it," Zigabenos snapped to the priests who flanked him.

They peered at the coffin with their sorcerously enhanced vision. "That is truly Ulror Raska's son within," Bonosos declared.

So Ulror had been a prophet after all, Zigabenos thought, and look what it gained him. Something else occurred to the Videssian general. "Is the rascal dead?"

Bonosos frowned. "A spell to ascertain that will take some little time to prepare, and in any case I mislike touching on death with my sorcery—see how such an unholy effort profited the northerner here. I suggest you make your own examination to satisfy yourself. If he is four days dead, you will know it."

"Something in the air, you mean. Yes, I take your point," Zigabenos chuckled. He added, "Who would expect such plain sense from a priest?" Bonosos' frown turned to scowl. The Videssian general approached the coffin. "Pry up the top of the lid, you," he told one of the northerners.

Shrugging, the Haloga drew his sword and used to it lever up the coffin lid; nails squealed in protest. Through the narrow opening Zigabenos saw Ulror's face, pale and thin and still. The death smell welled out, almost thick enough to slice. "Shut it," Zigabenos said, coughing. He drew Phos' sun circle on his breast, then saluted the coffin with the same formality he had offered Flosi.

Seeing how exhausted the pallbearers were, Zigabenos said kindly, "If you like, we will bury him for you here."

The Halogai drew themselves up; even in privation, they were proud men. One said, "I thank you, but we care for our own."

"As you wish." Zigabenos waved them on.

When the last northerner had left Sotevag Castle, the general sent in a crack platoon to search it from top to bottom. No matter what the priest said, no matter what he had seen and smelled, maybe Ulror had found a way to stay behind and then drop over the walls and escape. Zigabenos did not see how, but he took no chances where Ulror was concerned.

Only when the platoon's lieutenant reported back to him

that Sotevag was empty of life did he truly begin to believe he had won.

Hungry, worn, and battered as they were, the Halogai traveled slowly. Still, Kalavria was not a large island; by the end of the second day after they left Sotevag, they were at the end of the central uplands. They camped next to a swift, cool stream.

As the warriors shared the half-ripe fruits and nuts they had gathered on their march and hunters went into the undergrowth after rabbits, Flosi went up to Ulror's coffin. Wrinkling his nose at the stench emanating from it, he pried up the ends of a couple of boards with his dagger.

The coffin shook, as with some internal paroxysm. The boards Flosi had loosened flew up. Ulror scrambled out. The first thing he did was to dive into the water and scrub himself from head to foot with sand from the streambank. When he came splashing out, streaks of the mixture of chalk and grease with which he had smeared his face remained on it, but his natural ruddy color dominated once more.

One of his warriors threw a ragged cloak around him. "Food!" he boomed. "After two days with nothing but three stinking seagulls for company, even the rubbish we were eating back at Sotevag would taste good."

Flosi brought him some of their meager fare. He wolfed it down. One by one the hunters returned. Fresh meat, even a couple of bites' worth, roasted over an open fire was the most delicious thing he had ever eaten.

His belly was still growling after all the food was gone, but he had grown used to that in Sotevag. He looked around again and again, admiring the stream, the trees, the little clearing in which the Halogai were camped. "Free," he breathed.

"Aye." Flosi still did not seem to believe it. "I thought we were ruined when your magicking with Kolskegg failed."

"And I." Ulror longed for wine, but after a moment he realized triumph was a sweeter, headier brew. He laughed. "We get so used to using sorcery for our ends, we forget what we can do without it. Once I thought of the scheme, my biggest worry was that Zigabenos would attack before the birds got ripe enough to use."

"A good thing you whitened your face, even so."

"Oh, indeed. Zigabenos is too canny for me to dare miss a trick against him," Ulror said. A swirl of the breeze brought the carrion reek his way. He grimaced. "I was afraid of one other thing, too. He might have noticed something wrong if he'd heard my 'corpse' puking its guts out."

"So he might." Flosi allowed himself a rare smile. He rose and started over to the opened coffin. "The birds have served their purpose. I'll toss them in the creek."

"Eh? Don't do that," Ulror exclaimed.

"Why not? What do you want them for? I wouldn't eat the smelly things if I'd stood siege for years, not a couple of months. Throw 'em away and have done."

"I have a better plan," Ulror said.

"What's that?"

"I'm going to send one back to Zigabenos behind a shield of truce." Ulror's eyes glowed with mischief. "I wish I could be there to see his face when he finds out how" —he grinned a huge grin; it felt monstrous good to be able to joke again— "how he's been gulled."

"Gulled, eh?" Kypros Zigabenos nodded at the noisome pile of feathers the smirking Haloga herald set before him. He would not give the barbarian the satisfaction of showing he felt anything at all at finding Ulror alive and free. Never in his life, though, had he come so close to dishonoring a truce shield. The northerner would never know by how little he had missed the lash, the thumbscrews, the red-hot bronze needles, and the rest of the ingenious torments the Videssians had devised over the centuries.

But only a vicious fool struck the bearer of bad news. And so Zigabenos, his heart a cold stone in his breast, poured wine for the Haloga and laughed politely to hear how Ulror had duped him.

"Wait here a moment, if you will," he said to the warrior, and stepped out of his tent to speak to one of his guards. The man blinked in surprise, then saluted and hurried away, stringing his bow as he trotted.

Zigabenos returned to his unwelcome guest, refilled the fellow's cup, and went on with the urbane conversation he had briefly interrupted. Behind his smiling mask he felt desperation building. He had staked too great a part of the imperial forces on Kalavria to finishing Ulror here. The Videssians scattered over the rest of the island were ragtag and bobtail. With his victorious army as a core, they would have sufficed. Now the Halogai would mop up, not he.

And then they would come for him. He wondered how

fast his artisans could repair the damage his own engines had done to Sotevag, and what sort of supplies he could bring in. The Halogai were impetuous, impatient. They might not have the staying power to conduct a siege of their own.

But with Ulror leading them, they might.

The sentry with whom Zigabenos had spoken stuck his head into the tent. "I have one, your excellency."

"Very good. Bring it in." The general drew himself up straighter in his chair. Sometimes one won, sometimes one lost; no sane man expected nothing but triumph in his life. But win or lose, style mattered. He prayed the day might never come when he failed to meet misfortune with aplomb.

The bird the Videssian soldier brought in was smaller than the one Ulror had sent, with a deeply forked tail and a black cap. It was still warm. Zigabenos picked it up and ceremoniously offered it to the Haloga. "I hope you will be so kind as to present this to your master, with my compliments."

The northerner looked at him as if he had gone mad. "Just the bird, or shall I say something?"

"The latter." Zigabenos was an imperial, a man of anciently civilized race, and of high blood as well. This grinning blond lout here would never understand, but somehow he felt Ulror might appreciate the spirit in which he sent his message. "Tell him one good tern deserves another."

PASSAGE TO DILFAR

by *Roger Zelazny*

When Dilvish the Damned came down from Portaroy they
tried to stop him at Qaran, and again at Tugado, then again
at Maestar, Mycar, and Bildesh. Five horsemen had waited
for him along the route to Dilfar; and when one flagged, a
new rider with a fresh horse would replace him. But none
could keep the pace of Black, the horse out of steel, for
whom it was said the Colonel of the East had bartered a part
of his soul.

A day and a night had he ridden, to outpace the advancing armies of Lylish, Colonel of the West, for his own men
lay stiff and clotted on the rolling fields of Portaroy.

When Dilvish had seen that he was the last man standing
in the place of slaughter, he had called Black to his side,
hauled himself into the saddle that was a part of him, and
cried for an escape. Black's gleaming hooves had borne him
through a line of pikemen, their staffs turned aside like
wheat, and ringing, as their metal tips touched against his
midnight hide.

"To Dilfar!" he had cried, and Black turned at a right
angle in his course and carried him up the face of a cliff
where only goats can go.

When Dilvish came by Qaran, Black turned his head and
said to him: "Great Colonel of the East, they have mined
the air and the air beneath the air with the stars of death."

"Can you get by them?" asked Dilvish.

"If we go by way of the posting road," said Black, "I may
be able to."

"Then let us make haste to try it."

The tiny silver eyes, which looked out from the space

309

beneath space and contained the hellspecks of starstuff, blinked and shimmered ahead.

They turned off the road.

It was on the posting road that the first rider emerged from behind a boulder and called upon Dilvish to halt. His horse was a huge bay without trappings.

"Draw rein, Colonel of the East," he had said. "Thy men are slaughtered. The road ahead is seeded with death and flanked by the men of Lylish—"

But Dilvish had swept past him without making answer, and the man put his spurs to the bay and followed.

He paced him all that morning, up the road to Tugado, until the bay, who was all alather, stumbled and hurled the man to the rocks.

At Tugado Dilvish found his way blocked by the rider of the blood-red stallion, who fired at him a bolt from a crossbow.

Black reared high into the air, and the bolt glanced off his chest. His nostrils grew, with a sound like the cry of a great bird coming forth from them. The blood-red stallion leapt from the roadway then and into the field.

Black plunged ahead, and the other rider turned his horse and followed.

Till the sun reached the top of the sky did he give chase, and then the red horse collapsed in a heap of heavy breathing. Dilvish rode on.

At Maestar the way was blocked at the Pass of Reshth.

A wall of logs filled the narrow trail to twice the height of a man.

"Over," said Dilvish, and Black arced into the air like a dark rainbow, going up and across the fortification.

Just ahead, at the ending of the pass, the rider of the white mare waited.

Black cried out once more, but the mare stood steady.

The light reflected from the mirrors of his steel hooves, and his hairless hide was near blue in the bright light of noonday. He did not slow his pace, and the rider of the mare, seeing that he was all of metal, backed from out the pass and drew his sword.

Dilvish pulled his own blade from beneath his cloak and parried a head cut as he passed the other rider. Then the man was following after him and crying out:

"Though you have passed the stars of death and leapt the barrier here, you shall never make it to Dilfar! Draw rein!

You ride a nether spirit who has taken the form of a horse, but you will be stopped at Mycar or Bildesh—or before!"

But the Colonel of the East did not reply, and Black carried him on with long, effortless strides.

"You ride a mount which never tires," called out the man, "but he is not proof against other sorceries! Give me your sword!"

Dilvish laughed, and his cloak was a wing in the wind.

Before the day lapsed into evening, the mare, too, had fallen, and Dilvish was near Mycar.

Black halted suddenly as they approached the stream called Kethe. Dilvish clung to his neck to keep from being thrown off.

"The bridge is out," said Black, "and I cannot swim."

"Can you clear it?"

"I do not know, my colonel. It is wide. If I cannot clear it, we will never surface again. Kethe cuts deeply into the earth."

And the ambushers came suddenly forth from the trees then, some on horseback and others on foot, the foot soldiers bearing pikes; and Dilvish said: "Try."

Black was immediately at full gallop, going faster than horses can run, and the world spun and tumbled about Dilvish as he clung to Black with his knees and his great scarred hands. He cried out as they rose into the air.

When they struck the other bank, Black's hooves sank a full span into the rock and Dilvish reeled in the saddle. He kept his mount, however, and Black freed his hooves.

Looking back at the other bank, Dilvish saw the ambushers standing still, staring at him, then looking down into Kethe, then back up again at him and Black.

As they moved ahead once more, the rider of the piebald stallion fell in beside him and said: "Though you have ridden three horses into the ground, we will stop you between here and Bildesh. Surrender!"

Then Dilvish and Black were far ahead of him, and away.

"They think you are a demon, my mount," he said to Black.

The horse chuckled.

"Perhaps 'twere beter an' I were."

And they rode the sun out of the sky and finally the piebald fell, and the rider cursed Dilvish and Black, and they rode on.

The trees began to fall at Bildesh.

"Deadfalls!" cried Dilvish, but Black was already doing his dance of avoidance and passage. He halted, rearing; and he sprang forward from off his hind legs and passed over a falling log. He halted again and did it once more. Then two fell at once, from opposite sides of the trail, and he leapt backward and then forward again, passing over both.

Two deep pits did he leap across then, and a volley of arrows chattered against his sides, one of them wounding Dilvish in the thigh.

The fifth horseman bore down upon them. The color of fresh-minted gold was this horse, and named Sunset, and his rider was but a youth and light in the saddle, chosen so as to carry the pursuit as far as necessary. He bore a deathlance that shattered against Black's shoulder without causing him to turn. He raced after Dilvish and called out:

"Long have I admired Dilvish, Colonel of the East, so that I do not desire to see him dead. Pray surrender unto me! You will be treated with all courtesies due your station!"

Dilvish did laugh then and made reply, saying:

"Nay, my lad. Better to die than fall to Lylish. On, Black!"

And Black doubled his pace and the boy leaned far forward over Sunset's neck and gave chase. He wore a sword at his side, but he never had chance to use it. Though Sunset ran the entire night, longer and farther than any of the other pursuers, he, too, finally fell as the east began to grow pale.

As he lay there, trying to rise, the youth cried out:

"Though you have escaped me, you shall fall to the Lance!"

Then was Dilvish, called the Damned, riding alone in the hills above Dilfar, bearing his message to that city. And though he rode the horse of steel, called Black, still did he fear an encounter with Lance of the Invincible Armor before he delivered his message.

As he started on the last downward trail his way was blocked a final time, by an armored man on an armored horse. The man held the way completely, and though he was visored, Dilvish knew from his devices that he was Lance, the Right Hand of the Colonel of the West.

"Halt and draw rein, Dilvish!" he called out. "You cannot pass me!"

Lance sat like a statue.

Dilvish halted Black and waited.

"I call upon you to surrender now."

"No," said Dilvish.

"Then must I slay you."

Dilvish drew his sword.

The other man laughed.

"Know you not that my armor is unbreachable?"

"No," said Dilvish.

"Very well, then," he said, with something like a chuckle. "We are alone here, you have my word. Dismount. I'll do so at the same time. When you see it is futile, you may have your life. You are my prisoner."

They dismounted.

"You are wounded," said Lance.

Dilvish cut for his neck without replying, hoping to burst the joint. It held, however, and the metal bore not even a scratch to tell of the mighty blow that might have beheaded another.

"You must see now that my armor cannot be breached. It was forged by the Salamanders themselves and bathed in the blood of ten virgins . . ."

Dilvish cut at his head and as he had cut at him, Dilvish had circled slowly to his left, so that now Lance stood with his back to the horse of steel, called Black.

"Now, Black!" cried Dilvish.

Then did Black rear high up on his hind legs and fall forward, bringing his front hooves down toward Lance.

The man called Lance turned rapidly around and they struck him on the chest. He fell.

Two shining hoof marks had been imprinted upon his breastplate.

"You were right," said Dilvish. "It is still unbreached."

Lance moaned again.

". . . And I could slay thee now, with a blade through the eyeslit of thy visor. But I will not, as I did not down thee fairly. When you recover, tell Lylish that Dilfar will be ready for his coming. 'Twere better he withdraw."

"I'll have a sack for thy head when we take the city," said Lance.

"I'll kill thee on the plain before the city," said Dilvish, and he remounted Black and descended the trail, leaving him there on the ground.

And as they rode away, Black said to him: "When you meet, strike at the marks of my hooves. The armor will yield there."

When he came into the city, Dilvish proceeded through

the streets to the palace without speaking to those who clustered about him.

He entered the palace and announced himself:

"I am Dilvish, Colonel of the East," he said, "and I am here to report that Portaroy has fallen and is in the hands of Lylish. The armies of the Colonel of the West move in this direction and should be here two days hence. Make haste to arm. Dilfar must not fall."

"Blow then the trumpets," ordered the king, starting from his throne, "and muster the warriors. We must prepare for battle."

And as the trumpets sounded, Dilvish drank him a glass of the good red wine of Dilfar; and as meats and loaves were brought to him, he wondered once again at the strength of Lance's armor and he knew that he must try its invincibility once more.

NIGHT ON MISPEC MOOR

by Larry Niven

In predawn darkness the battle began to take shape. Helicopters circled, carrying newstapers and monitors. Below, the two armies jockeyed for position. They dared not meet before dawn. The monitors would declare a mistrial and fine both sides heavily.

In the red dawn the battle began. Scout groups probed each other's skills. The weapons were identical on both sides: heavy swords with big basket hilts. Only the men themselves differed in skill and strength.

By noon the battle had concentrated on a bare plain strewn with white boulders and a few tight circles of green Seredan vegetation. The warriors moved in little clumps. Where they met, the yellow dirt was stained red, and cameras in the helicopters caught it all for public viewing.

Days were short in Sereda. For some, today was not short enough.

As Sereda's orange dwarf sun dropped toward the horizon, the battle had become a massacre with the Greys at the wrong end. When Tomás Vatch could not longer hold a sword, he ran. Other Greys had fled, and Amber soldiers streamed after them, yelling. Vatch ran with blood flowing down his sword arm and dripping from his fingertips. He was falling behind, and the Ambers were coming close.

He turned sharp left and kept running. The swarm moved north, toward the edge of Mispec Moor, toward civilization. Alone, he had a chance. The Ambers would not concern themselves with a single fleeing man.

But one did. One golden-skinned red-haired man shouted

315

something, waved his sword in a circle over his head, and followed.

An ancient glacier had dropped blocks of limestone and granite all over this flat, barren region. The biggest rock in sight was twice the height of a man and wider than it was tall. Vatch ran toward it. He had not yet begun to wonder how he would climb it.

He moved in a quick unbalanced stumble now, his sword and his medical kit bouncing awkwardly at either side. He had dropped the sword once already, when a blade had sliced into him just under the armpit. The heavy-shouldered warrior had paused to gloat, and Vatch had caught the falling sword in his left hand and jabbed upward. Now he cradled his right arm in his left to keep it from flopping loose.

He'd reached the rock.

It was split wide open down the middle.

The red-haired Amber came on like an exuberant child. Vatch had noticed him early in the battle. He'd fought that way too, laughing and slashing about him with playful enthusiasm. Vatch thought this attitude inappropriate to so serious a matter as war.

Vatch stepped into the mammoth crack, set his back to one side and his feet to the other, and began to work his way up. Recent wounds opened, and blood flowed down the rock. Vatch went on, concentrating on the placement of his feet, trying not to wonder what would happen if the Amber caught him halfway up.

The red-haired man arrived, blowing and laughing, and found Vatch high above him. He reached up with his sword. Vatch, braced awkwardly between two lips of granite, felt the sharp tip poking him in the small of the back. The Amber was standing on tiptoe; he could reach no further.

The top was flat. Vatch rolled over on his belly and rested. The world whirled around him. He had lost much blood.

And he couldn't afford this. He forced himself to sit up and look around. Where was the enemy?

A rock whizzed past his head. A voice bellowed, "Rammer! Give my regards to the nightwalkers!"

Vatch heard running footsteps, fading. He stood up.

Omicron 2 Eridani was a wide, distorted red blob on the

flat horizon. Vatch could see far across Mispec Moor. He found his erstwhile enemy jogging north. Far ahead of him swarmed the army of the Ambers. Above them, the helicopters were bright motes.

Vatch smiled and dropped back to prone position. He was safe. No man, woman or child of Sereda would stay at night upon Mispec Moor.

On Sereda war is a heavily supervised institution. Battles are fought with agreed-upon weaponry. Strategy lies in getting the enemy to agree to the right weapons. This day the Greys had been out-strategied. The Ambers had the better swordsmen.

Seredan war set no limits to the use of medicine, provided that nothing in a medical kit could be used as a weapon, and provided that all medicines must be carried by fighting men. The convention was advantageous to an outworld mercenary.

Vatch fumbled the medical kit open, one-handed. He suspected that the gathering darkness was partly in his own eyes. But the Spectrum Cure was there: a soft plastic bottle, half-liter size, with a spray hypo and a pistol grip attached. Vatch pressure-injected himself, put the bottle carefully away and let himself roll over on his back.

The first effect was a tingling all through him.

Then his wounds stopped bleeding.

Then they closed.

His fatigue began to recede.

Vatch smiled up at the darkening sky. He'd be paid high for this day's work. His sword arm wasn't very good; he'd thought that Sereda's lower gravity would make a mighty warrior of him, but that hadn't worked out. But this Spectrum Cure was tremendous stuff! The biochemists of Miramon Lluagor had formulated it. It was ten years old there, and brand new on Sereda, and the other worlds of the Léshy circuit probably hadn't even heard of it yet. At the start of the battle he'd had enough to inject forty men, to heal them of any wound or disease, as long as their hearts still beat to distribute the stuff. The bottle was two-thirds empty now. He'd done a fair day's work, turning casualties back into fighting men while the battle raged about him.

The only adverse effect of Spectrum Cure began to show itself. Hunger. His belly was a yawning pit. Healing took metabolic energy. Tomás Vatch sat up convulsively and looked about him.

The damp air of Sereda was turning to mist around the foot of the rock.

He let himself over the lip, hung by his fingertips, and dropped. His belly was making grinding noises and sending signals of desperation. He had not eaten since early this morning. He set off at a brisk walk toward the nearest possible source of dinner: the battleground.

Twilight was fading rapidly. The mist crept over the ground like a soggy blanket. There were patches of grass-green on the yellow dirt, far apart, each several feet across and sharply bordered, each with a high yellow-tipped stalk springing from the center. The mist covered these too. Soon Vatch could see only a few blossoms like frilly yellow morels hovering at waist level, and shadowy white boulders looming like ghosts around him. His passage set up swirling currents.

Like most of the rammers, the men who travel the worlds of the Léshy circuit, Vatch had read the fantasies of James Branch Cabell. The early interstellar scout who discovered these worlds four hundred years ago had read Cabell. Toupan, Miramon Lluagor, Sereda, Horvendile, Koschei: the powerful though mortal Léshy of Cabell's fantasies had become five worlds circling five suns in a bent ring, with Earth and Sol making a sixth. Those who settled the Léshy worlds had followed tradition in the naming of names. A man who had read Cabell could guess the nature of a place from its name alone.

The Mispec Moor of Cabell's writings had been a place of supernatural mystery, a place where reality was vague and higher realities showed through.

Mispec Moor on Sereda had just that vague look, with darkness falling over waist-high mist and shadowy boulders looming above; and Vatch now remembered that this Mispec Moor had a complimentary set of legends. Sereda's people did not call them vampires or ghouls, but the fearsome nightwalkers of Mispec Moor seemed a combination of the two legends: things that had been men, whose bite would turn living or dead alike into more nightwalkers. They could survive ordinary weapons, but a silver bullet would stop them, especially if it had been dumdummed by a cross cut into its nose.

Naturally Tomás Vatch carried no silver bullets and no gun. He was lucky to be carrying a flashlight. He had not expected to be out at night, but the flashlight was part of his kit. He had often needed light to perform his secondary battlefield duties.

As he neared the place of the fallen soldiers he thought he saw motion in the mist. He raised the flashlight high over his head and drew his sword.

Thin shapes scampered away from the light. Tomás jumped violently—and then he recognized lopers, the doglike scavengers of Sereda. He kept his sword in hand. The lopers kept their distance, and he let them be. They were here for the same reason he was, he thought with no amusement at all.

Some soldiers carried bread or rolls of hard candy into battle.

Some of these never ate their provisions.

It was a repugnant task, this searching of dead men. He found the body of Robroy Tanner, who had come with him to Sereda aboard a Lluagorian ramship; and he cried, out here where nobody could see him. But he continued to search. He was savagely hungry.

The lopers had been at some of the bodies. More than once he was tempted to end his whimsical truce. The lopers still moved at the periphery of his vision. They seemed shy of the light, but would that last? Certainly the legends pointed to something dangerous on Mispec Moor. Could the lopers themselves be subject to something like rabies?

He found hard candy, and he found two canteens, both nearly empty. He sucked the candy a roll at a time, his cheeks puffed out like a squirrel's. Presently he found the slashed corpse of a man he had eaten breakfast with. *Jackpot.* He had watched Erwin Mudd take a block of stew from a freezer and double-wrap it in plastic bags, just before they entered the battlefield.

The stew was there. Vatch ate it as it was, cold, and was grateful for it.

Motion in the mist made him look up.

Two shadows were coming toward him. They were much bigger than lopers . . . and man-shaped.

Vatch stood up and called, "Hello?"

They came on, taking shape as they neared. A third

blurred shadow congealed behind them. They had not answered. Annoyed, Vatch swung the flashlight beam toward them.

The light caught them full. Vatch held it steady, staring, not believing. Then, still not believing, he screamed and ran.

There is a way a healthy man can pace himself so that he can jog for hours across flat land, especially on a low-gravity world like Sereda. Tomás Vatch had that skill.

But now he ran like a mad sprinter, in sheer panic, his chest heaving, his legs burning. It was a minute or so before he thought to turn off the flashlight so that the things could not follow its glow. It was much longer before he could work up the courage to look back.

One of the things was following him.

He did not think to stand and fight. He had seen it too clearly. It was a corpse, weeks dead. He thought of turning toward the city, but the city was a good distance away; and now he remembered that they locked the gates at night. The first time he had seen them do that, he had asked why, and a native policeman had told him of the nightwalkers. He had had to hear the story from other sources before he knew that he was not being played for a gullible outworlder.

So he did not turn toward the city. He turned toward the rock that had been his refuge once before.

The thing followed. It moved at a fast walk; but, where Tomás Vatch had to stop and rest with his hands on his knees to catch his breath before he ran on, the nightwalker never stopped at all. It was a distant shadow when he reached the rock; but his haste was such that he skinned his shoulders working himself up the crack.

The top of the rock was still warm from daylight. Vatch lay on his back and felt the joy of breathing. The stars were clear and bright above him. There was no sound at all.

But when his breathing quieted he heard heavy, uneven footsteps.

He looked over the edge of the rock.

The nightwalker came wading through the mist in a wobbling shuffle. It walked like it would fall down at every step, and its feet fell joltingly hard. Yet it came fast. Its bulging eyes stared back into Vatch's flashlight.

Why should a nightwalker care if it sprained its ankles at every step? It was dead, dead and bloated. It still wore a soldier's kilt in green plaid, the sign of a commercial war now two weeks old. Above the broad belt a slashed belly wound gaped wide.

Vatch examined the corpse with self-conscious care. The only way he knew to quell his panic was to put his mind to work. He searched for evidence that this nightwalker was not what it seemed, that it was something else, a native life form, say, with a gift for mimickry.

It stood at the base of the rock, looking up with dull eyes and slack mouth. A walking dead man.

There was more motion in the mist . . . and two lopers came lurching up to stand near the nightwalker. When Vatch threw the light on them they stared back unblinking. Presently Vatch realized why. They, too, were dead.

The policeman had told him that too: that nightwalkers could take the form of lopers and other things.

He had believed very little of what he had heard . . . and now he was trying frantically to remember details. They were not dangerous in daytime; hadn't he heard that? Then if he could hold out here till morning, he would be safe. He could return to the city.

But three more man-shapes were coming to join the first.

And the first was clawing at the side of the rock, trying to find purchase for its fingers. It moved along the base, scraping at the rough side. It entered the crack . . .

Three shadows came out of the mist to join their brother. One wore the familiar plaid kilt from that two-week-old battle. One wore a businessman's tunic; its white hair had come away in patches, taking scalp with it. The third had been a small, slender woman, judging from her dress and her long yellow hair.

They clawed at the rock. They began to spread out along the base.

And Vatch backed away from the edge and sat down.

What the hell was this? Legends like this had been left behind on Earth! Dead men did not walk, not without help. Ordinarily they just *lay* there. What was different about Sereda? What kind of biology could fit—? Vatch shook his head violently. The question was nonsense. This was fantasy, and he was in it.

Yet his mind clutched for explanations:

Costumes? Suppose a group of Seredans had something to hide out here. (What?) A guard of four in dreadful costumes might hold off a whole city, once the legend of the nightwalker was established (But the legend was a century old. Never mind, the legend could have come first.) Anyone who came close enough to see the fraud could quietly disappear. (Costume and makeup? That gaping putrescent belly wound!)

Out of the crack in the rock came a fantasy arm, the bone showing through the forearm, the first joints missing on all the ragged fingers. Vatch froze. (*Costume*?) The other arm came up, and then a dead slack face. The smell reached him . . .

Vatch unfroze very suddenly, snatched up his sword and struck overhand. He split the skull to the chin.

The nightwalker was still trying to pull itself up.

Vatch struck at the arms. He severed one elbow, then the other, and the nightwalker dropped away without a cry.

Vatch began to shudder. He couldn't stop the spasms; he could only wait until they passed. He was beginning to understand how the fantasy would end. When the horror became too great, when he could stand it no longer, he would leap screaming to the ground and try to kill them all. And his sword would not be enough.

It was real! The dead forearms lay near his feet!

Fantasy!

Real!

Wait, wait. A fantasy was something that categorically could not happen. It was *always* a story, *always* something that originated in a man's mind. Could he be starring in somebody's fantasy?

This, a form of entertainment? Then it had holovision beat hands down. But Vatch knew of no world that had the technology to create such a total-experience entertainment, complete with what had to be ersatz memories! No world had that, let alone backward Sereda!

Wait. Was he really on Sereda? Was the date really 2731? Or was he living through some kind of Gothic historical?

Was he even Tomás Vatch the rammer? Rammer was a high-prestige career. Someone might well have paid for the illusion that he was a rammer . . . and if he had, someone had gotten more than he had bargained for. They'd pull him out of his total-environment cubical or theater in total catatonic withdrawal, if Tomás Vatch didn't get a grip on himself.

Wait. Was that motion in the mist, off toward the battlefield?

Or more of his runaway imagination? But no, the mist was a curdling, swirling line, aimed at his rock.

That almost did it. He almost leapt from the rock and ran. If the city gates were closed he'd run right up the walls . . . But he waited. In a minute he'd know for sure, one way or another.

Within the crack the one he had struck sat slumped with its head bowed, disconsolate or truly dead. The other three seemed to be accomplishing very little.

The dead men from the battlefield streamed toward Vatch's place of refuge. They wore kilts of grey and amber. Less than a hundred of them, casualties in a war between two medium-sized companies, a war which would not have been fought at all if the cost could not be partly defrayed by holovision rights. When they came close Vatch began to recognize individuals. There was Erwin Mudd, whose stew he had stolen. There was Roy Tanner the Lluagorian, the rammer, the medic. Death cancels all friendships. There— Enough. *Forget about costumes, Tomás.*

Enough, and too late. The nightwalkers swarmed around the rock and began trying to climb. Vatch stood above the crack, sword ready. The sword was all he had.

Hands came over the edge. He struck at them.

He looked around in time to see more hands coming up everywhere along the perimeter. He yelled and circled madly, striking, striking. They were not climbing the rock itself; they were climbing over each other to reach the top. And his sword, its edge dulled by repeated blows against rock and bone, was turning into a club . . .

Suddenly he stopped.

Fantasy? Real? What kind of biology . . .?

He spilled his medical kit open and snatched at the bottle of Spectrum Cure. More than his life was at stake here. He was trying to save his sanity.

The pistol grip fitted his hand neatly. A nightwalker pulled itself over the edge and tottered toward him, and he sprayed Spectrum Cure between its eyes. An eroded face appeared near his feet; he sprayed Spectrum Cure into its mouth. Then he stepped back and watched.

The first one dropped like a sack. The second let go and disappeared from view.

Nightwalkers were coming up all around him. Vatch moved among them in calm haste, spraying life into them, and they stopped moving. In his mind he gloated. It should have worked, and it had.

For if anything in this experience was real, then it had to be caused by the biology of Sereda. So: something could infect the dead, to make them move. Bacterium? Fungus? Virus? Whatever it was, it had to have evolved by using dead lopers and other native life forms to spread itself.

It would walk the infected corpse until there was no sugar or oxygen left in the blood or muscle tissues of the host. That alone could carry the disease further than it could travel by itself. And if it found another host to infect along the way, well and good.

But the first step in infection would be to restart the heart. It *had* to be, or the bacterium couldn't spread throughout the host.

And if the heart was going . . .

The Spectrum Cure seemed to be healing them right up. He'd cured about eight of them. They lay at the base of the rock and did not move. Other nightwalkers clustered around them. For the moment they had given up on Vatch's rock.

Vatch watched some of them bend over the bodies of those he had injected. They might have been nibbling at the flesh above the hearts. A minute of that, and then they fell over and lay as dead as the ones they had been trying to rescue.

Good enough, thought Vatch. He flashed the light on his bottle to check the supply of Spectrum Cure.

It was just short of dead empty.

Vatch sighed. The horde of dead men had drawn away from the casualties—the *dead* dead ones—and gone back to trying to climb the rock. Some would make it. Vatch picked up his sword. An afterthought: he injected himself. Even if they got to him, they would not rouse him from death before morning.

The scrabbling of finger bones against rock became a cricket chorus.

Vatch stood looking down at them. Most of these had only been dead for hours. Their faces were intact, though slack. Vatch looked for Roy Tanner.

He circled the edge rapidly, striking occasionally at a reaching arm, but peering down anxiously. Where the blazes was Roy Tanner?

There, pulling himself over the lip of the crack.

In fact they were all swarming into the crack and climbing over each other. Their dead brains must be working to some extent. The smell of them was terrific. Vatch breathed through his mouth, closed his imagination tight shut, and waited.

The nightwalker remains of Roy Tanner pulled itself up on the rock. Vatch sprayed it in the face, turned the body over in haste, and found it: Roy Tanner's medical kit, still intact. He spilled out the contents and snatched up Roy's bottle of Spectrum Cure.

He sprayed it before him, and then into the crack, like an insecticide. He held his aim until they stopped moving . . . and then, finally, he could roll away from the choking smell. It was all right now. Roy had fallen early in the battle. His bottle had been nearly full.

For something like six hours they had watched each other: Tomás Vatch on the lip of the rock, seven nightwalkers below. They stood in a half circle, well out of range of Vatch's spray gun, and they stared unblinking into Vatch's flashlight.

Vatch was dreadfully tired. He had circled the rock several times, leaping the crack twice on each pass. "Cured" corpses surrounded the base and half filled the crack. He had seen none of them move. By now he was sure. There were only these seven left.

"I want to sleep," he told them. "Can't you understand? I won. You lost. Go away. I want to sleep." He had been telling them this for some time.

This time it seemed that they heard.

One by one they turned and stumbled off in different directions. Vatch watched, amazed, afraid to believe. Each nightwalker seemed to find a patch of level ground it liked. There it fell and did not move.

Vatch waited. The east was growing bright. It wasn't over yet, but it would be soon. With burning eyes he watched for the obvious dead to move again.

Red dawn touched the tops of glacier-spilled rocks. The orange dwarf sun made a cool light; he could almost look straight into it. He watched the shadows walk down the sides of the rocks to the ground.

When the light touched the seven bodies, they had become bright green patches, vaguely man-shaped.

Vatch watched until each patch had sprouted a bud of yellow in its center. Then he dropped to the ground and started walking north.

WARRIOR

by Gordon R. Dickson

The spaceliner coming in from New Earth and Freiland, worlds under the Sirian sun, was delayed in its landing by traffic at the space port in Long Island Sound. The two police lieutenants, waiting on the bare concrete beyond the shelter of the Terminal buildings, turned up the collars of their cloaks against the hissing sleet, in this unweatherproofed area. The sleet was turning into tiny hailstones that hit and stung all exposed areas of skin. The gray November sky poured them down without pause of mercy, the vast, reaching surface of concrete seemed to dance with their white multitudes.

"Here it comes now," said Tyburn, the Manhattan Complex police lieutenant, risking a glance up into the hailstorm. "Let me do the talking when we take him in."

"Fine by me," answered Breagan, the spaceport officer, "I'm only here to introduce you—and because it's my bailiwick. You can have Kenebuck, with his hood connections, and his millions. If it were up to me, I'd let the soldier get him."

"It's him," said Tyburn, "who's likely to get the soldier—and that's why I'm here. You ought to know that."

The great mass of the interstellar ship settled like a cautious mountain to the concrete two hundred yards off. It protruded a landing stair near its base like a metal leg, and the passengers began to disembark. The two policemen spotted their man immediately in the crowd.

"He's big," said Breagan, with the judicious appraisal of someone safely on the sidelines, as the two of them moved forward.

"They're all big, these professional military men off the

327

Dorsai world," answered Tyburn, a little irritably, shrugging his shoulders against the cold, under his cloak. "They breed themselves that way."

"I know they're big," said Breagan. "This one's bigger."

The first wave of passengers was rolling toward them now, their quarry among the mass. Tyburn and Breagan moved forward to meet him. When they got close they could see, even through the hissing sleet, every line of his dark, unchanging face looming above the lesser heights of the people around him, his military erectness molding the civilian clothes he wore until they might as well have been a uniform. Tyburn found himself staring fixedly at the tall figure as it came toward him. He had met such professional soldiers from the Dorsai before, and the stamp of their breeding had always been plain on them. But this man was somehow more so, even than the others Tyburn had seen. In some way he seemed to be the spirit of the Dorsai, incarnate.

He was one of twin brothers, Tyburn remembered now from the dossier back at his office. Ian and Kensie were their names, of the Graeme family at Foralie, on the Dorsai. And the report was that Kensie had two men's likability, while his brother Ian, now approaching Tyburn, had a double portion of grim shadow and solitary darkness.

Staring at the man coming toward him, Tyburn could believe the dossier now. For a moment, even, with the sleet and the cold taking possession of him, he found himself believing in the old saying that, if the born soldiers of the Dorsai ever cared to pull back to their own small, rocky world, and challenge the rest of humanity, not all the thirteen other inhabited planets could stand against them. Once, Tyburn had laughed at that idea. Now, watching Ian approach, he could not laugh. A man like this would live for different reasons from those of ordinary men—and die for different reasons.

Tyburn shook off the wild notion. The figure coming toward him, he reminded himself sharply, was a professional military man—nothing more.

Ian was almost to them now. The two policemen moved in through the crowd and intercepted him.

"Commandant Ian Graeme?" said Breagan. "I'm Kaj Breagan of the spaceport police. This is Lieutenant Walter Tyburn of the Manhattan Complex Force. I wonder if you could give us a few minutes of your time?"

Ian Graeme nodded, almost indifferently. He turned and paced along with them, his longer stride making more leisurely work of their brisk walking, as they led him away from the route of the disembarking passengers and in through a blank metal door at one end of the Terminal, marked *Unauthorized Entry Prohibited*. Inside, they took an elevator tube up to the offices on the Terminal's top floor, and ended up in chairs around a desk in one of the offices.

All the way in, Ian had said nothing. He sat in his chair now with the same indifferent patience, gazing at Tyburn, behind the desk, and at Breagan, seated back against the wall at the desk's right side. Tyburn found himself staring back in fascination. Not at the granite face, but at the massive, powerful hands of the man, hanging idly between the chair-arms that supported his forearms. Tyburn, with an effort, wrenched his gaze from those hands.

"Well, Commandant," he said, forcing himself at last to look up into the dark, unchanging features, "you're here on Earth for a visit, we understand."

"To see the next-of-kin of an officer of mine." Ian's voice, when he spoke at last, was almost mild compared to the rest of his appearance. It was a deep, calm voice, but lightless—like a voice that had long forgotten the need to be angry or threatening. Only . . . there was something sad about it, Tyburn thought.

"A James Kenebuck?" said Tyburn.

"That's right," answered the deep voice of Ian: "His younger brother, Brian Kenebuck, was on my staff in the recent campaign on Freiland. He died three months back."

"Do you," said Tyburn, "always visit your deceased officers' next of kin?"

"When possible. Usually, of course, they die in line of duty."

"I see," said Tyburn. The office chair in which he sat seemed hard and uncomfortable underneath him. He shifted slightly. "You don't happen to be armed, do you, Commandant?"

Ian did not even smile.

"No," he said.

"Of course, of course," said Tyburn, uncomfortable. "Not that it makes any difference." He was looking again, in spite of himself, at the two massive, relaxed hands opposite him. "Your . . . extremities by themselves are lethal weapons.

We register professional karate and boxing experts here, you know—or did you know?"

Ian nodded.

"Yes," said Tyburn. He wet his lips, and then was furious with himself for doing so. Damn my orders, he thought suddenly and whitely, I don't have to sit here making a fool of myself in front of this man, no matter how many connections and millions Kenebuck owns.

"All right, look here, Commandant," he said, harshly, leaning forward. "We've had a communication from the Freiland-North Police about you. They suggest that you hold Kenebuck—James Kenebuck—responsible for his brother Brian's death."

Ian sat looking back at him without answering.

"Well," demanded Tyburn, raggedly after a long moment, "do you?"

"Force-leader Brian Kenebuck," said Ian calmly, "led his Force, consisting of thirty-six men at the time, against orders farther than was wise into enemy perimeter. His Force was surrounded and badly shot up. Only he and four men returned to the lines. He was brought to trial in the field under the Mercenaries Code for deliberate mishandling of his troops under combat conditions. The four men who had returned with him testified against him. He was found guilty and I ordered him shot."

Ian stopped speaking. His voice had been perfectly even, but there was so much finality about the way he spoke that after he finished there was a pause in the room while Tyburn and Breagan stared at him as if they had both been tranced. Then the silence, echoing in Tyburn's ears, jolted him back to life.

"I don't see what all this has to do with James Kenebuck, then," said Tyburn. "Brian committed some . . . military crime, and was executed for it. You say you gave the order. If anyone's responsible for Brian Kenebuck's death then, it seems to me it'd be you. Why connect it with someone who wasn't even there at the time, someone who was here on Earth all the while, James Kenebuck?"

"Brian," said Ian, "was his brother."

The emotionless statement was calm and coldly reasonable in the silent, brightly lit office. Tyburn found his open hands had shrunk themselves into fists on the desk top. He took a deep breath and began to speak in a flat, official tone.

"Commandant," he said, "I don't pretend to understand you. You're a man of the Dorsai, a product of one of the splinter cultures out among the stars. I'm just an old-fashioned Earthborn—but I'm a policeman in the Manhattan Complex and James Kenebuck is . . . well, he's a taxpayer in the Manhattan Complex."

He found he was talking without meeting Ian's eyes. He forced himself to look at them—they were dark unmoving eyes.

"It's my duty to inform you," Tyburn went on, "that we've had intimations to the effect that you're to bring some retribution to James Kenebuck, because of Brian Kenebuck's death. These are only intimations, and as long as you don't break any laws here on Earth, you're free to go where you want and see whom you like. But this is *Earth, Commandant*."

He paused, hoping that Ian would make some sound, some movement. But Ian only sat there, waiting.

"We don't have any Mercenaries Code here, Commandant," Tyburn went on harshly. "We haven't any feud-fight, no *droit-de-main*. But we do have laws. Those laws say that, though a man may be the worst murderer alive, until he's brought to book in our courts, under our process of laws, no one is allowed to harm a hair of his head. Now, I'm not here to argue whether this is the best way or not; just to tell you that that's the way things are." Tyburn stared fixedly into the dark eyes. "Now," he said, bluntly, "I know that if you're determined to try to kill Kenebuck without counting the cost, *I* can't prevent it."

He paused and waited again. But Ian still said nothing.

"I know," said Tyburn, "that you can walk up to him like any other citizen, and once you're within reach you can try to kill him with your bare hands before anyone can stop you. *I* can't stop you in that case. But what I can do is catch you afterwards, if you succeed, and see you convicted and executed for murder. And you *will* be caught and convicted, there's no doubt about it. You can't kill James Kenebuck the way someone like you would kill a man, and get away with it here on Earth—do you understand that, Commandant?"

"Yes," said Ian.

"All right," said Tyburn, letting out a deep breath. "Then you understand. You're a sane man and a Dorsai professional. From what I've been able to learn about the Dorsai, it's one of your military tenets that part of a man's duty to himself is not to throw his life away in a hopeless cause. And this cause of yours, to bring Kenebuck to justice for his brother's death, is hopeless."

He stopped. Ian straightened in a movement preliminary to getting up.

"Wait a second," said Tyburn.

He had come to the hard part of the interview. He had prepared his speech for this moment and rehearsed it over and over again—but now he found himself without faith that it would convince Ian.

"One more word," said Tyburn. "You're a man of camps and battlefields, a man of the military; and you must be used to thinking of yourself as a pretty effective individual. But here, on Earth, those special skills of yours are mostly illegal. And without them you're ineffective and helpless. Kenebuck, on the other hand, is just the opposite. He's got money—millions. And he's got connections, some of them nasty. And he was born and raised here in Manhattan Complex." Tyburn stared emphatically at the tall, dark man, willing him to understand. "Do you follow me? If you, for example, should suddenly turn up dead here, we just might not be able to bring Kenebuck to book for it. Where we absolutely could, and would, bring you to book if the situation were reversed. Think about it."

He sat, still staring at Ian. But Ian's face showed no change, or sign that the message had gotten through to him.

"Thank you," Ian said. "If there's nothing more, I'll be going."

"There's nothing more," said Tyburn, defeated. He watched Ian leave. It was only when Ian was gone, and he turned back to Breagan, that he recovered a little of his self-respect. For Breagan's face had paled.

Ian went down through the Terminal and took a cab into Manhattan Complex, to the John Adams Hotel. He registered for a room on the fourteenth floor of the transient section of that hotel and inquired about the location of James Kenebuck's suite in the resident section; then sent his card up to Kenebuck with a request to come by to see the millionaire. After that, he went on up to his own room, unpacked his luggage, which had already been delivered from the spaceport, and took out a small, sealed package. Just at that moment there was a soft chiming sound and his card was returned to him from a delivery slot in the room wall. It fell into the salver below the slot and he picked it up, to read what was written on the face of it. The penciled note read:

Come on up—   *K.*

He tucked the card and the package into a pocket and left his transient room. And Tyburn, who had followed him to the hotel, and who had been observing all of Ian's actions from the second of his arrival, through sensors placed in the walls and ceilings, half rose from his chair in the room of the empty suite directly above Kenebuck's, which had been quietly taken over as a police observation post. Then, helplessly, Tyburn swore and sat down again, to follow Ian's movements in the screen fed by the sensors. So far there was nothing the policeman could do legally—nothing but watch.

So he watched as Ian strode down the softly carpeted hallway to the elevator tube, rose in it to the eightieth floor and stepped out to face the heavy, transparent door sealing off the resident section of the hotel. He held up Kenebuck's card with its message to a concierge screen beside the door, and with a soft sigh of air the door slid back to let him through. He passed on in, found a second elevator tube, and took it up thirteen more stories. Black doors opened before him—and he stepped one step forward into a small foyer to find himself surrounded by three men.

They were big men—one, a lantern-jawed giant, was even bigger than Ian—and they were vicious. Tyburn, watching through the sensor in the foyer ceiling that had been secretly placed there by the police the day before, recognized all of them from his files. They were underworld muscle hired by Kenebuck at word of Ian's coming; all armed, and brutal and hair-trigger—mad dogs of the lower city. After that first step into their midst, Ian stood still. And there followed a strange, unnatural cessation of movement in the room.

The three stood checked. They had been about to put their hands on Ian to search him for something, Tyburn saw, and probably to rough him up in the process. But something had stopped them, some abrupt change in the air around them. Tyburn, watching, felt the change as they did; but for a moment he felt it without understanding. Then understanding came to him.

The difference was in Ian, in the way he stood there. He was, saw Tyburn, simply . . . waiting. That same patient indifference Tyburn had seen upon him in the Terminal office was there again. In the split second of his single step into the room he had discovered the men, had measured them, and stopped. Now, he waited, in his turn, for one of them to make a move.

A sort of black lightning had entered the small foyer. It was abruptly obvious to the watching Tyburn, as to the three below, that the first of them to lay hands on Ian would be the first to find the hands of the Dorsai soldier upon him—and those hands were death.

For the first time in his life, Tyburn saw the personal power of the Dorsai fighting man, made plain without words. Ian needed no badge upon him, standing as he stood now, to warn that he was dangerous. The men about him were mad dogs; but, patently, Ian was a wolf. There was a difference with the three, which Tyburn now recognized for the first time. Dogs—even mad dogs—fight, and the losing dog, if he can, runs away. But no wolf runs. For a wolf wins every fight but one, and in that one he dies.

After a moment, when it was clear that none of the three would move, Ian stepped forward. He passed through them without even brushing against one of them, to the inner door opposite, and opened it and went on through.

He stepped into a three-level living room stretching to a large, wide window, its glass rolled up, and black with the sleet-filled night. The living room was as large as a small suite in itself, and filled with people, men and women, richly dressed. They held cocktail glasses in their hands as they stood or sat, and talked. The atmosphere was heavy with the scents of alcohol, and women's perfumes and cigarette smoke. It seemed that they paid no attention to his entrance, but their eyes followed him covertly once he had passed.

He walked forward through the crowd, picking his way to a figure before the dark window, the figure of a man almost as tall as himself, erect, athletic-looking with a handsome, sharp-cut face under whitish-blond hair that stared at Ian with a sort of incredulity as Ian approached.

"Graeme . . . ?" said this man, as Ian stopped before him. His voice in this moment of off-guardedness betrayed its two levels, the semi-hoodlum whine and harshness underneath, the polite accents above. "My boys . . . you didn't—" he stumbled, "leave anything with them when you were coming in?"

"No," said Ian. "You're James Kenebuck, of course. You look like your brother." Kenebuck stared at him.

"Just a minute," he said. He set down his glass, turned and went quickly through the crowd and into the foyer, shutting the door behind him. In the hush of the room, those there heard first silence, then a short, unintelligible burst of sharp voice, then silence again. Kenebuck came back into the room, two spots of angry color high on his cheekbones. He came back to face Ian.

"Yes," he said, halting before Ian. "They were supposed to . . . tell me when you came in." He fell silent, evidently waiting for Ian to speak, but Ian merely stood, examining him, until the spots of color on Kenebuck's cheekbones flared again.

"Well?" he said, abruptly. "Well? You came here to see me about Brian, didn't you? What about Brian?" He added, before Ian could answer, in a tone suddenly brutal, "I know he was shot, so you don't have to break that news to me. I suppose you want to tell me he showed all sorts of noble guts—refused a blindfold and that sort of—"

"No," said Ian. "He didn't die nobly."

Kenebuck's tall, muscled body jerked a little at the words, almost as if the bullets of an invisible firing squad had poured into it.

"Well . . . that's fine!" he laughed angrily. "You come light-years to see me and then you tell me that! I thought you liked him—liked Brian."

"Liked him? No," Ian shook his head. Kenebuck stiffened, his face for a moment caught in a gape of bewilderment. "As a matter of fact," went on Ian, "he was a glory-hunter. That made him a poor soldier and a worse officer. I'd have transferred him out of my command if I'd had time before the campaign on Freiland started. Because of him, we lost the lives of thirty-two men in his Force, that night."

"Oh." Kenebuck pulled himself together, and looked sourly at Ian. "Those thirty-two men. You've got them on your conscience, is that it?"

"No," said Ian. There was no emphasis on the word as he said it, but somehow to Tyburn's ears above, the brief short negative dismissed Kenebuck's question with an abruptness like contempt. The spots of color on Kenebuck's cheeks flamed.

"You didn't like Brian and your conscience doesn't bother you—what're you here for, then?" he snapped.

"My duty brings me," said Ian.

"Duty?" Kenebuck's face stilled, and went rigid.

Ian reached slowly into his pocket as if he were surrendering a weapon under the guns of an enemy and did not want his move misinterpreted. He brought out the package from his pocket.

"I brought you Brian's personal effects," he said. He turned and laid the package on a table beside Kenebuck. Kenebuck stared down at the package and the color over his cheekbones faded until his face was nearly as pale as his hair. Then slowly, hesitantly, as if he were approaching a booby-trap, he reached out and gingerly picked it up. He held it and turned to Ian, staring into Ian's eyes, almost demandingly.

"It's in here?" said Kenebuck, in a voice barely above a whisper, and with a strange emphasis.

"Brian's effects," said Ian, watching him.

"Yes . . . sure. All right," said Kenebuck. He was plainly trying to pull himself together, but his voice was still almost whispering. "I guess . . . that settles it."

"That settles it," said Ian. Their eyes held together. "Good-by," said Ian. He turned and walked back through the silent crowd and out of the living room. The three muscle-men were no longer in the foyer. He took the elevator tube down and returned to his own hotel room.

Tyburn, who with a key to the service elevators had not had to change tubes on the way down as Ian had, was waiting for him when Ian entered. Ian did not seem surprised to see Tyburn there, and only glanced casually at the policeman as he crossed to a decanter of Dorsai whisky that had since been delivered up to the room.

"That's that, then!" burst out Tyburn, in relief. "You got in to see him and he ended up letting you out. You can pack up and go, now. It's over."

"No," said Ian. "Nothing's over yet." He poured a few inches of the pungent, dark whisky into a glass, and moved the decanter over another glass. "Drink?"

"I'm on duty," said Tyburn, sharply.

"There'll be a little wait," said Ian, calmly. He poured some whisky into the other glass, took up both glasses, and stepped across the room to hand one to Tyburn. Tyburn found himself holding it. Ian had stepped on to stand before the wall-high window. Outside, night had fallen, but—faintly seen in the lights from the city levels below—the sleet here above the weather shield still beat like small, dark ghosts against the transparency.

"Hang it, man, what more do you want?" burst out Tyburn. "Can't you see it's you I'm trying to protect—as well as Kenebuck? I don't want *anyone* killed! If you stay around here now, you're asking for it. I keep telling you, here in Manhattan Complex you're the helpless one, not Kenebuck. Do you think he hasn't made plans to take care of you?"

"Not until he's sure," said Ian, turning from the ghost-sleet, beating like lost souls against the window glass, trying to get in.

"Sure about what? Look, Commandant," said Tyburn, trying to speak calmly, "half an hour after we hear from the Freiland-North Police about you, Kenebuck called my office to ask for police protection," He broke off, angrily. "Don't look at me like that! How do I know how he found out you were coming? I tell you he's rich, and he's got connections! But the point is, the police protection he's got is just a screen—an excuse—for whatever he's got planned for you on his own. You saw those hoods in the foyer!"

"Yes," said Ian, unemotionally.

"Well, think about it!" Tyburn glared at him. "Look, I don't hold any brief for James Kenebuck! All right—let me tell you about him! We knew he'd been trying to get rid of his brother since Brian was ten—but blast it, Commandant, Brian was no angel, either—"

"I know," said Ian, seating himself in a chair opposite Tyburn.

"All right, you know! I'll tell you anyway!" said Tyburn. "Their grandfather was a local kingpin—he was in every racket on the eastern seaboard. He was one of the mob, with millions he didn't dare count because of where they'd come from. In their father's time, those millions started to be fed into legitimate businesses. The third generation, James and Brian, didn't inherit anything that wasn't legitimate. Hell, we couldn't even make a jaywalking ticket stick against one of them, if we'd ever wanted to. James was twenty and Brian ten when their father died, and when he died the last bit of tattle-tale gray went out of the family linen. But they kept their hoodlum connections, Commandant!"

Ian sat, glass in hand, watching Tyburn almost curiously.

"Don't you get it?" snapped Tyburn. "I tell you that, on paper, in law, Kenebuck's twenty-four-carat gilt-edge. But his family was hoodlum, he was raised like a hoodlum, and he thinks like a hood! He didn't want his young brother Brian around to share the crown prince position with him—so he set out to get rid of him. He couldn't just have him killed, so he set out to cut him down, show him up, break his spirit, until Brian took one chance too many trying to match up to his older brother, and killed himself off."

Ian slowly nodded.

"All right!" said Tyburn. "So Kenebuck finally succeeded. He chased Brian until the kid ran off and became a professional soldier—something Kenebuck wouldn't leave his wine, women and song long enough to shine at. And he can shine at most things he really wants to shine at, Commandant. Under that hood attitude and all those millions, he's got a good mind and a good body that he's made a hobby out of training. But, all right. So now it turns out Brian was still no good, and he took some soldiers along when he finally got around to doing what Kenebuck wanted, and getting himself killed. All right! But what can you do about it? What can anyone do about it, with all the connections, and all the money and all the law on Kenebuck's side of it? And, why should you think about doing something about it, anyway?"

"It's my duty," said Ian. He had swallowed half the whisky in his glass, absently, and now he turned the glass thoughtfully around, watching the brown liquor swirl under the forces of momentum and gravity. He looked up at Tyburn. "You know that, Lieutenant."

"Duty! Is duty that important?" demanded Tyburn. Ian gazed at him, then looked away, at the ghost-sleet beating vainly against the glass of the window that held it back in the outer dark.

"Nothing's more important than duty," said Ian, half to himself, his voice thoughtful and remote. "Mercenary troops have the right to care and protection from their own officers. When they don't get it, they're entitled to justice, so that the same thing is discouraged from happening again. That justice is a duty."

Tyburn blinked, and unexpectedly a wall seemed to go down in his mind.

"Justice for those thirty-two dead soldiers of Brian's!" he

said, suddenly understanding. "That's what brought you here!"

"Yes." Ian nodded, and lifted his glass almost as if to the sleet-ghosts to drink the rest of his whisky.

"But," said Tyburn, staring at him, "You're trying to bring a civilian to justice. And Kenebuck has you out-gunned and out-maneuvered—"

The chiming of the communicator screen in one corner of the hotel room interrupted him. Ian put down his empty glass, went over to the screen, and depressed a stud. His wide shoulders and back hid the screen from Tyburn, but Tyburn heard his voice.

"Yes?"

The voice of James Kenebuck sounded in the hotel room.

"Graeme—listen!"

There was a pause.

"I'm listening," said Ian, calmly.

"I'm alone now," said the voice of Kenebuck. It was tight and harsh. "My guests have gone home. I was just looking through that package of Brian's things . . ." He stopped speaking and the sentence seemed to Tyburn to dangle unfinished in the air of the hotel room. Ian let it dangle for a long moment.

"Yes?" he said, finally.

"Maybe I was a little hasty . . ." said Kenebuck. But the tone of his voice did not match the words. The tone was savage. "Why don't you come up, now that I'm alone, and we'll . . . talk about Brian, after all?"

"I'll be up," said Ian.

He snapped off the screen and turned around.

"Wait!" said Tyburn, starting up out of his chair. "You can't go up there!"

"Can't?" Ian looked at him. "I've been invited, Lieutenant."

The words were like a damp towel slapping Tyburn in the face, waking him up.

"That's right . . ." he stared at Ian. "Why? Why'd he invite you back?"

"He's had time," said Ian, "to be alone. And to look at that package of Brian's."

"But . . ." Tyburn scowled. "There was nothing important in that package. A watch, a wallet, a passport, some other papers . . . Customs gave us a list. There wasn't anything unusual there."

"Yes," said Ian. "And that's why he wants to see me again."

"But what does he want?"

"He wants me," said Ian. He met the puzzlement of Tyburn's gaze. "He was always jealous of Brian," Ian explained, almost gently. "He was afraid Brian would grow up to outdo him in things. That's why he tried to break Brian, even to kill him. But now Brian's come back to face him."

"Brian . . .?"

"In me," said Ian. He turned toward the hotel door.

Tyburn watched him turn, then suddenly—like a man coming out of a daze, he took three hurried strides after him as Ian opened the door.

"Wait!" snapped Tyburn. "He won't be alone up there! He'll have hoods covering you through the walls. He'll definitely have traps set for you . . ."

Easily, Ian lifted the policeman's grip from his arm.

"I know," he said. And went.

Tyburn was left in the open doorway, staring after him. As Ian stepped into the elevator tube, the policeman moved. He ran for the service elevator that would take him back to the police observation post above the sensors in the ceiling of Kenebuck's living room.

When Ian stepped into the foyer the second time, it was empty. He went to the door to the living room of Kenebuck's suite, found it ajar, and stepped through it. Within the room was empty, with glasses and overflowing ashtrays still on the tables; the lights had been lowered. Kenebuck rose from a chair with its back to the far, large window at the end of the room. Ian walked toward him and stopped when they were little more than an arm's length apart.

Kenebuck stood for a second, staring at him, the skin of his face tight. Then he made a short, almost angry gesture with his right hand. The gesture gave away the fact that he had been drinking.

"Sit down!" he said. Ian took a comfortable chair and Kenebuck sat down in the one from which he had just risen. "Drink?" said Kenebuck. There was a decanter and glasses on the table beside and between them. Ian shook his head. Kenebuck poured part of a glass for himself.

"That package of Brian's things," he said, abruptly, the

whites of his eyes glinting as he glanced up under his lids at Ian, "there was just personal stuff. Nothing else in it!"

"What else did you expect would be in it?" asked Ian, calmly.

Kenebuck's hands clenched suddenly on the glass. He stared at Ian, and then burst out into a laugh that rang a little wildly against the emptiness of the large room.

"No, no . . ." said Kenebuck, loudly. "I'm asking the questions, Graeme. I'll ask them! What made you come all the way here, to see me, anyway?"

"My duty," said Ian.

"Duty? Duty to whom—Brian?" Kenebuck looked as if he would laugh again, then thought better of it. There was the white, wild flush of his eyes again. "What was something like Brian to you? You said you didn't even like him."

"That was beside the point," said Ian, quietly. "He was one of my officers."

"One of your officers! He was my brother! That's more than being one of your officers!"

"Not," answered Ian in the same voice, "where justice is concerned."

"Justice?" Kenebuck laughed. "Justice for Brian? Is that it?"

"And for thirty-two enlisted men."

"Oh—" Kenebuck snorted laughingly. "Thirty-two men . . . those thirty-two men!" He shook his head. "I never knew those thirty-two men, Graeme, so you can't blame me for them. That was Brian's fault; him and his idea—what was the charge they tried him on? Oh, yes, that he and this thirty-two or thirty-six men could raid enemy Headquarters and come back with the enemy Commandant. Come back . . . covered with glory." Kenebuck laughed again. "But it didn't work. Not my fault."

"Brian did it," said Ian, "to show you. You were what made him do it."

"Me? Could I help it if he never could match up to me?" Kenebuck stared down at his glass and took a quick swallow from it, then went back to cuddling it in his hands. He smiled a little to himself. "Never could even *catch* up to me." He looked whitely across at Ian. "I'm just a better man, Graeme. You better remember that."

Ian said nothing. Kenebuck continued to stare at him; and slowly Kenebuck's face grew more savage.

"Don't believe me, do you?" said Kenebuck, softly. "You

better believe me. I'm not Brian, and I'm not bothered by Dorsais. You're here, and I'm facing you—alone."

"Alone?" said Ian. For the first time Tyburn, above the ceiling over the heads of the two men, listening and watching through hidden sensors, thought he heard a hint of emotion—contempt—in Ian's voice. Or had he imagined it?

"Alone— Well!" James Kenebuck laughed again, but a little cautiously. "I'm a civilized man, not a hick frontiersman. But I don't have to be a fool. Yes, I've got men covering you from behind the walls of the room here. I'd be stupid not to. And I've got this . . ." He whistled, and something about the size of a small dog, but made of smooth, black metal, slipped out from behind a sofa nearby and slid on an aircushion over the carpeting to their feet.

Ian looked down. It was a sort of satchel with an orifice in the top from which two metallic tentacles protruded slightly.

Ian nodded slightly.

"A medical mech," he said.

"Yes," said Kenebuck, "cued to respond to the heartbeats of anyone in the room with it. So you see, it wouldn't do you any good, even if you somehow knew where all my guards were and beat them to the draw. Even if you killed me, this could get to me in time to keep it from being permanent. So, I'm unkillable. Give up!" He laughed and kicked at the mech. "Get back," he said to it. It slid back behind the sofa.

"So you see . . ." he said. "Just sensible precautions. There's no trick to it. You're a military man—and what's that mean? Superior strength. Superior tactics. That's all. So I outpower your strength, outnumber you, make your tactics useless—and what are you? Nothing." He put his glass carefully aside on the table with the decanter. "But I'm not Brian. I'm not afraid of you. I could do without these things if I wanted to."

Ian sat watching him. On the floor above, Tyburn had stiffened.

"Could you?" asked Ian.

Kenebuck stared at him. The white face of the millionaire contorted. Blood surged up into it, darkening it. His eyes flashed whitely.

"What're you trying to do—test me?" he shouted suddenly. He jumped to his feet and stood over Ian, waving his arms furiously. It was, recognized Tyburn overhead, the calculated, self-induced hysterical rage of the hoodlum world.

But how would Ian Graeme below know that? Suddenly, Kenebuck was screaming. "You want to try me out? You think I won't face you? You think I won't face you? You think I'll back down like that brother of mine, that . . ." he broke into a flood of obscenity in which the name of Brian was freely mixed. Abruptly he whirled about to the walls of the room, yelling at them. "Get out of there. All right, out! Do you hear me? All of you! Out—"

Panels slid back, bookcases swung aside, and four men stepped into the room. Three were those who had been in the foyer earlier when Ian had entered for the first time. The other was of the same type.

"Out!" screamed Kenebuck at them. "Everybody out. Outside, and lock the door behind you. I'll show this Dorsai, this . . ." almost foaming at the mouth, he lapsed into obscenity again.

Overhead, above the ceiling, Tyburn found himself gripping the edge of the table below the observation screen so hard his fingers ached.

"It's a trick!" he muttered between his teeth to the unhearing Ian. "He planned it this way! Can't you see that?"

"Graeme armed?" inquired the police sensor technician at Tyburn's right. Tyburn jerked his head around momentarily to stare at the technician.

"No," said Tyburn. "Why?"

"Kenebuck is." The technician reached over and tapped the screen, just below the left shoulder of Kenebuck's jacket image. "Slugthrower."

Tyburn made a fist of his aching right fingers and softly pounded the table before the screen in frustration.

"All right!" Kenebuck was shouting below, turning back to the still-seated form of Ian, and spreading his arms wide. "Now's your chance. Jump me! The door's locked. You think there's anyone else near to help me? Look!" He turned and took five steps to the wide, knee-high to ceiling window behind him, punched the control button and watched as it swung wide. A few of the whirling sleet-ghosts outside drove from out of ninety stories of vacancy, into the opening— and fell dead in little drops of moisture on the windowsill as the automatic weather shield behind the glass blocked them out.

He stalked back to Ian, who had neither moved nor changed expression through all this. Slowly, Kenebuck sank back down into his chair, his back to the night, the blocked-out cold and the sleet.

"What's the matter?" he asked, slowly, acidly. "You don't do anything? Maybe *you* don't have the nerve. Graeme?"

"We were talking about Brian," said Ian.

"Yes, Brian . . ." Kenebuck said, quite slowly. "He had a big head. He wanted to be like me, but no matter how he tried—how I tried to help him—he couldn't make it." He stared at Ian. "That's just the way, he never could make it—the way he decided to go into enemy lines when there wasn't a chance in the world. That's the way he was—a loser."

"With help," said Ian.

"What? What's that you're saying?" Kenebuck jerked upright in his chair.

"You helped him lose." Ian's voice was matter of fact. "From the time he was a young boy, you built him up to want to be like you—to take long chances and win. Only your chances were always safe bets, and his were as unsafe as you could make them."

Kenebuck drew in an audible, hissing breath.

"You've got a big mouth, Graeme!" he said, in a low, slow voice.

"You wanted," said Ian, almost conversationally, "to have him kill himself off. But he never quite did. And each time he came back for more, because he had it stuck into his mind, carved into his mind, that he wanted to impress you—even though by the time he was grown, he saw what you were up to. He knew, but he still wanted to make you admit that he wasn't a loser. You'd twisted him that way while he was growing up, and that was the way he grew."

"Go on," hissed Kenebuck. "Go on, big mouth."

"So, he went off-Earth and became a professional soldier," went on Ian, steadily and calmly. "Not because he was drafted like someone from Newton or a born professional from the Dorsai, or hungry like one of the ex-miners from Coby. But to show you you were wrong about him. He found one place where you couldn't compete with him, and he must have started writing back to you to tell you about it—half rubbing it in, half-asking for the pat on the back you never gave him."

Kenebuck sat in the chair and breathed. His eyes were all one glitter.

"But you didn't answer his letters," said Ian. "I suppose

you thought that'd make him desperate enough to finally do something fatal. But he didn't. Instead he succeeded. He went up through the ranks. Finally, he got his commission and made Force-Leader, and you began to be worried. It wouldn't be long, if he kept on going up, before he'd be above the field officer grades, and out of most of the actual fighting."

Kenebuck sat perfectly sill, a little leaning forward. He looked almost as if he were praying, or putting all the force of his mind to willing that Ian finish what he had started to say.

"And so," said Ian, "on his twenty-third birthday—which was the day before the night on which he led his men against orders into the enemy area—you saw that he got this birthday card . . ." He reached into a side pocket of his civilian jacket and took out a white, folded card that showed signs of having been savagely crumpled but was now smoothed out again. Ian opened it and laid it beside the decanter on the table between their chairs, the sketch and legend facing Kenebuck. Kenebuck's eyes dropped to look at it.

The sketch was a crude outline of a rabbit, with a combat rifle and battle helmet discarded at its feet, engaged in painting a broad yellow stripe down the center of its own back. Underneath this picture was printed in block letters, the question—"WHY FIGHT IT?"

Kenebuck's face slowly rose from the sketch to face Ian, and the millionaire's mouth stretched at the corners, and went on stretching into a ghastly version of a smile.

"Was that all . . .?" whispered Kenebuck.

"Not all," said Ian. "Along with it, glued to the paper by the rabbit, there was this—"

He reached almost casually into his pocket.

"No, you don't!" screamed Kenebuck triumphantly. Suddenly he was on his feet, jumping behind his chair, backing away toward the darkness of the window behind him. He reached into his jacket and his hand came out holding the slug-thrower, which cracked loudly in the room. Ian had not moved, and his body jerked to the heavy impact of the slug.

Suddenly, Ian had come to life. Incredibly, after being hammered by a slug, the shock of which should have immobilized an ordinary man, Ian was out of the chair on his feet and moving forward. Kenebuck screamed again—this time with pure terror—and began to back away, firing as he went.

"Die, you—! Die!" he screamed. But the towering Dorsai figure came on. Twice it was hit and spun clear around by the heavy slugs, but like a football fullback shaking off the assaults of tacklers, it plunged on, with great strides narrowing the distance between it and the retreating Kenebuck.

Screaming finally, Kenebuck came up with the back of his knees against the low sill of the open window. For a second his face distorted itself out of all human shape in a grimace of its terror. He looked, to right and to left, but there was no place left to run. He had been pulling the trigger of his slugthrower all this time, but now the firing pin clicked at last upon an empty chamber. Gibbering, he threw the weapon at Ian, and it flew wide of the driving figure of the Dorsai, now almost upon him, great hands outstretched.

Kenebuck jerked his head away from what was rushing toward him. Then, with a howl like a beaten dog, he turned and flung himself through the window before those hands could touch him, into ninety-odd stories of unsupported space. And his howl carried away down into silence.

Ian halted. For a second he stood before the window, his right hand still clenched about whatever it was he had pulled from his pocket. Then, like a toppling tree, he fell.

—As Tyburn and the technician with him finished burning through the ceiling above and came dropping through the charred opening into the room. They almost landed on the small object that had come rolling from Ian's now-lax hand. An object that was really two objects glued together. A small paintbrush and a transparent tube of glaringly yellow paint.

"I hope you realize, though," said Tyburn, two weeks later on an icy, bright December day as he and the recovered Ian stood just inside the Terminal waiting for the boarding signal from the spaceliner about to take off for the Sirian worlds, "what a chance you took with Kenebuck. It was just luck it worked out for you the way it did."

"No," said Ian. He was as apparently emotionless as ever; a little more gaunt from his stay in the Manhattan hospital, but he had mended with the swiftness of his Dorsai constitution. "There was no luck. It all happened the way I planned it."

Tyburn gazed in astonishment.

"Why . . ." he said, "if Kenebuck hadn't had to send his hoods out of the room to make it seem necessary for him to shoot you himself when you put your hand into your pocket that second time—or if you hadn't had the card in the first place—" He broke off, suddenly thoughtful. "You mean . . .?" he stared at Ian. "Having the card, you planned to have Kenebuck get you alone . . .?"

"It was a form of personal combat," said Ian. "And personal combat is my business. You assumed that Kenebuck was strongly entrenched, facing my attack. But it was the other way around."

"But you had to come to him—"

"I had to appear to come to him," said Ian, almost coldly, "otherwise he wouldn't have believed that he had to kill me—before I killed him. By his decision to kill me, he put himself in the attacking position."

"But he had all the advantages!" said Tyburn, his head whirling. "You had to fight on his ground, here where he was strong . . ."

"No," said Ian. "You're confusing the attack position with the defensive one. By coming here, I put Kenebuck in the position of finding out whether I actually had the birthday card, and the knowledge of why Brian had gone against orders into enemy territory that night. Kenebuck planned to have his men in the foyer shake me down for the card—but they lost their nerve."

"I remember," murmured Tyburn.

"Then, when I handed him the package, he was sure the card was in it. But it wasn't," went on Ian. "He saw his only choice was to give me a situation where I might feel it was safe to admit having the card and the knowledge. He had to know about that, because Brian had called his bluff by going out and risking his neck after getting the card. The fact Brian was tried and executed later made no difference to Kenebuck. That was a matter of law—something apart from hoodlum guts, or lack of guts. If no one knew that Brian was braver than his older brother, that was all right; but if I knew, he could only save face under his own standards by killing me."

"He almost did," said Tyburn. "Any one of those slugs—"

"There was the medical mech," said Ian, calmly. "A man like Kenebuck would be bound to have something like that around to play safe—just as he would be bound to set an amateur's trap." The boarding horn of the spaceliner sounded. Ian picked up his luggage bag. "Good-by," he said, offering his hand to Tyburn.

"Good-by . . ." he muttered. "So you were just going along with Kenebuck's trap, all of it. I can't believe it . . ." He released Ian's hand and watched as the big man swung around and took the first two strides away toward the bulk of the ship shining in the winter sunlight. Then, suddenly, the numbness broke clear from Tyburn's mind. He ran after Ian and caught at his arm. Ian stopped and swung half-around, frowning slightly.

"I can't believe it!" cried Tyburn. "You mean you went up there, *knowing* Kenebuck was going to pump you full of slugs and maybe kill you—all just to square things for thirty-two enlisted soldiers under the command of a man you didn't even like? I don't believe it—you can't be that cold-blooded! I don't care how much of a man of the military you are!"

Ian looked down at him. And it seemed to Tyburn that the Dorsai face had gone away from him, somehow become as remote and stony as a face carved high up on some icy mountain's top.

"But I'm not just a man of the military," Ian said. "That was the mistake Kenebuck made, too. That was why he thought that stripped of military elements, I'd be easy to kill."

Tyburn, looking at him, felt a chill run down his spine as icy as wind off a glacier.

"Then, in heaven's name," cried Tyburn. "What are you?"

Ian looked from his far distance down into Tyburn's eyes and the sadness rang as clear in his voice finally, as iron-shod heels on barren rock.

"I am a man of war," said Ian, softly.

With that, he turned and went on; and Tyburn saw him black against the winterbright sky, looming over all the other departing passengers, on his way to board the spaceship.

ABOUT THE EDITORS

Robert Adams lives in Seminole County, Florida. He is the author of the best-selling *Horseclans* series and the *Castaways in Time* series (both available in Signet editions), and is the co-editor, with Andre Norton, of an anthology series, *Magic in Ithkar*. Like the characters in his books, he is partial to fencing and fancy swordplay, hunting and riding, good food and drink. At one time Robert could be found slaving over a hot forge, making a new sword or busily reconstructing a historically accurate military costume, but, unfortunately, he no longer has time for this as he's far too busy writing.

Martin H. Greenberg has been called (in *The Science Fiction and Fantasy Book Review*) "The King of the Anthologists"; to which he replied—"It's good to be the King!" He has produced more than one hundred of them, usually in collaboration with a multitude of co-conspirators. A Professor of Regional Analysis and Political Science at the University of Wisconsin–Green Bay, he is still trying to publish his weight.

Pamela Crippen Adams is living proof of the dangers of being around science fiction writers. Originally a fan, she now spends her time as an editor and anthologist. When not working at these tasks, she is kept busy by her two dogs and ten cats.

THE FIERCE CHIEFS & FEUDING CLANS

· of the *Horseclans* Series by Robert Adams

(0451)

Buy them at your local
bookstore or use coupon
on next page for ordering.